THE NEWLYWEDS

"I've never been one to go by rules."

"You've never been married before." She hesitated. "At least, I don't suppose you have. You don't act like a man who's used to a woman around the house."

Matt trailed his eyes over Flame with such thoroughness, he set off the flutters inside her.

"It does take some getting used to," he said.

"I mean one who cooks and cleans," she snapped, with more spirit in her voice than she'd intended. "If you plan to eat elsewhere and carry on half the night—"

"I was tending to business."

"Ha!" She took another deep breath and gripped her hands for control. "I'm just thinking of the way things look. Is it necessary to show so openly that our marriage is a sham?"

"You'd rather everyone believe I'm keeping you occupied in bed?"

He had a devilish glint in his eye that Flame could not ignore. Her cheeks started to burn, but she refused to look away from him.

Matt stepped closer, studying the enticing way her skin had turned pink beneath the sprinkling of freckles. "Maybe if I had a reason for hanging around, I might do it."

Caught by his dark perusal, Flame could not take offense. "I cooked chicken stew for supper," she said, knowing as she spoke that the words must sound silly to a man of her husband's experience.

"Stew's not what keeps a man at home."

BOOKS BY EVELYN ROGERS

MIDNIGHT SINS
TEXAS KISS
A LOVE SO WILD
SURRENDER TO THE NIGHT
SWEET TEXAS MAGIC
DESERT FIRE
DESERT HEAT
WANTON SLAVE

EVELYN ROGERS

FLAME

ZEBRA BOOKS
KENSINGTON PUBLISHING CORP.

To Evan Marshall
with thanks

ZEBRA BOOKS are published by

Kensington Publishing Corp.
475 Park Avenue South
New York, NY 10016

First Printing: March, 1994

Printed in the United States of America

One

After weeks of worry, Flame Chadwick finally admitted that she was with child. For a single young woman, it was trouble of the worst kind.

Trouble she'd have to handle herself, since the man who'd gotten her in the family way was a thousand miles from Savannah, fighting Indians in the wilds of Texas. Lucky him, she thought with an admitted lack of charity as she paced in the privacy of her room, her anguish saved for her baby and the loving, soon-to-be-disgraced Chadwick clan.

The one thing she would not think about was the brief, uncomfortable act that precipitated everything. Considering the whispered promises and gentle hands preceding it, the ultimate intimacy had been a disappointment. But it had been enough to thrust her into the worst predicament of her twenty-three years.

Not that she deserved censure, she tried to reassure herself, fighting off a shame that never quite went away. She'd given her virginity to Second Lt. Robert Anderson on his last evening in Savannah, because she loved him—truly, deeply, eternally, for that was the nature of love.

But it was two months later now, long enough for her to know she was increasing. She knew, too, that with society being what it was, even in 1876, she and her baby would get the blame.

Her dear, precious, innocent baby. Already she felt as protective as any she-bear defending her cubs.

"Unfair," she wanted to cry out. But who would hear? And who would agree?

"I love you, Flame," Robert had whispered again and again on that fateful night. He'd certainly sounded sincere.

Of course, he'd been pulling her down onto the grass by a Georgia stream at the time, intent on unbuttoning her gown, and neither of them had been thinking clearly. And when he'd sworn she would one day become his wife, he asked that the betrothal remain a secret until he decided how to approach his father.

"Flame, face the truth," she whispered, "you were a fool."

But all was not lost, a small, more hopeful voice answered. Robert was an officer and a gentleman in the United States Army, as well as the lone son and heir of Sumner Anderson, one of Savannah's most prominent citizens. Robert wouldn't lie.

He might be serving his country at a place called Fort Hardaway, too busy fighting off savage Apaches to write, but she knew he'd left his heart with her.

Flame's slippered feet pounded a stretch of floral carpet beside her bed, while she pondered how she could make the rest of the world—most importantly, her family—realize that she had done nothing wrong. Foolhardy and certainly unwise . . . but for her baby's sake, she couldn't admit to being wrong.

If only the Anderson clan weren't so . . . so noble and aristocratic. Old Georgia money and old Georgia pride, that was the Andersons, untainted by commerce except when it came to selling plantation rice. They'd even made it through the War Between the States with most of their property intact.

In contrast, the Chadwicks were lower class. Thomas Chadwick, Flame's beloved, flamboyantly Irish Papa, ran a mercantile store, aided by wife Anne and their three daughters, the family home a simple frame structure at the rear. It mattered little to Savannah's gentry that Thomas was a fervently romantic and devoted family man, as well as a poet who could spin the most entertaining tales in town.

It mattered less that London-born Anne, who traced her lineage back to the time of Queen Elizabeth, could count an earl and a baron or two amongst her distant kin. For twenty years Thomas and his wife had owned Chadwick's Dry Goods and Clothing in Savannah, Georgia, employing each offspring in the operation as soon as she reached an age of responsibility. That made them merchants. Nothing more, nothing less.

As middle daughter, Flame had gladly accepted her tasks. Chadwicks pulled together. Always had, always would. They'd be on her side now. But they would be hurt when the news of her condition got about, and worse, when talk spread about how she was blaming the Anderson boy, trying to trap him into marriage.

Papa would be more than just hurt. Romantic though he was, he also possessed a terrible temper when he thought his girls were being slighted. She remembered the day the headmistress of Miss Lillian's Academy for Young Ladies had written to say that Miss Raven Chadwick was unsuitable for admission. Papa had blistered the walls with invective. It had taken all of Mama's considerable skills to persuade him that it was the academy which had proven unsuitable for the eldest Chadwick child.

If a letter drove him to fury, what would the ruin of his next-born lead him to? Flame shuddered from fear that he'd be reaching for his gun. To her, a shotgun wedding would be the ultimate disgrace, not so much for herself, but for the baby, who would suffer whispers and open innuendo for years to come.

A breeze fluttered the lace curtain at the bedroom window, bringing in a welcome waft of late September air. If only, Flame thought with a sigh, ideas could be wafted in the same way.

If only, she added with a touch of wistfulness, she hadn't gotten carried away by Robert's sweet words and warm hands. If only she were more like one of her sisters—Raven, older by two years and imminently sensible, or sweet young Angel, the baby at eighteen, who never brought anyone a moment's grief.

Flame was the impulsive Chadwick, the one who acted before she thought. Everyone in town knew it. Including Robert.

They'd made love only once. She'd heard it took at least three intimate encounters to start a baby, but she was heavy-hearted proof that the common girlhood belief was nothing but a lie, one probably perpetuated by overeager boys.

Someone raised a window in the adjoining room, and Flame's steps slowed. Raven had returned from her afternoon of working in the store. Practical, clear-thinking Raven, despite her impossible dreams. Mysterious Raven, too, at times harboring thoughts as dark as her natural coloring. Thoughts she never revealed to anyone.

Flame brightened. Raven could help sort out her problems—as long as she didn't know the exact nature of her sibling's predicament. No one must know, at least not until a plan of action had been determined.

Gathering her courage and smoothing her red locks into a semblance of neatness, Flame forced herself from the privacy of her own room to her sister's door and entered without knocking. Raven, reading by the window in a straight-backed chair, looked up from her book. As always, every strand of midnight-black hair was pinned in a neat coil away from her slender face. Flame thought self-consciously of her own disgracefully colorful hair that would not stay in place.

Raven would be reading Shakespeare, Flame knew without looking closely at the book. When her sister wasn't helping in the store or vocalizing her scales, she was most often found studying the works of the writer their mother called The Bard.

"What's wrong?" asked Raven, her black eyes instantly alert.

Flame took a deep breath. "What makes you think something's wrong?"

"Because you're pale as a cloud, and you've got a grip on your skirt a crowbar couldn't pry loose."

Guiltily Flame glanced down at her hands. They did, indeed, have a tight hold on her yellow gown. Attempting to smooth out the wrinkles, she looked back at Raven and shrugged.

"Just restless."

Raven nodded, not believing her for a minute. The middle Chadwick offspring was beautiful and charming and wonderfully talented with paintbrush and needle, but she couldn't lie to save her soul.

An uneasy silence settled between the two sisters, and Raven returned to her book, knowing she'd find out before long what troubled Flame's mind.

Flame cleared her throat. "I was thinking . . ." Her voice trailed.

"About what?" asked Raven.

"Silly thoughts," answered Flame with a wave of her hand, "the kind a girl sometimes has, about how the years are passing and maybe it's time we took ourselves a husband."

Raven set the book aside. "The same one, or are we allowed a man each?"

Flame grinned. "Oh, definitely one each."

"Count me out. I've got other plans for my life."

Flame kept her response to a nod. For some reason she couldn't understand, Raven was not interested in marriage and children. In truth, "not interested" was too mild a way to put it. Normally even-tempered, she had been known to fly into a rare rage if someone pushed the subject. A life of singing and acting upon the stage called to her, she claimed, even though the largest gathering she'd ever performed before was the Chadwick clan each Christmas Eve.

Flame was far more romantic. Like Papa. She wanted more than anything the kind of love her parents shared.

"What I really meant," she said, "was that it's time *I* settled down."

Raven studied her sister with what she hoped was objectivity. Fire-tinted hair that warranted her name; green eyes set wide apart and reflecting an intelligence she seldom used; a tall, willowy body that made subtle curves and graceful movements far more feminine than the obvious charms of buxom, big-hipped figures men claimed to prefer. Flame was a beauty, a fact she didn't seem to know.

"Any particular spouse in mind?" Raven asked. "You've got enough swains paying court to provide a dozen candidates." She didn't add that she feared they were after something far more disgraceful than a wife.

The Chadwicks, Raven knew as well as anyone in town, were decent folk, but not quite of a social class to join with Savannah's elite.

Flame wrinkled her nose. "They're boys. I was thinking more of a man."

"So you *do* have someone in mind."

"In a way."

"You either do or you don't."

"Sometimes, Raven, life's not that simple. It can't be broken down into yes or no. Black or white. Yank or Reb."

11

"Don't let any of the townspeople hear you say that. The war's been over more than ten years, but there are a thousand people around here who remember Sherman's march into town."

"At least he didn't burn it down," said Flame.

"No, just offered it to Lincoln as a Christmas present. There are hard feelings still. And rightly so, I might add."

Raven spoke with startling fervor, slipping briefly into the dark mode that brooked no argument, not even a response.

Moving deeper into the room, Flame sat on the edge of the bed and stared past her sister into a ray of early autumn sun outside the window. With all her heart she wished she could sprout wings and fly into the light.

"Robert Anderson," she said softly.

"Who?" asked Raven.

"Robert Anderson. The man I was thinking about. His father owns—"

"I know who he is. I just couldn't believe I heard right."

Temper flaring, Flame straightened. "Robert is perfectly respectable."

Raven snorted. "Oh, he's respectable, all right, but he's far from perfect. He's gentry. We're not."

"That didn't keep him from—" Flame bit at her lip.

"From what?" asked Raven, instantly alert.

Oh, dear, thought Flame, knowing she was an abominable liar. She must tell the truth . . . but not the whole truth, just enough to satisfy her sharp-eyed sister and to get some needed advice.

"If I tell you, I'm breaking a promise."

"So break it." After all, thought Raven, it was nothing more than a promise to a man, and an outsider at that. Except for Papa, she had little use for the opposite sex.

"He came by to see me the night before he left, and he . . . he asked me to marry him."

Raven sighed in relief. "I was afraid you'd say he did much worse than that."

Flame's cheeks burned. "I don't know what you mean."

"Oh, yes, you do."

Roughly crushing her conscience, Flame creased the folds of her skirt. "Well, maybe," she said, keeping her eyes downcast, "he did just a little more." Lifting her lashes, she met her sister's steady gaze. "The important thing is he asked me to keep our betrothal a secret until he gets back from Texas. Shouldn't be more than a year, he claimed."

"I see." Raven stood and paced the width of the room, black eyes flashing, her full lavender skirt swirling out with each turn. "And you're to remain true to him all the while."

Flame nodded, grateful her sister's anger kept her from more probing questions.

"Isn't that just like a man? I'll bet you he's not keeping his pants buttoned wherever he is."

"Raven! That's a terrible thing to say. He's out there in Texas, serving his country—"

"They've got women in Texas." Raven slapped at her thigh and halted before her sister. "So what's the problem? You want to do something crazy like tell his family?"

Flame stood to face her. The same height, the sisters adopted a similar stance—hands on hips, chins tilted in readiness for an argument.

"What's so crazy about a brief visit?" demanded Flame. "They'll be family before long."

"The Andersons linked with the Chadwicks? Not in a million years."

"Robert loves me."

"He'd be insane not to love you. Half the eligible men in Savannah—and most of the not-so-eligible ones—feel the same way."

"I love him. Not anyone else!"

"His father will say he should take you as a mistress, and save the vaunted Anderson name for someone worthy."

"Raven!"

"Don't act so shocked every time I present you with the truth. You know what the gentry believe. Thomas Chadwick is nothing more than a Philistine with a pretentious wife and three bratty daughters he'll have a difficult time marrying off well."

"Our mother is *not* pretentious!"

"Of course not. She's the dearest person in the world, but she's gentle and shy and she carries herself with an air she was taught from birth. So people misinterpret. And her girls? Oh, they're pretty enough, but they're just too much to take. Raven, far too dark-complected for decency, doesn't know her place. Angel, fair as a beam of sunlight, is suspected of being simpleminded because she's so sweet-natured, and as for that redhead, well, the less said about her the better."

"I'm not really simpleminded."

14

The softly spoken words came from the open door, and both Raven and Flame stared in dismay at their youngest sibling.

"Angel!" they said in unison.

"Well, I'm not."

"We know it," said Flame. "It's just Raven spouting off as usual."

Angel came into the room, her petticoats and white gown rustling as she moved. "About what?"

"About my marrying Robert Anderson."

"Sumner Anderson's son?"

"That's right."

"Ever hear of anything more absurd?" asked Raven.

Angel's blue eyes stared at Flame with gentle concern. "Do you want to marry him?"

"We're betrothed."

"Does Papa know?"

"No one does. Or at least no one did, until I decided to ask Raven if maybe I should go out and introduce myself to the family."

Angel's brow wrinkled in rare furrows. "I'm not sure that's a good idea."

"Exactly what I told her," said Raven.

Desperation ate at Flame's control. Hugging her middle, she stepped away from the two. "What if you're wrong? What if they welcome me, and say they are delighted with their son's choice?"

Raven reached out to stroke her sister's arm. "And what if they don't? Dearest Flame, we're only trying to save you from heartbreak. Wait until Robert returns. Let him break the news."

But I can't wait. The baby will be born long before then.

Flame fought the tears burning at the back of her eyes. The last thing in the world she should do right now was cry.

Pride came to her rescue, and she held herself erect. "I love you both very much and know you mean only the best. And, of course, you're right. A visit to the Anderson plantation would be a disaster. If I promise not to go out there, you must promise not to tell Mama and Papa I brought it up. And please don't mention the betrothal. Chances are it won't last long anyway."

"I promise," said Raven.

"So do I," said Angel, then added with a small smile, "but when you feel like talking, I'd like to know more about how and when you got engaged."

Impulsively Flame gave each of her sisters a hug, scurrying for the sanctuary of her room before the tears spilled down her cheeks. Leaning backwards against the closed door, she reached the decision she'd been hovering near ever since she started throwing up in the mornings.

As usual, Raven was right. A visit to the Anderson plantation would prove disastrous. But Flame had been right, too, when she'd assured them the betrothal would be finished before long.

Of course, it would. As soon as she and Robert were wed.

Goodness, it was a relief knowing she wouldn't have to hide her discomfort much longer. Masking daily bouts of nausea had been as difficult as maintaining a cheerful facade.

Like Raven and Angel, she had a small inheritance from one of her mother's distant cousins, a sum large enough to carry out her plan. And she had the determination to see it through. This was most definitely not an impulsive act. It was simply the only thing she could do.

Having settled her problem, she felt as though a weight had been taken from her shoulders. For the first time in days, it seemed possible that she could save her family from disgrace.

For her mother's sake, Flame had always wanted more than anything to be respectable. But she loved bright colors, and dancing, and laughter far too much to be dignified like Raven or quietly gentle like Angel. As a result, she suffered a reputation for wildness that was not entirely warranted.

Anne Chadwick had taught her daughters all the ladylike ways they could ever need, a necessary instruction since they'd been unwelcome at the snobbish Miss Lillian's. The dear lady deserved better than a bastard grandchild.

Papa, in his unconventional way, had sensed from the beginning that each of his daughters was unique. He'd named them for their coloring and for the personalities he knew they possessed. It was unfortunate that for her he'd chosen Flame. Not at all a dignified name. She didn't think he'd be too hurt if she chose another. At least not after a while.

She thought a minute before settling on Frances. Frances Chadwick Anderson had a nice ring to it, a name suitable for the lady Robert deserved, a name worthy of the wonderful child she would bring into the world.

Frances she would be.

Pulling paper and pen from the drawer of her

desk, she settled down to write the necessary letters. If her hand shook a little and the tears continued to blur her eyes, it wasn't because she was unsure of herself. As much for herself and her beloved kin, she worried about the welfare of her unborn babe.

Her daughter—somehow Flame knew the infant was a girl—must be protected at all costs. For such a cause she would do anything or go anywhere—even to a dangerous outpost that was known in the Army as Fort Hard.

Two

Matthew Jackson rode slowly through the West
Texas brush country, reins held loosely in his left
hand, the right resting on the handle of his holstered gun. Nerves prickled at the back of his neck.
Black Eagle lurked somewhere close. Matt could
smell the Indian's festering hate, the way a hawk
sensed carrion before it came into view.

Maneuvering his mount past a thicket of mesquite
and scrub oak, he searched in vain for signs of the
Apache warrior and his band. Matt knew all too well
that Apaches didn't give themselves away until they
were ready to be found. Seven years of his youth
had been spent in their captivity. Those years were
the reason he'd sought work as an Army scout.

He'd been on the trail for a week now, checking
waterholes and little-used trails, looking, listening,
meeting up with a few drifters and homesteaders,
but none had reported Indian trouble. Didn't happen very often in this year of 1876, not with most
of the savages living in the Indian Territory to the
north or on the reservations far to the west.

Except for the renegades, who over the years had established camps deep in the Sierra Madre of Mexico, raiding cattle ranches and haciendas on both sides of the border, then hieing for safety back to their impregnable homes.

Black Eagle was one of those renegades, as much an enemy to Mexico as he was to Texas. As soon as he was six feet underground, Matt would get out of this godforsaken country and get on with his life.

Edging a couple of yards into the chaparral, he reined the blood bay gelding to a halt. Thorns pulled at his buckskin trousers and tooled leather boots. Fringe from his buckskin shirt caught in a branch of mesquite. Thumbing his hat away from his brow, Matt looked slowly, carefully around him. Straight overhead an orange sun hung from a brilliant blue sky. Leaves stirred in the cool October breeze. A mockingbird's song greeted the noontime. It was, he decided, a beautiful day to die.

Except that Black Eagle wouldn't strike him from ambush. Their shared hatred went back too far, had dug in too deep in their guts, for anything but a direct confrontation to satisfy.

Something stirred in the grass to his right. Matt tensed and the Colt leapt to his hand, cocked and ready. The gelding Pigeon, a longtime companion, remained as motionless as his rider. Matt's keen eyes picked out the rounded rump and ratlike tail of an armadillo scurrying into the brush.

Matt slowly lowered the gun. The prickling at his nape ceased. No longer did he sense the presence of his enemy. Black Eagle had moved on. Whatever reason had brought the outlaw Apache across the river, it wasn't to meet up with Matt on this noonday.

One tug on the reins and Pigeon backed out of the chaparral, heading at a slow trot toward the road that wound through the countryside to Fort Hardaway. Matt felt no compulsion to hurry. Nothing of pleasure awaited him, if he didn't count Colonel Burr's overheated daughter . . . and he didn't count her for much.

Especially since Robert Anderson had reported for duty. Anderson occupied the lady's time, for which Matt was grateful. One tumble in the blankets with Miss Melody Burr had been all the harmonizing Matt wanted—harmonizing being the term she used.

"You know, sugar," she'd giggled as she reached for his belt, "in keeping with my name."

He'd almost lost the urge, but Melody had a pair of knowing hands that would serve a professional woman well, and he'd been a long time without a woman. Matt wasn't much for cuteness, but there was nothing cute about the lady's practiced skills.

He'd almost thought her approach an act of desperation, then backed away from that idea. She simply liked sex and didn't like to be denied.

As for his work, there were problems at Fort Hard, disappearing supplies, missing guns, but they were the problems of the soldiers. Matt was a loner, not a do-gooder, not a reformer. He'd signed on as scout with the proviso that he could leave at any time.

Which he would do when a scar-faced Apache

21

with an insatiable bloodlust no longer troubled his mind.

He thought, too, of Lieutenant Anderson, a fool of a young man with more daring than good sense. Just like Charlie . . . or the Charlie that Matt carried in his mind. In memory of Charlie, Matt had made friends with the officer—or as close to friends as Matt was likely to get.

Black Eagle . . . Charlie . . . Robert Anderson. He thought about all three as he rode toward the fort, the thick vegetation of the brush gradually changing to little more than wild grasses, and the land flattening from rolling hills and limestone escarpments to a sweep of flat plain.

There was nothing grand about Fort Hard—a parade ground surrounded by officers' quarters on the west, enlisted men's barracks on the east, headquarters and chapel on the north, the sutler's store on the south. Scattered around the perimeter could be found the stables, granary, storehouse, hospital, and a dozen other shacks necessary for maintaining the hundred and fifty men and the few dozen women who lived on the grounds.

Matt reined the gelding toward the shack next to the hospital, a two-room, adobe shelter that served as his home. Built for a former doctor and his wife, the place had become available when the new Army physician decided to take up quarters in the hospital.

The front of the house opened away from the rest of the fort, giving a privacy to the place that Matt liked, since he could come and go as he pleased without anyone watching. It also meant he could have unobserved visitors, a factor that in the case of one particular young lady didn't always work out so well.

He caught a blur of movement by the front window. It looked like he'd be welcoming the lady now.

Dismounting, he tied Pigeon to the porch rail that ran the width of the house. The front door opened. The first thing Matt noticed was the blue silk skirt, then the narrow waist, the full bosom, and at last the parted red lips of Melody Burr.

Matt's spurs jingled as he stepped onto the porch, but he didn't speak until he was inside with the door closed. "What the hell are you doing here?"

"Now that's a piss-poor greeting, if I ever heard one," whined Melody. "I'm waiting for you, sugar."

Matt hated flirty women, and he hated lovey-dovey names about as much as he hated women who schemed to get their way. Why he had ever gotten mixed up with the colonel's daughter, he couldn't imagine.

Melody stepped close, her full breasts brushing against his shirt, and he remembered.

Pouting, she puffed her mass of loosely worn, blond curls. "You sure do have a short memory, sugar. I'm just pleased as pudding it's the only thing short about you."

Sugar . . . pleased as pudding. He also remembered why he didn't let her catch him alone. At least not very often. Today she was proving a better scout than he.

"Melody, you're a good-looking woman, but I've been on the trail all day—"

"Humph!" She took a step backwards, hands on

23

rounded hips. "You sound just like Mother making excuses to Daddy. Except she usually says she's been working over a hot stove all day, when everyone knows she has a hired cook."

Everyone also knew that the colonel might well have been working over his hot mistress at her ranch just north of town, but Matt didn't figure the argument Melody would give him was worth the time it would take to calm her down.

Hell, for all he knew, she was acquainted with the woman, too.

He opened the door. She reached around him and slammed it shut.

"I got news for you," she said, a calculating light in her eyes, "and I didn't want you to take it wrong."

Matt viewed her warily. "What kind of news?"

"Oh, don't get in a dander, honeybunch. I'm not in the family way, if that's what you're thinking. Being the colonel's daughter, I know I've got to protect myself. Especially when the protecting involves a man like—"

She broke off and had the good sense to blush.

Matt leaned backwards against the door and enjoyed her discomfort. "A man like me?"

For a moment a faraway look darkened Melody's eyes. She blinked it away. "You know what I mean," she said, pouting once again. "You sure can curl a girl's toes, but that don't mean things ought to be permanent." The pout softened into a smile of invitation. "Don't mean they ought to be canceled, either."

Removing Matt's hat and tossing it aside, she played with the red bandanna at his throat.

"The news," he reminded her.

"Oh, that." She cringed. "I'm twenty, almost my majority, although you probably thought I was a little younger, seeing as how I look the way I do."

In truth, given the fine lines around her too-bright eyes and the set of her determined lips, Matt had thought her closer to twenty-five.

"Twenty's practically an old maid," she continued, her voice brittle, "and that's why I got myself engaged." Untying the bandanna, she sent it in the general direction of the hat. "He's a nice young man, got a big old plantation waiting for him somewhere back in the south, but, sugar, he don't do for me what *you* do."

She wound her fingers in the fringe across the front of Matt's shirt. "Tell me you're not heartbroken."

"I'm not heartbroken."

Her hands dropped to the buckle of his belt. "Nothing else broken, is there?" She looked up at him and licked her lips.

Despite his best intentions, Matt felt a tightening in his loins.

Melody's fingers trailed downward toward where matters were getting serious. "Maybe I ought to check it out." She lowered herself to her knees, her parted mouth inches from his crotch. "Sugar, you sure would taste sweet right now."

What the hell, he thought, half-deciding to join her on the floor.

From outside he heard someone call his name.

"Hell's fire," muttered Melody, sitting back on her heels. "It's Robert."

Matt's body cooled as quickly as it had heated.

"This engagement," he said, playing the gentleman as he helped the lady to her feet. "It wouldn't be to Robert Anderson, would it?"

"Robert said you two were close. I started to tell him it was something he and I had in common."

Matt shook his head in disgust. "Stay in here and keep quiet. No need to cause a ruckus."

"Don't you worry none. I'm not going anywhere."

Not a comfort, thought Matt as he stepped onto the porch, the door shut firmly behind him.

Robert stood a few feet away in the sun, a frown wrinkling his normally smiling face, a crushed piece of paper in his hand. "I've got woman trouble."

A contagious condition, thought Matt. "Looks like a telegram."

"It is. In all my life I've never known one to bring anything but bad news."

Having received no correspondence of any kind in his thirty years, Matt could only shrug.

"Damn, I didn't think she'd do it," said Robert. "Should have known her better." He grinned for a moment. "Not that I didn't know her, if you get my meaning."

Matt did.

"I know you don't have much use for women," said Robert, and Matt could have sworn he heard a giggle from behind the closed door. "Still, I was thinking you might suggest a way out of this mess."

Doffing the black felt uniform hat, he ran a hand through his dark blond hair. "I received a letter from her while you were gone. Said she was coming on out to get married. Hell, I thought one of her

26

sisters would talk her out of it. Should have known Flame better than that."

"Flame?"

"Some name, isn't it? Sounds like a fancy lady. She writes that she's changed it to Frances in recognition of her new status, but Flame suits her better. All that red hair and—"

Robert stopped himself. "I shouldn't be talking about her this way. She's a beauty, Matt. Sweet-natured, too, if a little wild. Her family owns a general store in Savannah. My father warned me against her. Well, not her exactly. 'Her kind' is what he said. Social climbers, that's what he called the Chadwicks. 'She'll get her claws into you, if you're not careful,' he warned me the last day I was in town."

Matt glanced at the telegram. "Looks like maybe she did."

"Maybe so, given a few things I might have said. At the time she could have put those claws anywhere she wanted." Robert shook his head. "She's not really like Melody. You know the colonel's daughter, don't you? We became engaged right before the letter arrived. Damned if I know how it happened, but we were out harmonizing one night—that's what she called it, when I was having success with the sweet talk—and bam, there I was, proposing marriage."

Matt pictured the colonel's daughter with her ear pressed against the door frame. If she heard anything she took exception to, he didn't doubt she'd come bursting outside to set her fiancé straight.

Untying the gelding from the post, Matt headed in the general direction of the stables, Robert in step beside him as they circled the house. "So what

27

about the telegram?" he asked when they were well out of Melody's earshot.

"Flame's made it to San Antonio all by herself, the little minx. As best as I can determine, she'll be on the westbound stage day after tomorrow."

Matt halted. "Damn."

"That's more or less what I said."

Matt stared at the young lieutenant. Blue eyes, even features, carrying himself with the air of a gentleman that Matt would never learn in a thousand years even if he cared to try. Like the youthful Charlie so many years before, Robert had a fun-loving way about him, so much so that Matt suspected he wasn't overly burdened with intelligence. But he'd never shown a sign of meanness to the men serving under him, and he seemed genuinely concerned about this woman Flame.

Except that he didn't understand the danger she was in . . . and it wasn't from Melody Burr.

Matt studied the far hills. "Apaches."

The one word was enough to widen Robert's eyes. "Black Eagle?"

Matt nodded.

"I thought he was somewhere down in Mexico! After the last raid, when you ran him off, I supposed he'd learned his lesson and wouldn't come riding back."

"You figured wrong. He's out there somewhere. Waiting for God knows what."

"Could be the stagecoach, couldn't it?"

"Could be."

Robert followed Matt's gaze to the hills. "We've

got to stop him. That's what we're out here for, anyway."

Matt gave the lieutenant credit for not flinching. Many a hardened soldier faltered at the thought of riding against a band of savages. Robert thought only of his duty.

Silently Matt cursed the woman who had invited herself out west. Probably some empty-headed flirt who'd expect the wealthy young lieutenant to surround her with luxury after he'd given her his name. At Fort Hard, for God's sake. She had a lot to learn.

A social climber, the elder Anderson had said. Sounded about right to Matt. He wasn't given to quick judgments against men, but women were something else. With the exception of a few hard-working homesteader wives, he'd never met a female worth the trouble to take care of.

This Flame woman hardly sounded like a homesteader. More like one of the saloon women in town. He thought of the newly engaged Melody back in his house. Robert had chosen one round-heeled, calculating bride; why not two?

"I'll talk to the colonel," said Matt.

Robert nodded. "Captain Davis is incapacitated with a bad leg, but there's nothing to say I can't lead." Unused to making decisions of a military sort, he hesitated. "I don't suppose we'll need the whole company."

Matt figured it would take only one man to bring down the elusive Apache. Himself. That he'd failed to do so in the past year of scouting ate at his gut.

"My advice is to pick out two dozen of your best

shots," Matt said. "If the colonel says okay, we'll ride at dawn."

Robert nodded, then headed at a run toward the enlisted men's barracks across the parade ground.

An edge of dark excitement cut at Matt as he veered his course toward the headquarters building, Pigeon trailing without protest at his heels. Something told him that this time he'd find the man that had evaded him for so many years.

This time one of them would die.

"Frances Chadwick," said the traveler, the name rolling out like thunder from his barrel chest. "Sounds mighty familiar."

Flame, sitting on a long bench inside the stage-coach relay station, barely heard him, so weary was she. Ignored, too, were the ten fellow passengers who either sat on the bench or milled about the small, dusty room.

"Little lady, you ever been to St. Louie?"

Feeling the nudge of an elbow, she sat up and straightened the feathered bonnet that had slipped over one eye.

"Are you speaking to me, sir?" she asked with what she hoped was dignified disdain. But it was difficult to be dignified when she'd gone two days without sleep, and it was impossible to be disdainful when all the world knew that properly raised young ladies did not travel alone.

"Frances Chadwick. That's you, all right. Heard the driver say your name. Ralph Dunderway here."

He stuck out a thick-fingered hand, which she ignored. "You ever worked in St. Louie?"

Suspecting the kind of work he meant, Flame stood, eyes wide and angry, this time having difficulty with neither dignity nor disdain. Smoothing her dusty green traveling gown, she strode to the far end of the crowded bench and found a place next to a married couple—Sam and Ethel Rylander—who had been bickering ever since they left San Antonio.

On this occasion the Rylanders were arguing about how long the journey would take into Fort Hardaway, but Flame paid them no mind. So close to her destination, she was fighting to convince herself that her decision to come west had been right.

At least the nausea was gone. She hugged her middle. Little Annie was resting peacefully for a change.

Maybe it was silly to name the baby so soon, but Flame felt such a love for her firstborn, that she could already picture her. A small replica of her maternal grandmother, that's what Annie would be. Fair like Robert and blue-eyed—everyone would say she inherited his looks—but Flame would know where she really got them.

She sighed, and again the bonnet drooped. Removing it, she placed it in her lap. Her hair tumbled down from the Raven-like coil she had attempted, but weariness kept her from pinning it neatly back in place. Might as well look disreputable for a while, since that was the way everyone viewed her anyway. She'd have time enough to make herself respectable before they arrived at the fort.

The main thing she must do was remember her name was Frances. That's what she would put on the marriage certificate. Ignorant of the law, she hoped that would make the change legal. Maybe the preacher would know . . . if they could find a man of the cloth in this godforsaken land. There was one on the stage, headed for a church in El Paso, but he was so pinch-faced and obviously disapproving of her that she didn't much feel like asking for his advice.

She was about to doze off when one of the passengers burst into the crowded room. "Soldiers a-coming," he yelled. "Driver says maybe we got ourselves an escort right into Fort Hard."

Flustered, Flame stood. Soldiers? Could Robert possibly have ridden out to see that she arrived safely?

Her heart filled with joy, and all the doubts subsided. Of course, he had. He hadn't lied when he said he loved her. She hadn't misjudged.

Forgetting the bonnet, which had fallen to the floor, she joined the other passengers trying to squeeze out the door. She exited face-to-face with Ralph Dunderway. It was not, contrary to the grin on his face, a pleasant experience. They popped out of the room like cork from a bottle of port, and Flame hurried to the driver who was standing by the stage overseeing the change of horses.

"Is it true, Mr. Caplin?" she asked. "Are soldiers really on the way?"

Caplin spat a stream of tobacco juice into the dirt. "True enough. You can just make 'em out down yonder. That'll be some troops from Fort Hard."

He didn't add that they rode escort only when there was trouble in the area. He had worries enough without getting the passengers riled.

Flame looked past him toward the distant cloud of dust that formed on the rise of a far hill.

"Annie," she whispered where no one could hear, "it looks like everything's going to work out all right."

Excited chatter rose around her, and she separated herself from the others, walking away from the stagecoach and the fresh team, not stopping until she came to a fenced corral by the side of the road a dozen yards away.

Like a sentry, she waited and watched the troop of soldiers gradually take shape. A blur of horses and blue uniforms for a long time, at last they became individuals to her tired eyes . . . individuals who would look her over and who would judge the reason for her presence. Impetuous floozy? Pitiful, abandoned girl from back home? In truth, she felt as though she were a little bit of both, and the shame she'd tried to leave behind in Savannah returned.

When they were a quarter of a mile away, she picked out the man in the lead. Curiously, he wasn't in uniform. Leather, it looked like, clothing she associated with earlier days in the West.

He wore a hat pulled low on his forehead. Black hair fell to his shoulders; it was not, she felt certain, the regulation Army length. Tall and lean, he sat easily in the saddle as though he'd been born to ride. For some unexplainable reason she couldn't pull her eyes away from the picture he presented . . . even when he was close enough for her to make out the weathered skin pulled taut over sharply hewn features, the thick, black brows, the strong nose, the square jaw. Not at all handsome like Robert, yet she could not look away.

"Miss Chadwick," said Ralph Dunderway at her elbow. "I might've known I'd find you out here greeting the troops."

As though she'd been bitten, Flame jumped away. Too late she remembered her disheveled appearance; too late she tried to smooth her hair.

And then the troops were riding into the yard of the relay station. Two horses drew near, and she raised her eyes to see the leather-clad leader and, belatedly, the none-too-welcoming scowl on the face of her betrothed.

Robert's broad-brimmed, black felt hat bore a not-so-jaunty broken red plume, the dark blue of his uniform carried a pound of dust, and the brass trim on the jacket had long ago lost its shine. All in all, he was not the rescuing knight she'd pictured in her mind. But he was here, she told herself, and that was all that mattered.

Or was it?

She looked from man to man, the one dark and forbidding as a thundercloud, the other usually as cheerful as sunshine, only on this midday he wasn't cheerful in the least.

Heart pounding against her ribs, she stepped forward, away from Dunderway, away from the past. In a curious way it seemed as though she walked toward her future, and she wondered that at this long-awaited moment she could summon little joy.

Instead, an embarrassed shyness took over, and

she wished with all her heart she'd waited inside the relay station for a more intimate reunion.

"Lieutenant Anderson," she said, all formal politeness as the men dismounted, "what a welcome surprise this is."

"Damned if I'd call it that," Robert replied, and Flame's heart quit its pounding, indeed quit beating altogether.

Suddenly light-headed, she gripped a corral fence post and turned to Robert's companion, as though he could provide equal support. She caught him studying her from head to foot, the way he might study a strumpet who was offering herself for sale. When at last they stared at one another, she read nothing but taunting scorn in the depths of his brown eyes, evidence of an assessment not too different from the view she held of herself.

Flame took an instant dislike to him, not caring that he openly exhibited an equal dislike of her.

Three

Matt settled back in the saddle and considered the tall, slender woman whose presence so irritated the usually affable lieutenant: wrinkled green gown that matched the color of her eyes, faint shadows beneath thick lashes, fiery hair half-pinned into a coil, the other half tumbling to her shoulders.

Flame Chadwick looked as though she'd just crawled out of a man's bed. Not a bad way for a woman to look, unless she was pretending to be a lady concerned only with getting wed.

The woman who wished to be called Frances was no more a lady than Myrtle at the Kitty Cat Saloon.

He grinned at the hostility in her stare. She had spirit, too, standing there next to the corral in the middle of nowhere, chin tilted upward as if she dared anyone to question her presence, from head to toe a splash of color against the October browns of the countryside. For all her buxom charms, Melody Burr paled in comparison.

If it was rowdy good times Anderson wanted, he should have shown more patience and stayed engaged to this one. If it was a loyal, loving wife, he should have run from the both of them as though they carried the plague.

Slowly Matt shifted his gaze from the Georgia beauty to the portly man standing behind her. "We'll be leaving as soon as the horses are fed and watered. Pass the word."

After a speculative glance at the two men and Flame, Dunderway retreated.

Flame shook her head at the sight of the buckskin-clad stranger. Who did he think he was, sitting so high on his horse, a dust-colored hat pulled low on his forehead above a pair of far-too-watchful brown eyes, black hair brushing against a pair of wide and obviously muscled shoulders? A scarlet bandanna encircled the column of his strong neck, brighter than the broken plume in her fiancé's black felt hat.

Something tingled inside her, and she told herself it was disgust.

What a boor the man was, she thought, giving orders when it should have been Robert's place to take charge. And why had the air suddenly become so warm and still?

She forced her eyes to Robert, who was signaling the men behind him to move toward the back of the relay station. Here was the one she loved. Truly, deeply, eternally—the way she'd told herself ever since he sailed from Savannah harbor. She could not allow herself to believe anything less.

As the troops rode past, saddles creaking, dust stirred in their wake, Robert dismounted. The last soldier in line took the reins from Robert's hands, leading the horse to the waiting hay and water.

Robert turned to Flame. She caught him staring at her middle, a sharp reminder of why she was here. Not because she loved him, although that was certainly how she felt, but because of the way she had proven her love.

I don't show yet. Realizing now was not the time for delicacy, she would have said the words aloud, if the dark-eyed man hadn't been hovering so near.

"Could we talk in private?" she asked Robert.

The boor grinned, tipped his hat, and without a word reined his horse in the direction of the retreating troops. Flame watched until he rode out of sight behind the station, unable to ignore the easy way he sat the saddle. Not knowing the correct procedure in such a situation as this, she felt a moment's irritation that Robert hadn't introduced them. As if he were ashamed of one of them, and she didn't much think it was the boor.

"Who is he?" she asked her fiancé, who stood not two feet away, hands at his side.

"Matt Jackson. He's a scout for the fort."

"What does he scout?"

"Indians."

"Oh." Flame thought that one over. "Does he find them very often?"

"He did yesterday. That's why we're here."

Not, she thought with a heavy heart, to welcome the soon-to-be Mrs. Robert Anderson to the West. On the contrary, Robert didn't seem at all pleased that she was here. Perhaps she should be more alarmed at the thought of savages in the area, but she could handle only one disaster at a time, and it looked very much as though she were faced with one now.

He loved her, she told herself. He had to. Just as she loved him.

She studied the man who had occupied her dreams. He looked as tired and dirty as she felt, and she missed very much the flash of golden smile and admiring glance that had always greeted her when they met.

A soulful sigh escaped her lips. Robert didn't love her. Or if he did, it was not with the ungovernable passion he'd shown by a Georgia creek.

Her thoughts went back to that warm summer evening, when they'd lain together in the wild soft grass. Too well she remembered what they had done—remembered with an unexpected ability to recall every detail. Even the act itself. Suddenly shy—and more ashamed than ever—she gripped the top rail of the corral fence and looked toward the faraway hills.

Robert stepped close. "Is it true?"

A lump formed in Flame's throat, and her eyes burned with unexpected tears. Goodness, but she was becoming a crybaby lately. Blinking the tears away, she concentrated on Annie. Robert might not hold her in great affection, but surely he would love their child.

"It's true," she said softly.

"Damn," said Robert.

Flame held still for a moment, her tears dried, the burden of self-pity relieved by Robert's single word. Instead of feeling sorry for herself, an object of pity and disgrace, she was grateful for her fi-ancé's reaction, since it gave her the backbone she needed. Once again she was a she-bear, and Robert had joined the residents of his faraway home as a threat to her unborn child.

She tapped her foot against the dusty ground. The son and heir of Savannah's noble and aristo-cratic Anderson clan was not behaving in the least noble or aristocratic. In truth, he resembled the Army scout more than he did the gentleman who had left Georgia two months before.

"I suppose Mr. Jackson knows about my condi-tion. And got a good laugh out of it," she said.

"Of course, he doesn't know. He doesn't have much to do with women, and I couldn't see the point in telling him."

Flame remembered the way the Army scout had looked her over. He'd known just where to linger to bring a tightness in the pit of her stomach and a burning to her cheeks. Compared to him and his all-too-obvious knowledge of women, Robert was a monk.

"Besides," Robert went on, "I was too embar-rassed to speak of the matter."

"Embarrassed!" Everything Robert said was wrong, and Flame's temper rose to the boiling point, along with the pitch of her voice. "How do you sup-pose *I* feel?"

Robert looked at her in alarm.

"Now, now," he said. "Don't cause a scene. We'll work something out. We have to. Father—" He stopped, and the color drained from his face. "You haven't told Father, have you?"

40

"I've told only one father," Flame said tightly, "and that's you."

She felt light on her feet and ready to fight. If Robert made one more remark that seemed in the least disparaging, she would go for his eyes.

In that moment, she was very much her Papa's daughter. Robert was lucky she didn't pack a gun.

"If you're waiting for me to say I'm sorry about coming out here, you'll have to wait a long time," she said, looking at him straight on with unblinking eyes. "We both may have said and done some unwise things, but that doesn't mean our child should pay the price."

"Our child—"

Robert stared at her stomach as though he could see the growing baby.

"For heaven's sake, Robert, you might as well hold up a sign announcing the impending birth."

"It's just that when we were together, I didn't think—"

"Neither of us was doing much thinking," said Flame, her voice more forceful than his. Somehow over the past few minutes she had become the strong one, the one in control. It was a role she was unused to. She would have preferred resting her head on Robert's shoulder, feeling comforting arms enfold her, hearing words of assurance that everything would be all right.

She wanted above all else to be told she was loved.

But Robert wasn't enamored; he was embarrassed. So much, she thought, for noble aristocracy.

Removing his hat, he wiped a dusty blue sleeve across his forehead, then ran his fingers through his

41

hair. The normally neat, fair curls were left spiked out of place, darkened by sweat. As tired as he looked, he seemed no more than a boy . . . a youngster playing grownup in an Army suit. His weeks at the fort had not toughened him to the hard life, Flame realized, had not added a single line or done more than darken his skin. Somehow he seemed younger than when he had left.

Robert Anderson would be one of those lucky men who never grew old.

Which wasn't his fault. He'd been coddled since birth, and she saw with sudden insight that he'd never learned to stand on his own or, worse for her, accept the responsibility for his mistakes.

"How long have you been on the road?" she asked, gentling her tone even while she felt something die deep inside.

"We left the fort at dawn." He studied the sky and the position of the sun. "We should be able to get back there soon after dark. If we leave right away and don't meet with any trouble."

Flame turned from him to look at the fresh team hooked to the coach, the milling passengers, the soldiers who had drifted on foot to the front of the relay station. Most of the men had cups of coffee in their hands. Matt Jackson was nowhere in sight.

Looking back at the conveyance that would take her to the destination where she was not wanted, Flame suddenly felt old as the awaiting hills.

"Let's go rest while we can," she said. "I don't imagine it's any more comfortable in that Army saddle of yours than it is crowded with six other people inside a stuffy coach."

Taking his proffered arm, she realized with a start that it was the first time since he arrived that they had touched. Like his words, the warmth and support he provided were not particularly comforting.

She attempted a smile. "If there really are Indians awaiting us as Mr. Jackson suspects, we need to conserve as much strength as we can."

She spoke lightly, not really afraid of any attack by savages. Already having faced more than enough disaster for one day, she simply refused to consider the possibility of anything worse.

They got under way within the hour. Matt would have preferred a quicker departure, but the horses needed the rest, and so did the men.

He watched in silence as the lieutenant's woman climbed into the coach. The portly man he'd seen with her by the corral was close by to offer assistance. She tried to pull away, but the man wouldn't be denied. Grabbing her elbow, he stepped close to lift her onto the high first step, and Matt got the idea he was debating whether to pinch her rear.

The man glanced over his shoulder . . . caught Matt watching . . . and winked.

Matt wondered what Miss Chadwick had done to encourage the fellow. Hell, looking the way she did was enough.

With Anderson busy getting the troops in line, Matt dragged his thoughts to the open road. Maybe Black Eagle wouldn't be waiting. Maybe when he'd disappeared yesterday, it was to take his men back across the Mexican border fifty miles to the south.

43

Maybe. But Matt didn't believe it for a second. Somewhere ahead the Apache was waiting for something . . . for someone . . . possibly for them. It was up to Matt to see that the Indians didn't take them by surprise.

With seven passengers crammed inside the stage and four more riding precariously on top, they headed west. Matt rode well ahead of the coach; the soldiers scattered to the sides and rear. Anderson took up his post in front of the team.

A horse approached from behind him, and Matt turned to watch the hulking figure of Sergeant Gibson draw near. A grizzled Indian fighter, skin like oak bark, eyes hard as flint, Gibson had been serving in this part of Texas since right after the war.

They rode side by side in silence, Gibson shifted a fraction to the side of his saddle, a grimace of pain screwing his features. The tough old sergeant could ride into a band of armed Apaches without fear, but on occasion hemorrhoids, the common cavalry complaint, got him down.

Gibson scratched at his bristled chin. "You figger Black Eagle's out there some'eres?"

Matt scanned the rolling hills awaiting them . . . the scattered boulders and trees behind which an Apache might lurk.

"That's what I figure," he said.

"Expectin' trouble?"

"It's always best to expect it. That way you don't get taken by surprise."

Gibson spat to the side. "I was wonderin'—" He hesitated. "Don't mean to question the officer in charge, you understand. Still, crossed my mind that

44

maybe the lieutenant ain't got the grit to handle trouble."

Matt kept his eyes on the road ahead. "Hard to tell such a thing about any of us. Until we're tested."

"He's got the woman to think of. Men saw the two of 'em talkin'. Must 'a knowed one another from back East."

Matt nodded.

"Woman like that, lookin' the way she does, has a way of confusin' a man, know what I mean?"

"The lieutenant will be all right."

Gibson shifted his weight cautiously to the opposite side of the saddle. "I ain't questionin' the officer in charge. Ain't my place. Just wonderin' is all."

"A man can't help wondering," said Matt. No need to tell the sergeant he'd been wondering much the same.

How much was Anderson like Charlie, the lad he so closely resembled? Was he as brash and brave? Matt hoped today wasn't the day to find out.

"Tell the others there's no reason to worry. They're all crack shots and well armed. Black Eagle rides with a small band, and the last time they tried a raid around here, half their guns misfired. He'd be a fool to attack."

The sergeant dropped back. Matt spurred the gelding Pigeon to a gallop, separating himself from the dust and inevitable noise of the stagecoach and troops. The road looped and straightened, wound over hills and cut across a couple of creeks where they stopped to water the horses, ran along the base of a limestone escarpment that got Matt's special concern.

During the next few hours he saw no sign of Black Eagle or his men. Maybe he had been wrong about a threatened attack.

In case he wasn't, however, he dropped back once to suggest to Anderson that they take a high road off the main route and ride down into the fort from a back way. "Fewer trees. Less chance of ambush."

Anderson seemed distracted at first. Matt had to make the suggestion twice.

"That would add hours to the ride," the young lieutenant said, as he glanced briefly over his shoulder toward the coach. "Wouldn't that give more time for them to attack us?"

"Apaches seldom attack at night," said Matt.

"You've said yourself more than once that Black Eagle doesn't do what's expected of him. Let's get on into Fort Hard as soon as we can. Flame—" He caught himself. "The men and horses are tired. It's been a long enough day as it is."

So it was Flame that Anderson worried about; Matt could see it in his eyes. The woman looked healthy enough to him, but she must have convinced her bridegroom otherwise.

No doubt about it. Women were trouble. Especially this one.

They were an hour's ride from the fort—the sun close to setting behind the distant hills, casting an orange glow to the land—when the back of Matt's neck prickled. He was riding twenty yards ahead of the stagecoach, as they moved through a copse of oak and cottonwood near a small stream. He reined to a halt, eyes darting, senses alert.

46

He detected no sign of the Apache . . . except for the tightness in his neck.

He reached for the Spencer carbine holstered against Pigeon's neck, propped it across his lap, fingered the trigger. The troops would be carrying the newer Springfield rifle, a sturdy, dependable gun, but it fired only one shot. Matt preferred the older Spencer with its seven rounds.

He also liked the .45-caliber Colt "Peacemaker" strapped to his thigh. He liked the pistol enough to carry it with him at all times.

He slowed Pigeon to a walk; to the rear he could hear the creak of the stage, the snap of the driver's whip, the clop of a hundred hooves against the hard ground.

Slowly he reined toward the stagecoach, ever watchful, dropping in beside Anderson as he rode in front of the team. To the right the land sloped upward through a thickening of trees, to the left downward toward the stream.

"Bring the troops in closer," he said in a low voice. An upward glance at the driver was enough to bring a rifle to the man's hand. Hurried whispers spread topside across the coach; as if by magic guns appeared. Matt considered warning the five men and two women who rode inside, then decided if trouble came, they'd know soon enough.

Besides, there was no telling what Miss Flame Chadwick would do. Fall into hysterics, maybe. Matt didn't want to take the chance.

Cursing the hilly woods through which they rode, Matt spurred the gelding back into the lead. Since he couldn't advise Anderson to safety, he would serve as a target, draw Black Eagle's fire away from the stage.

If it was Black Eagle that awaited. Maybe it was just Matt's imagination that ate at him. Maybe he'd been chasing the bastard too long. Maybe—

A chilling *hi-yi* drifted from somewhere down by the creek, filling the air. Matt's blood ran cold, even as he snapped the rifle into place. An open stretch of land beckoned ahead, a low-rolling plain without trees and creeks. He fired a warning shot toward the savage cry, reined toward the rear, and leaned low over Pigeon's neck as the gelding flew toward the approaching stage.

"Ride fast," he yelled as he sped past Anderson, then motioned for the driver to do the same. No such order was needed as the whip snapped over the already racing team.

The Apaches came at them through the trees on both sides of the road, rifles cracking in the gloom. Matt galloped to the rear of the coach, circled behind the fast-turning wheels, and as he came up on the opposite side, fired one shot after another at the marauders.

Gunfire exploded like dynamite in the once peaceful grove. Indians and soldiers fell, their mounts loping onward riderless. Matt's Spencer came up empty; he holstered it in favor of the Colt, counting each shot as he rode a twisted route, saving one bullet for the unseen leader of the raid.

The road angled to the left, and he spotted his enemy directly ahead astride a spotted horse, bare-chested, his long black hair bound by the scarlet band encircling his forehead. He waited in the narrow path the stagecoach must take, waited beside a fallen log that blocked the roadway. Even in the gloom of approaching night and the fury of the moment, Matt could see the wide smirk on the Apache's scarred and hated face.

He drew a bead on Black Eagle.

"God damn!" the driver yelled behind Matt as he spied the blocked road. He pulled back sharply on the reins, but the team was lost to him, thundering on toward disaster, their pounding hooves almost covering the cries of fear coming from inside the swaying stagecoach.

Matt saw the danger. It took all the strength he could muster to forget Black Eagle, to holster the Colt, to race the gelding alongside the team, nudging them off the road, toward the trees and the hill, knowing their chances were better there than in a collision with the downed log.

The team of horses took his lead, veered to the right, almost clearing the blocked road. Only the back left wheel of the stagecoach failed to pass safely. As it crashed against the thick trunk of the fallen tree, the top-heavy conveyance teetered, lurched, sending the outside passengers flying through the air.

For an eternity the coach balanced on the two right wheels, then came crashing onto its side, dragged up the hill for a half-dozen yards before Matt could bring the terrified team to a halt. Screams came from inside. Matt jumped to the ground, attempting to quiet the frightened horses as they tangled themselves in their traces.

On the ground beside the toppled coach lay the

moaning driver, his arms clutched around a twisted leg.

Above the screams of panic from the coach, Matt heard racing hooves, watched in horror as Black Eagle reined to a halt by the coach's left rear wheel spinning wildly in the air. Dismounting, the Indian scrambled nimbly up on the door and dropped to his knees, a rifle pointed downward into the open window.

"No!"

The hoarse, wild cry seemed to come from hell, echoing above the roar of the gunfire, and out of the smoke and confusion rode Robert Anderson, hunched low over his galloping horse.

"No!" he cried again, as he thundered up the hill straight for the Apache.

Black Eagle lifted the rifle from the window. The lieutenant bore down upon him, his gun wielded overhead like a club, his visage twisted into the triumphant grin of an avenging angel. Matt palmed the Colt, but as he stared up at the young officer, he was thrown back in time to another day of horror . . . to another fair-haired young man bearing down on a killer Apache with nothing more than a club in his hands.

"Charlie," cried Matt in anguish, once again a terrified and helpless eight-year-old, and the name reverberated through the woods.

The sound of his own voice jolted him to the present. The Colt belched fire just as the Apache jumped to the ground, but for once in his life, Matt's aim was off. The bullet grazed Black Eagle's arm too late to stay the rifle fire that came a split second later.

Anderson's horse reared, pawing the air at the same time Flame Chadwick thrust her head and shoulders through the stagecoach window.

She saw the look of pain on her betrothed's face, saw the red stain spread across his shirt, saw him pitch sideways in silence toward the flattened grass.

Bereft of all control, Flame screamed. And screamed and screamed.

Four

The Army horse reared over Robert Anderson's fallen body, hooves thrashing, then took off at a gallop down the hillside, leaving behind the echoes of Flame's shrill, mournful wail.

Hands clasped over her mouth, she swallowed the cries, but she could not move from her place in the upturned window of the coach, could not shift her eyes from the motionless, twisted form on the ground.

Matt tossed the empty Colt aside and launched himself toward Black Eagle.

Crouched by the undercarriage of the overturned conveyance, a scant three feet from Anderson, closer still to Matt, the Apache whirled toward him, his rifle brandished in triumph. Matt hesitated, then watched in helpless horror as the rifle shifted toward Flame.

Looking down the death barrel of the savage's gun helped Flame marshal her wits, and she dropped like a stone back into the mass of humanity thrashing about in the coach.

Once again the two longtime enemies eyed each other. Blood trickled from the slash Matt's misdirected bullet had dug into Black Eagle's upper arm, but the Apache showed no sign he suffered pain.

"*Sikisn,*" he said derisively above the crack of distant guns, "we will meet again."

"I am not your brother," Matt spat back, but the Indian was already scurrying away, his moccasined feet carrying him swift as the wind to the spotted horse waiting downhill on the road. He vaulted over the animal's rump, and with one quick, insistent whoop, he disappeared into a low-lying fog that had settled amongst the trees by the creek.

Like warrior puppets pulled by strings, the remaining half-dozen Apaches gave up the battle and followed him into the mist, taking their dead with them.

Shaking with hatred, Matt shifted to the still body on the ground, and he gave up all thought of pursuit. His stupidity . . . his weakness had killed the lieutenant, and he knew an anguish he had not suffered in years. Sergeant Gibson crunched through the fallen October leaves toward the coach, and Matt pulled himself to the unwanted position of command.

"Help them," Matt ordered, gesturing toward the passengers struggling to free themselves from their toppled prison.

A sick sadness overcame him as he knelt and turned the young lieutenant over on his back, cradling his head in his arm, feeling at his throat for a pulse. Blood stained the front of the blue uniform to black.

If his aim had been true, thought Matt, if he hadn't been caught up in his own tortured past, the blood would not have been spilled.

Aided by Gibson, Flame was the first to emerge from the stagecoach into the gloom of approaching night. Dropping to the ground, she settled close to Robert and stared in shock at the stain.

Trembling fingers reached out to touch his face. "Is he—"

"Alive," answered Matt curtly. "Barely. Get some water."

It took a moment for Flame to realize what he had said. She looked toward the creek, her thoughts turned briefly to the Apaches and where they might have gone.

Robert moaned once, then fell silent. Now was not the time for the vapors, she told herself. She'd already disgraced herself with childish screams. Gripping her torn skirt to keep from tripping, she fought a rising panic and hurried downhill to do as Jackson bade.

From his position atop the coach, the sergeant whistled for one of the men to accompany her, then helped the remaining passengers to freedom, using his massive strength to lift them, one by one, through the high, open door.

A young soldier came to give support as they jumped to the ground. Matt gestured for them to give the lieutenant room. Still in shock, they stumbled away without argument, receiving succor from the remaining troops.

Robert's eyes fluttered open. His skin was as white

as parchment, and when he parted his bloodless lips to speak, only a faint whisper came out.

Matt leaned close.

"Looks like this is it," Robert managed.

Matt didn't respond except to loosen the lieutenant's collar and to brush the damp, matted hair away from his face.

"Favor." The one word seemed to take much of Robert's strength.

"We can talk later," said Matt.

Robert shook his head angrily. "No time."

"All right," conceded Matt. "You want a favor, you've got it." At that moment he was ready to concede anything the lieutenant asked.

"Flame—" Robert paused, eyes closed, and a deep sigh shook his body. Matt thought for a moment that he was gone, but the lieutenant rallied, his eyes open wide, his voice stronger than before.

"She needs help."

Matt forced his dislike of the woman to the back of his mind. "She'll get it. I'll escort her personally back to San Antonio."

"Not that kind." He hesitated. "Can anyone hear us?"

Matt hid his surprise. "No one."

"I'm not a good man. A weakness for women, that's my problem. Strange how I see it now. Here, at the end." The phrases came out in spurts, like the blood darkening his chest.

"You rode unarmed at an Apache gun," said Matt, puzzled, almost angry. "That's the bravest action I've ever seen."

Robert ignored him. "The baby. He'll need a name."

Matt thought he heard wrong.

"There's no baby, Robert," he said, using the lieutenant's given name for the first time. He wished he'd done so earlier . . . wished he had more openly returned the young man's ready friendship.

"There will be. My son must have a name."

"Your son—"

"And Flame's."

At last Matt understood, and he glanced down the hill in time to see Flame Chadwick and a pair of soldiers emerging from the mist onto the road.

He watched her approach, saw the solicitude of the men who flanked her, saw the ease with which she accepted their help, and he felt a disgust for her that equalled the harsh feelings he held for himself. If she were with child and not just using the story to get a rich young man to the altar, he doubted she could identify the father with certainty.

In Matt's mind, there was no question about her pretended virtue. There hadn't been since he spied her waiting for the troops by the relay station corral.

"Marry her," whispered Robert.

Matt's eyes darted back to him. "What did you say?"

Robert managed a smile. "Old bachelor like you, I don't suppose you ever planned on a wife."

"No, I never did," Matt said with honesty.

"I've not been a gentleman to the lady," said Robert. "Too late to change, but I can't have my son born a bastard." A sudden frenzy took hold of him, and he gripped the fringe on Matt's shirt, pulling himself up with startling strength. "You owe me, Matt. Promise."

A sense of helplessness washed over Matt as he stared down at the dying man. Once before he'd knelt like this to hold the victim of an Apache attack. He'd been unable to save his brother Charlie . . . to do anything except sob over his body after he took his last breath.

But he could help Robert Anderson die in peace.

"I promise." The words almost caught in his throat.

"Promise what?" asked the woman under discussion, as she dropped to the ground beside Robert.

Matt shot her a look of disgust, but she was too busy staring down at Robert to notice.

"Here's the water," she said, holding forth an Army canteen. Matt propped Robert higher, pressing the water to his lips. He swallowed once, coughed, then settled back.

Robert's eyes drifted to Flame. "I'll take care of you. Don't worry."

She took one of his hands between hers, blinking back tears. The world whirled in confusion around her and she felt empty and lost . . . but she thought not of herself, only him.

"I'm not worried. We'll get you back to the fort and into a doctor's care. Everything will be all right."

"How are the troops?" he asked. "Hell of an officer I am to lead them into this."

Flame knew she could not lie. "The soldiers said two were . . . fatally wounded." The words sounded stiff and unnatural on her lips, but she had no experience in reporting death. "The Apaches lost the same."

"And the wounded?" he asked.

"None seriously," she said.

He closed his eyes, then opened them to look at Matt. "I should have done what you said . . . should have gone the long way around," he said. "Thought short was better."

"It might have been," said Matt hurriedly. "I didn't put up much of an argument, did I?"

Robert's lips twitched, as if he would smile. He spoke to Flame. "Matthew Jackson's a good man. A little rough-natured, but good. Promise you'll do what he says."

Flame hesitated, having none of the faith her fiancé had in his companion.

"Promise," he said with greater insistence, stiffening as though he would rise from the ground.

Robert gave her little choice. "I promise," she said, feeling the scout's hard stare on her as she spoke.

"Sumner Jackson's a good name," said Robert.

"A beautiful name," said Flame, puzzled.

"Glad you agree."

"Of course, I do," said Flame, looking over him to Matt, wishing she could understand Robert, wishing, too, she could understand the stark, forbidding expression in the scout's dark eyes.

A look of peace settled on Robert's face, and this time he managed to smile. "I'd like to be buried right away. The post cemetery is no place to spend eternity." He stared up for a moment into an overhanging branch thick with autumn leaves. "It's almost like Savannah out here."

"See here, Robert Anderson," she said, "I'll not have you speaking of burial. We've already decided everything will be all right."

"That we have." He looked at Matt. "There should be a preacher somewhere around. He still alive?"

Matt nodded, remembering he was one of the passengers who had scrambled from the coach.

"Have him perform both ceremonies. Don't wait 'til you get to the fort."

Matt could do nothing else but nod.

A sudden sigh shook Robert, and with a whispered, "God bless you, Matthew Jackson," he was gone.

Flame felt the life leave his body, felt his hand fall lax in hers. Tears streamed down her cheeks, as she remembered how only a few hours ago she had thought Robert Anderson would never grow old.

But she hadn't meant he'd keep his youth this way. God knew she hadn't meant this way.

Head bent, she offered a prayer that the once-golden man would find his shining place in Heaven, and that there he would find eternal peace.

Robert was buried by lamplight on the side of the hill beneath a spreading oak. The Rev. Mordecai Mason, his destination aboard the ill-fated stagecoach a church in El Paso, officiated.

In private and for a substantial fee, Matt arranged with the reverend for the second ceremony. He did

59

it quickly before he could think much about the consequences of his actions . . . before he could reconsider and back out.

Twenty-two years ago he'd made a deathbed promise to avenge his brother's slaughter, something he'd never carried out to his satisfaction. He couldn't go back on his word tonight.

Trouble came from the woman when he took her aside and informed her what was about to take place.

"Never!" she said, hands on hips. "How can you suggest such a thing with Robert—" Her voice broke, and she looked away to blink back the tears. She'd stopped crying only in the last few minutes, and here she was, going at it again.

"You can be damned sure it wasn't my idea," he snapped.

"Then why—" She stopped, her grief replaced by a newly dawning horror. "Oh, no. That's what Robert meant by all that promise business." She slapped at her forehead. "And Sumner Jackson. I should have figured it out. Robert thought he would have a son, and he wanted him to have a name. So he told you everything."

"Smart woman," said Matt. He looked her over the way he'd done by the corral. A hell of a lot more travel-worn and weary than she'd been a few hours ago, she still managed to hold appeal.

"But then," he added with a smirk, "I never figured you for stupid. Anderson's kin have money, right?"

Flame slapped him hard, the imprint of her hand forming fast on his cheek.

Matt didn't flinch. "Try that again and you'll get slapped back."

"Don't worry. I don't plan on touching you. Ever. And I'll burn in hell, before I'll become your wife."

"Think again, Miss Frances Chadwick." He made the name a sneer. "I made a promise, and by damn you're not going to make a liar out of me. Whether or not your bastard is really Robert's, he's going to have the Jackson name."

The words struck her with more brutality than his hand would have done. But she was beyond crying, beyond so much as a whimper. She was not, however, beyond rage. It filled her so completely that she wondered if it couldn't somehow harm her child.

Shaking with fury, she looked away and tried to shove all thoughts of Matt Jackson outside the ragged edges of her mind. This was all insane. Not just the cruel, unfair words that had been flung at her, nor the indecent proposal of marriage—if that's what it could be called—but the whole of her existence over the past few months.

Her arms wrapped about her middle. "Oh, Robert," she whispered, sick inside with a kind of despair she could barely contain. Consumed with the frenzy of the moment, she had yet to truly grieve for him.

Noble beyond all past recalling, Robert had ridden to her rescue, and his last thoughts had been of his son, not of himself. At the end he'd accepted the responsibility of his actions, and in so doing he'd paid with his life.

Whether or not she had truly loved him, she realized how much she liked him—more than she had ever done before. Despite all the ugliness that was assailing her, she felt a tenderness in her heart that was closely allied with love.

And then she said, "Annie." She carried a girl. Despite the father's belief.

If she were wrong and the baby turned out to be a boy, she would most certainly name him Sumner.

But Sumner Jackson? She shuddered at the thought.

She turned back to the hard-edged man who would be her husband . . . the last man on earth she would ever have chosen to wed.

"I'll pretend Robert and I married," she said, her chin tilted against his skepticism, her voice stronger than her resolve. "That way his child will have the proper last name."

"And you will have the proper money and the proper right to all his holdings. Think again, lady. Robert's daddy will never let you get away with such a lie."

Flame hated him for speaking what she already knew in her heart. She thought of the love she had wanted, the sharing of life's good times and bad, the tenderness, the understanding. There were no signs of tenderness in Matthew Jackson, no indication he would be willing to share his life, certainly no signs that he knew the meaning of love. How could she ever be his wife?

You promised, a small voice inside her said.

But I didn't know what the promise meant, she came back.

The voice was still. No more argument was

needed. Flame had been taught the importance of keeping her word. Every one of the Chadwicks would know what she had to do.

And her baby needed a last name. By her calculation, they would be married only six months before Annie was born, but dates on marriage and birth papers could be altered, and anyway, she doubted anyone back in Savannah would bother with checking such fine details on anyone so insignificant as a member of the Chadwick clan.

She glanced into the night sky, and then at Jackson. A full moon and a thousand stars shone down, the silvery light joining with the glow from the stagecoach lamp higher on the hill. The scout was hatless, his black hair thick against his shoulders, his dark eyes sunken. He stood so close that even in the dimness she could see the lines etched into his lean face . . . lines that seemed deeper and more numerous after the long and terrible day.

Despite his obvious weariness, he carried an untamed air about him. Maybe it was the buckskin clothing or the set of his lips or the unyielding way he held himself, even in this time of death. Regardless of the reason, he frightened her in a way no man had ever done.

All his harsh words came back at her like rocks thrown by a villainous child. He believed she coveted money and social standing, and she wanted them enough to use the basest kind of lie.

For a moment she saw the situation from his point of view. He, too, had been trapped by a deathbed promise, and he was reacting out of frustration and ire. His feelings were natural, even understandable. But he did not have to be so cruel.

In the background she could hear hammering as the driver and soldiers attempted to repair the coach. She thought with a trace of irony that it would take more than simple carpentry to repair all the things broken in her.

She could start by facing the situation straight on, by accepting it for the time being and making the best of it. For that, she needed to establish some rules.

"Mr. Jackson—"

"Under the circumstances, don't you believe Matt would be more appropriate?"

"Mr. Jackson," she continued, "you know, of course, this will be a marriage in name only."

Matt started. He hadn't given any thought to that particular aspect of the relationship. Now that he was thinking about it, he didn't much like it that a woman of Flame Chadwick's experience rejected the idea of sharing his bed.

He stopped himself. Hell, was he crazy? The fewer entanglements their union involved, the better off they'd both be.

"Miss Chadwick," he said in complete sincerity, "I wouldn't have it any other way."

"Good," she said. And meant it, although she felt a strange disturbance because he had agreed so readily.

"We can get the divorce as soon as the baby's born," he said.

"You've been reading my mind, Mr. Jackson. That's exactly what I hoped you would say."

"So we've got a deal."

Flame stared at the hand he offered. If she took it, would this be just another of her impetuous acts, a rash decision that led to more and more trouble?

No, she knew that wasn't true. Annie told her.

"Deal," she said, shaking his hand. Briefly, quickly letting go lest she be burned by the heat from his palm.

Their eyes met for a moment, the man and woman who would soon be husband and wife, looking at one other as though they were strangers. No, worse . . . far worse. Strangers could at least hold out hope for an eventual friendship. Matt Jackson could never be her friend.

The opinion was enforced beyond all doubt when, high on the hill overlooking the creek, the Rev. Mordecai Mason began the ceremony. Sergeant Gibson and the bickering Mrs. Rylander stood up as witnesses. The most Flame had been able to do in preparation for her wedding was wash her face and pin up her hair.

"Matthew Jackson and Frances Chadwick, we are gathered—" the reverend began.

"Flame," Matt said, interrupting.

"I beg your pardon?" the reverend asked. From the beginning he hadn't liked the idea of this hasty marriage, the groom being little more than a heathen ruffian and the bride a floozy with sinful hair. Fortunately, the coins in his pocket would come in handy at his El Paso church.

"The woman's name is Flame Chadwick," said Matt. "Not Frances."

Flame's cheeks burned. "I'm changing it," she said, trying to keep her voice to a whisper, fearing that it carried to the small congregation of soldiers and travelers who stood nearby. "I like Frances better."

"Flame's what your family called you, right? Then Flame it will have to be."

Trying to inject a much-needed note of dignity into the occasion—since it was impossible to inject it with joy—Flame gave up the argument, and the reverend continued, using the name her papa had given her at birth.

"I'm keeping my promise, Robert," she told herself as the reverend's voice intoned what seemed a hundred verses from the Bible. "I promise, too, to make you proud of your child."

At last it came time for her participation. Paying scant attention to the marriage vows, she stumbled as she said, "I do."

There, it was done, even though she and the bridegroom agreed mutually—and somewhat awkwardly—to forego sealing their union with a kiss. For her part, Flame would rather kiss a badger, and she knew Matt Jackson felt the same.

As she walked down the hill with the bridal party—Lord, she thought, why did she insist upon giving any part of this farce a formal name?—she felt curious stares upon her and the groom. No one could begin to figure this out, and neither she nor Jackson had given any clues. They must be wondering if she had known him before today. If not, was it love at first sight? And why didn't the newlyweds at least deign to hold hands?

Dunderway, looking as puzzled as anyone, helped her into the stagecoach while her husband assembled the troops. The two fallen soldiers were placed across their respective saddles, and the wounded assured Matt that they could take care of themselves.

The stagecoach was one of the few around operating by night as well as day. With a full moon and cloudless sky overhead, Matt decided they should get on into the fort. The driver Caplin, his sprained leg bound tight and barely throbbing, agreed.

Matt hated like hell leaving Robert Anderson's unmarked grave, although he didn't know why. In his years of roaming, he'd buried more than one man beside the trail.

Maybe it was because he hadn't been able to tend to the burial of his own family, the Apaches not wanting to hang around long enough for an eight-year-old to dig the necessary graves. A mother and father, a baby sister, and older brother Charlie. He hadn't thought of them all at once in years. On his own for so long, even during those dark days when he'd been an Apache captive, he sometimes forgot he once belonged to a warm and loving home.

Maybe the memories came to him now because it was his wedding night.

Or maybe not. As he sat wearily in the saddle and stared at the long, winding road ahead, his thoughts turned to the stagecoach behind him and to one of the women inside.

A temptress for sure, and a slattern, too. Matt was human enough to appreciate the sweet pleasures she would offer, and smart enough to know they were pleasures he could never taste. Flame Chadwick might call herself Flame Jackson now, but Matt swore there was no way she would ever be his wife.

Five

What's brave, what's noble,
Let's do it after the high Roman fashion,
And make death proud to take us.

Flame had never understood these lines from Shakespeare, no matter how often Raven recited them. They came from *Antony and Cleopatra*, one of her sister's favorites. She'd often acted out the parts on winter evenings before the family fire.

As Flame quoted them now in a letter back home, she saw what the poet had been getting at. Robert's courage and unselfishness at the end of his life must surely be in the high Roman fashion, for death could be nothing less than proud to take him to the after-life.

It was an idea she was trying to get across as she let everyone back home know at least part of what had happened. Maybe it was foolish to work at such a difficult task tonight, but she'd been unable to sleep after the long ride into the fort.

Barely nodding to the Fort Hardaway staff who'd

awakened to greet them, she'd been too weary to protest as Jackson took her into his house. She'd fallen into bed and awaited the oblivion that Raven promised "knitted the raveled sleeve of care."

But her eyes wouldn't close and her mind wouldn't rest, and so she'd thought of the letter. But what to say? In a farewell note to her family just before sailing for Galveston, she'd written only that she was joining her true love—nothing about why the journey must be made right away. She couldn't bring herself to reveal her impending motherhood, not even to explain her hasty marriage so soon after Robert's death. They'd just have to believe that in wedding a man she'd known only a few hours, she was wilder and more impetuous than ever.

She didn't feel in the least wild and impetuous, not propped up in a narrow, lumpy bed on her wedding night with an unwanted mate lying on a bedroll in an adjacent room.

She glanced around the small bedroom. *His* bedroom, which he'd insisted she take. The place looked like him—rough, unadorned walls, curtainless windows, crudely hewn bureau and chair. Not even a rug to take the cold from the plank floor.

The best she could say was that the bedclothes were clean, and her husband was leaving her alone.

In truth, she had never felt more alone in her life.

For a long while she stared at the paper in her lap, before once again taking up the missive. *I never imagined this kind of emotion,* she wrote of her relationship with Jackson, knowing her beloved parents and sisters would misinterpret. *Please do not hate me. Try to understand.*

She brushed away a sudden rush of tears, before they fell and ran the ink. This was too hard, she thought, but she forced herself to finish, ending with heartfelt expressions of love for each of the Chadwicks and a plaintive plea that they continue to feel the same about her.

Setting the writing materials aside, she turned down the lamp and pulled the covers tight to her chin. Each time she closed her eyes, she relived the attack and all that had followed—the tumbling about inside the coach, the crash, the panic as men fought the women and each other to get out.

She herself had thrown a fist or two in self-defense.

Dunderway had been the one to thrust her half-way through the window, and she'd like to think it was only because he wanted to be kind.

But the worst memories weren't of the coach. They belonged to Robert . . . the gunfire . . . the screams that she hadn't realized at first were coming from her. She thought, too, of the way her one-time lover had given his last thoughts to their unborn child. After that evening by the creek, he must have continued to care for her, must have planned to return and honor his vows as soon as his Army service was done.

Surely this was so. Tonight she could allow herself to believe nothing less.

They'd been apart too long, that was the problem, but he would have realized the depth of his feelings . . . if he had lived.

She clasped the thought hungrily to her bosom, for sanity's sake needing to believe he'd been true. Above all else, she had to know that in coming west she had done the right thing, even if it had turned out all wrong.

So very, very wrong. All the tragedies of the evening renewed their assault, and Flame feared very much that if she continued to lie like this in the dark, recalling each grievous moment, she would again begin to scream.

She turned up the light and, crawling from the bed, fetched the half-completed shawl she had begun to make after leaving Savannah. The wool was dark as the night outside the window, dark as her husband's eyes.

What a ridiculous comparison, she thought, as she settled back under the covers and put the needles to work. As if Matt Jackson's eyes did anything except to unnerve her, to let her know his scorn and his—

She couldn't go on, finding it hard to put into words what those eyes revealed. It wasn't exactly interest in her—he'd not once touched her after they became man and wife. But he touched her with his glance, sometimes with such intensity that it seemed he was touching her with his hands.

Flame shivered at the memory. As soon as Annie was old enough to travel, mother and child would leave this harsh land—and the harsh man she'd been forced to marry. It would go against all her mother's teachings, but she had no choice but to obtain a quick divorce.

In the adjoining small rectangle that served as parlor, dining room, and kitchen, Matt lay on a pile of blankets and watched the light go off and on under the bedroom door. Sharing the restlessness of his bride, he shifted uncomfortably in the direction of the dying coals in the fireplace and, for the hundredth time, counted the ways he could have made the day turn out differently.

No matter how hard he tried to blame Flame Chadwick Jackson, he ended up blaming himself.

And a man could curse himself for only so long. Then it was time for action. In public he would play the honorable role Robert Anderson had assigned him, the newlywed father awaiting the birth of his first child. Not well, he knew, but he'd do the best he could, considering how things were between him and the mother. He'd count it penance for failing at his job, but it wasn't all he would do.

He'd got the stagecoach and troops back to the fort shortly after midnight, settled the passengers and driver into a couple of empty quarters, then decided to wait until morning to file a report with Colonel Burr. Matt needed some time to decide what to say.

Not about the route they'd taken or the attack or the way the lieutenant had lost his life. For all of these, Matt was prepared to take full blame. He'd even take heat for bringing back a trouble-making wife. But he wasn't going to cover up the nature of the firepower the Apaches had used against the troops.

Matt stared at the rifle leaning against the stone fireplace, moonlight from an open window glinting against the polished gunmetal gray. A Winchester

Model 1876, fresh from the factory, bound for Fort Hardaway, according to talk Matt had heard.

Except that this particular gun had not made it to the fort. Somehow it had wound up in the hands of one of the Apaches who had died. Matt had found it on the ground, recognized it as the same make and model Black Eagle used to kill the lieutenant. He'd brought it back as evidence that someone connected with the Army was running guns to the Indians. The culprit probably completed his transaction a couple of days ago, while Matt was searching the brush. He was planning to show the gun to the colonel, relay his suspicions, and wash his hands of the affair.

Lying on the hard floor, thinking over all that had happened, he began to wonder if maybe he wasn't acting hastily. Tell the colonel about the gunrunning? Not a good idea, since there was no telling how far up the chain of command the rot had eaten. There could be some festering right at the top, Army pay at any level not being much. Money didn't mean a great deal to Matt, but he'd seen too much of the world to believe other men felt the same.

Much as he wanted to walk away from Army problems—much as he'd been planning to before today— he couldn't forget the way Black Eagle had brandished the contraband gun in triumph, and the way he'd turned on the lieutenant and fired.

If Matt's aim had been true—if he hadn't been caught in his own private suffering—he could have saved Robert. Marrying his pregnant, discarded woman wasn't enough to avenge his death. Especially when Matt was far from certain about who had done the dirty deed that got her in the family way.

Matt did a lot of thinking during the early morning hours, two images burning into his mind: the savage, triumphant grin of Black Eagle before he'd turned to run, and the constant, scornful glance of his bride. He hadn't been asleep long when he heard a pounding on the door.

He woke with a start, sat up, shook his head to figure just why the hell he was lying on the floor. Stiff, he pulled himself to his feet and staggered toward the pounding. Trailing a hand through his hair, he flung open the door and blinked into the morning sun.

"Hell's fire, Matt, you'd make a town drunk look good," a woman's sharp voice complained. "You look like you've been sleeping in your clothes."

Matt groaned. "Melody, what are you doing here so early?"

"It's after eight o'clock. You know things get started early on the post." She flounced into the room, then turned to face him. "Better close the door, sugar. Wouldn't want anyone passing by to see us, would we? Even though this time I've come in a good cause."

Matt managed to focus on the picture she presented. Dressed in black, her blond curls tamed into a respectable bun, she cast a curious glance at the blankets on the floor, then at the closed door leading to the bedroom.

When she looked back at him, she did not try to hide a smirk.

"I thought we could share our mourning."

Matt looked at her in disgust. "For Robert, you mean."

"Don't look at me like that, Matthew. I *am* sorry he got shot. The troops are saying he died a hero, saving your life and the lives of a stagecoach full of passengers."

"They're right."

She shook her head, her young features settled into what appeared to be an expression of self-derision. "Finally got myself a good man, and he goes and gets himself shot."

"I can see your heart is broken."

For a moment she looked serious, almost sad. "I'm not hypocrite enough to claim that, but I really do regret what happened. Believe what you will, but that's the truth."

Again she glanced toward the bedroom. "Is the new Mrs. Jackson still asleep?"

Matt ran a hand through his rumpled hair. "You heard about her."

"Hell's fire, Matt, I imagine the news is in El Paso by now, and that's a hundred miles away." Her full red lips pulled into a pout. "Why didn't you tell me you were sending for a woman? You're a secretive one, that's for sure."

She sidled closer, glanced down, then slyly raised her lashes. "It was gonna be good, wasn't it? Me being respectable with my new husband, behaving myself like a lady and visiting you on the side. No one would suspect a colonel's daughter and a lieutenant's wife of playing around, now would they?"

"They might, if they knew the lady in question."

A hard glint darkened her blue eyes. "Don't play

75

any holy-moly games with me, Matt Jackson. There's no way you can stand there and say you'd have kept your hands off me if I came around during the night, and it wouldn't have mattered that I was wearing a ring."

Matt backed away and looked her over, trying to remember what he'd seen in her, then decided it was her availability that had been her main charm.

"Get out," he said. "You'll have to grieve someplace else. I've got business to tend to."

"Husband business? You gonna do a little pokin' with the bride?" She gestured toward the blankets by the hearth. "Why did she have you sleeping out here? Can't be much of a woman to treat a man like that."

"It's none of your concern, Melody. She's in there resting. Surely you've got sense enough to know that being caught with me would be a mistake."

"Why, sugar," she said, pulling a handkerchief from her pocket and dabbing a dry eye, "I'd just declare I've come here to accept condolences and to pass on my best wishes." She eased close to him, her fingers stroking the fringe on his shirt. "Sort of killing two birds with one stone, as the saying goes."

The door to the bedroom creaked open, and the two of them jumped apart. Matt didn't know why he felt so guilty, but he caught a look of satisfaction on Melody's face.

Flame stood in the doorway, a white gown covering her from neck to toes. It should have been innocent-looking, but Matt couldn't help noticing the way it followed the sweep of her legs and the curves of her body. Her hair was a jumble of fiery curls tumbling to her shoulders, and her green eyes had a just-out-of-bed dark cast.

Sexy as hell, that's what she was.

"I've been waiting for you two to finish whatever it is you're up to," she said, all politeness, "but I decided that unless I interrupted, you might not be finished before lunch."

Melody's eyes narrowed. "So this is the blushing bride. Matt, sugar, aren't you going to introduce us?"

Flame stepped boldly into the room. "That won't be necessary, *sugar,*" she said to her husband, pleased that he had the good sense to look distressed. It was the only thing about the moment that pleased her, since she felt that her heart would break.

She held out her hand. "I'm Flame Chadwick Jackson, the newest resident, it would seem, of Fort Hardaway. And you? I assumed when I first heard your voice that you were a servant come to clean Matt's quarters, but something you said indicated I was wrong."

Her directness took Melody aback.

"Well!" the colonel's daughter said.

"I don't imagine there's much that's well on this day," said Flame, giving way for a tremulous moment to despair. Catching herself, she smiled at her husband, but she put nothing warm or humorous into the look. "I suppose you'll have to do the honors after all, since the lady has suddenly gone tongue-tied."

Matt shifted, uncomfortably aware that among his

wife's several characteristics was the close resemblance to a tigress when she was aroused.

"Miss Melody Burr," he said, "this is Flame."

Melody found her voice. "Colonel Burr is my father," she said. "I don't suppose Matt has told you much about me, the devil. He's certainly never told me about you."

"Matt's a devil, all right," said Flame, casting a sideways glance at her husband. "He's probably got a hundred secrets he keeps from you besides me."

Melody opened her mouth to speak, then changed her mind, deciding the new Mrs. Jackson was not worth tangling with so early in the morn.

"I'll leave you two lovebirds alone." She glanced at the pile of blankets beside the hearth, then smiled sweetly at Flame. "I can't imagine Matt sleeping on the floor, but I guess there are some details of your marriage you haven't worked out yet."

So saying, she skirted around Matt and exited, slamming the door behind her. The noise echoed through the small room.

Husband and wife stared at one another.

"In case you didn't know it," said Flame, still holding tight to her control, "sound travels very well from room to room."

"I was afraid that's the way it was."

"Robert had become engaged to her." She spoke the words flatly, hoping Matt didn't realize each one was a knife in her heart.

"He'd have changed his mind."

"And found someone else."

Her eyes were wide and stark, and Matt could see the trouble she was having keeping calm. For the

78

first time since he'd met her, he felt a spark of sympathy for her plight. Maybe she wasn't the floozy he'd taken her to be. Or if she was, that didn't mean she was totally without a heart.

Turning from him, she walked slowly toward the privacy of the bedroom. A sudden, painful thought forced her to pause in the doorway, and she shifted back around.

"I'd like to ask a favor of you, Matt. Maybe I'm not in much of a position to do so, but I'm asking anyway. It's no business of mine who you sleep with, but considering the baby on the way, I'd prefer you keep your assignations more discreet."

"My what?" he asked, losing the sympathy fast.

"Assignations. You know, your—"

"I know what they are. Never heard screwing around put quite so delicately."

Pink stained Flame's cheeks. She tried to stand tall and dignified, but being barefooted and clothed in a nightgown, she found dignity hard to attain.

"I'm sorry you find it necessary to be crude, but that's your nature, I suppose. I know I'm supposed to be grateful you've taken in a disgraced woman and given her your name, but you'll have to excuse me if I have a hard time expressing that gratitude this morning. All I want is for you and the colonel's daughter to choose another place to meet. Or at least let me know when you'll be here, and I'll make certain to be far away."

"You've got things all worked out, haven't you?"

"I've got very few things worked out, but before long I will."

She looked so damned sure of herself, Matt had

to fight the urge to take her by the shoulders and shake some of the confidence away.

"And how about you?" he asked.

He walked across the room, daring her with his eyes to retreat, but she held her ground. Up close, he saw the faint sprinkling of freckles across the porcelain smoothness of her cheeks, saw the golden flecks in the depths of her green eyes. He heard her intake of breath as he stared down, saw the parting of her lips.

"What about me?" she managed as a wave of heat washed over her.

He propped one arm against the door frame close to the tangle of fiery curls and leaned down, feeling her breath on his cheek, catching the scent of her rose perfume, knowing if he stayed this close to her much longer, he'd be totally aroused.

"What do you plan to do about getting sex?" he asked.

Flame could barely believe she heard right, and she stared up at Matt in astonishment. Black hair, brown eyes, bristled cheeks—he looked like a prince of darkness, and she decided on the instant that he was evil personified.

"Don't look so innocent, Flame," he said, his mouth twisting into a half-smile. "As if you don't know what I'm talking about. You're a beautiful woman who must have no trouble attracting men. And you couldn't have gotten yourself pregnant without lifting your skirts."

"You are a bastard," she hissed.

"Could be. Bastards are something you'd know about."

Flame raised her hand to slap him. He caught her by the wrist.

"No, not this time. You wanted an officer and a gentleman, but surely you know by now that's not what you got."

"I know exactly the kind of man I married," she said, putting all the hate she could into the words.

"Good." He looked past her to the unmade bed and the clothes lying on the floor where she'd dropped them in her exhaustion the night before.

"There won't be a maid coming around to pick up after you," he said. "You'll have to fend for yourself."

"I'll manage."

She stepped backwards, but she did so proudly, wanting him to know she was not in retreat. Hugging her middle, she looked him straight in the eye. He stared back with open scorn.

"I'm sorry," she said, "that we don't like one another. It's going to make the next few months go by very slowly. You needn't worry that I'll disgrace you by asking the troops to share my bed. It will be difficult, of course, given my wanton nature, but until I ride out of here, I'll force myself to concentrate on motherhood."

Something in her eyes renewed Matt's suspicion that he might be wrong about her.

"Flame—"

"I'm not finished. Last night you said something about the hospital being right next door. When the time comes—and that should be a little more than six months away—I'll just walk right over, do what's

81

necessary, and be out of here with my baby on the next stage."

Matt almost smiled at the bravery of her words. "Don't you think childbearing is a little more complicated than that?"

"If so, I promise you won't be bothered."

Without waiting for a response, she slammed the door against his insolence, almost catching his hand before he jerked away. For a minute all was quiet in the house, then she heard his boots strike the floor, heard the front door open and close, and she knew that he was gone.

Weary, she sat at the side of the bed and thought how badly the first day of her marriage had begun. About as badly, she admitted to herself, as possible. If only Robert had remained true . . . if only Melody Burr had not captured his heart . . . if only she hadn't come around so early this morning to stake a claim on the second man in Flame's life.

There she went again with another string of *if only.*

She saved the biggest one for last: if only this nightmare in which she was caught would come to an end.

But such was not to be. With Matt Jackson hovering close by day and night, taunting her with his words and with his glance, unsettling her in strange, dark ways she didn't like nor understand, she knew with sad certainty the nightmare had barely begun.

Six

"Mr. Jackson to see you, sir," announced Fort Hardaway's post adjutant, First Lieutenant Abraham Lilly, as he stood in the doorway of Colonel William Burr's office.

Close behind, grumpy and grizzled as a bear, Matt half-expected the freshly shaven lieutenant to click his heels for punctuation. For damned sure Burr would have approved.

Not much on military protocol, Matt entered the room without waiting for permission. Lilly frowned and glanced toward his commanding officer for instruction. Receiving none, he exited, closing the door behind him.

Burr glanced up from his seated position behind the desk. A longtime Army man, short and wiry, his full head of hair and moustache the color of rain-clouds, the colonel showed anger in the pair of faded blue eyes assessing the buckskin-clad newcomer.

"Figured you'd have some questions about yesterday," Matt said, looking sideways at the tall, gaunt uniformed figure standing by the open window at the side of the room.

"In private," Matt added, not wanting a witness to whatever he decided to say.

Captain Arnold Davis held his silence as he fingered the smoking cigar in his hand, a superior smile on his pale face.

Burr cleared his throat. "As a matter of fact, the captain and I were discussing that very thing. An officer dead, three men wounded. And Black Eagle still on the loose. No excuse for that kind of skirmish. No excuse."

For once, Matt agreed with the commanding officer. True, Robert Anderson had chosen the fatal route for the stagecoach and patrol, but it was also true Matt hadn't put up much of a fight.

Details of the attack flashed through his mind—the unexpected *hi-yi* from the lurking Apaches, the volley of gunshot blasts, the twisted, triumphant sneer on the Apache warrior's face when Matt's aim proved false.

Most of all he remembered Robert Anderson's brave ride to his death . . . and the screams of the woman who had journeyed west to be his bride.

Frances Chadwick, she'd called herself. Now Flame Jackson. Matt's bride, not Anderson's, a final twist of irony that made the disaster of the day complete. He thought of the way she'd stood in the doorway to his bedroom less than half an hour ago, and glared defiantly up at him. Wild curls the color of fire, a freckled nose and green taunting eyes, a slender nightgowned figure . . . these were details that Matt also recalled.

"It won't happen again," he muttered, not knowing whether he meant the Indian attack or the insolence of his wife.

"Speak up, Jackson," said Burr. "Need to have conviction in your voice, if I'm to take your word. Got to admit it'll be difficult. Blackie's made a half-dozen raids into Texas over the past year, and damned if he hasn't made it back across the river every time."

"Rather an old habit of yours, isn't it, Jackson?" said Captain Davis. "Letting him get away, I mean."

Rage took hold of Matt, and his fists knotted. He'd get great satisfaction from knocking the smile off Davis's face. Trouble was, there was truth to the bastard's comment. Black Eagle's raids had proven progressively less destructive since Matt took the assignment as scout a year ago, but they hadn't decreased in frequency. Worse, the renegade Apache always seemed to know where he was, and to conduct his raids somewhere else.

Until yesterday, when he'd shown up well armed.

Matt considered a connection between the captain and the Army guns that had ended up in Indian hands. No reason to link the two, except that someone inside the fort must be providing information to the Indians' suppliers, and Matt disliked the captain enough to wish it were he.

As for the colonel, the stories about his adulterous affair were too numerous and consistent not to have some basis in fact. The woman would want something for her troubles, besides an occasional hour or two in bed.

And he had a daughter who wasn't hesitant to

outfit herself in expensive finery. Matt didn't know much about the wife, but she probably came with a high price tag, too. With three women to take care of, Burr could very well be running up more expenses than his Army pay would cover.

Still, Matt remained inclined to suspect the captain.

"How's your leg, Davis?" he asked.

"My leg?"

"Anderson said it was giving you trouble. Otherwise you'd have been leading the patrol."

"Oh, yes," Davis said. He rubbed at his thigh. "An old injury from the war. Acts up every now and then, and the doctor advises me to favor it when it does." He glanced at Burr. "You can imagine, colonel, how frustrated I was to miss out on a chance to capture that Apache villain."

"I'm sure you were," said Burr.

Matt caught a trace of sarcasm in the commanding officer's voice.

The colonel shifted to Matt. "So tell me what went wrong. My daughter's beside herself with grief—engaged to the lieutenant just recently, as a matter of fact—and I'd like to comfort her with some details about his bravery."

Matt could have told the colonel just what kind of comforting Melody most appreciated, but again he saw little value in revealing all the truth.

"Lieutenant Anderson died a hero," said Matt. He filled in with particulars, including how his aim had gone astray just as Anderson was riding up the wooded hill toward the overturned stagecoach.

He left out nothing but the harsh memories that

had assailed him at the time, and the screaming presence of the woman who had journeyed to Texas demanding the lieutenant's name.

"Not like you to miss," said Davis. A thin ribbon of smoke issued from between his lips. "Not like you at all."

"You hinting at something?"

"Only what I've overheard the men say."

"Now, now," said Burr, "no need to go into that. Rumors always persist on an Army base."

"But these seem particularly well founded," said Davis, keeping his small brown eyes pinned to Matt. "We all know of your hatred for the Apache, Mr. Jackson. At least, that's what we've always believed to be the case. You did spend much of your youth among the Indians, did you not? It seems curious that when you had your enemy within gun range, you let him go. It seems very curious indeed."

Matt seethed all the more, his rage fed by the realization that the rumors were not unjustified, even if they were not true.

Smacking the cigar into Davis's smug face would offer little more than temporary satisfaction, he reminded himself as he glanced at the colonel. "You can get yourself another scout anytime you want. Just let me know and I'm out of here."

"With the new bride?" asked Davis.

Matt should have seen the comment coming. He cursed under his breath.

"I must say," said Burr, "news of the ceremony took us by surprise. Never considered you a ladies' man. And here you go tying yourself down to just one of them. Thought you had better sense."

Matt shrugged. "Took me by surprise, too."

"Oh, I can understand," said Davis. "The excitement of the moment led to other excitements." His eyes lit with a new fervor. "I hear she was friendly with Anderson at first, and then after his death turned to you."

Matt leapt to his wife's defense, giving no thought to why. "If you're hinting at something, say it. Otherwise leave her out of this."

Davis shrugged. "Just passing on what I've heard. If the woman is as beautiful as the men claim, I'm surprised you've risen so early from your wedding bed. Surely"—he puffed again on his cigar and the smoke curled around his sunken features—"there's not trouble already under the Jackson roof. Disappointment, perhaps, on one part or the other?"

Matt considered snapping the captain in half.

Instead, he shifted his attention to Burr. "As I said, anytime you want a replacement just let me know. Mrs. Jackson and I can be out of here by noon."

It was a promise Matt wasn't certain he could deliver, given the obstinacy and dubious character of his wife, but saying it felt good.

"Don't be a damned fool," said the colonel. "Although I must say, it seems strange that so much happened in one day. Including burying the body of that young lieutenant in unsanctified ground."

"Savage, I'd call it," said Davis with a sniff, his ferret eyes taking in Matt's unorthodox garb.

"We're all savage, captain," said Matt, "if you scrape enough civilization away. Besides, the burial was Anderson's idea. And I wasn't savage enough to deny his dying wish."

Which, as it happened, involved something in addition to the burial, something rather more demanding that he'd be living with for a while.

Matt forced his thoughts away from a redheaded woman and onto the Winchester rifle back in his cabin. "There's a great deal strange about this whole thing, Colonel. You're not the only one with questions."

He looked at Davis, then back at Burr. Instinct told him he was right not to mention the Army-issue guns that had been turned on the soldiers of the patrol. If either or both of the officers were guilty of running them, he wanted them to think the crime hadn't been discovered.

"Rest assured," he said, "I'll find the answers I'm looking for."

He left the way he'd entered, without awaiting permission, his boots turning by habit toward the hospital and on to the adobe shack that was his home. If he had to choose between the colonel and the captain as the culprit, he'd pick the latter. But only because the man was a cowardly bureaucrat more concerned with appearance than substance.

Not once had Matt seen him turn a hand to anything more strenuous than his cigar.

Proof was what Matt needed. Proof was what he would get.

At the same time he brought Black Eagle to justice. That he'd failed to do so before now ate at him like a cancer. It was past time to carve it out.

As soon as he walked through his front door, he

caught the scent of roses, and forgot Davis and Burr and even the Apache. The blankets were gone from the hearth, and the floor had been swept, but otherwise all was the same as he'd left it.

Except for the rose-scented air. With that one addition, everything seemed changed.

He could tell from the stillness she was gone. Nothing had yet been this quiet when Flame was around. He glanced in the bedroom . . . and at the neatly made bed. Big enough for two, if they slept in each other's arms. Hell of a thing to think of, since he'd sooner cuddle with a rattler.

He'd have to tell her to cut out the perfume. Didn't go with the adobe walls.

And where the hell was she? His conscience struck him. He'd left her with no food, and little knowledge about the fort. He didn't know if she had a dime to her name. She wasn't his responsibility, that was for damned sure. Yet he couldn't let her starve.

He thought of the way she'd confronted Melody, and he almost smiled. Oh, she was a feisty one, all right.

And too good-looking to be out on a frontier fort unchaperoned, men being men, and lonely men at that. Wherever she was, more than likely trouble was close by.

"Not my problem," he told himself.

But he knew that she was. Matt raked a hand through his hair. Hell of a thing for a man to deal with. Too bad he didn't keep liquor on the premises. A swallow of whiskey would go down smooth right now.

His eye fell to the Winchester propped against the

stone fireplace. Feeling the urge to shoot something, he decided the targets on the range would have to do. Find out just how good the gun was . . . do a little thinking in the process, decide on a plan for bringing the guilty to justice, including Black Eagle.

And forget that for the time being he was no longer a single man.

Left to fend for herself, Flame found the privy modestly tucked away behind a grove of trees a dozen yards from the front door. A young soldier passed her as she was trying to steal out with only her gown and wrapper as covering.

She blushed in embarrassment, but no more than the young man.

"It's thataway, Mrs. Jackson," he said, avoiding her eye as much as she was avoiding his. "Seeing as how it's close to the hospital, we keep it limed and everything. Don't hardly stink."

"Thank you," she said, although she didn't know exactly what she was thanking him for. For knowing who she was already? For being so polite in showing her the way? Maybe for hurrying on past her and leaving her to her mortification.

A zinc-lined tub was propped against the side of the house, prompting dreams of a proper cleaning to rid her body of the soil from the road. It proved too heavy to move. Gathering water from a cistern located on past the privy, she settled for a sponge bath in front of her husband's bureau.

She dressed with care in a modest, two-piece, lavender cotton gown, her hair tucked demurely beneath a matching feathered bonnet, and set out on a stroll along a worn footpath that outlined the perimeter of the fort. Seeing no other women, she tried to remain undaunted, tried to keep her footsteps firm, her back straight, her thoughts optimistic.

Still, she couldn't help wondering if perhaps she wasn't supposed to be out like this without escort . . . or even simply out at all.

Maybe the only acceptable behavior at Fort Hardaway was to sneak into a man's cabin the way that witch had done this morning . . . the one Robert had betrayed her with.

Tears welled in her eyes, but she forced them away. It was all too clear that Matthew Jackson and the woman were on intimate terms. And she the commanding officer's daughter, too, with her betrothed lying miles away in a cold and newly dug grave.

A lump formed in Flame's throat. Did no one in this land have honor?

Certainly not her husband, who'd left her with no food and only a little money remaining from her traveling funds. Money she hadn't mentioned. For all he knew, she was destitute.

Oh, how she hated the man. And yet she felt a tight squeezing of her heart that he could be so thoughtless. They'd argued, true enough, and she'd sent him away, but he'd been the one to insinuate she was a wanton. Just because she'd been forced to wed.

Whatever sympathy she got for her plight would not come from him.

"Raven," she whispered to herself, "what would you do?"

But she couldn't imagine her sensible sister in such a situation. And if she were, she'd brood about it in private, keeping her worries—and her solutions—to herself.

Flame refused to put the question to Papa or Mama or Angel, even in her mind. They would be too hurt.

Halting on the footpath well away from her new home and the neighboring hospital, she stared around her—at the hard-packed ground with its scattering of dying grass, at the stone buildings she couldn't begin to identify, at the stretch of land with the flagpole in the center . . . and on to the surrounding hills.

Only the hills held charm, and that because she couldn't see them up close. Loving beautiful things, she imagined trees and flowers and singing birds, shrubs and creeks and wild deer bending to drink. These were the images she must keep in her mind, not the pebbled dirt beneath her feet.

A line of soldiers marching past startled her from her reverie. She counted a dozen as they trod close by, and she didn't think it was her imagination that they stood straighter and kept to a brisker pace while they were in her view.

She didn't want to watch them, but she couldn't help it. And she caught more than one casting a sideways glance in her direction. What were they thinking? What was *anyone* at the fort thinking about a traveling woman who'd married a rough-hewn Army scout hours after they met?

Her cheeks burned. Wanton would be the kindest thing they would call her. She decided then and there that if her husband didn't blab about the baby to everyone around, she would keep the news to herself, until the truth became obvious. Not even the doctor at the hospital would be told.

Annie was her secret, as well as her strength. She'd keep going because of her.

Flame's stomach rumbled, and she realized the morning nausea she'd suffered for weeks was replaced by a ravenous hunger. If she didn't find sustenance soon, she'd be gnawing at the feather in her bonnet.

Somehow she doubted a place called Fort Hard would offer a tea room where she might dine. But, having done a little reading about her destination, she knew there were general stores on the frontier forts, establishments much like the one her family owned.

Fort Hard would have such a place, run by a sutler, and she did have a few coins in her purse. Maybe some bread and cheese, a glass of milk, fresh fruit—strawberries, perhaps. Oh, how she craved a bowl of berries and cream. But she'd settle for bread and cheese.

There were other meals to think of, too. Meals that as a wife she must provide. Where to find the store?

She spied three soldiers strolling toward her. Not marching as the others had been, but walking slow, watching her just as she was watching them. Each carried his own long-handled gardening tool—a shovel, a rake, a hoe—angled over a shoulder, the way another trio of soldiers might hold their guns.

How young they looked, not one more than twenty years of age. Dusty blue uniforms fit loosely on their lank frames, and their black caps were much too small to hide the fact that each and every one had hair much the color of hers.

Three redheads meeting a fourth. In her desperation she took it as a good sign.

As they approached, she smiled a nervous greeting. "Gentlemen, good morning," she managed when they halted in front of her.

"Thank ye for the compliment," said one, "but you'll not find a gentleman in the bunch. Foot soldiers, we are, and privates, t' boot. A trio of hapless youths from the Emerald Isle. Lost in this wasteland, struck dumb by the sight of an angel awaiting us on this glorious morn."

Flame couldn't help but grin. "Struck dumb? Only an Irishman would claim such a thing after that speech."

The second soldier slapped his free hand over his heart. "The voice of an angel, too. Me heart is filled with love."

The third leaned against his hoe and thumbed the cap to the back of his head. "Brendan falls in love every time he journeys to town. Now me, I'm the constant sort. You'll not find me eyes straying to another lass. Pray tell, dearest darlin', when can we wed?"

Flame glanced at her bare left hand, easing it into the folds of her skirt, feeling naked without the respectability of a ring. Somehow the joy of the moment was gone.

"A cloud has bedimmed the sunshine in our angel's face," said the first. "Have we displeased ye with our brazen ways?"

"You've not displeased me, not in the least. It's just that my sister is called Angel and I miss her very much."

"We'll be thinking of another name for ye, lass." He stood up smartly. "Michael Mallon at your service. These be me mates Brendan Faulkner and Ian Craig. All Irish lads as ye might can tell. Would we be talking to a colleen by any chance? You've a voice soft as summer wind and lacking the brogue, but the locks peeking beneath the fair bonnet give us hope."

"I'm half and half. Papa says his ancestors go back to Ireland's earliest days. Mama was born in London to old English stock."

"I forgive ye," said Brendan, "for the London connection."

"Nothing to forgive," said Ian, shooting his friend a censorious glance. "Welcome to Fort Hard, Miss . . ."

"Chadwick. Oh, no, I'm sorry. It's Mrs. Jackson. I'm recently wed, you see, and I've not introduced myself very often."

Brendan's brow furrowed. "Jackson . . . You'd not be speaking of Alonzo Jackson over in B Company by any chance?"

"Ye dunce," said Ian. "What would the likes of her be doing wed to that old bas—" He caught himself. "Sorry, lass, but we're not used to speaking with ladies such as yourself."

96

"No apologies, please. My husband is a scout at Ford Hardaway. Matthew Jackson."

The three looked at her in wide-eyed surprise.

"Is something wrong?" she asked.

"Beggin' your pardon," said Michael, "but we'd not put the two of you together in a thousand years. You being a lady and all."

Flame thought of the man whose name she shared . . . remembered the dark smoldering suggestions in the depths of his eyes when he'd looked at her this morning, the twist of his lips when he'd asked what she would do for sex. He was so close, so overpowering she'd felt lightheaded, needing to touch him for strength.

But the only touching possible was a slap to that smirking face.

"Are ye feeling well, Mrs. Jackson?" asked Michael. "The sun is bright today, and you've no parasol to protect yourself from the rays. Even in October, a Texas sun can sap the strength from your bones."

"I'm fine," she said, even managing a bright smile. "But I appreciate your concern. Tell me, where can I find a store to make a few purchases?"

"You're on the right path," said Ian. "The building down the way to the right is where the sutler plies his trade. Don't let him cheat ye, now. He's one to boost the prices, if he thinks he can get away with it."

"I'll be careful. Thank you for your kindness." She put out a hand.

"Michael," said Brendan, elbowing his friend. "We've trouble a-comin'."

97

Michael looked past him. "Begorra, ye speak the truth fer once." He looked at Flame. "We'd best be gettin' to our tasks. Cowards we are, but we've not the intestines to face down the colonel's wife so early in the day. And we'd not be doin' ye a favor if we did."

The three smiled a cautious goodbye, and with tools once again propped against their shoulders they hurried on down the path, leaving Flame to watch the approach of two black-clad women, the elder grim of face, the younger with an openly curious expression on her face, as if she wanted to understand this latest newcomer to the fort.

She seemed at the moment like a different woman from the hussy who had approached a day-old bridegroom in the confines of his home. Flame looked at her more closely, wondering if there weren't more to the woman than she'd previously suspected.

"Mother," Melody said when Flame was within earshot, "this is the woman we've heard about. The one that married Daddy's scout."

She spoke with surprising meekness. Flame looked at her closer still.

"Well," said Mrs. Burr with a sniff, her voice carrying clearly on the still morning air, "she's no better than she should be. Marrying that barbarian was bad enough, but she's already consorting with the troops. And redheaded! What else can one expect?"

Flame's temper flared, and she forgot her musings about the daughter. She knew that on occasion she was talked about back in Savannah, simply because she didn't always behave with propriety, but at least the hometown folks had the decency to keep the talk behind her back.

She also knew the polite way to cut someone she considered beneath her consideration. It was a skill taught at Miss Lillian's Academy for Young Ladies, one every Southern girl learned early, one the Chadwick daughters had picked up through observation on the Savannah streets. Mama considered such behavior as rude and refused to condone it, but sometimes polite rudeness was the only approach to take.

Lifting her skirts slightly, she planted her feet firmly on the path and headed straight for the enemy.

"Miss Burr," she said with a bright smile, slowing her step when they were near, "what a surprise to see you again." She glanced at the mother. "Lovely day, isn't it? I do hope it doesn't rain."

She swished on past, leaving the mother's, "Well, I never!" in her wake. She also heard the woman question Melody as to how and when she'd met "that dreadful creature."

If she thought the answer could be anywhere near the truth, she'd slow her step to eavesdrop, but something told her Melody Burr was well practiced at prevarication, and Mrs. Burr equally practiced at believing what she was told.

A few steps more and her anger dissolved, in its place a return of desolation. She had to get along at this place, at least for the upcoming months. Any satisfaction she received from speaking her mind would be temporary at best.

Oh, but her temper and impetuous ways would prove her downfall yet. To think that back in Savannah it seemed clear as her mother's prized Waterford crystal that she had fallen as far as possible. A half continent away, she feared that there was still some distance to go.

Bitter memories assailed her, thoughts of how she'd longed for a newfound respectability to emerge from her disgrace. The short life of Frances Chadwick seemed a long time past. She was Flame Jackson now, wife of a close-to-savage Army scout. Despite what he believed, she didn't care in the least that he wasn't an officer, but she minded terribly that he would never be kind.

It struck her that her new bridegroom didn't seem anymore acceptable than his bride. To the gentry of Fort Hardaway, if not to the hardworking foot soldiers, Mr. and Mrs. Matthew Jackson were a well-suited pair.

It was a most discomforting thought.

Seven

Five loaves of bread ought to keep them for the week. And they looked so pretty lined up on the checkered tablecloth Flame had bought at the sutler's store, five fragrant brown-crusted loaves worthy to be set before a king.

Four and a half loaves, to be exact. She hadn't been able to resist a healthy sampling when she popped the first warm loaf out of the pan.

And they weren't prepared for royalty, unless she considered Matt Jackson king of all boors.

Flame brushed a damp curl from her face. Cooking was hard work, but that was something she'd never avoided. And, since she hadn't laid eyes on her husband after he stormed out earlier in the day, it helped to pass the time.

So she expected a servant to wait on her, did she? Little her husband knew.

Bread baked, chicken stew simmering on the lone burner of the wood stove, even a yeast jar on the shelf for when it was baking time again—all products of a long afternoon. She'd considered cooking up some kind of dessert, but he might expect similar treats every night. Papa always did.

In truth, she didn't want to do so much as see Matt Jackson, but with the way her luck was running, an autumn storm would flood the fort and they'd be stranded together for a week.

No matter how much he upset her, somehow they had to get along, at least for the next few months. Flame wouldn't have it said she didn't do her part.

The truth was she hated being surrounded by anything less than the love she'd always known in her Savannah home. Love was, of course, out of the question, but right now she'd settle for civility.

She'd tried to make amends for the scene with Melody Burr and her mother as soon as she'd gone into the sutler's, behaving with all the propriety the strictest stickler for deportment could demand.

"Mrs. Jackson, you say?" the proprietor had asked when she introduced herself. "Surely not married to the scout."

The half-dozen customers milling about the store—four women and two uniformed soldiers—had immediately perked up, reminding Flame of hound dogs cornering quail.

Flame forced a smile. "Yes, I am. I arrived at Fort Hardaway late last night."

The sutler, a small, fox-faced man with piercing brown eyes, looked her over in a most uncomfortable way. "Asa Underwood here. I'll do what I can to make your stay a pleasant one."

Flame shivered. Mama would want her to thank Mr. Underwood for the offer, but something in his eyes and in his voice kept her from saying the words.

She pulled a folded paper from her reticule. "I've made a shopping list. Staples, mostly." She laid it on the counter.

Underwood scanned the list. "No fruit, sorry. And the beef is a mite ripe, but I got a fresh-killed chicken that'd do you. Don't happen every day, understand. It'll cost you some."

Mentally Flame counted the coins in her purse. "Chicken would be fine," she said, aware that everyone was listening to the conversation. As if they had nothing better to do than find out what the Jacksons would be eating tonight.

While the sutler filled her order, she had browsed among the tables, pleased to see bolts of cloth and a rainbow variety of threads available for purchase.

Not that she could buy anything so frivolous today. Matt's empty larder gave evidence she'd best save her money for food.

A swath of bright red had caught her eye. Red silk, as fiery as her name. Redheads weren't supposed to wear the color well, but it had always been Flame's favorite. One day she'd get up the nerve to make herself a crimson gown.

Certain that day was at best far in the future, she had thrust all thoughts of sewing aside. Until she outgrew her wardrobe, the dresses she'd brought with her would be sufficient.

But she hadn't been able to resist the red-and-white checkered tablecloth. It would be the one bright spot in her new, albeit temporary home.

Hours later, viewing the bread, she congratulated herself on the purchase. And where was her spouse to admire it?

Flame sighed in exasperation. The little she knew of Matt Jackson, he didn't seem the kind to take notice of tablecloths.

She glanced through the bare window. Night was coming on. Her stomach rumbled. She stirred the stew, then sat on the bench beside the table, assuring herself—with little success—that he wasn't off with a crowd of men complaining his new bride had run him out of his home.

Or equally bad, locked in a heavy embrace with the commanding officer's daughter.

Not that she should care. It wasn't as though she'd sought out this arrangement. Marriage had been Robert's idea, and Mr. Jackson had seemed willing, if not exactly pleased.

Well, she silently admitted, *willing* might be putting it a tad inaccurately. He'd been madder than a Reb facing Sherman, as Papa might have put it. She felt the same way. But she couldn't dwell on the negative aspects of her situation. Annie must have a last name.

Flame tapped her slipper against the plank floor. She was trying to be accepting, trying to be cooperative, trying to keep from bursting into tears, all inordinately difficult when she was fighting a sense of abandonment and desolation.

Most difficult of all to handle was a nagging feeling that because he'd been so much against marrying her, she ought to be grateful to Jackson for doing it anyway. By his action she would not return to Savannah in disgrace. Or at least not totally.

She truly ought to be grateful. Somehow she had to be.

Outside the shadows lengthened. She got up to stir the stew, adding liquid to keep it from scorching, then lit the lamp by the hearth. At last she set the kettle away from the heat and spooned a serving of chicken into the lone tin plate. She'd need to eat first and clean up anyway, before her husband could dine.

She sat at the lonely table and forced down the stew, for Annie's sake, not for herself. It tasted good, she had to admit. Mama had taught her girls to cook.

And to clean and to sew and more than anything to expect a loving family of their own when they were grown.

A piece of bread caught in Flame's throat, and she forced herself to swallow. She could have that family yet. It wasn't impossible. Just not at Fort Hard. And not with the stranger she had wed.

More than ever she swore he would be her husband in name only. Any other arrangement went beyond all boundaries of gratitude. There were young women who might take to his dark rugged looks. But not her. He was too unnerving ever to be considered her soul's mate.

Robert could have been. She brushed a tear from her eye. Sweet-talking Robert with the gentle, loving hands.

The unwanted image of a buxom blond flashed in her mind, and she faced the truth. Robert had been sweet-talking, all right, a privileged Southern gentleman who had loved the ladies more than he should. But she couldn't think ill of him, not after he'd ridden to her rescue, daring the devil Apache to fire, bravely falling, then giving his last thoughts to his unborn child.

For those reasons she would always love him and hold his memory dear. Someday, perhaps when Annie was old enough to understand, she could tell her just how brave her father had been.

But she didn't love him the way Mama loved Papa—truly, deeply, eternally—even though she had once tried.

As to her current arrangement, the best she could manage was to tolerate her husband. If he bothered to show up again.

She stared at the kettle of stew on the stove, and with the minutes slowly crawling by, she watched as it slowly cooled, the fat congealing across the top.

The longer she waited, the angrier she became, and the more completely she forgot about cooperation. Here she was, doing all she could to make the best of this sham arrangement, but it was clear the effort would go unnoticed and unappreciated.

A mournful trumpet sounded over the stillness of the fort. Taps. Day was done.

Flame's temper flared. Grabbing the kettle, she slammed out the front door, stepped down from the porch, and unceremoniously dumped her bridegroom's supper onto the bare ground. She'd much rather feed the strays that would be along soon than offer a forkful of sustenance to him.

Or, what was more likely, give him an opportunity to turn it down. Whatever he'd wanted to eat, from main course to dessert, he must have already been offered somewhere else.

Inside she cleaned up the supper mess, stored the

bread, and, with a night chill coming on, started a fire from the pile of wood stacked at the end of the porch. She was seated beside the hearth, knitting the black shawl, when Matt strode inside. Her back was to him, and she didn't bother to look around, but she could feel his presence the way she might if a wild creature had stalked into the room.

Her heart pounded with unexpected intensity. She'd long ago given up her anger, in its place an aching sadness that was much more difficult to tolerate. So why feel something akin to excitement because he'd returned?

Standing just inside the door, studying the way gentle light washed over her, Matt was caught by the picture she presented. She sat straight, her hair piled atop her head, her long slender neck curved gracefully as she worked at her knitting.

Something inside him twisted. He was struck by a long-forgotten memory of another woman sitting before the fire, then turning to welcome a small boy who'd been helping his daddy build the corral.

Matt had never before recalled the scene, not once since his capture, yet it came clearly to him now, as though it had always been at the back of his mind, waiting for the right moment to appear.

He cursed himself for being a fool. The memories of his mother in no way resembled the woman he had taken to wife. It was just the whiskey he'd been drinking that was muddling his mind.

"Thought you'd be in bed," he said as he propped the Winchester beside the fireplace, resting his hat over the stock, running a hand through his hair.

107

Flame didn't drop a stitch. "Sorry to disappoint you. I'm not used to retiring so early."

"Out here we don't waste fuel."

She gripped the needles. "I'll buy what I need."

"Not a matter of buying. The supply sometimes runs low."

Flame felt a sudden urge to cry, and she didn't like it one bit. What had taken possession of her to bring on tears at every moment of distress? Pregnancy, she supposed. It certainly wasn't because of the brusqueness of her spouse.

She laid the shawl aside and stood to face him, husband and wife alone for only the second time in their brief marriage. Strangers, too, sharing nothing but a name. It was a thought that produced an emptiness around her heart.

In one glance she took in the tall, lean figure, the broad chest beneath the fringed leather shirt, the hollowed cheeks dusted with bristle, the unkempt black-as-night hair. Her breath quickened. In the flickering light he looked as dangerous as when he'd held his ground before the Apache's gun. She'd never seen such eyes on a man. Brown as Georgia loam, yet deep and watchful, judging, she knew, searching out all her faults.

But he didn't find fault with her appearance, not if the scrutiny he was giving her provided any proof. He looked her over more carefully than any Savannah man had ever done, at least while she was watching. She wanted to smooth her skirt, to fasten the top button of her lavender top, to pin the stray curls back in the topknot where they belonged.

Mostly, she wanted to get rid of the tightness in

her stomach and the shortness of her breath. Why had she ever lit that fire? The room was much too warm.

At last his eyes met hers.

"You're a healthy-looking woman, Flame."

Healthy! As though she were a horse he'd bought at market. The tension snapped. "I've got all my teeth, too, in case you were considering a look-see in my mouth."

Ah, yes, thought Matt, not knowing whether to smile or frown, he was definitely back with his wife. What was he supposed to tell her? That looking the way she did could drive a man crazy? That standing there with her breasts heaving in indignation, her chin tilted, her green eyes flashing fire, she teased with enough promised pleasures to keep him tossing every night until she was gone?

Two hours on the firing range, another two spent riding in the brush, his usual supper in the mess, a session of whiskey and poker until taps, while he ignored the curious glances of the men . . . nothing had kept her totally out of his mind. Not even the long walk he'd taken before returning home. He was trying to give her time and freedom to herself. What in hell else did she want?

"I take it you got something to eat," he said, well aware of the scent of fresh-baked bread mingling with the sweetness of her perfume. Damned if he didn't like them both, a fact that added to his frustration.

"Do not concern yourself about my welfare, Mr. Jackson. I'm quite able to take care of myself."

109

Matt thought of her claimed pregnancy. "I'm certain you are."

"What do you mean by that?"

"Just agreeing with you, dearest."

"Don't call me dearest. It sounds like Melody's 'sugar.'"

Matt almost smiled. "Good point. I'll never call you dearest again."

"That's fine with me."

"And with me."

Goodness, thought Flame, they sounded like a couple of squabbling children. She took a deep breath to steady her temper. "We've got to set out some rules for what we expect of each other."

"I've never been one to go by rules."

"You've never been married before." She hesitated. "At least, I don't suppose you have. You don't act like a man who's used to a woman around the house."

Matt trailed his eyes over Flame with such thoroughness, he set off the flutters inside her.

"It does take some getting used to," he said.

"I mean one who cooks and cleans," she snapped, with more spirit in her voice than she'd intended. "If you plan to eat elsewhere and carry on half the night—"

"I was tending to business."

"Ha!" She took another deep breath and gripped her hands for control. "I'm just thinking of the way things look. Is it necessary to show so openly that our marriage is a sham?"

"You'd rather everyone believe I'm keeping you occupied in bed?"

He had a devilish glint in his eye that Flame could not ignore.

"Better that, I suppose, than what they're thinking now."

"Which is?"

Flame had to swallow her pride before she continued. "That I obviously displease you, or you displease me, or we don't even try to please each other." Her cheeks burned, but she refused to look away.

Matt stepped closer, studying the enticing way her skin had turned pink beneath the sprinkling of freckles. "Maybe if I had a reason for hanging around, I might do it."

Caught by his dark perusal, Flame could not take offense. "I cooked chicken stew for supper," she said, knowing as she spoke that the words must sound silly to a man of her husband's experience.

"Stew's not what keeps a man at home."

The words sent a rush of heat to fill the hollowness she felt inside. She swayed toward him, and then she caught the look of satisfaction in his eye. In an instant the heat was gone, and she stood erect and apart.

"Too bad. It's the best you're likely to get."

Grabbing up her knitting, she headed toward the door leading to the adjoining room. "I suddenly find myself with a roaring headache," she said from the doorway. "I'm sure you'll pardon me, if I don't continue this ridiculous conversation."

She disappeared into the bedroom, emerging once again with the blankets he'd slept on the night before. She set them on the table—the covered table, he noted—and disappeared once again into the bedroom—his bedroom, he also noted—slamming the door behind her.

Matt stared at the blankets, at the tablecloth, at the closed door. Damn it, she was rearranging everything to suit her purposes, all because she'd gotten herself knocked up.

Never one for much patience, Matt lost the little he had retained.

In three strides he was across the room, throwing open the door, catching her unbuttoning the front of her gown. She started and raised startled eyes to his. Matt's gaze shifted downward. A wisp of white lace showed amidst the lavender muslin, and a tempting curve of breast, visible just before she clutched her clothing closed, hiding her charms from his view.

Stronger than his anger was a jolt of hunger for her, an urge to rip aside the rest of her clothing and inspect with more than just his eyes exactly the package he had wed.

The fire in her eyes turned to fear as she stared at him, and he was bastard enough to like it. Until now he hadn't known she could be afraid of anything.

He walked slowly toward her. She backed up until she was stopped by the bed.

"Don't ever slam that door on me again," he said.

"I'll do what I please," she said. Proud words, but the trembling in her voice was clear for them both to hear.

"And what if I said the same? What do you think would please me, wife?"

Flame swallowed, but she kept her stance straight and proud. If her legs were weakening, it was not for him to know.

"I wouldn't try to guess," she managed. "It's obvious civilized intercourse is not to your liking."

He grinned. Flame longed to retrieve the words.

"Civilized conversation, I meant to say."

Matt was close enough to count the golden flecks in the emerald depths of her eyes . . . close enough to catch the quickening of her breath and the return of a blush on her cheeks.

"I kind of like the way you put it first. Not knowing exactly what civilized intercourse could be, I'd have to guess maybe you're right. Doesn't sound overly exciting, but if you'd like to give it a try—"

"You promised."

"I agreed to what you asked in a very difficult time. I'd hardly call it a blood oath."

Oh, how those eyes bored into her, somehow managing to take on at the same time a devilish twinkle. Panic seized her.

"This is entirely unacceptable."

Matt glanced down at the death grip she had on her clothes.

"Yeah, I'd have to agree."

"See here, Mr. Jackson—"

"Matt."

Her chin tilted a notch. "Never."

It was enough to challenge the good will of a saint. He held her by the shoulders. How slender she felt, how fragile, but he knew the fragility was deceptive. Flame Chadwick Jackson had the will of a wild mus-

113

tang filly. She had to know that she was bringing out some equally wild urges in him.

"Matt," he repeated. He pulled her close until he felt her knuckles brush against him. So slight a touch, even through his leather shirt, almost cost him his control.

No woman had ever taunted him this way, not even Melody Burr when she was putting her experienced hands and mouth to work.

But Flame was experienced, too, he reminded himself, despite the frantic, trapped look in her eyes.

"Say it," he demanded, anger joining with the hungers she'd already aroused.

"Matt," she whispered. "Now will you leave me alone?"

"First we seal the marriage."

"We do *what*?"

"You heard me. We don't want this thing to be a sham, do we? I believe that's what you were worried about."

"I don't want people to know it's a sham, which isn't the same thing."

She tried to jerk free, but his grip tightened and he held her close against him, his mouth inches from hers. He could have crushed her until she was broken in body and spirit, but he didn't want her crushed.

He simply wanted her. Hell of a note, wanting what by any law known to man and God was his to have.

"A kiss, that's all, wife." He bent his head closer. "We forgot it after we said the vows."

"No—" she began.

But his mouth covered hers, and his tongue slipped between her partially open lips. His arms enfolded her, trapping her hands between them. She offered warm, sweet goodness, whether or not the offering was her idea. Matt tasted the honey, dark and rich and pure, and as his tongue brushed against hers, he felt her stiffness lessen, felt her soften in his arms and lean into him, felt her hands flatten against his chest, as if she wanted to explore him the way he wanted to explore her.

Hot promises, unspoken, but conveyed all the same, erased the harshness of his world. He would have her . . . here, now . . . and let the consequences be damned.

He broke the kiss, pressing his lips against her eyes, her cheeks, her throat, feeling her rapidly beating pulse, at last whispering, "Oh, baby," into her ear as he stroked her slender back.

She stiffened. "No," she cried out, and she was out of his arms so quickly he had no chance to tighten his embrace.

Edging away from the bed, away from him, not stopping until she was across the room, she stared at him in horror, one hand pressed to her mouth as though she would hold in a thousand curses against them both.

Matt swayed, shaken by the suddenness of her action. If she glanced downward, she would see how she had aroused him, but she kept her eyes pinned to his, accusing him in silence of unspeakable acts.

Under such a look, Matt cooled fast.

"Sorry to disappoint you, Flame, but one kiss is

all I wanted. There's no reason for pretending to fight."

"Why, you—" she sputtered.

"You'll have the night to think of a finish."

"Good. That means you won't bother me again."

"Unless you can't get me out of your mind. And remember, the wedding vows are now sealed. Love, honor, and obey, you said. Right now I have only one order. Don't slam the door against me again. In my own house, I'll sleep where I want."

Tough words and empty ones, he thought as he left her, heading back toward the bed he would make beside the hearth. This arrangement wasn't going to work. There was something between the two of them, and they both knew it. It had been there from the start.

What in hell he was going to do about it was something else entirely. Stay out of her way, to begin with, even though everyone at Fort Hard would have a damned good idea how things were between them. If he caught her undressing beside his bed again, he couldn't guarantee they wouldn't end up naked on the mattress, in every way man and wife.

For damned sure he'd carry on with his gunrunning investigation, the rifle having proven itself worthy of the highest praise. Over poker he'd asked questions about the weaponry, but the officers he'd chosen to play with hadn't been able to tell him a thing that would help.

He would also scout around for signs of Black Eagle's return. He didn't plan on being taken by surprise again.

Except by his wife, of course. He'd proven to them

both that they had a dangerous situation on their hands, damned dangerous if they wanted to dissolve the union without its being consummated.

Yeah, he'd stay out of her way as much as he could, and to hell with appearances. She'd said she could take care of herself. He'd give her the chance to do just that.

Flame stood in shock for a long time after Matt had left. What had come over her? If he hadn't called her *baby*, hadn't reminded her of her plight, she would have continued opening up to him . . . wantonly, shamelessly, eagerly, proving beyond all doubt that she was everything he already believed her to be.

Perhaps she was, a niggling voice claimed.

"No," she whispered into the quiet of the room.

Yes, the voice insisted. In all her twenty-three years, only two men had kissed her, and she'd reacted to both in disgracefully promiscuous ways.

But it hadn't been the same. Robert had been promising her love and marriage, and she had wanted them both very much. Matt was different— oh, how different. Their mating would be perfectly legal, acceptable, certainly expected in the eyes of the world. And yet with him the lovemaking would seem illicit, forbidden, and somehow all the more erotic.

With the taste of him still on her tongue, she knew to her complete shame she would enjoy it far too much.

Oh, she was truly little more than a tramp.

Had he really said he would sleep where he chose? Did he mean that after tonight they would share a bed?

Impossible. And she didn't believe him, not when he'd chosen to sleep on the floor once again.

But he'd looked so sure of himself. He always did.

Maybe she could buy him a cot. There were some for sale at Asa Underwood's store, but she could imagine the rumors her purchase would arouse. There was a town nearby, a place called Little Sandy. If she could get a ride, she would go there tomorrow and see what was available.

Something told her Matt wouldn't approve of her going off without telling him, but that bothered her not one whit. Love, honor, and obey, was it? As though she'd really meant her vows.

She hadn't. No more than he.

Matt Jackson was obviously too used to getting what he wanted. If he put her on his list of desires, he would find himself disappointed indeed.

Eight

An opportunity to journey into town came three days later, when the three Irish soldiers, crowded onto the seat of an Army buckboard, rode right up to Flame's front door shortly after breakfast. She'd been worrying over a few new physical discomforts, and their arrival came at a perfect time.

Matt was gone as usual. He always left at dawn and didn't return until she had retired for the night, a practice that irritated more than it pleased. What did he think she was going to do, scream *rape* if he came at her the way he had done once or, worse, throw herself into his arms and tear off his clothes?

If she didn't know better, she'd think he was afraid of being alone with his wife. But, of course, she did know better.

One kiss was all I wanted.

Oh, how she'd been remembering his words. *One kiss.* Maybe that's all it was to him, but sometimes as she lay in her lonely bed, she could feel his lips on hers and all the sensations of that moment returned in a velvet flood. *You can't get me out of your mind*. Matt had been right. No amount of self-chastisement could make the memories go away.

And no amount of speculation could convince her *he* would ever experience anything resembling such a remembrance. He'd kissed her to show that he could, and then he'd backed away. In truth, Matt Jackson wasn't afraid of her. He was simply bored.

It seemed their arrangement was not going to be an amicable one. Worse, just as she'd predicted, everyone at Fort Hardaway must know of the animosity between them. Otherwise, they must be asking themselves, why would a bridegroom spend so little time with his bride?

And so it was, after three days of knitting and cleaning and cooking lonely meals, of isolating herself from the rest of the fort, including a couple of wives who'd made friendly overtures at the sutler's, and, worst of all, of worrying whether Annie was all right, Flame felt a return of her old enthusiasm when she heard the creak of the wagon and the laughter of the three soldiers who had come to call. Springing from her chair, she walked onto the front porch and grinned up at the trio sitting high in the buckboard, a brilliant sky at their backs.

"Good morning to ye," one returned cheerily, the reins to the dray horse held loosely in one gloved hand, while he tipped his cap with the other.

"The same to you, Private Mallon."

She curtsied, holding between her fingers the edges of her lemon yellow skirt. How glad she was to have chosen the gown, with its ruffle of delicate lace around her throat and wrists. Full-sleeved and wide at the hem, it boasted a fitted bodice with a dozen tiny tucks over the bosom and a narrow waist that was her particular pride.

She'd sewn it with her own hands, and even persnickety Raven had proclaimed the effort an example of her best.

It fit her almost too snugly now, and she knew it was only a matter of weeks before she would have to put it aside until Annie's appearance.

"I'm pleased to see you on this lovely morning," she added, taking in all three of the men with her smile.

"Michael, she remembers," said Brendan Faulkner, who was wedged into the middle of the seat. "'Tis for sure I'm in love."

Ian Craig nudged him, while he held onto his precarious position on the outside. "Don't be frightening the lass. She's got enough t' contend with, as things be."

Michael scowled at his two companions. "Hush, you two. Remember our agreement."

Flame's pleasure faded, replaced by a sense of dread. "What are you talking about? Is there something I ought to be worried about?"

"Nary a thing," said Michael, a look of innocence in his round, brown eyes.

"Excepting the loneliness of the land," said Ian.

"And three Micks who've taken it upon themselves t' be your protectors," said Brendan.

"I need protecting?"

Brendan caught Michael's warning frown. "Lass, every mother's son and daughter needs protectin' at Fort Hard."

"From Indians and the weather, he means," Ian

hastened to add. "You've yet to experience the hell-ish heat of summer or a winter's storm sweeping out o' the hills, but ye will. 'Tis impossible to choose which is worse."

Flame looked from soldier to soldier to soldier, and they all looked blandly back at her. She was certain they kept something to themselves. She was also certain that if she talked to them long enough, she would find out what it was.

Flame sighed. It didn't take a confession from the three to know what they were hiding. It was pity for the woman who was the talk of the fort—Matt Jackson's abandoned bride.

"There's a purpose to our calling on ye this morning, Mrs. Jackson," said Michael, his voice taking on a formal tone. "We've a bit of shopping to take care of in town, and wondered if there was anything we could do for you while we're there."

Fate, that's what it was, Flame decided, her spirits lifting.

"No," she said, smoothing a lock of hair away from her face, "but you can take me along. I'll ride in the back and won't make a sound."

A look of dismay crossed Michael's face. "Sorry, lass, but 'tis against all the rules."

"Aye," added Ian. "Sergeant Gibson would nail our Irish hides to the barracks wall, if he were to find out. Only in a moment of rare weakness did he allow the three of us the possession of the supply wagon. We've strictest orders to return as fast as the wind."

"I won't hold you up. In fact, I'm ready to go right now."

The soldiers studied her, their eyes held determinedly to no lower than her face and shoulders. Not that she didn't look perfectly respectable in her long-sleeved, high-necked gown. She'd even pinned her hair away from her face, allowing only a few soft curls to tumble loose against her forehead; the rest hung in ringlets down her back.

"No offense, lass," said Michael, "but you'd be needin' an armed guard to protect you from the vermin in Little Sandy."

Flame had a difficult time believing he was right, but she didn't think now was the time to start arguing.

"All I want is to go to the general store. Surely that can't be too dangerous? Besides, I've got a shawl I just finished that'll cover half of me. I'll stay so hidden in it no one will give me a second look."

Brendan shook his head in disagreement. "They'd be lookin', Mrs. Jackson, if you buried yourself in a tent."

"Aren't there any women in the place?" she asked.

"Saloon wh—" Ian caught himself. "For certain there's women, but there's also a decided absence of ladies, if ye know what I mean."

Flame certainly did, and she turned the information to her own ends. "Which means they have female companionship readily available. So that a standoffish matron like me, with a black shawl draped over her person, won't draw the least attention, certainly not if she keeps to the general store. I promise, on my honor, not to walk into a single saloon."

"You're showing your Irish half this morning,

123

lass," said Michael. "'Tis certain you could talk the bark from the trees."

"Thank you for the compliment, although it's ill deserved. I guess it's just that I've been rather lonely since I arrived, and I've been thinking up ways to decorate the Jackson abode."

Like buying her husband a cot to sleep on, instead of his own bed.

A small sigh escaped her lips as she lowered her lashes and allowed her shoulders to slump, the picture, she prayed, of even more loneliness and despair than she already felt. Oh, what a despicable fraud she was. And a rather fine actress. Raven would appreciate the skill, if not its use.

"Chances are, Michael, we won't be found out," said Ian. "Unless it's the colonel himself or Captain Davis that spies us, there's nary a man at Fort Hard who would tell."

"After all," said Brendan, "we're doing nought but giving the wife of our trusted scout a ride into town. There's not a more popular man at Fort Hard. Be a pleasure to serve him, and without his having to ask."

"'Tis for certain he'd be grateful," said Ian.

Flame almost laughed out loud. Matt, grateful for a favor to his wife? How mistaken the Irishman was, or maybe he was just talking. She recognized rationalization when she heard it, having often gone through the same quick reasoning process in order to do something she knew was unwise.

"Should I get the shawl?" she asked, casting her eyes up at Michael.

"Aye," he said with a grin. "I worry too much.

We've only to use the brains God gave us, and take care of our business fast. We'll be in and out of Little Sandy so fast, there's precious little that can go wrong."

The woman pushed Matt's hat aside, sat on edge of the saloon table, and leaned her fleshy body close, a low-cut, black satin gown pressing tight above her nipples, forcing the white, mounded breasts to crowd close to her throat.

"How about buying Myrtle a whiskey?" she said, offering him a mottled smile as she brushed a strand of brown hair toward an untidy bun at her nape. The seams of satin strained to hold in her most obvious charms, as she took a deep breath. Everything about her reeked of perspiration and heavy perfume, earthy smells to some men. Matt had lately decided he preferred the scent of a rose.

He considered the construction of the saloon woman's clothing at the same time he thought over her question. Surely the gown was painful, cutting in the way it did. Yet when he looked up at Myrtle's full, painted lips and narrow, blinking eyes, he saw no signs of pain other than the fear of rejection.

He understood her problem. She had to bring in enough money or the proprietor of the Kitty Cat Saloon would toss her onto the street.

A final disgrace, being thrown out of the Kitty Cat in Little Sandy, Texas.

Matt glanced around the saloon with its splintered tables and dirty plank floor. A dozen gamblers and drinkers, most of them drifters and out-of-work cowboys, slumped over their bottles in the smoky dimness, joined at a couple of tables by women who could have been Myrtle's kin. A lone man worked behind the counter. No mirrors to back him or brass rails or pictures of naked ladies, like the big city saloons.

In his traveling days, before old memories began to haunt him, Matt had sampled the distractions in the plushest watering holes in the country, from San Francisco to New York and down to San Antonio. At the Cat and a couple of similar establishments in Little Sandy, patrons got down to basics: gambling and drinking and whoring, none of which had enticed him through the swinging doors.

Myrtle smoothed the gown over her broad hips, and tried to look provocative as she perched on the table's edge. Unfortunately, both gown and woman had seen better days. She couldn't be out of her twenties, but despite her fixed smile, Matt saw about her a weariness as old as the hills.

He signaled to the bartender. "One drink, Myrtle, but you'll have to take it to another table. I'm waiting for someone."

Myrtle pouted. "A woman, ain't it?"

Not necessarily, Matt could have said, not with a bride warming his bed, but the declaration would be carrying the farce of his marriage too far. Damned peculiar how the arrangement kept eating at him, especially since it wasn't permanent.

"Man like you needs female companionship on a regular basis," said Myrtle, tugging at the red bandanna at his throat. "Not like some of 'em around here. I could tell you tales, Matt, that'd make you

126

give up on the human race. Almost do myself, some-times.''

For a moment her thoughts turned inward, then she smiled, shaking off whatever bothered her. "Whoever she is, I can do more for you than she can. You won't let me show you, Matt, but I just know I can."

Matt pictured his wife the way she had looked when he had kissed her, lips swollen, eyes rounded, her body soft and ripe against his. The kiss had been days ago, but damned if he couldn't still taste her.

Flame could do something for him. Just thinking about her made him hard.

He pulled away from that line of thinking, as suddenly as she'd pulled away from his embrace. She was doing something already. She was making his life hell.

The drink arrived. Matt flipped a coin to the bartender, and when he was gone pressed another into Myrtle's damp hand. "That ought to take care of your quota for the day."

"Oh, Matt," Myrtle gushed. She leaned closer and gave him a big hug, almost toppling them both to the floor. While he struggled to keep them upright, she planted a wet kiss on his cheek.

"Thanks, honey," she said. "There ain't enough whiskey in this glass of water to drown a Kitty Cat cockroach. I'll get me a real drink later and think of you."

She winked broadly as she stepped away, leaving strong traces of perfume clinging to his buckskin shirt and a smear of red paint on his face. "Whenever you want it, for you it'll be free."

Matt watched her sway away and approach another lone drinker toward the back of the long and narrow room. Free, she said. Matt finished his whiskey. Nothing in this life came free.

He turned toward the man he sensed walking through the Cat's front door.

A small Englishman of forty, Nigel Wolfe was as much a dandy as ever in his tailored vested suit. With his black hair slicked back from his face, pencil moustache, and hard, dark eyes, he looked like what he was—a cardsharp who made his living gambling with the drifters traveling through town and the soldiers who came illegally into the Cat.

At least rumor had it that he earned enough at the tables to get by. Matt had never seen him win more than modest sums, hardly enough to pay for his suits or the diamond stickpin in his tie.

Which was why he was here. The money had to come from somewhere, and through his poker-playing, if not elsewhere, Wolfe had contacts at the fort.

"Wolfe," Matt said in greeting.

"Good morning, Mr. Jackson," the man returned. "I received word at the hotel that you wanted to see me."

The gambler coughed into a monogrammed handkerchief, then took a chair opposite Matt. "Dreadful place, your American West."

"It's not mine to defend," said Matt.

"More's the pity. I rather imagine you'd run a more orderly country." His dark eyes glinted briefly. "Although there is something of the savage in you, isn't there?"

Without waiting for a reply, Wolfe signaled toward

the bartender. "I left London looking for an arid climate, you understand." Again he coughed. "Little Sandy is rather more than I bargained for."

"So why stay around?"

"A question I might easily put to you." The gambler's eyes flicked over Matt's attire. "Really, Mr. Jackson, isn't buckskin rather *passé*? An affectation, I should think. Come now, don't deny it. You dress like a bumpkin, and even while it suits you in a feral sort of way, I suspect a swallowtail coat might do the same."

"I'm not here to discuss my sartorial choices."

"Ah, you prove my point. What barbarian uses a word like sartorial? None, I assure you."

The bartender arrived to set before him a snifter of brandy. "Ah, thank you, my good man. Put it on my bill." Wolfe glanced at Matt's empty glass. "Would you care for another? Perhaps a sample of this fine nectar. Unfortunately, I've provided the Kitty Cat—dreadful name, don't you think?—with only one appropriate piece of glassware, which the proprietor is kind enough to reserve for me."

Matt shook his head. "None for me."

Wolfe eyed him over the edge of the crystal glass, and Matt was reminded of the animal that shared the gambler's name. He glanced toward the back of the room and saw Myrtle staring at the Englishman, her painted face darkened by a look of revulsion that even the smoke and poor lighting could not obscure.

"No idle chatter? No brandy?" said Wolfe, giving no indication that he noticed her—or, if he did, that

129

he cared how she felt. "You arouse my curiosity. Just why are you here?"

Slowly Matt returned his attention to the gambler. "You heard about the attack on the stagecoach a few days ago?"

Wolfe shuddered. "Most certainly, yes. Dreadful brutes." He flicked an invisible speck from his lapel. "Isn't it your responsibility to see that such incidents do not occur?"

Matt ignored the question. "A lot of talk gets passed around in a place like the Cat."

"Men are, after all, greater gossips than the fairer sex. But I fail to see your point."

"Some of the talk involves you and the Apaches."

Wolfe looked genuinely alarmed. As well he might, Matt thought, if there had been anything to the claim.

"Explain yourself, sir."

"I—"

A woman's scream stopped him. It seemed to come from somewhere down the street. Distance muted its resonance, but not its particular pitch. It was a scream he'd heard before. No one else in the Cat paid the cry any mind.

But then no one else in the Cat had only days ago been standing beside an overturned stagecoach during an Apache attack, listening to that anguished sound close by.

Matt shook his head. It couldn't be. A second scream assured him that it was.

Bounding from the chair, he pushed through the swinging doors and came to halt on the wooden walkway. Even in the blinding morning sun, he could see the dirt street held only a few tethered horses in front of the neighboring saloons and a couple of wagons close to the general store across the way.

A third scream. This time it seemed to echo from the alleyway between the row of saloons and the stable. Matt lit out toward the sound. He rounded the corner of the alley in time to see three soldiers moving in on the hulking figure of Buck Grady, one of Little Sandy's resident drunks.

Grady faced away from the street. On past him stood Flame, her back pressed to the stable wall. Instead of cowering, she glared up at him with hands on hips, chin tilted, in a way Matt recognized.

"For gawd's sake," her pursuer growled, "stop yer caterwauling. I ain't laid a hand on you yet."

"You do so, sir," Flame snapped, "and you'll regret it until the day you die. Which might very well be today."

Grady hitched his baggy britches. "I'll take a heap of enjoyin' first, little lady. Come give ole Buck a little kissy-face."

"I most certainly will not."

The first of the soldiers launched himself at Grady's broad back, and then the second and the third. One by one, he tossed them aside onto the trash-strewn ground, but they jumped up to come at him again.

If Matt hadn't been so angry, he would have enjoyed watching the second assault. He knew these boys, knew them to be scrappers, but the three of them couldn't match their opponent's bulk.

One gunshot fired into the air was enough to get everyone's attention.

"Saints alive, it's Jackson," said one of the soldiers, and the three of them scrambled to get out of the line of fire.

Grady blinked over his shoulder at Matt, but there was little comprehension in his eyes.

"Leave her alone, Buck," said Matt, holstering the gun.

Flame peered around her attacker in disbelief. "Don't just stand there, Matt. Shoot him! At least in the foot or something."

"Hush, woman. Now do what I said, Buck. Leave her alone and get on out of here."

"But I found her, just walking the street."

"I was not—" Flame began. A glance from Matt silenced her.

"You can't pick up stray women the way you can stray dogs," he said.

Buck thought that one over. "Don't see why not. I warn't gonna hurt her or nothing."

"I'm sure you weren't."

"Matthew Jackson," sputtered Flame.

Another glance, and again she fell silent.

Grady looked at her and grinned. "Corraled her the way I used to do the dogies in my workin' days. Maybe just one little kissy-face? Ought to get that for my trouble."

"Only one thing wrong," said Matt. "She's already taken. This is my new wife." Something made him add, "Frances Chadwick Jackson. A lady, Buck. We don't see her kind very often out here in Little Sandy."

He shifted his eyes to her for a moment. Not having seen her in three days, he'd almost forgotten what a beautiful woman she was. No wonder she was dragged off the street.

"Your wife?" asked Grady.

"That's right."

"You always treated me good, Matt. Least I can do is leave your woman alone." He couldn't resist one last look at her. "But she shore is tempting."

"Of course, she is. Otherwise, I wouldn't have married her."

A sigh shook the big man's body as he shuffled past Matt, disappearing around the corner in the direction of the row of saloons.

Silence descended as Matt studied the three young soldiers, who stood sheepishly nearby. Red-headed, every one of them. He was learning to be suspicious of the trait.

"Michael," he said, directing his attention to the trio's leader. "You bring her into town?"

"Aye, sir, that I did," the Irishman said briskly, as though he were addressing an officer. Matt had corrected him about that error more than once.

"We were coming in for supplies," said Ian, "and she asked for a ride. Promised t' stay in the store, she did." He sent Flame a look of regret. "Something must have happened to bring her out."

"It's my fault, Mr. Jackson," said Brendan.

"And how is that?" asked Matt.

No answer was immediately forthcoming.

"Work on it," said Matt. "Maybe you'll think of something."

His dark gaze shifted to his wife. Oh, yes, she presented quite a picture in her yellow gown, her fiery hair tumbling to her shoulders, her eyes wide with what should have been fright.

Except that she wasn't afraid. She was furious.

"I could have handled him all right," she said.

"What, no embrace of gratitude?" asked Matt, sauntering toward her. "No kissy-face for the rescuer?"

She opened her mouth for a retort, then glanced at the three silent soldiers who were taking in every word.

"You boys go on and get the wagon," Matt instructed. "She'll be out in a minute for the ride back."

"The escorted ride," he added as he turned back to his wife. "But first I'd like to greet the little woman. We've had so few chances to be alone, haven't we, Flame?"

"What happened to Frances?" she snapped, trying very hard to be brave.

"Ah, yes, indeed, what happened to the respectable Frances? Did she ever exist? It hardly matters now. It's time, wife, for a little show of thanks." He moved in close, well aware the witnesses had not yet departed. "Don't be shy. Show me how glad you are that I'm here."

Nine

Flame smelled another woman on him as soon as he got close.

"Get away from me, Matt."

"Why, dearest, remember your admirers are watching. Wouldn't want to arouse any suspicions, would we?"

"You promised not to call me that again," she hissed, pressing harder than ever against the rough wall at her back.

"The way you promised those hapless soldiers you wouldn't leave the store?"

He had a hard, taunting look in his eye as he stared down at her, but Flame refused to be intimidated.

"I promised not to go into a saloon. And I didn't. Which is more than I can say for you." She wrinkled her nose in disgust. "At least I suppose that's where you met her. And don't pretend you haven't been with someone. You still reek of her, and the light's not so bad I can't see her mark on your cheek. Was it a little kissy-face? To seal some kind of vow?"

135

"You've got a sharp tongue on you, woman," he said, not entirely without admiration.

"Everyone used to think I was sweet-natured and kind. But, of course, that was before I met you."

He edged closer, until his trousers brushed against her skirt and she could practically feel the fringed buckskin touching her bodice. Heart pounding, she sent a frantic look past him in search of her three Irishmen. Like Buck Grady, they had fled. Some protectors, she thought in disgust.

"I guess we bring out the beast in each other," he said. He'd meant the words to be teasing, but as he gazed into her upturned eyes, wide and bright and thick-lashed, he experienced the hard twist of desire that was beginning to be natural whenever she was around.

His rage returned, directed as much at himself as at her. Circumstances had forced him into this marriage, including his own bad aim when he'd had the chance to stop Black Eagle, but he'd be damned if a physical weakness for his pretend-wife would get the better of him. If it did, he'd only be following the path of every other man who came near her.

"You're a real little temptress, aren't you?" he said, making no attempt to sound complimentary. His gaze locked onto her full, parted lips. "I understand Buck's wanting under your skirt."

The words cut her like a whip, and she could summon no defense against them, no ready retort. He made her feel cheap and tawdry, when all she had done was walk down the street.

She closed her eyes and forced back the tears. She would not cry. She would not cry.

But Matt wasn't the only reason for the debased feelings; she brought them on herself—heating up the way she was because he was so close, filled with self-hate even as she wished he would say something sweet to her, something apologetic, and maybe, just maybe, nuzzle her neck.

Oh, what a hussy she was turning into! Matt Jackson might be her husband, but he had no husband's rights. Given the harshness of his nature, there wasn't a hint of a chance that the situation would change.

Lifting her hands, she shoved against his chest. Beneath her palms, he, too, was hot. And he did not budge.

He placed a hand against the wall on each side of her head, fingering for a moment the strands of her fiery hair. His bride was taller than most women, but slender and, in her own special way, delicate, despite the willfulness of her nature. He had the sensation that if he were to hold her tight, she might simply fade away in his arms.

Or maybe he feared she would leave. He brushed the idea aside as absurd. She'd be leaving, all right, after she bore another man's child.

The thought made him mean.

"Kiss me, Flame. Show me you're grateful."

He spoke harshly, and there was nothing sweet in his words.

Flame could hardly draw breath. "Let me go."

"I didn't ask to find you here, but I'll damned sure set the conditions for when you can leave."

"Oh, how manly you are. Having to threaten your own wife for a kiss."

"Don't think you can talk your way out of this alley. Talk's not what I want. I'm after something else."

Flame stared at his lips. "This is absurd, Matt. Someone will come along."

"The Micks are watching out for us, don't you know? And don't look so disapproving. That's what they call themselves. The Three Micks. They're good boys. We've got a little time."

"You want to punish me with a kiss."

"Put any name to it you want. The result will be the same."

Flame closed her eyes, and for just a moment she was aware only of his physical presence and the hot yearnings—the hot *shameful* yearnings—he aroused within her. If only he didn't carry the perfume of someone else, she would take this moment as something far different from punishment.

But the scent was there, and so was her growing perception of the man she had been forced to wed. What did she really know about him, except that without any sign of grace or understanding, he'd kept his word to Robert? And, too, the three Micks liked him. They'd said so on the ride into town.

But what did they know? They liked her, too, and right now she didn't feel very likable.

Where was the hope-filled young woman who'd journey west to find the kind of eternal love her parents shared? Somehow she'd gotten lost along the way.

She looked at her hands pressed against his broad chest. She concentrated on the left hand, particularly on the lone piece of jewelry that she wore. A stab of pain came upon her unexpectedly, and worse, an irrational, burning shame.

She tried to draw her hands away from him, but he was too close, and he had her pinned tightly into place. He must not see what she had done so impulsively this morning. Was it still before the noon hour? Surely it must be close to night.

Panic took hold and she fought to get away, but Matt's strength was too much to overcome.

"I hate you," she whispered.

He flinched under the sincerity in her voice. "Not quite the words of thanks I was after, wife."

"Don't call me that."

"So many forbidden names. You'll have to make out a list."

"Don't call me anything. Just let me go."

Matt sensed the change in her, from rebellious anger to near-acquiescence to something close to despair. If by some twist of fate they stayed married into the next century, he doubted that he would ever understand her.

He took her hands in his, and he felt the ring.

Stepping back, he lifted her left hand into a ray of sunlight that fell into the alley. "What's this?"

In vain she tugged to free herself. "Let me go."

"How long have you had it?"

So many questions he asked. She stood straight and let him inspect the narrow band as long as he wished. Despite the sentimental glow she'd experienced after slipping it onto her hand outside the store—the stupid, inexplicable glow, as though a true love had placed it there himself—the ring didn't mean anything to her. Nothing at all. If it did, she would be proving herself nothing more than a romantic fool.

"It's not gold. The storekeeper said he thought it was brass; otherwise, I couldn't have afforded it, not with the other things I bought."

Including, she might have added, wool to knit a blanket for Annie. But he wouldn't care.

Suddenly Matt felt like something he might scrape off the bottom of his shoe.

"You bought yourself a wedding ring."

"I'll be showing soon. It seemed there would be fewer questions, if matters between us seemed"—she swallowed hard—"more in the usual way of things."

"I see," he said, easing away so that she might step from the confined space against the wall.

"I can throw it away, if you prefer. It doesn't have much value. Maybe the storekeeper will take it back."

Her voice was flat, devoid of all emotion. Matt didn't know what to say. That he felt like a bastard? Under the circumstances of their marriage, it was a term best unsaid.

"I'll reimburse you."

"You'll what?"

"I should have thought of it myself. There's no sense in your being out the money."

"Of course, there is. I'm the one who saw the need in the first place. Now, if you don't mind, I'm really feeling tired and there's still the ride back to the fort."

Flame spoke the truth. Usually filled with enough energy for herself *and* her sisters, she was overcome with a weariness that threatened to send her to her knees.

Matt heard the exhaustion in her voice and saw for the first time the shadowed half-circles under her eyes. Something stirred inside him. Something close to care.

"You doing all right?" he asked, then added, awkwardly, "You know—with the baby."

Flame's eyes darted to his. Must be the dim light in the alley that made her think she saw concern. But that was impossible. He didn't care for her anymore than she cared for him. If she trembled when he touched her—if his nearness created warm yearnings deep inside—it was simply because of the emotional turmoil she'd been going through lately. And the fact that just maybe she had a weakness for men.

"I'm doing fine," she said, the edge back in her voice. And she was, too. It mattered not that her body seemed to be telling her something else. She stepped past him and picked up the black shawl she'd worn over the yellow dress. Shaking it clean, she wrapped it about her shoulders. A fascinator, the garment was called in this part of the country. A woman in the store had told her, but she hadn't known the reason for the name.

Matt watched every movement she made, unable to turn away. She had a natural grace about her that reminded him of a wild deer in the forest. Try as he might to think of her as cold and calculating, she kept presenting herself as fragile. And desirable.

As he fell into step behind her, wanting to wrap his arm around her and give her his strength, it seemed as though the ground were shifting under

141

him, just the way their relationship always seemed to be shifting.

Damn it, he reminded himself, it was a relationship that didn't exist.

Listening to Matt's booted footsteps, Flame walked onto the street. Blinding sunlight greeted her, and she blinked.

"Down this way," said Matt, taking her by the arm. It was by far the most gentlemanly gesture he'd made toward her. How tired did she look? Tired enough, it seemed, to make him think she was going to collapse at his feet. He wouldn't like her showing such a weakness. He liked to think she could care for herself.

Nodding her thanks, looking no higher than the red bandanna at his throat, she walked alongside him down the narrow, broken sidewalk. All seemed peaceful around her, only a few riders coming down the rutted street at a quiet pace, the town's dozen ramshackle buildings hiding whatever activity was going on within their shabby walls.

Ahead she could see the Micks waiting by the wagon in front of the general store.

Suddenly the peace was broken by the painful *yip* of a bony yellow dog tearing down the street toward them, a tin can tied to his tail.

A figure darted from between two buildings on the far side of the street and ran after the dog. A boy, Flame saw, shirtless and barefooted, his trousers little more than rags. Mostly skinny arms and legs with black hair longer than Matt's streaming down his back. He couldn't have been more than fourteen.

It seemed impossible that he could catch the terrified mongrel, but somehow he did, launching himself in the air and throwing his arms around the dog's hindquarters.

Flame cringed and waited for the animal to turn on the boy, snarling and snapping and tearing his fangs into the fleshless arms. It didn't happen. As the boy whispered indistinguishable words into the canine's ear, he removed the tin can and tossed it aside. They were no more than a dozen yards away, close enough for her to hear the dog-whine of gratitude as the animal crouched by the boy's feet.

She watched in amazement as the dog licked the boy's face.

"Matt," she said, "did you see that?"

"Half-breed," he answered in disgust. "They've got a way with animals."

She looked closer at the boy, who continued to hug the animal, and saw the high cheekbones and the coppery tone of his skin.

"Apache?" she asked.

"Yeah. Now let's get out of here." He started off down the sidewalk. She had to hurry to catch up.

Another flurry down the street brought her once again to a halt. A half-dozen youths, most of them bigger than the half-breed, came running and yelling and tossing rocks at the boy and dog. The youth in the lead, pudgy and red-faced, moved fast in spite of his size, staying well ahead of his compatriots.

The air filled with their obscenities, and the rocks found their mark more than once.

The half-breed scrambled to his feet. He looked so scrawny, so helpless, standing there without shelter or defense, and Flame's heart went out to him.

143

"Matt, we've got to stop them," she said with a tug on his shirtsleeve.

"He can take care of himself."

She started to argue, but there was something implacable in his expression that said this was one argument she was not going to win.

By the time she glanced back toward the street, the half-breed and the dog were gone, and the crowd of youths had dispersed. It had all happened so fast, she could barely believe she'd seen right. But the look of disgust in Matt's eyes told her she had. The look came not, she knew, because of the gang of bullies, but because of the boy they had attacked.

He really hated Apaches. Even children with white blood in their veins.

No longer holding her arm, he strode down the street toward the wagon. Halting beside the trio of soldiers, he said, "Watch her. I'll be right back."

He disappeared into one of the nearby saloons and emerged a minute later, his hat firmly in place low on his forehead. She'd been right, Flame thought with a heavy heart. That's where he'd met the woman. His wife's scream of defense had interrupted whatever he'd been up to, bringing him running into the alley. Frustrated at the interruption, he'd demanded a kiss in return.

Matt wasn't a man to let an opportunity go to waste.

Flame would be forever proud that this time his demands hadn't been met.

On the half-hour return journey to the fort, she rode in the back of the wagon beside Brendan, Matt astride the gelding directly to the rear, as though he were serving as guard. What did he think she was going to do, Flame asked herself in irritation, as she watched the easy way he sat in the saddle, jump out and run back into town?

In truth, she hadn't the energy, even if she could manage the feat.

She pictured their arrival at the adobe shack—the Micks helping her to the ground and handing her the packages, Matt watching her walk inside, the sounds of the departing wagon and gelding abandoning her to another stretch of lonely solitude.

She felt a sickness in the pit of her stomach, and a burgeoning sense of rebellion that managed to dispell her weariness. The house should be her sanctuary, yet the closer she got to it, the more she felt like a bird who'd known an hour's freedom out of its cage. She could no longer close herself behind bars, no matter how invisible they might be.

Some serious amendments to this arrangement must be made. It really wouldn't take more than one, if it was drastic enough.

She had just such an amendment in mind, one that involved separation and distance. This afternoon she would check it out. Without, of course, saying a word to Matt. If things worked out as she hoped, she would present him with her plan as an accomplished fact. And there was nothing he could do to stop her. Nothing at all.

"I'd advise against traveling all the way back to Georgia. As a matter of fact, I'd advise against any travel at all."

145

Flame stared in dismay at the fort's doctor, Maj. Edmund Kirby, as he prounounced the dreaded words.

"Not even to El Paso? Or San Antonio? They're not so far away."

"For the time being, the farthest you should ride—even in the best-sprung carriage money can buy, is Little Sandy. And I can assure you, Mrs. Jackson, there's little chance you could get such a conveyance in this part of the country, until long after the baby is due."

Flame and the major were seated in his small, crowded office in the hospital, not more than twenty yards from Matt Jackson's home. Immediately after arriving back from town, she had slipped next door and asked, with great embarrassment, if maybe the doctor could talk to her about a very personal matter. He had readily agreed.

She hadn't meant to confer with him until closer to the time of Annie's birth. But that was when she was planning to stay in Matt's house. And it was before she'd started feeling bad.

He'd given her an examination, too, adding to her humiliation. Women certainly did have to go through a lot to bring a new life into the world.

Not that he'd been anything but kind. A short, paunchy man, Major Kirby had a ring of gray hair around his bald pate, wire-frame glasses propped on the end of a prominent nose, a pair of kindly blue eyes, and an understanding, ready smile. If she was going to be poked at in such a clinical way, she was grateful that it was a man like this doctor who was doing the poking.

He'd made the examination fast, then listened to her talk about the morning sickness and the oncoming of fatigue. She'd also told him about the latest development, something she'd been pushing to the back of her mind. Since yesterday she'd been spotting a little blood on her undergarments. Woefully ignorant of what her condition involved, she'd thought it was natural. But before she set out on the long road across Texas, she'd felt the need to check her condition with someone who knew more than she.

And now that someone was telling her that she had to stay put.

"Is something wrong with me?" She hated the tremor in her voice as she put the question to him, but she had to know.

"Nothing that rest won't cure."

She tried to read the truth in his eyes, but all she saw was a kindly smile. She prayed he was telling her everything, in part because she liked him. Not once had he said anything about her being almost three months' pregnant and only one week wed.

Pulling the fascinator tight around her shoulders, she thought over what he'd been telling her.

"What do you mean by rest, Major Kirby? It seems that's all I've been doing since I got here."

"Call me Doc, Mrs. Jackson. Men around here hardly know my rank. If they hear you, they'll be thinking I'm trying to get military on them. As to the rest that I'm recommending, you ought to spend the next few days in bed. Let that healthy husband of yours wait on you. Matt won't mind."

Flame didn't know whether to laugh or to cry.

Matt not mind caring for her needs? He could hardly stand to be with her in the same room.

But that was her problem, not the doctor's, and she attempted a reassuring smile. "We'll work things out somehow."

"Good," said Doc, but he didn't put much vigor into the word. "Best thing of all to do is not worry. Haven't read much in the medical books about attitude, but it seems to me the soldiers who don't fret about their problems heal the fastest."

This time Flame almost laughed out loud. Not worry? Doc could have advised her to repaint the fort and come closer to getting what he asked.

She stood, thanked him for his help, and opened her reticule.

"I don't know how the payment works. What do I owe?"

"Not a penny, Mrs. Jackson. It's part of my job."

"Please call me Flame," she said, and almost added he could call her anything, as long as it wasn't Mrs. Jackson.

They shook hands. Doc held on for a minute, looking into her eyes, at the shadows beneath them, at the crinkles to either side.

"I'll drop by in a couple of days to see how you're doing."

"That's too much to ask," she said.

"No trouble. We're neighbors, after all. Follow my instructions, and everything ought to be just fine."

The doctor's kindness and reassuring words sent a warm comfort stealing through her, even though she was skeptical about his advice. For Annie's sake, she had to listen and to respond. Rest, he said. That would be harder to come by than he knew, but she would do the best she could.

As to the not worrying, just thinking about it caused her stomach to knot.

"Thank you again, Doc," she said, shaking his hand across the desk. "I certainly won't forget a word you've said."

"One thing more." Kirby cleared his throat and decided he'd rather treat Sergeant Gibson's hemorrhoids than deal with the delicate matters between a man and wife.

"Yes?"

"I know you're a bride and all, but for the time being, you better not have relations with your husband."

Flame kept a straight face, but she felt the burn of a blush on her cheeks.

"That won't be a problem, I promise."

Kirby didn't like the positive tone in her voice. So it wasn't a problem, was it, keeping Matt out of her bed? If that were really true, human nature being what it was, there was more trouble under the Jackson roof than even a skeptical old physician would have guessed.

Assuring her once again that he'd be checking on her, he watched as she let herself out. In the following stillness he leaned back in his chair and stared solemnly at the closed door. Flame Jackson was carrying a heavy burden around with her, secrets that darkened those remarkable green eyes. More than once he'd wanted to ask if she cared to talk. But there was something about the way she held herself and met his gaze straight on, that said she was a proud woman and he'd be best off not to pry.

Kirby didn't give a hoot in hell that the baby had been started a long time before she said *I do*. And it sure wasn't his business that the husband couldn't be the father. Matt Jackson had been working as a scout at Fort Hard for more than a year; his wife had only just arrived.

But what did concern him was that the woman was unhappy, just at a time of her life when she should be filled with joy. A first baby was a special experience. He remembered well the birth of his son.

Kirby Junior was working now as a doctor back in Kentucky. Mrs. Kirby must be looking down from her place in Heaven as pleased as she could be over the boy.

And Kirby Senior? He was out here in a hard and lonely land, patching together soldiers who got into scrapes or took ill or got in the way of an Indian's gun.

He treated the women on the fort, too. A hardy breed, most of them. But not Flame Jackson, for all her pride. If she carried this baby to term, he'd consider it a miracle.

And if her husband didn't do all he could to see that everything went right, he'd need a thrashing within an inch of his life. Matt Jackson was a good man, but he was rough around the edges.

"I might be bald and gone to paunch," Kirby said as if Matt were in the room, "but if you let that girl come to harm, I'll see you get everything that's coming to you."

Ten

Knowing she was disobeying Doc's orders, Flame couldn't bring herself to return immediately to the confines of her husband's home. Instead, she strolled along the pathway that wound around the fort, her step quickened by a brisk wind out of the north. Nearing the parade grounds, she spied a line of marching soldiers in the middle of the grassy field. High overhead the United States flag snapped lustily, and as she stopped to watch the troops, she held the black, crocheted fascinator tight against her shoulders for the warmth it would bring.

The brightness of the morning had long passed, and gray, fingerlike streaks of clouds darkened the afternoon sky, a fitting background for the mood she was in. It was halfway through October. Winter would be here before long. Winter was her least favorite season of the year.

She did a lot of thinking as she stood there on the path, the wind whipping her hair loose from its pins and molding the yellow gown against the slender lines of her body. Memories of Papa and Mama and her sisters assailed her, and of her pretty room with its floral carpet and high feather bed, of the family store and the simple, clear-cut chores she performed.

At home she knew what was expected of her, and she knew that she was loved. At Fort Hard no such assurances comforted her. And now she was having trouble with the one aspect of her existence that brought her joy: the bearing of her child.

She looked around the flat, brown land, at the squat government buildings, and on to the surrounding hills. She'd once pictured them covered with flowers and wildlife and trees, but now she imagined only rock cliffs and boulders and dying grass, all natural extensions of the flat plain from which the hills rose.

No wonder Fort Hardaway had been shortened to Fort Hard. There wasn't one thing restful or consoling about it, nothing pretty nor suggestive of hope. Doc had said she must remain here, and the words had sounded more like a judge's sentence of confinement in jail.

Funny, that's what they called a woman's seclusion during pregnancy, wasn't it? Confinement. It was a most appropriate word.

It wasn't Flame's nature to be so cynical, but her weariness consumed her usual good cheer . . . weariness and the thought that she would have to deal with her husband for the next six months, just when she'd decided another day was too much to ask.

How serious Doc had been in warning her against relations with Matt! How hard it had been not to laugh.

She played with the ring on her finger. At least she wouldn't have to deal any longer with the foolish longings her husband stirred within her. Because of the doctor's admonitions, those longings were a thing of the past.

She was certain of this until languid, retraced steps brought her back around the hospital and to the front of the adobe house. Pigeon, Matt's gelding, was tied to the front post. Her husband was home.

Immediately her blood quickened, and she felt the usual twist in the pit of her stomach. Whatever the invisible pull Matt had over her, it was as strong as ever. And only a minute ago she'd been thinking it had already passed.

Flame sighed. It was a deep-felt sigh that came from her soul. Everything in her life was far too complicated, from the mixed-up, unbidden feelings inside her, to the way the world viewed her hasty marriage. She didn't know how to view it herself.

The Micks respected Matt and wanted to help him by helping her. Melody Burr, seeing right away that the Jacksons slept in separate rooms, wanted Matt for herself. Not permanently, Flame was certain, just on loan, the way she might draw money from a bank. For all Flame knew, her husband was already making deposits for the colonel's daughter to enjoy.

Doc was the farthest off the mark, assuming that the rest he recommended would be helped along by Matt. Doc assumed wrong. She couldn't ask her husband to wait on her. He'd already given her his name, and for both of them that was as far as his obligation went.

And she couldn't ask him to be faithful. He gave no indication of tolerating celibacy, and she could give him no reason why he should. If he wanted Melody Burr or the women at the Kitty Cat, she had no justifiable cause to say nay.

Except that, all her rationalizing to the contrary, she had the urge to scratch the eyes out of any female who came near him.

Nothing made sense to her anymore. Least of all her husband and the way he was upsetting her. And she wasn't supposed to worry? Doc didn't know what he asked.

Drawing closer to the house, she stared at the gelding and pictured Matt astride the horse—the way he'd looked the day they met. She'd reacted then pretty much as she was reacting now, with a tightness inside that wasn't entirely unpleasant. Her husband wasn't handsome in the traditional sense of the word, but he had a dark, brooding air about him—and a hint of just-under-control savagery—that made every other man seem foppish in comparison.

What a worthless, foolish thought. Again Flame sighed. Pregnancy, it would seem, did nothing to enhance a woman's good sense.

Matt strolled onto the porch, a cup of coffee in his hand, and she started. Hatless, the red bandanna at his throat, the leather clothing fitting his muscular body far too well, he was a formidable sight for a woman with a weakness for such things. It was a description that obviously applied to Flame, since she felt a decided frailty in her knees as she neared the porch.

Matt watched her hesitant approach. "Where have you been?"

She flinched, and he silently cursed himself. He hadn't meant the question to sound so harsh—he'd simply been concerned, since fatigue had overtaken her in town—but she looked so vulnerable staring up at him that way, with her hair blown by the wind and her eyes round and somehow wounded, as though by coming home unexpectedly during the day he'd done something wrong.

I've been to the doctor, and he said you were to care for me during the next six months, and see that I get lots of rest, without once claiming your husband's rights.

Flame wondered what his response would be if she actually spoke the words. He'd be sputtering coffee all over the porch.

"I've been for a walk."

"Thought you were tired."

"I was restless."

He looked at her closer. The shadows were still there under her eyes, darker than ever. And there was something else that bothered him. She was answering him the way she usually did, with brief responses that told him little. But the fight was missing. Her voice sounded flat.

"Are you sure you're all right?"

"I'm fine. Is there any more of that coffee left?"

She stepped onto the porch, circled around him so that not even their clothing touched, and went inside.

Pouring a cup, she stood by the stove and let a sip of the bitter brew settle for a moment on her tongue, then trickle down her throat. After the brisk wind, the warmth was soothing. Matt liked his coffee strong. She'd have to remember that if she ever made him a pot.

But not once had he stayed around for something as ordinary as a cup of coffee. He came home only to taunt her, and then he was gone.

The front door opened and closed, and she turned to face him across the cloth-covered table.

"What are you doing here in the middle of the day?"

Matt's lips twitched. "Why, is my presence awkward?"

Flame did not like the hint of a smile. "What is that supposed to mean?"

Good, thought Matt. The fight was back.

"Forget it," he said with a shrug. He gestured with his cup toward a roll of canvas on the floor by the hearth. "Is that for me?"

The cot, she thought with a sinking feeling. She'd forgotten about buying it in town. And she'd forgotten about her worry over how he would accept it.

"I thought you might be more comfortable at night."

Damned little chance of that, he thought, not with her sleeping a few feet away behind a closed door. Bedding her was out of the question, but that didn't mean his body didn't keep thinking about it. If bodies could think. In his case, randy thoughts heated him up every night.

And she expected a cot to satisfy him. Was she really so simpleminded? He didn't know a hell of a lot about her, but he'd never taken her as weak in the head. On the contrary, she was outsmarting him every day—and night—of the week.

"I won't be needing it for a while," he said.

"Oh?" She hated the tremor in her voice.

"There's a patrol going out. I'll be with them."

Memories of the Apache attack on the stagecoach rushed into her mind. Once again she was in the midst of yells and bullets and falling men.

At that moment Matt no longer looked strong and invincible. No one could when riding against a blaze of guns. If anything happened to him—

She couldn't finish the thought.

"Has that Indian returned?" she asked, not wanting to know, but at the same time needing to find out how bad the situation was.

"Black Eagle? It's possible."

An icy fist squeezed Flame's heart. "Oh," she managed.

If Matt didn't know better, he'd think she was concerned.

"And it's also possible that he's safe down in Mexico, laughing because we can't get to him."

Flame liked the second response better. "Do you have any idea where he hides?"

"Yeah, I've got an idea." Matt knew exactly where. It was the place he'd lost his childhood, the place where he'd learned to hate.

Flame watched the harshness tighten his face. He seemed carved from rock, not flesh and blood. The look of him frightened her, more than his gaze of taunting arousal had ever done. It spoke loudly of how little she knew him, and of how she never would.

157

But that was worry for another time. Matt was riding into possible danger—the same danger that had taken Robert's life. She was stunned by how much she cared.

She could not let him know. She could hardly understand or deal with it herself.

"You can't just take everyone at the fort and ride down there?"

"Treaty between the governments forbids it. We have to be actually in pursuit of him, not leading a search party. If possible, we even have to let the Mexican authorities know we're on our way."

"Then it seems to me *they* ought to stop him."

"They've tried. Hundreds have been slaughtered for the effort. Whole villages wiped out."

"That's terrible."

"That's Black Eagle's way."

He spoke as though he were saying it was the way of a wolf or bear. Not the way of a man. She remembered how he'd viewed with contempt the half-breed in town, as though the boy carried in his blood the same murderous traits as Black Eagle. Matt carried burdens she couldn't begin to guess at. The fact that he would never confide in her . . . never let her share the weight . . . filled her with sadness.

More than ever she realized what a farce their marriage was.

She stared into the remains of her coffee. "So you're riding out to look for him on this side of the river."

"There's a new settlement west of here. Colonel Burr wants us to see that they get a decent start."

She tried to picture the settlement, the houses

much like this one rising out of the rocky ground, the men and women who would be building them, the peril they would face.

"Why do people come out here, when there is so much danger?"

"Hard to say. Why did you come out?"

The question took her by surprise, and she raised her eyes to stare at the man who dared ask it.

Because I believed myself in love with the man who fathered my child, and because I believed that he loved me.

So many thoughts she could not speak aloud. Matt had once questioned whether or not she could be sure Robert caused her condition. Perhaps he thought she could have settled on another possible husband, closer to home. She didn't want to find out if he truly suspected such duplicity. The mere idea of it hurt more than she believed possible. She didn't want to find out if it were true.

"We're not talking about me."

Their eyes locked. "That's right," he said. "And we shouldn't. It wouldn't be very smart for us to get to know each other better."

"Not smart at all."

Neither spoke for a moment. They simply stood there, staring at one another across the table. If he had said one kind word, if he had gestured in any way, Flame knew she would be fool enough to hurry around to him and let him hold her in his arms. She needed to share both comfort and kindness more than she'd ever needed them in her life, and at that moment she needed to share them with him.

But he continued to stare, as though he wanted

159

to see into her soul. And there were thoughts and feelings hidden there which she didn't want him to know about . . . thoughts and feelings she didn't understand herself.

Confused, she looked away. "When are you leaving?"

"Before dawn. I'll be with the troops tonight."

"Oh." Not even the late night return and the early departure were to remain in his routine.

"You'll be all right?" He pulled a small leather pouch from a pocket and set it on the table between them. "Here's some money. Buy what you need."

Something about the gesture angered her. What she needed could not be found tucked in a pouch with her husband's cash.

"I'll be all right." She faced him once again. "It's just that I'm more tired than I thought. If you need anything from the bedroom, go ahead and get it. I'll rest awhile, after you're gone."

"You don't sound all right."

"Don't worry about me, Matt." Tired as she was, she stood as tall as she could. "I said before that I could take care of myself. Since I've arrived, nothing's changed."

During the next couple of days, Flame had ample time to wonder if she'd been right in keeping from him the nature of her condition. She did the best she could to follow the doctor's advice, eating the food she'd put aside for storage instead of cooking fresh, skipping the morning sponge bath to keep from hauling water from the cistern, letting the sweeping and dusting go so that she might stay in bed for much of the day.

She passed the time working on Annie's blanket, and when that was finished, she used the leftover wool to knit a pair of booties, so tiny, they barely covered the palm of her hand. The sight of them brought tears to her eyes, and not because she'd done a poor job.

On the contrary. She'd never seen anything prettier. And she kept picturing them on her baby's little feet.

The only trouble was, after the knitting was finished and packed away in her trunk, she was left with nothing but slow-passing time and little with which to fill it. Except thinking over all that had happened to her, which did not put her in a cheerful frame of mind.

Remembering Mama and Papa and Raven and Angel, she got so homesick she thought her heart would break. If only she had someone to listen to her remembrances . . . to sympathize and maybe pass the time with remembrances of his own. That's what went on between a real man and wife, not just the physical loving.

But that was when true, deep, eternal love existed in a home. Too well she remembered the way her husband had departed, with only a brief nod as a goodbye. It had seemed to her that he couldn't wait to get out the door.

True love between Mr. and Mrs. Jackson? What an absurd idea. She and Matt hadn't even reached the tolerance level.

And they weren't likely to, not with the schedule

161

he'd been keeping before he left, rising early from his blankets by the fire and returning late after she had turned down the bedroom lamp. He must have thought she was sleeping, but she never really began to rest until he was back under the same roof with her.

She could tell he had tried to be quiet and not disturb her, but it wasn't in his nature. Papa was like that. Bumping into things, dropping his boots on the floor, where they landed as heavy as cartons of food tins that needed unloading at Chadwick's Dry Goods and Clothing. Sometimes the noise Matt made forced her to smile.

And the snoring. Nothing loud and snorty like Papa's, but kind of low and rumbling and soothing. Most nights Flame had fallen asleep to the sound.

She knew it was sheer foolishness on her part, and she'd die if he knew, but never in her life had she slept alone in a house, and she was finding it impossible to start now.

After two days of rest and little sleep, the fatigue that had come on her still refused to go away. But the blood spots had ceased. Doc hadn't seemed overly concerned about them, but she didn't know him well enough to determine if he'd been telling the truth.

On the third day of her solitude, he came to see her, and as he stood beside the bed she put the question to him outright.

"Why would I be passing blood?" she asked.

Doc adjusted the glasses over his nose. "That still a problem?"

"No. I just wanted to understand why it happened."

"Hard to say. Glad it's stopped, though. Now there's something I'd like to know. Why didn't you tell me that Matt rode out on patrol?"

"Because I didn't think you needed to know."

"You're the one with the need. How have you been taking care of yourself?"

"I've done all right."

"Don't try to lie to old Doc. You're as white as that sheet. Ever see a raccoon up close? That's the way your eyes look, just like a baby coon's."

"Give me time. I'll be all right."

"I'm not worried about what you're *going to be*. It's right now that's the worry."

Fright seized Flame. "Is the baby all right?"

"Near as I can tell, the baby's fine. It's the mother that's giving me trouble. Tell you what. I'll have one of the soldiers assigned to the hospital put water and food on your front door every morning. If you've not got too many foolish sensibilities about it and there's a chamber pot around here, put it out and he'll take care of that, too."

"I'm not a child," said Flame, embarrassed.

"No, but you're bringing one into this world, and we want to see that everything goes all right."

It was the one argument she couldn't refute. Except that she refused to consider the chamber pot. The privy wasn't far. And it offered the one excuse she had to get out of the house every day, however briefly.

Doc left, and the next few days passed even more slowly than the previous ones. Every morning she

163

found a bucket of water and a plate of food at the front door; every night she placed them back outside, empty.

In between times she stared at the four walls and the ceiling, and tried not to think about what was happening to Matt . . . tried not to consider whether or not he would return.

Early on the morning that marked the tenth day since his departure, with the air so close she could barely breathe, thunder rolled in over the hills, and within minutes she heard the rustly sound of fast-falling raindrops on the thatch roof. Pulling herself from the bed, she tiptoed to the window and peered into the dark. The only thing she could make out was a solid sheet of water washing down the windowpane.

Flame hadn't seen such rain since she'd left Savannah, and she didn't find it welcome now, even though it would replenish the dwindling water supply in the cistern. She hugged herself. Not long ago she'd thought that the worst thing to happen out here in this wilderness would be a storm keeping her isolated in the house with her husband. In a moment of complete honesty, she prayed she could be isolated with him now.

Staring at the wall of water, she imagined what he would look like if he really were sleeping in the next room, lying on top of a blanket on the cot, and maybe under a cover, too, since the weather was turning cold, his hair mussed, his face bristled, his long, lean body maybe without a stitch of clothing . . .

She stopped herself. Too many details could confuse a woman.

Crawling back into bed, she pulled the covers tight under her chin, and with thunder rumbling in the distance, she admitted to a longing that she could not accept in the bright light of day. Shameless she might be, but she was lonely and lost, and she needed Matt's strength and his . . . his companionship. She could think of no other word.

She wanted to feel his arms around her and his hands stroking her body and his lips warm against hers. She wanted to hear his husky voice taunting her, she wanted to see his dark eyes assessing her in ways that set her on fire.

Impossible yearnings, of course, even if her condition would allow such intimacies. But in the dark with the air close and damp and the storm raging against the rattling windowpane, she found it equally impossible to deny them. Crazy as it seemed, she knew that with him close by, she could not come to harm.

"Please keep yourself safe," she whispered, and with a sigh of desolation, thought how he would scoff at her caring.

Sleep came slowly. She awoke to the light of a gray day. Something had disturbed the troublesome dream that set her heart to pounding. The dream was fading fast . . . something about a baby crying in the dark and no one to hear, and Flame racing after the cry but unable to locate the exact place from which it came.

It had all seemed real, drawing her down into a thick and misty dream world, so that she had a difficult time rising to the surface of the day.

"Good morning," a deep, familiar voice said.

165

Flame bolted upright in the bed and stared at the tall, lean figure standing in the doorway. A shiver ran down her spine, and she was filled with a rush of joy that almost sent her springing from the bed.

Just when she needed him most, her husband had returned.

Eleven

Shirtless and barefoot, Matt propped his arm against the door frame. Even in the gray light of a stormy morning, he made quite a picture. Flame couldn't shift her eyes away.

One sweeping glance took everything in, from the uncombed hair black as pitch to the watchful brown eyes and bristled cheeks, to the strong neck and broad shoulders, and down past the hairy chest she'd never before seen and the fitted breeches she'd seen all too often to the bare feet on the plank floor.

Oh yes, quite a picture.

Relief shot through her, and more than that, a sense of happiness she hadn't known for a long while. Matt was alive and well. Very much alive, and from the looks of him, very well.

And she no longer had to face the storm and the emptiness alone. Feeling suddenly fluttery inside, she quickly moved back to his eyes. No longer watchful, they held the smile that was on his lips.

Trouble lay behind that smile, trouble for her, and

she clutched the covers close to her chin, as though she might cover her joy. When this moment had seemed impossible, she'd wanted it above all others. Certainty turned her into a coward.

"What are you doing here?" she asked.

Matt's smile faded.

"I live here, remember?"

As if she could forget.

"You're undressed," she said, feeling foolish, as though by admitting she'd noticed, she was giving his naked chest a special importance.

"Got back during the night. Didn't want to wake you."

She cast an eye to the window and the gloom of the day. "Before the storm?"

"Had to stable Pigeon first. Barely made it in the front door, before the rain came."

So he'd been in the next room just when she'd been picturing him there, lying on the blanket, un-clothed . . .

The thunder hadn't awakened her. Matt's presence had brought her out of a shallow sleep.

"Did everything go all right?"

He shrugged, and the motion did interesting things to his naked shoulders and chest.

"No sign of the Apaches. Just lots of hard riding and sleeping on a harder ground."

She pictured Matt stretched out under the stars, his head angled awkwardly against a rigid leather saddle, his long, lean body finding little comfort on the rock-strewn Texas soil. He needed—and he de-served—the comfort of his hearth and home.

And the comfort that a wife was supposed to provide. An ordinary wife. Which she was not.

Wives, too, needed comfort when they'd been left behind with no word of their men. Ordinary wives, that is.

What would it be like to live as an ordinary wife with Matt? Her experiences, brief though they had been, brought a few particulars to mind.

Had he stopped by the saloon in Little Sandy, before continuing his journey to Fort Hard? Had he been with Melody Burr only minutes before? Something about the look in his eye told her that wherever wanderings had taken him, his hungers had not been satisfied.

Flame had hungers, too, curling, insistent pangs impossible to ignore or deny.

With the rain continuing to pound against the adobe walls of her husband's home, she pulled the covers tighter. Every part of her was tingling with a heat that had nothing to do with the closeness of the air. She could not will the reactions to abate.

Matt felt the tension as he walked into the room, one bare foot in front of the other, his body growing harder with each step. It was his house, by God, and his room, and his bed. And it was his wife, who lay beneath the covers as if she were welcoming her man to a sanctuary from the tempest.

And just how welcome was he? He wasn't so aroused by the sight of her that he missed her distress. Either Flame wanted him the way he wanted her, or she regretted his return. It was time to find out which guess was right.

It mattered damned little that she carried another man's child.

He stopped at the foot of the bed and leaned down to put his hands flat on the cover beside her feet. Flame's hair was a disarray of long, loose curls, the color of morning sun against the white of the sheet, and her eyes, for all their greenness, were wide and alert, reminding him of a frightened doe.

The shadows were still there; he'd been wanting to see her so much, that he decided they gave her a sexy look. Funny thing his missing her. It had taken him by surprise. For the first time on one of his patrols to find Black Eagle, he hadn't wanted to continue the fruitless search. He'd wanted to get back home.

He let his eyes trail down the figure outlined beneath the shielding quilt. Her arms hid her breasts, but he saw the narrow waist and flaring hips and the impossibly long, shapely legs. He'd heard that redheads had the same color hair between their legs. The natural redheads. He'd slept with women from San Francisco to New York, some of them redheads, but he'd never been intimate with one who didn't get the color out of a bottle.

Speculation about his wife was making the fit of his trousers damned uncomfortable.

But that was the condition he'd awakened to every morning before he left, just knowing she was behind the closed door, lying in his bed. A cold dousing in cistern water had become part of his daily routine. In all his life Matt had never been so clean.

Slowly he let his gaze return to her face and to the frightened deer eyes. She could be a tigress, too,

170

he remembered. And he remembered what it took to bring that wild, hungry look back to her lovely face.

With the rain pounding down outside, sheltering them from intrusion by the world, he wanted to work on some of the unfinished business that lay between them. Ten days away had seemed forever. Teasing her might have its torturous effects on his celibate body, but it was a sweet kind of torture that seemed right for a day like today.

And maybe things would go beyond teasing. Flame wasn't an innocent. And she was legally his.

The grin returned to his face.

"Where's my good morning? We've been married almost two weeks, and I've yet to hear you say it."

She brushed an errant curl from her face. "I say it all right. Into the mirror right after dawn, when I'm combing my hair. I say it so I can hear the sound of a human voice."

"Do I hear a little irritation in your tone? Kinda hard to know what I'm supposed to do and not do as a husband. Would you like me to hang around every morning to watch you get dressed?"

Yes . . . no. Flame had no answer. She didn't know what she wanted.

What she did *not* care for was him standing at the foot of her bed, half-naked, looking at her as though he were starving and she was a platter of roasted beef.

Suddenly her fatigue left her. She'd spent ample time at rest, more than Doc probably thought she would get. All her symptoms were gone. Annie was fine. But no matter how healthy she was, one stric-

171

ture of the doctor's would be kept: she would not have relations with her husband.

With that thought in mind—and her eyes carefully turned away from the formidable sight of him—she threw back the covers and stood. The hem of the white lawn nightgown brushed against her feet, and she felt adequately covered from neck to ankles.

"I'll cook some breakfast, if you'll give me a minute to get dressed."

Matt could see the outline of her body beneath the gown, especially the shape of her high, firm breasts. If he put anything in his mouth right now, it would be the pebble-hard nipples of those breasts.

Matt moved around the edge of the footboard. "I like to be served in bed."

Flame cleared her throat, cast him a sideways glance, and quickly looked away again. She hadn't married a prettily handsome man the way Robert had been; she'd married the manliest man she had ever seen. And her woman's body knew it from the suddenly tight and tingling breasts, down her stomach to her thighs, and in a very strange and intimate place that had suddenly taken on a sensitivity all its own.

He'd set up throbbings of a new and dangerous kind just by looking at her from under those thick black brows, his eyes velvet brown, his lips beckoning in silence with a message as loud as a shout. His hands couldn't have much more effect on her sensibilities than the look he was giving.

What a wanton she was, and the worst thing of all was that she couldn't dredge up the least amount of shame.

He eased closer and touched a lock of hair brushing against her shoulder. Until that moment, Flame hadn't realized hair had feelings. Until that moment, she hadn't realized every part of her had feelings of a kind Matt Jackson aroused.

She tried to remember if Robert had made her feel this way, but she couldn't even remember what he looked like right now . . . and she knew for sure she'd never experienced this kind of heat.

"Our agreement—" she began, but her voice broke as she stared at the set of his mouth.

"Yeah. Right." His fingers touched the side of her neck, and she trembled. "Cold?" he asked.

She hurriedly shook her head.

He caressed the damp curve of her nape, his hand fully buried beneath the blanket of red curls. "I could warm you if you want."

"No!" she practically shouted, twisting away from his touch. She flushed with embarrassment. She spoke too quickly, too loudly, and she knew he recognized her response as a lie. Only a short while ago she'd been tossing in bed and thinking about how lonely she was . . . how much she would welcome any kind of comfort . . . even her husband's caress.

Her own conscience labeled her liar. She'd especially yearned for Matt.

Thunder boomed and bright light filled the room. She jumped and he took her in his arms.

"That was close," she said, her eyes directed to the pouring rain outside the window, her mind distracted by the storm.

"Yeah. You're safe with me."

His words, deep and thick with layers of meaning, brought her gaze back to him. She saw the workings of his throat as he spoke, the tightness of copper skin across muscled shoulders and chest, the curls of black hair swirling across the contours of his body, and she breathed in the scent of musky maleness that clung to him.

Flame forgot the elements outside the room. The storm raging within her breast was all she could handle.

Enfolded in his arms, hands trapped between their facing bodies, eyes directed to the pulse point at his throat, she had no choice but to let her fingers press against his chest. The feel of taut warmth tingled the tips. She felt that warmth all the way to her toes.

"Look at me, Flame."

Reluctantly she lifted her eyes. He stared back with startling intensity. She could not turn away.

"Kiss me," he said.

She swallowed. Gone was her loneliness. Faded was her despair. One kiss. What could it hurt?

She touched her mouth to his.

Matt's manhood threatened to split the seam of his trousers.

He touched her teeth with his tongue. She opened herself to him. The kiss deepened.

Flame's breasts grew tight and hard-tipped. Easing her hands to his shoulders and around his neck, she thrust her lawn-covered body against his bare chest. The hardness of him extended from the sinewed shoulder down to the thighs pressing against

174

hers. She was especially aware of his arousal teasing her abdomen.

If she stood on tiptoe, if she eased her legs apart, she could settle that very special part of him into the valley where it belonged.

Taunting her tongue with his, Matt trailed his hands down the slopes of her body, easing from the sides of her breasts to the narrow waist to the flaring hips. He settled his palms against her thighs and with great restraint left her legs to return to the hips. There were so many parts of her he wanted to explore. Desire burned in him. It would take more than a kiss, no matter how thorough, to quench the flames.

He pulled at her gown, slowly lifting the hem as he eased his mouth from hers. The kiss moved down her throat, across the rise of her breasts tantalizing him beneath the soft white gown, and his fingers kept working toward the hem. At last he felt the smoothness of her upper thigh. No underdrawers, he realized, and he fell deeper into the conflagration of desire.

Flame was cool and warm at the same time, and he felt her tremble as he eased his fingers to the curves of her buttocks, grasping her tight against him, his lips seeking out the tip of one high, beckoning breast.

Flame's head fell back, and she gave in to the storms that raged within her. Matt was here, stroking, kissing, holding her tight, and she was no longer alone. This was right, she thought as her hands explored the splendor of his shoulders and back. Husband and wife, nothing of shame in that.

Husband and wife and baby. The remembrance knifed through Flame. Was she insane? Oh, yes, most definitely so. This must not continue . . . somehow she must pull away.

But he felt so good, and he felt so precious, and she had been so alone. Tears burned her eyes. She wanted him above all else, and he wanted her.

But Annie needed her protection.

She grew still, and that was when she heard the slam of the front door.

Matt, too, quietened, his lips easing from her breasts, his hands shifting to allow the hem of her gown to fall once again to the floor.

He let her go, fast, and spun toward the door, disappearing into the adjoining room. Dizzy from his sudden departure, she sat on the edge of the bed. He was back in a minute, a covered plate and a bucket of water in his hand.

Standing in the doorway, he stared at her. Something sharp clawed at his gut, something he had never felt before, and it didn't help his well being that he was still aroused.

"These were inside. Caught only a quick look at the man who left them. He was hurrying too fast through the rain. What's going on?"

Flame flushed with guilt. She'd let Matt ride out without telling him of the doctor's orders for bed rest. It hadn't seemed important to let him know. And she hadn't wanted to hear him say he didn't care.

"Nothing's going on," she said.

"Then why won't you look me in the eye?"

There was sharp accusation in his voice, and when

she met his cool regard, she saw the same sharpness hardening his expression.

All the hungers of a moment ago shriveled inside.

"What do you *think* is going on?" she asked, matching his sharpness.

Matt shook his head in frustration. "How the hell should I know? I leave for a few days, and a strange man starts delivering my wife gifts."

"He's not a strange man. He works at the hospital."

"You're getting service I never got."

"Maybe you didn't ask in the right way."

"What the hell does that mean?"

Flame hadn't the vaguest idea. But she couldn't let him stand there like a crusading judge and accuse her of infidelities she would not so much as contemplate.

Besides, how could she be unfaithful, when there was nothing to be faithful to?

She stood. The dizziness returned, but she ignored it. One glance out the window told her the rain had at last abated.

"I'll tell you what, Matt. Let's get him back here and ask him to explain."

"Don't be stupid."

Nothing he could have said would have emboldened her more. She closed the distance between them, took the plate and bucket, and eased past him through the door. Setting the offending objects on the table, she turned to face him once again.

"The stupid thing was almost giving in to you a moment ago. I'll not make that mistake again."

"Don't bet on it."

"You really are a beast."

"I've been told that before."

Fury consumed her. She wanted nothing else but to slap the uncompromising glint from his eyes. Always their tender moments ended like this. If what had passed between them beside the bed could be called tender.

There was certainly nothing tender between them now.

His eyes told her he still wasn't sure just who had fathered her baby. He believed she was a slattern who slept around. She believed the same thing about herself, because she wanted only to sleep with him.

The air in the house became unbreathable. She must get out. Annie wanted the same thing, else why the sharp pains low in her abdomen?

Hugging her middle, Flame headed for the door.

"Come back here," Matt said.

She glanced over her shoulder at him. "Don't order me around, Matt. You haven't the right."

She shoved open the door and emerged onto the porch. A cool, damp breeze brushed across her cheek.

Matt followed, and she whirled to face him.

"Let's face it, Matt. This isn't working. You don't like me, but you want me. And I feel the same about you. Except that I've decided not to want you anymore."

"You're not dressed, for God's sake. Get back inside."

She could have believed there was concern in his eyes, concern for her, but she still felt light-headed and her abdomen still hurt, and Matt had never once shown anything toward her but carnal desire.

"Since I've already obviously shamed you, what possible difference could it make that I parade around in my gown?"

She had a crazed look in her eye that he had never seen before, and he thought only of her safety. Knowing nothing about women who carried babies, he realized nevertheless that she must be brought back into the house, must be calmed, must get some rest.

He took a step toward her. She had a wild urge to flee from him, to take a path that would lead her into the rain-washed woods and up the nearest rocky hill.

Turning, she stepped from the porch onto a patch of slippery mud. Her foot went out from under her. She twisted in an attempt to keep from falling, and Matt watched in horror as she came down hard on her face and stomach.

He was beside her in an instant, kneeling in the mud, turning her to her back, cradling her close to his chest. It was the way he'd held his brother Charlie and, much later, Robert Anderson. Both of them had died.

Matt caught himself trembling. Flame wouldn't die. He wouldn't let her.

But why wouldn't she look up at him with orders to leave her alone? He wanted to hear the rebellious words issue from her lips.

But she remained silent and still, thick lashes resting against bruised cheeks. He brushed the muddied hair from her face. She moaned a single word that sounded like *Annie*.

He loosened the high collar of her gown, its pristine whiteness stained black from her fall.

And then he saw the slash of red across a twisted swath of material below her waist. His eyes darted back to her face. She looked so pale, so helpless, so dependent on him.

Somehow, so was her baby.

Anguish twisted his heart. Holding her close, he stood and hurried toward the hospital only twenty yards away. It might have been twenty miles. Already he knew that as skilled as Doc Kirby proved himself to be, help for Flame Chadwick Jackson would arrive too late.

Twelve

"She would have lost the baby anyway." Doc Kirby twirled the inkwell on his desk and peered through a pair of wire-frame glasses at the man sitting opposite him. "Wasn't anything you did wrong."

"Like hell," said Matt. Unable to relax, he sat on the edge of his chair and stared into open space. "We had a fight just before she fell."

"You hit her?"

"Good God, no!"

"Didn't think so, but I had to ask. And I'm not lying to make you feel better about the miscarriage. After my examination, I feared it would happen. Some things just aren't meant to be."

Matt looked over at Doc in surprise. "Flame didn't say anything about seeing you."

"It was the day you rode out—what was it, more than a week ago? She sat right where you're sitting, and I wanted to tell her how things would likely go."

Doc sighed and pushed the glasses more firmly on the bridge of his nose. "Except miracles sometimes happen. Guess the good Lord was fresh out of miracles today."

"You say it was the day I left. What time?"

"Right after noon, best I can recall."

Matt thought back to that day. They'd returned from Little Sandy after he'd rescued her in the alley. They hadn't been getting along too well.

Hell, when did they ever?

He raked a hand through his hair. "Why did she come see you?"

Doc didn't respond right away, taking time to ponder the ethics of the situation. What passed between a doctor and his patient—even if the patient was a married woman—ought to be confidential. But this particular patient was lying behind a screen in the Fort Hard hospital ward, sleeping restlessly, and when she awoke her husband would have to tell her something that would tear her apart.

And it wasn't just the loss of the baby. There was more bad news even Matt didn't know.

All right, so he probably wasn't the baby's father. But there was pain in his eyes, enough to tell Doc that it didn't much matter to him who the real father was, that the loss was a tragedy for everyone concerned.

Doc had been wrong to question whether Matt was a good man or not. He was, although he didn't seem to know it.

"She hadn't been feeling well," said Doc. "Tired, she said. And she was passing some blood."

That was enough to say. No good in letting him know his wife had been asking about whether she was in condition to take a long journey away from the fort.

Matt shifted in his chair, uneasy with the facts Doc was telling. He knew damned little about the workings of a woman's body, except what he'd wanted to know. And he'd never been interested in the bringing of life into the world, except how to avoid it. That's why he'd stayed with experienced women who made him spill his seed on the bed, or who claimed childbearing was a part of their past.

If the subject came up. He left the mention of that problem to them.

He'd been thinking Flame was experienced, that through her condition she'd been trying to fool a wealthy Army officer into marriage. But she'd wanted that baby more than anything, even after Robert Anderson was no longer around.

Matt was thinking now that maybe he'd been wrong about her motivations.

Funny thing about him and his wife. They didn't mean anything to each other—hell, they hardly knew each other—but she had a way of making him feel as lusty as he'd ever felt in his life . . . or as low as a skunk. Sometimes the two feelings came at the same time. There never seemed to be anything in between.

"I told her," said Doc, "that she needed rest, that she shouldn't worry. And that the two of you needed to sleep apart for a while. She seemed a little doubtful about the first two, but she said that last wouldn't be a problem. Seemed mighty sure."

"She would be," said Matt with a sharp, humorless laugh.

He thought about his wife lying in a screened-off hospital cot down the corridor outside Doc's office door, her face as white as the sheet on which she lay. One of the soldiers who served as orderly was watching over her. Could very well be the soldier he'd seen running from his front door.

"You sent over food and water every day, didn't you?" he asked.

"Sure did, when I found out she was all alone. Stubborn woman you've got there, Matt. Didn't let me know she was trying to care for herself."

Matt caught the accusation in the doctor's voice. He saw no purpose in discussing why he hadn't known she was having trouble. No need to say they weren't really man and wife.

He cursed the day he'd ridden out with Robert to guard the woman who was writing troublesome letters. Since the moment he'd spied her standing tall and proud by the corral at the stagecoach relay station, like a long-stem rose growing out of place in the desert, he hadn't drawn an easy breath.

But then, he reminded himself, neither had she.

Upset as he was, he'd be a genuine bastard to lay it off on her. Rousing her from her bed of rest the way he'd done, pawing her like she was one of the women at the Kitty Cat, he'd already been bastard enough for a troop's company.

"How long will she be asleep?"

"Her body's worn out. Probably won't be fully awake until tomorrow morning."

"Does she realize what's happened?"

"It's doubtful."

"That means someone will have to tell her."

"Sure does," Doc said.

The two men stared at one another in silence, each waiting for the other to volunteer.

Doc removed his glasses and rubbed at his tired eyes. He set the wire-frames on the cluttered desk.

"I can do it, if you like," he said.

Matt came close to accepting the offer. Flame might take the news better from Doc.

The idea didn't sit well. Somehow it seemed like the coward's way out. Somehow it seemed right that she hear the bad news from the man who'd practically chased her out of the house and caused her to fall.

He wasn't her husband, not in any way other than legal, but somehow his doing the telling seemed right.

Once a long time ago, Matt had run from his problems. He didn't run anymore.

He stood. "Thanks for everything, Doc, but she'll hear it from me. I'll wait by her bed 'til she's awake."

"Don't be a fool, Matt. You don't look much more rested than that brave little woman lying out there. Go on home and try to get some sleep. We'll get you here as soon as she starts to stir."

Matt shook his head. "I'm staying."

Doc opened his mouth to argue, but there was something in the scout's eyes that stilled his protest.

Since the examination more than a week ago, he'd been worrying about more than Flame Jackson's pregnancy; he'd been worrying about her marriage, pondering just how unorthodox it could be, coming on as suddenly as it had. But there was real concern in her husband's eyes, and it spoke well of his feelings that he was taking on a spouse's responsibilities in a time of such stress.

Doc was more convinced than ever that Matt Jackson was a good man.

"At least let me get you some food. We don't have much of a cook here, but it's healthy, and it'll give you a little strength. You're going to need it, Matt. I'm afraid there's more bad news."

Matt shook his head wearily. "Shouldn't be surprised. It's been my experience that once the bad times start, they just keep on coming."

"You may be right." Doc stood and escorted him out the door. "It's too close in here. The rain's long gone. Let's take a stroll outside, and I'll fill you in on exactly what's happened to your wife."

Flame woke to darkness. She hurt all over, and she felt lost and alone. Drifting in space, it seemed, on a hard, narrow bed. Fright seized her.

"Mama!" she cried out, the way she'd done as a child, and she tried to sit up so that Anne Chadwick could find her daughter in the dark.

A warm, strong hand clasped hers, and a deep, strong voice said, "I'm right here. You're safe. Don't be afraid."

The words eased her panic, but as she lay back on the bed, her heart continued to pound.

"Matt?" she asked in a small voice.

"Yeah, I'm right here."

She squeezed his hand, fearful that he would let go, despite his assurances. Gradually she made out the outline of his tall, lean presence close by her side. The sight of him, the feel of his hand, and the sound of his voice brought a calming relief.

Gone was the sense of drifting, but the hurt wouldn't go away. She'd never hurt so bad . . . across her shoulders, down her arms and legs, as though she'd been working hard out in a field somewhere, and most of all in the part of her body where Annie was growing, and in the part where Annie would be born.

She wanted to ask about all that hurt, but when she started to do so, the fright returned.

"Where am I?" she said instead, her eyes concentrated on the shadowed figure of her husband.

"In the hospital where you can get some rest."

"The hospital?"

"Doc thought it best. He must have been right. You've been asleep for a long time."

More than fifteen hours, he could have said, but that would require an explanation of her condition he wasn't ready to rush into.

"Then why am I so tired?" she asked.

"Maybe because you haven't rested enough."

Flame fell silent, and Matt hoped his answer eased her for a while.

"I fell, didn't I? Outside the house. It was muddy, and I slipped and fell."

"That's right."

Without letting go of her hand, he dragged his chair nearer to the bed and sat where he could look more closely at her. His eyes were used to the dark, and he could make out the contours of her face and the splay of her hair against the pillow.

Lying still in the dim light, she looked so damned

187

young, so dependent on him. So fragile. It was difficult to take, since he'd grown used to thinking of her as tough.

Tough, he could handle. Fragile came harder.

He felt awkward and helpless and more than a little angry at the way things were working out, but he also knew that he could be no place else on earth except by her side.

Even though she'd cried out for her mother when she'd awakened. Damned stupid idea to even consider she should be calling for him.

Flame sensed his distress. Why was he here, anyway? Come to think of it, why was she? For rest, the way he had said? She could get that at home.

She caught herself and felt a moment's anguish. She didn't really have a home, at least not one close by. Matt's adobe house might shelter her from an occasional storm, but it also was the scene of monumental tempests within its walls.

Which brought her back to the question of why the hospital? The fall hadn't been all that far. With her rambunctious ways, she'd taken far greater tumbles all her life.

But not as an expectant mother. She'd been right to panic when she first awoke. Something must be terribly wrong. She wanted to reach down and touch her stomach. Annie wasn't big enough to show her presence much, but Flame always imagined she could feel her baby's body growing. Maybe if she touched herself, she could know that everything really was all right, just the way Matt was saying.

But she couldn't seem to make the necessary

188

moves, no more than she could believe he told the truth.

"I guess it was the falling that made me so sore."

"It was hard on you."

Neither spoke for a minute. Flame could hear soft footsteps somewhere in the distance, and whispering voices drifting out of the dark. She and Matt were not alone. For some reason everyone was being awfully quiet.

"Was it hard on Annie?" she said at last, barely able to speak, barely able to breathe. All she could feel was the hurt and the fear and the cold that had her in their grip.

Matt knew she spoke of the baby. He hadn't known she'd given it a name.

He leaned closer and stroked her hair, hoping it was the right thing to do. Suddenly he felt like an impostor, sitting here the way a real husband would do, trying to pass on the news that would tear his wife apart, and his hand dropped back to his lap.

"It was hard on the baby," he said. "But that wasn't what caused it to happen."

Flame pushed him away and lay rigid in the bed. "Caused what to happen?"

Matt couldn't bring out the words. Doc ought to be here. Better, Flame's Mama. Anyone but him.

"You don't have to tell me." Her voice was flat, without emotion. "I lost Annie."

Her throat closed over the last words, and the tears streamed from her eyes. All the separate hurting dissolved into one tremendous pain that settled around her heart.

Matt let his silence answer for him. He hadn't felt

so helpless since the day he'd watched his family die.

In a way it seemed like he was losing them all over again. It was a crazy thought. He must be more exhausted than he'd realized.

He sensed his wife was crying, but she didn't make a sound. Awkwardly he sat on the edge of the bed and took her in his arms. She felt limp as a doll, weightless, without will either to push him away or to cling to his support.

Flame had no strength to fight or return his embrace. He meant to help her—she knew he did and maybe later she would be grateful—but for now she could do nothing more than mourn for all her shattered dreams.

She hadn't handled anything right . . . not from the moment Robert Anderson asked her to ride with him in the country, to the time she'd run away from her yearnings for Matt.

Mama and Papa would be ashamed, and Raven and even sweet Angel.

But those were considerations she must leave for another time. Right now her grief was centered on a fair-haired infant she would never hold in her arms. Right now she grieved for a life that would never be.

When Flame awoke a second time in the hospital, it was to the solemn face of Doc Kirby standing beside her bed. Daylight brightened with cruel efficiency the corner of the ward where she lay, but she had no idea of the time or even the day.

All the horrors of her condition rushed in on her, and she thought she could not contain the pain. Little did time or day matter. Nothing mattered, not with Annie gone. How much better it would be if the fall had taken her life, too.

She felt so weary that she could think of nothing better than to close her eyes to an eternal sleep.

"I was about to wake you," said Doc. "You need a little nourishment, if I'm to get you on your feet again."

She gripped the covering sheet to her breast and shifted her gaze toward the wall directly behind him. Doc looked so kind, so sympathetic. She couldn't handle kindness and sympathy. She wanted nothing but to be left alone.

"I'm not hungry," she managed, surprised she could get the words out so strongly.

"Don't imagine you are. But Cook's fixed a little soup for you that ought to go down smoothly enough. Try to swallow a few spoonfuls, and later I'll help you walk around."

"Thanks, but I'm really not hungry."

"Doesn't matter. You've got to eat. You want me to get Matt in here to force the soup down you?"

Flame looked back at him with alarm. He sounded brusque instead of kind. The change surprised her, took her mind off her misery for a second.

She thought of the way Matt had been here to give her the bad news. She also remembered the way he held her when the pain had become too much and she'd broken down. Doc must have forced

191

him to do it; he never would have shouldered such a delicate task on his own.

But she would have given a great deal to have him back right now with his strong arms around her. The realization took her by surprise. In her weakness she was idealizing him as a real husband. He wasn't. And he never would be.

"I'll try the soup," she said in resignation.

"Good."

She was surprised when Doc himself braced her back with an extra pillow, fetched the bowl from behind the screen, and sat at the edge of her bed.

Looking into his kind, blue eyes, she tried to smile. "I can feed myself."

"Nonsense. Haven't done this since I was an intern back in Boston." In went a spoonful of broth. "Feels kind of good to get back into practice."

Flame let the warm beefy liquid trickle down her throat. It tasted surprising good.

"Do you have any children, Doc?"

Another spoonful, and then another. "A son. He's a doctor back in Kentucky."

Watching as she continued to eat, he debated whether to tell her more. He didn't say another word until the soup was gone and he'd set the bowl aside.

"My wife lost another child. A daughter."

Flame's eyes filled with tears. "I'm sorry. Where is she now? Your wife, I mean? I didn't know you were married."

"Widowed. Mrs. Kirby passed on five years ago."

Flame brushed the dampness from her cheek. "I guess everybody suffers loss. It's just that this is my first time, and I—"

Her voice broke, and she bit at her lower lip to get control.

"Don't try to hold back. Crying is the Lord's way of letting out the grief that builds inside us. Maybe it's not the professional way to handle it, but I've shed a tear or two over your baby."

She stared at Doc through blurry eyes. "Why did it happen? I did everything you said. Except maybe running out the way I did."

"Don't blame yourself, young woman. Bunch of nonsense. You were having troubles, remember? I was praying for you, but it's my guess you were going to lose that baby no matter what. I told your husband the same thing. Some things just aren't meant to be."

Flame traced a circle on the bed. "I guess you're trying to console me."

"I don't imagine there's much I could say that would do that. I'm just telling you the way I view things. And it would be a mistake to blame either yourself or your husband."

She glanced up at Doc in surprise. "I'm not blaming him."

"Glad to hear it. He's blaming himself enough for the two of you."

Flame didn't know whether to believe him or not. The picture Doc was presenting of Matt was not one she could readily bring to mind.

"Doc," she said in complete sincerity, "I've done impetuous things all my life. Running out of the house and slipping in the mud is just one of them. The problem is, always before *I've* been the one to suffer. I should have been thinking of more than just myself."

Doc stood, and for the first time since they'd met, he looked truly angry.

"Flame Jackson, I'm going to tell you this one more time, and I want you to listen carefully. Falling didn't cause the miscarriage. You were carrying the baby wrong. Remember the bleeding? That was almost a sure sign there would be trouble, that and the fatigue."

"You said everything would be all right if I rested. Was that a lie?"

"It's what I prefer to call a caution. There was a chance, slim though it was, that things would work out the way you wanted. Matt said you were planning on a little girl. Could very well have been. You go right ahead and grieve for her, the way the Lord intended, and then you get on with your life."

She hugged herself and stroked at her upper arms. "That's a great deal to ask."

"Sure it is. But you're a strong woman, and you're married to a good man."

If Doc only knew the way things really were between the Jacksons . . .

And then Flame realized that she and Matt could now get an annulment. She should have been pleased, but the thought did nothing to ease the ache in her heart.

"Where is he?"

"Getting some sleep. At least that's what I ordered. He's gone a day and a half without rest."

Doc thought of the bleary-eyed man he'd sent home not more than two hours ago. He'd not been the sure-of-himself, closemouthed scout the fort had grown used to over the past year. Not that he'd lost any of his intensity. He'd picked up something in addition. Doc didn't want to call it a gentleness, exactly—Matt Jackson was hardly a gentle man—but gentle came as close as he could get.

"Matt doesn't know quite how to handle all this," said Doc, "but give him time. He'll be close by if you need him."

He left her to ponder his words. He could have told her more, but somehow it seemed like the wrong time. Let her grow strong again, and then he'd tell her what he'd already told Matt.

He would let her know as kindly as possible that more than likely she would never bear another child.

Thirteen

Over the next few days, Matt went to see Flame every morning and every evening, but neither had much to say.

He tried to talk about what had happened when she lost the baby, but he wasn't very smooth about apologizing, and she gave no hint that she understood what he was talking about. Or maybe it was that she didn't want to hear what he had to say.

As usual, they ended in an argument, which wasn't at all what he had intended.

Once she brought up the subject of an annulment, saying that only the two of them and Doc knew she had been pregnant. Doc promised to say she was being cared for because of "female trouble," and surely Matt would go along with the story, since everyone would know the baby couldn't be his.

He told her they could discuss it later, when they were alone.

So she was already thinking of getting out of the marriage. Good. The sooner the better, as far as he was concerned. He could get back to finding Black

Eagle and whoever was selling him guns, and then Matt, too, would be leaving, getting the hell away from this part of the country.

A long time ago, a few years after escaping the Apaches, he'd tried to get away from Texas, traveling from New York to San Francisco, stopping at points in between. When he left the next time, he wouldn't return.

On the third morning of Flame's hospitalization, he caught her walking up and down the center aisle of the ward with the three Micks, talking to them with an animation he hadn't seen since her fall. The hospital's only other patients, a couple of privates who claimed food poisoning from the previous night's stew, watched her white-robed figure move back and forth past their beds.

Whatever the severity of their ailment, it wasn't bad enough to keep them from following her every step. But who could blame them? She made quite a picture with all that red hair loosely covering her shoulders and a good portion of her back. And she was dressed in her bedclothes, for God's sake.

To him she still looked tired and pale, with a brightness in her eyes that was not natural; he knew her better than they.

Neither of the laid-up soldiers looked at her as though she were just another patient. Neither did the Micks.

And no one bothered to notice the presence of her husband at the entrance to the ward. Especially not Flame.

"We've been missing your smiling face around the

fort," Michael Mallon declared where all could hear.

"Aye," said Brendan Faulkner. "Me heart's about to break from the dreariness of it all."

"Don't you have work you're supposed to do?" asked Flame. "I don't know much about the Army, but it seems to me you have a great deal of free time on your hands."

" 'Tis an illusion," said Ian Craig with a shake of his head. "You see before you a trio of hardworking Irish lads. Beyond the barracks we've tilled every square inch of soil that doesn't have a building on it, in preparation for spring planting. If Sergeant Gibson had his way, we'd be working at our hoes all the way to El Paso."

Flame thought about the hard-packed, rocky ground that was so different from the rich loam of southern Georgia. "I'm surprised you can get anything to grow."

"You're looking at three magicians from County Cork, lass," said Michael. "We're mixing in the animal droppings from the stables, and carting up some of the dirt around Little Sandy Creek."

"There's an underground pool, too, we've tapped into," added Ian, "not far from the parade grounds. Wait until spring. That's when you'll see the handiwork of our magic."

"Spring," said Flame. On her lips the word sounded sad. She looked into the empty air beyond them and thought of all that the season meant, with its promises of reborn life. April, especially, would be cruel this year.

"Spring's a long time away," she said, but not, she could have added, long enough.

" 'Tis right at November now," said Brendan. "Not so far."

Flame shook off her melancholy. She'd be gone well before the first shoots poked through the ground. Doc said she would need an extended period of rest to gather her strength for any journey she might be contemplating. She didn't tell him she'd be heading back to Georgia as soon as she could get an annulment.

And she certainly didn't tell him why.

It wouldn't be to escape the memories of her loss. Grief was a portable emotion; she would take it with her wherever she went. But her relationship with Matt was different. The greater the distance between them, the less he would occupy her mind.

As the Micks talked on about their gardening, her thoughts wandered to her husband and the ought-to-be-simple relationship between them. As in so many other areas of her life, this particular ought-to-be was in truth a never-was.

She couldn't fault Matt for ignoring her, but she could see his daily visits were made because he supposed it was the right thing to do. He never had much to say, except to contradict her, and the wall between them rose as high and impenetrable as a Texas limestone bluff.

What had they ever had in common but forced promises to Robert, and an attraction to each other that was hardly honorable?

The promises had been rendered unnecessary— among Flame's regrets was that Robert left no part of himself behind—and she couldn't imagine Matt's being attracted to her again, not when she had regularly changed her mind about just how she felt about him. Or at least how far she had been willing to let those feelings take her.

Anyway, he'd not been interested in her because of anything personal. She was simply the woman close at hand.

Doc said she would be able to "serve as a wife," as he put it, within a couple of weeks. Flame almost laughed. As shameless as she'd grown to view herself, she couldn't imagine wanting any man.

Not even Matt.

Doc also told her that it was about time she was going home again. He meant, of course, Matt's house. Images of a dark-eyed, virile man hovering over the bed loomed in her mind. She was putting off the return as long as she could.

In moments of rationality, she admitted to inconsistent thoughts. Matt wouldn't want her . . . he'd be stalking her in his bed. She didn't know which attitude she preferred.

"Glad to see you're doing so well this morning."

She whirled in place and saw her husband, hat in hand, standing only a few feet away at the entrance to the ward. Her breath caught at the sight. As usual, he wore the fringed buckskin shirt and trousers, not much darker than the color of his skin, and just about as form-fitting. A red bandanna circled his throat, and a gun holster was strapped to his thigh.

His tooled leather boots were polished for a change, he was clean-shaven, and his thick black hair was combed away from his face. Despite the groomed appearance, he still had a savage look about him. At least, he did to her. Maybe it was because she knew the intensity with which he did everything.

Everything. She could imagine the way he would make love.

She flushed at the thought and turned away. What had come over her? The weakness of body and spirit that she was fighting had obviously traveled to her brain.

"I think it's time for you to go," she said to the three Irishmen, who'd fallen into an unaccustomed silence.

"You'll fare well?" asked Brendan, his young, freckled face lined with concern.

"I'll fare well." Flame attempted to smile, but she didn't meet with much success. She wondered if she would ever manage to laugh again.

But that was a maudlin thought. Sometime in the past two days, between bouts of desperate tears and searing desolation, she'd come to the conclusion that Annie deserved more than a self-pitying mother as her lone mourner.

Raven always said that if the rest of the one-time Confederacy had as much resilience as her middle sister, the South would never have lost the war. Papa said her Irish heritage gave her fortitude. She hoped that the two of them were right, but it would take the strength of a heritage dating back to St. Patrick himself to control the pain that burned like a furnace in her heart.

But there she went, getting close to teary-eyed again. Memories of Annie and what might have been must not always stir her grief to the surface.

Somehow, some day, she must remember her baby with an outpouring of comforting love.

In the meantime, she thought as the Micks said a quick goodbye, she would concentrate on handling a problem very close at hand. Matt Jackson. They stared at one another as the Irishmen hurried out.

"If you'll look the other way, ma'am," one of the bedridden soldiers said, "I'll be headin' out for the privy. I'm in my longjohns, understand, and I wouldn't want to give offense."

"I'll go with you," the other announced.

Flame turned her head and waited while they pulled on their Army trousers that had been hooked to the wall beside them, then the Army boots beside their beds. They departed noisily, leaving her alone in the ward with her husband, and she retreated to her refuge behind the screen. She had barely tossed the robe aside and scurried beneath the covers, before Matt was beside the bed.

"Good morning." He tossed his hat on the covers at her feet, and with great thoroughness she studied the wide brim and the jaunty red feather stuck in the band.

"Good morning." She did not try to meet his eye.

"Glad to see you up and about."

"Are you?"

She couldn't keep from glancing at him once, briefly, but the glance turned into a full-scale stare. His velvet brown eyes always had a magnetic effect on her, no matter the expression in them. Right now he was looking at her as though she had lost her mind.

"You don't look in the least bit glad," she said.

"What I don't like is the show you were putting on."

She sat up, and the cover fell to her waist. Despite his best intentions, Matt lowered his gaze to the sight of her breasts beneath the soft gown. She'd been sexy when he knew she was carrying a child, and even in her time of trouble, she was sexy still.

Damn, he was a bastard.

But he kept on looking.

She pulled the cover all the way to her chin.

"I wasn't putting on any show."

"Ask the men when they get back. Whatever is wrong with them, it's not affecting their eyesight, or their—" He caught himself, swallowing just in time the vulgar term that came to mind. "Let's just say that they'd probably rather Doc not give them a close examination for a few minutes. Not if he looks between their legs."

"How nice of you to clean up the observation."

"Ever the gentleman, ma'am."

She rolled her eyes at his exaggerated politeness. "What do you want?"

"Damned if I know." He spoke the truth. It shouldn't have meant a cursed thing that she was parading around the hospital as entertainment for the troops. But he'd grown furious when he saw the way they were looking at her.

In view of all that had happened to her, he was trying to think of his wife as an innocent victim of circumstance. The trouble was, she kept putting herself in circumstances where she didn't look innocent at all.

Flame smoothed the sheet over her legs. "I suppose you're seeing to your husbandly duties."

Matt thought that one over before replying. The last time he gave attention to his husbandly duties, his wife had gone running from the house.

Where she had fallen. A tight, sick feeling settled in his gut as he remembered the sight of her lying in the mud, her gown stained with blood. No matter what Doc said, he held himself to blame for the fall.

But she had already rejected his apology. He wouldn't give it again.

"I came by to let you know that when you leave here, you'll have the house to yourself."

The news did not fill Flame with joy, as she might have expected.

"And where will you be?"

"I'll find a place to sleep."

"I'm sure that you will."

"What's that supposed to mean?"

"Nothing." Flame waved a hand airily. "I have confidence that you won't be out in the elements, that's all."

Matt shook his head. He had a comeback, but it would only lead to an answering comeback from her, and they'd be at it again.

What was happening to him? Normally he kept his peace with most everyone outside an Indian camp.

Not anymore.

And he wasn't proving much of a hospital visitor, not if the purpose was to help the patient pass the time in pleasant talk.

What he'd like to do was hold her, not kiss her

or stroke her or get intimate—at least he told himself that was the way he felt—just hold her and listen as she talked out the heartache she must be carrying. The only times she'd allowed him to approach anything close to a gentle embrace was when she'd been unconscious, or when she'd been crying her eyes out.

One time had been about as torturous for him as the other; he didn't want to go through that hell again. Matt faced the truth. He wasn't cut out for this role as sympathetic spouse. A loner, a creature for the outdoors, a traveling man, that's what he was. And about as comfortable beside a convalescent's bed as a stray wild goose at the colonel's Christmas ball.

Grabbing his hat, he settled it low on his forehead. "I'll ask Doc to send word when you leave. If you want me around, let him know."

He left so quickly Flame had no chance to respond. Perhaps it was a good thing, because she didn't know what she would have said.

Oil and water, sun and rain, fire and ice. And, of course, Matt and Flame. The two of them simply did not mix.

Any pleasure she experienced in his presence came solely because he looked at her in such unsettling ways and said such outrageous things that she couldn't think about anything else.

The sound of a rustling skirt jerked her from the reverie. "Sugar," she heard from the far side of the screen, "I thought I might find you here."

Melody Burr. Flame sat straight up in the bed.

"What are you doing here?" Matt asked.

205

A low, throaty laugh.

"Not nearly as much as I'd like."

Silence.

"Cut it out, Melody."

Cut out *what?* Flame's temper as well as her curiosity prickled.

"Doesn't sugar like to be touched? I was thinking you would be in the mood for some harmonizing, seeing as how your wife's laid up and all. You married a sick one, Matt. Too bad."

"Shut up, Melody."

A silver giggle raised Flame's ire another ten degrees.

"Shut me up. You know how. After all, we're alone."

"Not quite."

"Is the little woman behind that screen over there? Oh my, I guess I've been indiscreet." Her voice rose. "Mrs. Jackson, if you're listening, I was only teasing. Matt and I always tease this way. It helps to pass the time out here in all this wasteland."

Flame listened to every word, imagined the sly smile on the young woman's face as she spoke, wondered what kind of smile was on her husband's face. All her reasoning and planning and worries about what to do in the immediate future disappeared as if in a puff of smoke.

She threw back the covers and without bothering to slip on her robe, stepped around the screen.

"Good morning, Miss Burr." She flipped back her hair. "I know exactly what you mean. Matt is such a jokester. I never know when he's serious or when he's just playing me along for his own enjoyment. I'm sure you have the same trouble."

Melody's lips tightened briefly, then settled into her more typical pout. "Why, Flame, honey, don't all men toy with a woman's affection? The thing is, we just have to toy right back."

A sharpness in the young woman's voice almost stopped Flame, but when she looked at her closely, all she could see was wide-eyed innocence. Or as close to innocence as Melody could get.

Smiling sweetly, Flame shifted her attention to Matt, who stood very close to the blond curls and voluptuous figure of the colonel's daughter, staring at his wife in bemusement from beneath the low brim of his hat.

"Oh, Miss Burr, I'm sure you've learned the art of toying. I'm sure you've learned to give my husband just what he wants."

"Flame—"

"Don't let me interrupt anything, Matthew." She put the full force of Miss-Lillian's-Academy-for-Young-Ladies dignity in her voice. "I'll slip on out and leave you two alone."

She attempted to walk past them. Matt caught her by the arm.

"Just where do you think you're going?"

She fluttered her eyelashes, glanced at his hand as though he were bruising her—which he could be doing, given the hold he had—and looked innocently into his eyes.

"To find Doc. I've decided I've recuperated from my female trouble as well as can be expected. You were right a minute ago, when we were talking. It's time, my precious *sugar,* I was back in your bed."

By nightfall, with Matt in some unknown quarters she didn't want to think about and with the dark closing in on her, Flame regretted the impetuous declaration that her temper had caused. She hadn't been ready to return to this room and the closeness of these four walls. But Melody had made her angry. Would she never learn?

It didn't help that she'd found waiting for her a letter from Mama. Flame had been so certain that no one at home had known of her condition. As in so many other things, she'd been wrong.

Her mother had known of her morning sickness, had suspected the cause, had waited for her middle daughter to confide the worries that must have been wracking her soul.

You chose to take care of your problems alone, Mama had written. *How like you. I pray your hasty marriage is bringing you the happiness you deserve. Most of all, I pray that your confinement is going well. I have spoken of these things to no one, dearest Flame. Your secret is yours alone to reveal.*

Papa sends his love, although you must know that he is understandably hurt. You are the most like him, and he fears your rashness will bring you to harm. I have assured him we must place our trust in your good judgment. Angel and Raven send their love. We miss you. You have only to say the word, and I will travel to wherever is necessary to be with you at the birth.

How like Mama to think of her daughter before

she thought of herself. Flame had shed tears until she thought she must surely never cry again. And then she had done the most difficult thing of her life. She'd written Mama the truth . . . about Robert's unhappiness over her arrival, his deathbed concern for his child, the promises he had extracted, the nature of her marriage to Matt.

And she'd written, too, about the loss of Annie. That had been the hardest part. She'd left out any mention of her feelings during the events of the recent past. Let Mama read between the lines.

Tell everyone what you think is best they know, she had concluded. *I want to hurt no one more than I have already done. My family means everything to me. I plan to return to Savannah as soon as the doctor says I can, which shouldn't be long considering the rapid improvement in my health.*

Once her answering letter was sealed and set aside, she found the confessions it included had helped to soothe her troubled spirits. Still, she didn't get a wink of sleep, and early the next morning, fighting lethargy, she decided to clean the bedroom where she would be spending the next few days . . . or weeks, at the most. Perhaps, she told herself, she could overcome the chill of the room with a little physical exertion.

And, too, she might forget for a moment the hollow, lost feeling in her heart, the furnace of sorrow that burned in her soul.

Dressed in the lavender skirt and blouse, with a pillow slip pinned over her clothes as an apron, she twisted her hair loosely off her neck and surveyed the awaiting challenge. As a start, she decided to delve into the dust under the bed. It wasn't an especially pleasant task, not with the boxes Matt had crammed underneath, but she would have rethatched the roof to keep from going through her own trunk, where the knitted baby clothes were stored.

She hadn't meant to open any of the boxes, just dust around them and put them back. But they weren't very well constructed, and when the first one virtually fell apart as she scraped it against the bedsprings, she found herself doing what Mama and Raven would have been appalled to witness.

She found herself going through her husband's private things.

Clothes, mostly. A black wool suit, several waistcoats (one made of red velvet with narrow black lapels), a wide cravat still sporting an ornamental tiepin, and a half-dozen shirts, most of them white linen with high collars and wide, full sleeves. One even featured ruffles down the front.

Not one item was made of buckskin, and there wasn't a red bandanna in the lot.

Flame sat back on her heels and surveyed the array scattered on the floor around her. Matt Jackson was a gentleman . . . or at least he dressed like one. Maybe the clothing was some sort of disguise. As creative as she could be at times, there was no situation in which she could imagine such to be the case.

Perhaps the garments belonged to someone else. She picked up one of the shirts and held it close. The linen fibres were redolent of Matt.

She closed her eyes for a moment. She'd never realized how personal a thing scent could be, marking a man as surely as the spread of his shoulders or the color of his eyes. But this shirt, though obviously cleaned before it had been packed away, still held the outdoor, manly aura of her husband.

The realization stirred something deep inside her, and she cradled the garment close to her bosom, her eyes closed, her mind picturing the way he would look wearing it. Her fingers tingled as she sensed how the linen would feel resting against his muscled chest, the white a glorious contrast to the rich tan of his skin. The chill of the room receded as a special kind of warmth settled all the way to her bones.

"What the hell are you doing?"

She started and her eyes darted toward the door. "Matt!"

Swallowing hard, she attempted to stand, but she could not find the strength. The way he just stood there staring at her, and at the shirt she held close, told her more clearly than words could ever have conveyed, that she had done something terribly wrong.

Fourteen

Matt stared down at the clothes and the open boxes and the woman who sat in the middle of it all, a stricken look on her face as though she were a naughty child.

Except that Flame wasn't a child. He looked at the thick lashes, the full, parted lips, the slope of her throat curving downward to the greater curve of her breasts. No, he thought, his blood thickening, she definitely was not a child.

He'd been angry at the sight of her rummaging through his belongings, instinctively rebelling against her intrusion into matters he considered private. Until she'd looked up at him . . . until she'd tried to stand. Gone was her toughness. The fragility had returned, and with it, Matt's view of himself as an insensitive clod.

She was just out of a hospital bed, for God's sake . . . and she had the widest, greenest, most soulful eyes he'd ever seen. Eyes that asked for tender care. And what did a few clothes matter, anyway?

You're a traveling man, Matt Jackson, a loner, a man not meant for domestication.

It was a truth he'd need to keep repeating, especially if he stayed around Flame much longer. She had a look about her that made a man forget what or who he was.

His long stride brought him close to the bed, and he stared down at the remnants of his past. "What a mess," he said, extending a hand to help her up.

Flame waved it away. Still clutching the shirt, feeling foolish and tongue-tied, she managed to stand on her own.

"I decided to clean house—" she began, smoothing her hair from her face, but she broke off. He'd think she was behaving like a real wife. She buried her left hand in the folds of white linen. Under the circumstances, there seemed little need to flaunt the ring she'd purchased for herself.

Matt caught the movement. "You decided to snoop," he said, reacting to her rejection more than he'd intended.

"I decided to clean house," she repeated, more firmly. "You had enough lint and dust under the bed to start a fire."

Matt's eyes glinted. "That's one way to get heat in here."

Flame sighed in exasperation. "Do you ever think of anything besides sex?"

"That's hard to say." He thought a moment. "Back in '72—"

She held up the badly wrinkled shirt. "What were you wearing at the time, leather or this?"

He took the garment from her. "This. Definitely

213

this." Dropping the shirt on the bed, he surveyed the floor. "Anything else you'd like to ask about?"

"The red velvet waistcoat. I can't picture you wearing it."

"A Christmas present from a lady in San Francisco."

She looked at him in surprise. *What lady*, she wanted to ask. *What did she mean to you?*

Instead, she managed an inane, "You've been in San Francisco?"

"And New York. Never as far south as Savannah, though."

"But I thought—"

"That I was a half-savage Texan who'd stayed in the wild?"

Flame shook her head. "There's nothing halfway about you, Matt."

"Then it's all the way to savage, is it? Sorry to disappoint you. I've spent most of my life in civilization."

Wandering, gambling, trying his hand at different endeavors, looking for a place that might be home. Until he'd given up the search. Until he'd admitted he would never find whatever future he wanted, without settling the troubles of the past. The problem was that since his return to Texas, he hadn't taken care of anything very well.

Flame watched the darkness come and go in his eyes, and wished she could read the thoughts that caused the shiftings of his mood. He'd seemed so easy to understand when she first saw him riding along a Texas trail. Arrogant, uncivilized, more than a little dangerous to anyone who got in his way. Man or woman.

She hadn't changed her original assessment. Except that now she realized he was a great deal more.

"I really wasn't snooping," she said. "The first box came apart, and then there were the others." She paused. "What I should say is that I didn't *start out* snooping. But that's how I ended up."

She shrugged prettily. A man would have to be a genuine rogue to get angry at such a confession. For the moment Matt couldn't summon even a mild irritation.

"Why the buckskin?" she asked.

"What are you talking about?"

"You went from ruffled shirts to fringed leather. Why?"

Matt didn't know if he could explain it, except that it was the kind of clothing he'd worn in the years of his captivity, and it had seemed appropriate in his quest for his Apache enemy. Not only would the explanation be difficult, he couldn't see a reason to attempt it.

A loner. A traveling man.

"I'll get this," he said as he knelt and began cramming everything back into the boxes. He didn't try for neatness, didn't try for order.

Flame watched him for a minute, wondering why he hadn't answered a simple question.

Perhaps because he wasn't a simple man.

She dropped to the floor beside him. "Let me. I'm the one who dragged everything out."

She reached for the waistcoat he was holding. Her

hand brushed his. An accident. She hadn't meant to touch him. Burned as if by fire, she jerked away.

Matt watched her from the corner of his eye, far too aware that she didn't care to touch him. "I said I'll take care of this," he said. "You must have other things to disturb."

The rebuff came at her as sharp as a slap. Everything she did was wrong. Everything. Standing, she turned her back to him, and for just a moment she gave in to the despair that was never far away.

He glanced up at her slender frame, at the easy flow of the lavender gown against her shoulders and narrow waist and the gentle flair of her hips. Her hair was inadequately pinned into a knot at her nape, and crimson tendrils curled carelessly against her neck.

He'd been without a woman too damned long. Otherwise, why was he tempted to pull her down beside him and kiss her until she begged for more?

Which he couldn't give her. Doc had told him this morning that she was still bleeding from the miscarriage, that she might be sore for another couple of weeks. He didn't like details like that. A woman's body should remain a mystery, except for the mating part.

A woman's heart and a woman's mind were equally foreign to him. Or maybe it was just his wife's heart and mind. He'd always figured out most women, especially the ones like Melody Burr and Myrtle at the Kitty Cat.

He shoved the last of the boxes back under the bed and stood. "You're not crying, are you?"

"No," she said in a small voice.

"Good," he said, willingly accepting what he knew was a lie.

Her back straightened. "Why did you come by this morning? I thought you were going to stay away for a while."

"To bring you this." He held out a pouch of coins.

She glanced over her shoulder at the offering. "I haven't spent what you left the last time."

"I don't want you doing without what you need."

Her eyes lifted to his. "What I need, money can't buy. Take your coins. I'll be all right."

The baby. He didn't have to be hit in the head to know that was what she needed. Certainly not a buttoned-trousers husband getting in the way. It wasn't for him that her eyes were rimmed in red. He'd tried, he told himself, letting anger overcome frustration. He'd done the best he could.

This time when he left, he didn't come running back the next day. He didn't even think about returning for over a week, riding out on patrol during the day, sleeping in the barracks at night, checking in with Doc to find out if there were any emergencies at home he needed to take care of.

Doc assured him everything was all right, and he chose to believe him.

Once he rode into Little Sandy looking for Nigel Wolfe, but the British gambler was nowhere to be found. Matt got the idea he was being avoided, and his suspicions that Wolfe was involved in a gun trade with the Apaches drew strength.

Throughout all this forced activity, he grew restless, grouchy as a bear, angry, he told himself, because Black Eagle didn't return from across the river and give him another chance at settling their private war.

As for the men, they gave him a few curious looks, as if to ask what he was doing in the barracks with a wife like Flame warming his bed. No one approached to put the question into words. In the mood he was in, he would have chewed the tail off anyone who tried.

The colonel sent him on a week's expedition, which lengthened into two. Still no sign of the Apache, but he turned up some interesting information concerning one of the wagon drivers who brought Fort Hard supplies up from the port at Indianola. Supplies meant, too, for the sutler.

It was nothing conclusive, but his curiosity became aroused. And it gave him something to think about other than a green-eyed redhead who was becoming more and more a part of his life.

The next time he saw Flame was a mild morning in early November, when he went to the sutler's store to talk to Asa Underwood right after his return to Fort Hard. He didn't trust the sutler, didn't like the calculating look in his small brown eyes. Underwood was gaining as a candidate for gunrunner, but he hadn't yet supplanted Wolfe, Captain Arnold Davis, Colonel Burr, and just about anyone else he could think of besides Flame.

He could blame a lot of things on her, but not selling Winchesters to the Apaches who attacked her stage.

When she entered the store, he was standing in the shadows at one of the far tables, waiting while the sutler finished unloading supplies in the back.

Her laughter drew his attention first. He had never heard her laugh like that, silvery, the way the moon might laugh, if it could. But right away he knew it was her, and a surge of pleasure shot through him.

The spontaneous reaction took him by surprise. He wasn't a man to find such pleasure on a regular basis, except sometimes in the solitary beauty of a Texas sunrise, or the sight of a doe and her fawn drinking in innocent unawareness at a woodland creek. Flame's laughter brought the same kind of warmth.

As if she had called out to him, he took a step toward her. And then he noticed the man by her side. Tall, thin, looking more like a store clerk than a captain at a frontier fort.

What the hell was Arnold Davis doing with his wife? And what the hell had he said to make her laugh that way?

She was wearing the yellow dress and the black crocheted shawl that she'd worn that day he found her in a Little Sandy alley, fending off Buck Grady's unwanted regard. She'd done what she could to pin up the mass of red hair, made herself look ladylike. Made herself look good.

Davis certainly thought so. The bastard. He was looking at her the way only a husband ought to. Not that Matt should give a damn. Still, he had to fight a razor-sharp rage that rose from the ashes of his initial warmth.

"Captain Davis," she was saying as they came to a halt inside the front door, "thanks for the escort."

"If you have many packages, I'll be glad to carry them home for you. All I'll be buying is a package of cigars Underwood was supposed to order for me. Being a bachelor, I don't do much shopping, you understand."

Matt watched the smile on her face die. More than once he'd brought the same sad-pensive expression to her eyes that he could see across the length of the store. Or maybe he just imagined it. In some ways he didn't know her at all; in others, he knew her far too well.

"Papa runs a store back in Savannah. Sometimes I work there. Or at least, I used to."

"Really?" Davis's eyes narrowed in disapproval.

Flame didn't seem to notice. "Lots of bachelors used to come in to buy things."

"And you thought it was because they needed to shop? Come, come, Mrs. Jackson—"

Matt could have sworn she flinched at the name.

"—surely you realized there was a special attraction besides whatever was offered for purchase."

Flame looked down and did not answer.

Had Matt known anything about her family? He couldn't remember, except that part about the store, which he'd learned from Robert Anderson. Oh yes, there were sisters, too. The lieutenant had made mention of them.

Flame had certainly never volunteered any information, and here she was giving her life history to a man who was practically a stranger.

Or was he? Maybe during his absence, Flame had set her sights on Davis as the proper officer to replace Anderson. Matt decided to find out.

He stepped out of the shadows, moved closer, saw

that on this cool, damp morning they were the only customers in the store.

He saw, too, that his wife had not completely lost the shadows under her eyes.

"Matt!" Flame exclaimed as she caught sight of him, looming out of the dark. Her heart beat in double time, and a smile flashed across her face. Something in his expression gave short life to her joy, but nothing stilled the stirring of her blood.

He looked a little leaner and a little browner, maybe a little more grizzled than usual with his hair longer than she remembered it, and his cheeks darkened by the beginnings of a beard. He remained altogether the manliest man she had ever seen. Her first instinct was to rush toward him and let him know she was glad he'd returned without harm.

But she'd learned to question her instincts around her husband. With him she was losing her impetuous nature. Maybe, she told herself with the weight of resignation, she was finally growing up.

At twenty-three, she was long overdue for the change.

"Flame," he said with a nod. "Davis."

"When did you get back?" she asked, unable to look away from him.

"This morning."

"Oh," she said, aware that Davis was looking back and forth between them, trying no doubt to figure out just how matters were between the Jacksons. So after weeks of being away, Matt had not cared to check on his wife or even drop by and tell her he was back, or ask if she were doing all right or . . .

She could almost read the captain's thoughts. She could have added a million other things Matt had neglected to do, including showing the least sign he was glad to see her.

Something devilish . . . or lonesome . . . or maybe even a little childish awakened a spirit of defiance in her soul.

"Well," she said with a broad smile, "I'll just have to revise my shopping list. Anything in particular you want for supper? Oh, that's all right. I'll be sure to have something on the table that you like. And don't worry about staying around, either of you two gentlemen. I'll take care of everything just fine."

So saying, she whirled from the men—glad for an excuse to get away from the far-too-solicitous captain as well as the far-too-unnerving scout—and set about studying the rows of canned goods on the far side of the room. She'd fix the best meal the Jackson adobe house had ever seen, and if Matt hadn't the sense to come home and join her at the table, she knew someone else who would.

She wasn't the same pitiful creature her husband had visited in the hospital, not even the restless woman he'd caught rummaging through his clothes. Healed in body, her spirits slowly healing despite the sad memories, she had made several changes in her day-to-day routine.

More important, she'd made a new friend.

Matt watched as she scurried about the store, pulling cans from shelves, reaching into barrels, conferring with Underwood at the back of the store. He liked the sight of her, no matter what she was doing. He couldn't look away.

Neither could the man beside him. "Don't you have something else to do?" he said to Davis.

The two men stared at one another a moment. At length, with a shrug, the captain started toward the door, hesitated, then turned back to Matt.

"You have a charming wife, Jackson. A real delight out in this hellacious place." His thin lips twitched into a smirk. "She's certainly made the time go by fast, for which I and several of the men should offer thanks. Until this past week I had never thought to be grateful to you for anything."

Matt stared at the door closing behind him. What the hell was Davis getting at? He glanced back at his wife, who remained in conference with the sutler. A picture of innocence. But he remembered the way she responded to kisses she claimed not to like.

Several of the men. Damn. Without a husband around to get in the way, she was apparently recuperating just fine.

He decided to show up for the meal she promised. Hungry in more than one way, he had a strong urge to find out just what sweetmeats his wife would offer tonight.

He had a strong urge to find out how her offerings would taste.

Men liked meat three times a day. Mama always said it, and Papa cleaned every plate that was set before him.

Flame was determined that her husband, too, would lap up everything she prepared for him. If he bothered to show up. Why she had issued the invitation was a puzzle. She certainly wasn't eager to have him back under the same roof.

As she worked at the stove, she admitted the truth. Even with the changes she'd made in her life over the past couple of weeks, she hadn't made the nights a great deal easier to get through. And there were far too many moments in the day, when the stillness and the solitude became as oppressive as the storm that had struck the day she lost Annie.

The problem lay in her inability to stay busy every moment of the time. Like now, when she allowed her thoughts to wander away from the tasks at hand.

As usual, they wandered not to her loving family back in Georgia, but to the very unloving man who filled the role of her family out here in the middle of nowhere.

What had Melody called it that day in the hospital? A wasteland. But it wouldn't be a wasteland—no place ever need be—if the person you cared for most in all the world was near.

Well, that wasn't the situation at Fort Hard, and she'd best not waste sentimental minutes brooding over it.

True, deep, eternal love wasn't necessarily lost to her forever—she couldn't allow herself to believe such a terrible thing—but it wasn't in her immediate future, either.

She threw herself into the preparations for supper, and when she was confident she could satisfy at least one of Matt's appetites, she retired to the bedroom to do what she could with her person. Earlier she'd washed her hair in cistern water. Now, only shortly before the hour she was expecting her husband, she set about scrubbing everything else.

Studying her meager wardrobe, she settled on the two-piece lavender gown, not because Angel had once said it brought out the color in her cheeks and eyes, but because she'd washed it only yesterday at the creek, working alongside the fort's laundresses, by far the nicest people she'd met outside of the Micks.

Her undergarments were the best lace-trimmed camisole and petticoat she owned. Even her under-drawers featured lace around the bottom of each leg, an addition she'd made last week as she sat one evening before a lonely fire.

She tried a dozen different ways to fix her hair, then settled on wearing it free and loose. Confined to the small mirror on the wall above the bureau, she couldn't get an overall idea of how she looked, but she wasn't fixing herself up special, anyway.

Just because it would be the first meal she'd prepared for her husband since the chicken she'd thrown out almost two months ago, didn't mean there was anything exceptional about tonight. If he bothered to show up. She hadn't given him a chance to decline.

She was giving dinner a final inspection, when she heard a footstep on the front porch. Her eyes darted over the room. It had never looked better. The floor and hearth scrubbed clean, new curtains at the window, sprigs of sweet-smelling grass in a vase on the table, the glassware sparkling, a special bottle of brandy at one end beside the freshly baked apple pie.

She had been extravagant in this single meal, but she had a modest income now. And she didn't cook for Matt just any day.

She was facing the door when he entered. He'd shaved since this morning, didn't look half so grizzled in his clean buckskins, but his dark, manly presence filled the room and robbed it of air.

She'd been wrong to think anyone else could take his place tonight. No one could take Matt Jackson's place. For the first time she doubted that anyone ever could.

"I'm glad to see you," she said, unable to lie.

Matt stared at the woman the world called his wife. She was everything that he called beautiful—sunrise and dove songs and wild bluebonnets in the spring. Everything clean and pure. His blood heated and pulsed erratically through his veins. What was happening to him? He didn't even know why he was here.

Except that he'd grown tired of hardtack and Army grub, and it was time to find out if his wife knew how to cook.

He laughed to himself. She could serve up dirt tonight and he'd eat it, if she continued to look at him like that.

Had she been serving others while he was gone? Arnold Davis wanted him to think so, but Matt would be a poor example of a man if he allowed the captain to tell him how to think.

Right now all he wanted to concentrate on was the scent of roses she carried on her skin. What did roses taste like? He planned to find out.

"Are you hungry?" she asked.

"Yeah."

He seemed to put a great deal into the brief answer, and she felt fluttery inside.

Turning from him, she dished up the peppered beef she'd fixed, one of Papa's favorites, and the rice and tomatoes, wishing there had been more fresh vegetables from which to choose at the sutler's.

Maybe Matt wouldn't notice the omission.

Indeed, he hardly seemed to look at his plate, as she set it across the table in front of him.

"Something wrong?" she asked.

He went from staring at her hand to the way the lavender sleeve fit her long, slender arm, to the rise of breasts, to her lips, to her eyes. "No."

She swallowed. "You haven't looked at your food."

"I know."

The jitters took control. She turned toward the stove. "I thought you said you were hungry."

"You didn't ask for what."

Shaky hands spooned up a second plate she'd bought just for the occasion. She forced herself to take her place opposite him.

"Eat," she said. "I've been working on this all day."

Matt liked the bossiness in her voice, and he turned his attention to the food. It looked as good as it smelled. He almost forgot the scent of roses.

He sampled everything, grinned at her, and just as she hoped, he cleaned his plate, even accepting a slice of pie, and then a cup of coffee and glass of brandy. The sight of him brought a cuddly feeling inside Flame. Maybe her husband wasn't a total savage after all.

Turning down the lamp—to conserve fuel, she told herself—she joined him in the coffee and brandy. They sat looking at one another across the table, the light from the fireplace flickering over them both.

"I talked to Doc this afternoon," he said, watching the display of changing color that was her glorious hair.

"Oh? What about?" she asked, marvelling at the way Matt's eyes melted her composure until she could hardly put two coherent words together.

"You."

Flame sipped at the brandy and decided it was like drinking fire. "Me?" she asked when she could speak.

"Yeah."

"But he's been telling me there's nothing wrong."

Which wasn't exactly what he'd been telling Matt. They'd both decided she had to be told the complete truth.

"Doc's a good man. He knows what he's doing."

"I think so, too." She swirled the liquor in her glass. "He said I could travel without any problems."

"You're thinking of moving on?"

His voice was hard, and her eyes darted to his.

"Isn't that what you want?" she asked.

"Winter's coming. Weather's been mild so far, but in these parts, that can change overnight."

She could almost believe he didn't want her to go.

"There's nothing to keep me here anymore."

Not unless someone asks me to stay.

Matt finished his brandy. The burning liquid did nothing to cool a flare of anger.

"Not even Arnold Davis?" Matt surprised himself with the question. He'd decided not to mention the captain, but around his wife, plans kept changing.

"What does he have to do with anything?" she asked.

"You two seemed mighty friendly this afternoon. Have you been seeing him while I was gone?"

He might as well have struck her. Flame slapped her glass onto the table, and the amber liquid splashed onto the red and white cloth.

"And what's that supposed to mean? Oh, don't tell me. You asked me once what I planned to do about sex. Now that I'm healed and available once again, I must be looking around for a partner. Matt Jackson, you will never change."

Fighting tears, she pushed away from the table and hurried into the bedroom. The door slammed behind her, but it opened right away.

"A neat maneuver, Flame. When asked a tough question, you just flare up in anger and stomp away."

Flame refused to turn around. "Oh, I'm filled with neat maneuvers, aren't I? You probably didn't figure out why I worked all day cooking. It was to get you full and then mellowed on brandy, and when you fell asleep in front of the fire, I could go through your pockets and rob you."

He stepped in front of her, leaving scant inches between them. "I should have thought of that. But I don't have pockets." He took her by the wrist and

229

pressed her hand against his side. Her fingers burned against the smooth nap of the leather.

"Feel anything?" he asked, his voice husky. He moved her hand lower, to his groin, and then suddenly her palm was against his sex, hard and full and extended.

She gave an involuntary jerk, but he cupped her hand hard against him.

"That's what I've got for you. But you've got to give me something in return."

Flame couldn't breathe, couldn't think. Every part of her turned to liquid heat. She closed her eyes and wet her lips.

He leaned near and tasted the dampness.

"Oh," she said.

"Yeah," he said. "Oh."

She tried to put her thoughts in order, tried to remind herself why this was so wrong.

But all she could think of was the fullness against her palm and the way his whisper-kiss made her want to kiss him in return.

"I'm going to make love to you," he said into her parted mouth. "And you're going to make love to me."

Her thick lashes lifted, and she gazed into his eyes. He lifted the hand he'd been holding against him and he kissed the fingers, one at a time.

In that instant of unexpected tenderness, Flame knew she was lost.

Fifteen

Matt folded back the cuff of her sleeve and kissed her wrist. A rapid, irregular pulse pounded against his lips.

He glanced into her eyes. The heat in their green depths sent a bolt of desire shooting through him, and he pulled her into his arms. She slipped easily into their sanctuary, weightless as a cloud, yet when his lips met hers, he felt the heat of her flesh burning into the full length of his body.

He kept the kiss light, unwilling to give free rein to the passions that trembled within him. She frightened easily, this woman who was and was not his wife. Before Flame, there had never been anything refined in his lovemaking, but he saw the need in being different with her.

He *wanted* to be different, because she was different from any woman he'd ever known, full of passions and inconsistencies, intriguing and enraging and seductive all at the same time.

Flame moved her lips under Matt's, and forgot all the reasons that this was wrong. Nothing could be wrong with fighting the loneliness. Nothing could be wrong with forgetting despair.

Nothing at all could be wrong, when everything felt so right.

She felt a thrill of discovery. This is what husbands and wives were supposed to do . . . break bread together, and then retire into each other's arms. An eternity ago in Savannah, when Flame was considering the desirability of her own marriage, she had thought of the ethereal aspects of love—the eternal union, the melding of separate spirits—but Matt's hands and Matt's mouth and the hardness of his body pressed against hers gave heady testimony to the carnal aspects as well.

For one night they would know what it was to be husband and wife.

Her fingers twisted in the fringe of his shirt. She'd seen him bare-chested only once, but she could recall with inspiring clarity the swirl of chest hairs, the flat nipples, the tightness of his stomach just above his belt.

Oh, she truly was wanton, and what a pleasure it was to be in such a state.

His lips dragged reluctantly from hers, moved to her throat, then to the soft, vulnerable spot behind her ear.

"Matt." Her voice was low, husky, barely discernible over the beating of his own heart.

He gripped her shoulders, to steady himself as much as to steady her.

"Matt, please." Her voice became more urgent.

"I aim to please," he whispered against her neck. "Didn't you know?"

His warm breath tickled. She shivered in delicious anticipation of how that same warmth would feel elsewhere on her body. In her lone other experience, she had not been kissed below the rise of her breasts.

In truth, she'd barely been touched. Robert's groping hands at her skirt and underclothes . . . a quick thrust, and then another and another . . . for her, after the quick, sharp pain, a teasing, a hint of the pleasures mating could bring. That had been the total of her memories from the evening by the creek.

That and all those sweetly whispered promises that she had accepted into her heart.

She knew that with Matt, everything would be different. Everything would be wild.

But there would be no promises from him. And there would be no involvement of the heart.

She was beyond caring.

"The light," she said, nodding to the lamp beside the bed. "Aren't we wasting fuel?"

He eased just far enough away to look down at her. "Not to my way of thinking. Looking sometimes is almost as good as touching."

She put his declaration to the test, studying the thick black hair and brows above his deep-as-forever brown eyes, counted the wrinkles in the corners, considered how a prominent nose and strong jaw could keep a man from being pretty, but might make him beautiful at the same time.

Savagely beautiful, a prime example of nature in the wild.

"I'm not going to change my mind this time," she

said softly, her fingers stroking through the thick hair resting against his nape.

"If you won't, I won't."

Was he grinning at her? Oh, yes, in a funny, hot kind of way, and she found herself grinning back at him, like some silly fool.

But as they continued to stare at one another, the grins died. Flame melted inside.

Matt gave up on refinement. There was nothing delicate about the kiss he gave her, nothing subtle in the way his tongue pressed between her lips to taste the honeyed warmth inside her mouth. He wanted to possess all of her, inside and out, to ease the frustrations of the past weeks, to do everything that had flashed through his mind the first moment he saw her standing with windblown hair beside a dusty corral.

She moaned, but it was not a sound of submission or regret. He sensed her urgency, and the last vestiges of control dropped away. Desire became a wild animal within him, clawing for satisfaction, silent screams of hunger exploding in his mind and in his loins.

He fumbled with the button at her throat. God, he was no good at this undressing of a woman, when he was mad with wanting her naked in his arms.

Flame covered his hands with hers, guiding him in the delicate maneuvers, at last taking control and unfastening the front of her blouse until it parted, and he could trail his hot lips against the rise of her breasts, his tongue licking the satiny skin, the lace edge of her camisole, the hard nipples erect beneath the soft cloth.

Under his assault, she felt the growing heaviness of her modest bosom, she felt voluptuous, she felt eager for him to rip her clothing aside and rake that wonderful tongue over all of the fullness that existed because of him.

Slipping the blouse from her shoulders, she let it fall to the floor. Next came the straps of her camisole. She eased the garment past the pebble tips of the breasts, until she was exposed to his eyes and his hands and his mouth. Her head dropped back, and she closed her eyes, as if to say, *Here I am. Do what you will.*

Matt took a moment to feast on the sight of her, the thick lashes resting against pale cheeks, the full lips, the graceful throat, and at last the blue-veined breasts with the hard pink tips that he'd been picturing the past two months.

He'd pictured wrong. She was better than his most inspired imaginings.

He eased his tongue across the offered sweetness, and Flame experienced delicious curls of warmth opening inside. His hands traced the length of her spine, clasped her waist, then glided lower until he cupped her buttocks, all the while his lips and tongue worked with enthralling diligence at her breasts.

Her body pulsed at a spiraling pace, and she arched convulsively against him, closing the rare spaces that separated them, willing his hands to keep at their intimate explorations. As if she had spoken the order aloud, he eased his hold until he touched the backs of her thighs, until his fingers probed into the layers of skirt and petticoat, until he felt the division of her legs. She parted for him. His hand relaxed between her thighs, lifting until he was holding against his palm the most intimate place of all.

She cursed the clothing that separated his hand from her throbbing heat, even while she gloried in the waves of pleasure he aroused.

Bending her head, she kissed his hair and wished she could kiss the tautly contoured expanse of back and shoulders taunting her hands. She grew feverish from the frustration.

"Matt," she whispered into the stillness of the room, "I want you naked."

Matt heard her plea and gave her what she wanted, pulling away to finish the undressing of her, this time his hands more sure and knowledgeable, then undressing himself, the lavender gown and flesh-toned buckskin intertwined on the floor the way husband and wife would soon be in the bed.

Flame had not known what it would be like to stand in such a way before her husband. She was not so bold as to stand for long. Turning from him, she crawled beneath the covers, but not before he caught a seductive glance of curved hip and thigh and a more thorough study of the long legs, just as she covered them with the quilt.

And, too, he saw the thatch of wiry red hair between her legs. A natural redhead. A natural lover, too, he figured as he followed her into the soft, warm haven.

The springs squeaked ominously beneath them.

"Is the bed too small?" she asked.

He showed her how the two of them would fit,

Flame on her back, Matt on his side, his body melded to hers as though they were truly one, his erection firm against her thigh, his hands stroking the sweep of her body, his tongue outlining her lips. Matt showed an incredible attention to detail, and Flame writhed beneath it all, at first embarrassed by the noise of the springs, and then, without realizing just when, becoming totally oblivious to everything except where he touched and where he kissed.

Matt couldn't stop touching or kissing her. She obsessed him. For once in his life he didn't mind losing control, especially since she was in the same condition, letting him know with soft moans and whisperings and kisses of her own that she wanted everything he gave, and more.

When she parted her legs, he settled himself in place and entered her slowly. She gasped once. He eased back, but then she clutched at his buttocks to hold him close. He slipped one hand between them, rubbing between her thighs to make sure her pleasure did not cease as he buried himself in her wet, tight cavity.

Flame had never experienced such sensations before, had never known they existed. She pulsed against his fingers. Her hips lifted from the bed in silent, rhythmic demands for something stronger, something imperative, something she did not rationally understand.

Her body knew what her mind did not. The pulses became one transcendent explosion. She trembled against him, held him tight, cried out his name again and again, until the single syllable matched the timing of the hard thrusts of his own body into hers. She felt a mighty tremor shudder through him, and knew he experienced what she was feeling. Tears burned her eyes, but they were tears of excitement because of what they shared.

They clung to one another, their breathing ragged. Flame simply could not let go. To do so would be to slip from the surface of the earth . . . or far worse, to fall into the aftermath of this night, to face the consequences of what she had done. She wasn't ready. And he gave no evidence he was inclined to end the embrace.

Their skin was hot and slick wherever they touched, and she could feel the residue of his seed between her legs.

His seed . . . the part of him that made babies.

The thought was like a chill wind blowing across her heart. She grew still, and her mind filled with thoughts she could not will away, no matter how she tried. She'd been so lonely, so eager for him, at the same time she'd been telling herself that she'd grown past all the impetuosity of youth. Her lecture had been a lie. He'd only to look at her across the dinner table, and she'd been impatient to tear off her clothes.

But lovemaking didn't end with a brief explosion in bed. Sometimes the result could last a lifetime.

And sometimes it lasted only three months.

What if she were pregnant again? What if she went through the same excitement, the same blossoming of love and hope for an unborn, only to go through the same troubles, the same loss, the same pain?

This time she knew that she, too, wouldn't survive. In that moment Flame hated herself.

She could not bring herself to hate Matt. This terror that seized her was not his fault. He'd told her what he planned to do. As she had done once before, she could have run from the room, and it wouldn't have mattered if she'd slipped and fallen. Whatever damage resulted would be only to her.

All these terrible thoughts skittered through her brain in a scant minute or two, and she was dimly aware of Matt's pulling away, his turning her to her side and pulling her back against him, his arm around her waist, his lips pressed to the warmth of her nape.

Everything that was happening seemed right, yet terribly, terribly wrong. Her fears were not irrational, no more than her yearning for the comfort of her husband's arms.

But Matt did more than comfort her. In showing her what lovemaking was all about, he'd created a hunger in her that she suspected would not go away. Making love to Robert—if that brief coupling could be called such a thing—had been like wading in a stream. With Matt, it was a plunge into a sun-warmed ocean, where she was buoyed and drowned at the same time, suspended in the deep by passions she had never known.

Oh, she was a wanton, all right. Weak. Foolish. And afraid.

Matt felt the change in her, the stiffness even while she lay in his arms, the deep sigh that seemed to shake her soul. He'd satisfied her, damn it. What more did she want?

And then he cursed himself. She'd satisfied him, too. And in the doing, she'd sacrificed the chance at the annulment she wanted. Divorce was her only option now.

At least it was the only option either one of them would consider, the severing of a marriage that neither one had sought, and neither one wanted to endure.

Strange circumstance, he thought, to be considering the way they would part only minutes after the first time they'd really been together. But then, life was full of strange twists and turns, in his experience most of them unwelcome.

Hell, he never should have taken her to bed. But he'd had little choice. He'd do it again, too. Probably would.

He felt his body begin to harden against her buttocks. No probably to it. He was ready for her now.

His fingers began to play at the tips of her breasts.

"No," she said. Flatly, and unmistakably sure of herself.

He eased his hand back to her waist and tried to imagine what was wrong. She'd been eager enough all night to take everything he had to give.

"I hurt you, didn't I?" he asked. "I'm sorry, my fiery little bride, but you drove me out of my mind."

"You didn't hurt me." Her voice was small and low.

He tried some more thinking.

"You're not trying to tell me you didn't like it, are you?"

Her laugh was short and filled with self-derision. "You wouldn't believe me if I did."

"You're right about that."

Silence.

He listened to the steady pace of her breathing, and tried to decide if whether holding her naked body like this was worth all the torture it was bringing. He decided it was.

"If it's the annulment you're worried about," he said, trying again, "hell, we can lie and say tonight didn't happen. The trouble is, I'm not certain there won't be other nights we do the same thing."

"One time is all it takes."

"You think so? Considering the way you cooperated, I'm surprised you feel that way."

"I meant one time is all it takes to make a baby. I always thought conception took three tries, but with Robert I found out different."

Goddamn. He should have guessed.

"I can't go through it again, Matt." Flat, to the point. She spoke the truth in every word. But not the entire truth. She could have added that she couldn't go through it again right away, and with another man who did not plan to remain by her side.

Matt rested his hand lightly at her waist, but he kept her back curled against his front, and he watched the play of lamplight on the incredible sunset color of her hair.

He'd rather face Black Eagle's Winchester rifle a dozen times than do what he had to do. The only consolation he got out of the situation was a certainty that she hadn't been sleeping with anyone else, not feeling the way she did about carrying another baby so soon.

"You're not pregnant," he said.

He sounded so sure that she could not suppress a short, humorless laugh. "Are you the expert in such matters?"

"Sort of."

"There's no way you can make such a statement—" She stopped herself. "Unless you can't—"

Her sigh was a mingling of embarrassment and regret. "Oh, Matt, I didn't mean to bring up something you weren't willing to talk about. I know there are some men who can't, well, be fathers. Raven said she was reading—"

"There's nothing wrong with me," said Matt, interrupting. "At least, not so far as I know." He hesitated, called himself a coward, and blundered on. "Something happened when you lost the baby, Flame. Something inside you."

He tried to turn her so he could see her face, but she held herself stiff and he continued to talk into the tangles of thick red curls.

"Doc thought it a good idea if we waited to tell you—"

"No!"

The denial came out a mournful cry as she bounded from her side of the bed, propelling herself from Matt's embrace so quickly he had no chance to hold onto her. The sudden act of standing left her dizzy. She hugged herself and stared at the plain rough wall in front of her, past caring that she was unclothed.

In an instant, Matt was beside her.

"Don't touch me," she said. "You're lying because you want to do it to me again."

Matt's anger flared. He told himself she spoke without thinking, wanting only to disprove what she'd just been told. Never himself planning on having a family, he could only guess at the agony his news brought. Women—some of them, at least—saw children as their purpose in life. Flame could be one of those.

He felt a stab of jealousy. She'd come looking for Robert to give her baby a father. Now she'd have no need for any special man.

Hell, why was he thinking this way? There was no good reason for her to have him turned inside out. It wasn't his business to do the telling tonight. He should have informed Doc that the job belonged to someone who dealt with such problems as part of his trade.

The only things Matt had ever pursued in a professional way were gambling and wrangling and killing Indians, nothing that had prepared him for tonight.

Except he'd learned not to be a quitter.

And whether he liked it or not, the woman standing naked beside him was his wife.

"I'm telling you the truth, Flame."

Leaning against the bedroom wall, she covered her ears with her hands. "Be quiet," she said, and the tears began to flow. "I'm not listening to you anymore. I'm going to have a dozen babies, and they're all going to look like Mama or Papa. I'm going to love them and nurture them and I—"

Her voice broke. She stood slumped, all energy spent, and when he took her in his arms, she didn't

243

resist, not even when he eased her back into bed and held her close.

Each thing he did—holding her gently, stroking her arm, telling her everything would be all right—was because he didn't know what else to do. Leaving would be easy. Staying was hard.

At least that's the way it was at first. But she rested against him, did some crying, then rested some more, and he decided providing comfort to his wife wasn't as troublesome as he'd thought it might be.

Truth to tell, he liked this sharing of pain . . . well, not liked it exactly, but admitted that somehow it felt right, almost natural. The realization took him by surprise.

Matt still was a loner. But maybe not all the time.

Sometime in the middle of the night, just when he decided she was finally falling asleep, she stirred in his arms, facing him, not moving away when he rested his leg across hers and stroked her hair.

"Make the thoughts disappear, Matt," she whispered against his throat. "Make love to me."

She kissed his chest and laved a nipple. It was all the urging Matt needed. He didn't bother to ask if she was sure.

If he'd been the wild one before, she was the wild one now, kissing him hard, thrusting her tongue into his mouth with the same urgency he'd shown when he was kissing her. Hungry hands, hungry lips, everything about her hot and hungry. She rubbed her breasts across his chest, brushing her nipples against his, straddling his thigh and stroking her damp sex against his hairy leg.

Her fingers explored his throbbing shaft and the

heavy sacs beneath. By the time he thrust her back onto the bed and plunged inside her, both of them were caught in the mindless savage splendor of ecstasy.

Matt had never climaxed so fast, his pleasure multiplied by the way she climaxed along with him, their separate cries blending and drowning out the creak of the bed. For him, some women came first, some came later, and a rare few didn't come at all.

His wife was different.

But then, she always was.

Flame welcomed each glorious shiver of satisfaction. Her only regret was that the end came too soon. And thoughts rushed in.

One primary thought was that she was not much of a woman, if she could not bear a child. But then, she'd brought her sure-of-himself husband to a state of mindlessness, hadn't she?

It took a woman to do that.

And she could do it again—if she concentrated enough and cleared her mind of everything else.

His sex was limp and damp when she touched him.

"Woman," he growled into the side of her neck, "what are you up to?"

"You're the one that's supposed to be up, aren't you? I'm not good at dirty talk, but I think that's the way it's said."

He heard the flippancy in her voice, and he heard the desperation as well.

"You're good enough, Flame," he said. "And the talk's not dirty. Just to the point."

She continued to massage him. "Speaking of a point—"

Matt sighed in frustration. "Maybe I ought to explain how a man's body works."

"Go right ahead," she said, stroking and fondling and insinuating one of her legs between his.

Matt felt the familiar stirrings of desire.

"Then again," he said, taking up some stroking and fondling of his own, "maybe you could explain a few things to me."

Which sounded like a good idea, only neither of them did much explaining to the other for a long, long time.

When at last they rested in each other's arms and Flame listened to the low, even snore of her husband, she wondered if now were not the right time for tears. But she was dry-eyed—sated, yet empty inside—exhausted, yet restless for things she could never have. Each time when she believed she'd reached the bottom of despair's deep well, she discovered another excavation of darkness awaiting her.

Mama and Angel said God never gave a person more to bear than he or she could handle.

Lying naked in the arms of a man for whom she held strong, unnamed feelings, knowing he didn't want her except in specialized ways, realizing that in her damaged condition he had every right to feel that way, she knew that this time Mama and Angel were wrong.

Sixteen

Matt woke to bright daylight and knew right away something was amiss. No naked woman curled in warmth beside him. No fiery locks lay spread across the pillow by his own dark head.

The bedside lamp had been extinguished sometime during the early morning hours. He was alone.

The springs creaked under him as he sat up. Flame's clothes were gone from the floor beside the bed, and his were folded neatly next to a pitcher of water atop the bureau.

Damn. He liked it better knowing where she was.

The smell of coffee drifted into the room. Ignoring the complaints of a well-used body, he dressed quickly and hurried out to greet his wife. He found only a warm pot awaiting him on the stove. Remembering that the stage from El Paso would be traveling through this morning, he returned to the bedroom and caught sight of his wife's trunk. Inside were her clothes. She hadn't decided to take off for Savannah without saying a word, or at least if she had gone on, she'd left her belongings behind.

Which she could have done. He didn't put much past her, and she seemed to have money of her own.

And how would he feel, if she'd left for good? It was a hard question to answer. For sure his life would be a hell of a lot less complicated, but then he recalled the particulars of last night. Complications, he decided, were not without their compensations. Besides, Flame owed him at least a goodbye.

Matt shook his head in self-disgust. He wasn't used to thinking about what people did or didn't owe him. Loners didn't look at things that way.

Returning to the stove, he poured himself a cup of coffee and came close to spilling it as the front door eased open. He turned to view Flame in a white smock that covered most of her lavender gown. Her hair was pulled back in a neat bun. Too neat. He preferred the wild tangles of last night.

Still, he was glad to see her. Glad didn't say it all. He almost bounded over the table to give her a reminder of what had passed between them during the past few hours. A lifetime of restraint held him back.

"You're awake," she said. She didn't try to sound pleased. In truth, she wasn't in the least bit eager to see him. Not right away. Not when she could still feel his hands upon her, not when the memories of last night were vividly clear.

All the memories . . . the good and the bad. She swallowed the lump in her throat.

"Yeah, I'm awake," he said, almost growling. "What's going on?"

It wasn't, she decided, a particularly loverlike

greeting, but then maybe it was typical of men who weren't in love. It certainly seemed typical of Matt.

"Nothing," she said, feeling awkward, refusing to meet his eye. "I needed to post a letter before the stage left and set out some clothes for the laundresses, before I reported to work."

"Reported to work?" he asked, feeling more than a little stupid.

And, he finally admitted to himself, more than a little sore. Flame had put him through his paces last night. He looked for signs she was feeling some of the same symptoms. All he could detect was a tightness around her mouth and a brightness in her eyes that gave no evidence of contentment.

"While you were gone the past few weeks, I started helping Doc at the hospital. The pay's not bad—"

"No wife of mine is going to work."

Flame stared at him in disbelief. "Don't be ridiculous, Matt. We both know I'm not your wife."

"You could have fooled me a few hours ago."

Flame almost welcomed his stubbornness and his taunting words. Here was a Matt she was used to. Not the gentle lover of the night.

"You know what I mean," she said.

Matt sipped at his coffee. "Yeah, I guess I do."

Flame continued to look past him, all businesslike. From the way she was acting, he could believe last night had been a dream. Except for his personal soreness and that brightness in her eye.

"It's certainly not necessary for you to support me," she said, "not if I can earn money on my own."

"That's the damnedest idea I've heard out of you yet."

"What you mean is, it's the most sensible and you just didn't expect it. I can be imminently sensible and practical, if I'm given the chance."

"You weren't too sensible last night. How are you feeling this morning? I lost track after three times, but it seems to me we—"

"Really, do men keep count?"

She looked at him wide-eyed and censorious. In her heart she was terrified he would want to talk some more about what had gone on between them. She could have told him they'd made love four times with some playing around in between. Except it wasn't play. Not for her.

And it wasn't anything on which to build a future. With her pregnancy she'd allowed her hopes to rise too high. She wouldn't make that mistake again.

Now, if only she could get through the next few minutes without breaking down . . .

She dug her nails into her palms.

"I've got some breakfast warming on the stove," she said. "I don't know what you'll be doing today, but it certainly would be done better if you attempt it on a full stomach."

Matt shifted uncomfortably. It wasn't his stomach he was thinking of right now.

He glanced at the two cloth-covered plates sitting toward the rear of the stove behind the single burner.

"You're eating with me?"

"Oh, no. That's for you and Keet."

"Who the hell is Keet?"

"A friend of mine. He's been showing up about this time every morning."

Flame twisted her hands at her waist.

Matt saw that she'd turned nervous.

"A friend of yours," he said, picturing a tall, muscled soldier, or maybe an officer, someone fair and polished like Robert Anderson. He didn't like the picture at all. He especially didn't like it when this Keet bastard was seated at *his* table eating with *his* wife.

What kind of name was it anyway? Maybe something to rhyme with *sweet.*

Sweet Keet.

He was liking the turn of events less and less.

"I've got to run," she said. "The laundry can wait." Her voice was crisp, almost brittle, as though at any moment it might break. "I assume that you'll be home tonight. There'll be supper on the table. Try not to be too late."

The door slammed behind her. He started to follow. But what if he caught up with her? What was he going to say?

We're going back to bed, baby. It's the one place we seem to get along.

He wasn't entirely sure she wouldn't agree. Either that or she'd light into him with a tongue-lashing he'd never forget.

Worse, she might turn a pair of tear-filled green eyes up at him and make him feel lower than a Texas skunk.

Tonight they'd talk about going back to bed. It was damned certain he wasn't slinking back over to the barracks, and he'd spent his last night on the floor by the hearth.

Turning his attention to the stove, he cleaned one of the plates of the still-warm eggs and bacon. It tasted damned good. He was considering the second plate when he heard a knock at the door.

Must be this Keet, he thought.

"Come in," he said, wondering if the shock of a man's voice would send the newcomer hightailing for the woods.

The door opened, and Flame's new friend stepped inside. Matt saw two dirty bare feet, then scrawny legs extending from a pair of ragged trousers, a narrow naked chest, arms to match the legs, long hair streaming past the shoulders, wide black eyes, and last, the high cheekbones and copper skin he recognized too well.

It was the half-breed street kid from Little Sandy, the one who'd rescued the tortured dog.

"She ain't here?" the boy asked as he took in the room with one glance. "Shit. I had something I wanted her to see."

He proceeded to let loose with a few more obscenities, while Matt considered whether to scrub the boy's mouth with soap before he threw him out of the house.

"You're a coward, Flame Chadwick."

Flame directed the self-lecture out loud as she hurried down the corridor leading to the hospital ward. She knew all too well that she should have stayed to serve as peacemaker between Keet and

Matt, but she was weary of figuring out how to behave around the man who had made love to her
throughout the night.

Maybe if he had said or done something different
this morning, but he'd held himself apart, keeping
a room's width between them, staring at her with
those watchful brown eyes over the coffee cup, assessing, judging, and in the end just standing there
as though he, too, didn't know how to behave.

He probably didn't, not with them both upright,
dressed, and bathed by daylight streaming in
through the window.

"A true coward, Flame Chadwick," she said, then
hastened to correct herself with a muttered "Jackson" added on.

After last night, she was most certainly Matt Jackson's wife.

But she would never be the mother of his child.
Her throat closed at the thought. She didn't want
to consider the brutal truth, not in such a knife-
sharp way, not right now, not when she was still dealing with Annie. All the injustices of the world
seemed layered on her shoulders, and she questioned her strength to carry them one step more.

Self-pity numbered among those burdens. She
must cast it off—and she would, later. For the time
being it offered a curious kind of solace, a temporary balm for her troubled soul.

She wondered if there were a line from Shakespeare that covered her situation. Raven would
know. Raven ought to be here to tell her what it was.

And Papa and Mama and dear, sweet Angel. But
she couldn't think about them long. Homesickness

was an anguish she couldn't handle just yet. Nor could she deal right away with writing another letter to her mother, this time revealing the sad news of her state of health.

Mama wanted grandchildren. With Raven vowing never to wed, that put the burden on Angel to provide the next generation of the Chadwick clan.

"Good morning, Flame."

She came to a halt, forcing her eyes to the good doctor blocking her path.

The doctor who had known of her altered condition and who had chosen to tell Matt instead of her.

"Good morning," she said, uncertain as to how she felt toward him.

He stared at her longer than he usually did. She shifted nervously.

"You're looking different today," he said, thinking she looked even more tired than usual, and somehow harder, too. As though she'd been given very bad news.

Flame wondered if a night of sex showed on a woman. Maybe there were signs only a physician would recognize. If so, those signs ought to be fairly screaming out at Doc.

"I didn't get much sleep." She paused. "Matt told me."

"Figured that's what it was. Want to come into my office? Seems to me you might have questions to ask."

Flame swallowed hard. "He told it in plain enough language, I'm sure the way you told him."

"It's hard news to soften. And I could be wrong

254

about the diagnosis. A woman's body is a complex thing."

"You're a good doctor, aren't you?"

"I like to think so."

"Then be good enough not to hold out any false hopes. If you've got any other bad news, I'd appreciate hearing it now. Might as well get everything out where I can deal with it at once."

Doc would have liked to take the young woman in his arms, so she could rest her head on his shoulders and maybe have a good cry. But that hardness about her, added to the flushed cheeks and unnaturally bright eyes, spoke loud and clear that she wouldn't be interested.

"You're a brave woman."

Flame almost laughed. She'd been called a lot of things in her life, but brave had not been among them. And she certainly didn't feel very brave right now.

She straightened the white smock covering her lavender dress. "Any patients this morning?"

"I'm surprised they're not marching in columns through the door, considering the changes you've made around here."

"Don't try to make me feel better, Doc. It won't work."

"Only speaking the truth. Best food on the fort, clean sheets, a beautiful woman fluffing the pillows. Damned if the whole regiment won't be coming down with the plague any day."

"All I did was talk to the cook a little."

"You're a modest woman, Flame." He patted his

255

rotund belly. "If I'm not careful, by Christmas I won't be able to find my feet."

Flame's cheeks warmed at his kind words. "And the sheets were already clean."

"Must be the way you tuck 'em around the men."

Her flush deepened. "I thought that's what I'm supposed to do."

"Oh, it is. You've got those hearts to beating strong as ever. Better than I could have done. Had to send yesterday's contingent back to the barracks. We've only got one so far today. A bad sprain, keep him laid up a few days. Lieutenant Abraham Lilly, the colonel's adjutant. Maybe you know him. Young man. Crisply military, if you know what I mean. He's already complaining about being confined to bed."

Flame recalled the lieutenant, the Micks having pointed him out one day when she'd been talking to them outside the sutler's. Tall and lean and fair-haired handsome, like a host of the young men she remembered from back in Savannah, he'd been walking alone across the parade grounds, his steps high and measured, as though he were leading a platoon.

"Kinda stiff-necked," Michael had said. "But not a bad sort. Nary a thing wrong a little time in County Cork wouldn't cure."

A visit to the home of Papa's family had seemed enticing to her at the time. It seemed even more enticing now.

"Why is he here?" she asked. "Couldn't he recuperate just as well at his own quarters?"

Doc adjusted the wire-frame glasses on the bridge of his nose. "Sort of man he is, he'd be up and

256

walking too soon, thinking he was shirking his duty to the colonel and the Army. Here I can keep an eye on him, at least for a day or two. Otherwise, he's liable to do permanent damage to himself."

"Can you keep him down?"

Doc's blue eyes twinkled. "Gave him a little something to make him sleep. Doubt if even you hovering over him will stir him much this morning."

"I don't hover," Flame said, then hurried on down the corridor to begin putting fresh linens on the beds.

Just as Doc had predicted, Abraham Lilly did not awaken during her period of work. Instead, with his leg propped up on a couple of extra pillows, he lay quietly beneath the covers, a shock of dark blond hair resting carelessly across his forehead, looking for all the world like the young boy he must have been.

Flame had worked her way down to the far end of the ward, when she was surprised by an unexpected visitor.

Melody Burr, clad in a rich blue velvet gown and matching feathered bonnet, her fair hair twisted into curls that brushed against her face and neck, strode into the hospital ward as though she did so every day. Flame had never seen her look so good. No wonder Matt had taken notice of her.

Flame stopped herself. From everything she had observed and overheard between the two, he'd done a great deal more than just take notice of her. And she had certainly done more than simply take notice of him.

Which really wasn't Flame's concern, even though the certainty of it twisted her heart.

And why was she thinking solely of Matt? Her ersatz betrothed had gotten himself engaged to the girl. If she were to match up the very busy Melody with anybody, Robert should be the one.

Flame's eyes dropped to Melody's waist and abdomen, and an unbidden thought almost crushed a cry from her throat. The colonel's daughter had a fertile look about her. She could have provided Robert with a healthy baby . . . or two or twelve, as many as the Anderson plantation could hold.

If Matt were a family man, she could provide the same for him. It was something Flame could never do.

Anguish tore at her, and an unreasonable hatred for the girl. She drew upon an untapped strength to keep her misery under control. Not once had she broken down because of Matt's revelations—it was as though she'd used up all her tears over Annie—and she refused to break down now.

Her hurt was too raw for rational reactions, she told herself. In time she'd handle such foolish jealousies better. Perhaps in a decade or two.

Oblivious to the turmoil within Flame, Melody walked into the middle of the ward, stopping when she was at the foot of the lieutenant's bed. She gave the patient a quick look, and then another. The tightness around her eyes softened, her lips parted, and she looked like nothing other than a lovely young girl who'd dressed up for her beau.

But only for just a moment. When she looked at Flame, a false-sweet, older-than-old smile was firmly in place. The familiar attitude was better, thought Flame, easier to deal with than the innocent vulnerability of a second ago.

"Mama said you were working here now," she said.

Flame couldn't see that the comment deserved a reply. During her hospital stay, the colonel's wife had not bothered to visit, and neither had the other officers' wives, not even the ones who'd been friendly at the sutler's. Not that she'd wanted or expected them. Flame knew her position as wife of a scout put her in a sort of social limbo, but that wasn't much different from her position back in Savannah.

She didn't care. Her aspirations had always been different. A man to love, a home, a family of her own . . .

There she went again, dangerously close to spinning out of control. But she couldn't allow herself the luxury, especially with the sole witness her husband's mistress.

If that's what she was. Flame didn't know all the correct terms for people involved in love affairs.

Melody smoothed her lace-trimmed gloves. If Flame hadn't known better, she would have sworn the girl was nervous.

"I just couldn't imagine what you'd be doing here," Melody said with a little laugh. "I see you've only got one patient."

"Doc has the patient. I'm just here to help out where I can."

"Well, I'm sure you do a very fine job."

Flame stared at Melody in open surprise.

"Goodness," the girl continued, brushing at her forehead, "it's warm in here."

"We try to keep out the drafts of air."

"As I said, I'm sure you do a very fine job."

An awkward silence descended.

"Could I help you with something?" Flame asked, wishing she could dislike the girl as much as she had the first morning they met. Strange how she could hate her at this moment, and feel a sudden sympathy for her at the same time.

"I had this silly little idea." Melody opened her purse and pulled out a small, leather-bound volume. "I thought some of the men might like to hear some poetry."

"You did?" Flame did not try to hide her astonishment.

"Well, I thought I might offer to read to them. And here the only one who might listen is fast asleep. Do you think he might wake up before long?"

"Doc said he'd sleep much of the day."

"Oh." A forced smile graced the girl's face. "It's probably just as well."

"You could come back later this afternoon."

Melody waved the volume carelessly. "If I've got the time." She seemed to be considering adding a comment, then changed her mind. The indecision faded, and she looked about her with all the old calculation in her eyes. It was, Flame thought, like watching a chameleon adapt its protective coloration as it leapt from bark to leaf.

"I guess you'll be taking care of the lieutenant, anyway," Melody said. "Where's Matt while you're here? I ought to go see if he needs someone to help him pass the time. I miss the hours we used to have together, before he decided to get himself a wife. That sugar knows how to talk to a girl, but I guess you've found that out by now."

It depends upon what you mean by "talk."

Banning all sympathy from her heart, Flame forced a Melodylike false-sweet smile on her face. "It was good of you to drop by the sick ward. So few choose to do so, when they might expose themselves to a contagious disease."

"There's one thing you don't know about me," Melody said as she turned to leave. "I'm not afraid of anything."

But Flame could see the lie even as the girl spoke. Her nervousness had not been faked. In the stillness that marked her departure, Flame wondered what had been the true purpose of the visit. She glanced at the sleeping lieutenant. As the colonel's adjutant, he worked inside the headquarters building. And Melody wouldn't hesitate to visit her daddy whenever she wished.

The lusty Melody and the upright Abraham Lilly? Impossible.

Just as impossible as Flame and Matt.

"Oh, Annie," she whispered, "there are strange things in this world to contemplate. I wish I had more experience, so I could figure them out. Trouble is, experience comes at too high a price."

The whispering seemed natural, yet it caught her by surprise. She'd quit talking to Annie after the fall, and here she was at it again. She felt no sadness or regret, or at least only a little bit. To Flame, Annie had been a real person once, and she couldn't see why that situation had changed. Somewhere there was a spirit of the child who had never been born. Somehow Flame knew that spirit was very close by.

With that realization, her despair lifted, and she didn't feel quite so alone.

Doc came in shortly and said that with only one patient, there was really not much for her to do.

"Go on home and rest. You're looking tired."

"I didn't get much sleep last night," she said, then realized what she might be revealing and blushed. "If the plague strikes, you'll let me know? I wouldn't want you faced with caring for a ward full of sick men all on your own."

"I'll let you know," said Doc, grinning.

He really was a kindly man, she thought. She couldn't hold it against him that he'd confided in Matt instead of in her. Men were supposed to care for the weaker sex, to handle the difficult times in life, or so they thought.

It was up to women to let them maintain the myth and to keep the world moving along. Or at least the responsibility was left to most women. Right now Flame didn't understand her part in the human race.

Leaving her smock on one of the hooks by the door, she forced herself to walk to the adjoining house. She was stepping onto the porch when she heard a familiar, "Flame."

She turned to see the half-breed boy who had become her friend. Three weeks ago she'd caught him trying to steal a plate of food one of the Micks had placed at her front door. They'd shared the repast, and they'd been sharing meals ever since.

Her conscience struck her that after the first few minutes away from the house this morning, she hadn't thought of him one time.

"Keet," she said, coming as close as she could to smiling, "I'm glad to see you."

"No more'n I am to see you."

"Did you come by earlier?"

The scowl on his dirty brown face told her the answer.

"I take it you met my husband."

Keet muttered a string of words she couldn't make out, but *bastard* came up several times. Which was clean talking for him. The orphan son of a saloon girl who'd been raped in an Apache raid—the boy had openly told the story—he'd been raised around his mother's acquaintances. He'd picked up a vocabulary that would make the most hardened soldier blanch.

Flame didn't always understand exactly what he meant, but she usually caught the general tenor of his words.

She would have liked to explain her husband's aversion to the Apaches, but since he'd never fully explained it to her, she didn't think she could do a very good job. Most of all, she would have liked a description of just what had taken place when the two had met. She'd have to let the several *bastard* comments in the space of a minute be her guide.

Besides, whatever Keet told her, Matt would tell her something else. Since there would be no knowing who came closer to accuracy, she was better off not hearing either version right away. There were just so many things she could handle, and a battle between her husband and her new young friend did not number among them.

A coward for sure, she thought. And Doc had called her brave.

"Did you get something to eat?" she asked.

Keet kicked at the dirt. "I took care of myself."

Which meant he hadn't had a bite, or at least he hadn't been served the breakfast plate she'd left for him.

"Well, I'm hungry. It would be nice if I didn't have to eat alone."

The boy considered the offer. "First, I'd like to show you something."

"All right."

Hitching up his ragged trousers, he led the way around the side of the house away from the hospital, past the zinc-lined tub propped against the adobe wall, to a clump of shrubbery a short distance away, his bare feet treading over sharp rocks and dirt and grass as if they were all the same. They marched one after the other—one whose coloring blended with the earth, the other a splash of gaudiness in the expanse of earth and autumn shrubs.

Flame glanced toward the far line of trees that marked the eastern edge of Fort Hardaway. Beyond, Little Sandy Creek bounced and rippled over its pebbled base, pooling occasionally to unexpected depths, then turning shallow again as it hurried toward the Rio Grande.

The laundresses would be at work by one of those pools. Wives of the enlisted men, most of them, a few of the single women earning extra money in a profession older than even soldiering.

But they had been good to Flame, when she'd joined them at their washing chores. And so had Keet, who regaled her with saloon tales the likes of which would never be heard at Miss Lillian's.

She studied the thin figure in the lead. Shoulder blades protruding like wings from the brown naked back, trousers hanging loose on thin hips, ankles thin as twigs. For all his angularity, he had a strength to him, too, the kind that came with steel wire. She'd never seen him weary, never seen him down.

As they neared the shrubs, the boy's pace slowed to a creep. Coming to a halt, he grinned at her over his shoulder, startling white teeth in a copper brown face. He smiled so seldom that her heart turned.

"In there," he whispered, pointing to a clump of wild grass at the base of the nearest shrub.

"What is it?" she whispered back.

"You'll see. Shit if I can figure it out. Shouldn't be here this time of year."

He knelt and she dropped beside him. He eased the grass and the bottom leaves of the shrub aside. Nestled in the shadows of a dirt hollow was some kind of small baby animal. Just one was all she could make out. One all alone.

"Couldn't be more than three weeks old at the most," said Keet. "His eyes were open when I found him. No mama around to take care of him, and I thought of you. Seeing how you like to take in strays and all."

Flame knew the boy referred to himself.

With studied care Keet lifted the animal and held him into the light for Flame to admire.

She looked in astonishment at the offering. Resting in the boy's hand, fitting into his undersized palm with ease, was a black and white ball of fur that was unmistakably a baby skunk.

Seventeen

William Burr's weathered hand snaked along an amply endowed ridge of naked hip and thigh. The Widow Rowena Latrobe grinned encouragingly in response.

"You're a beautiful woman, Weenie," he said, patting her ample rear. He liked a woman with some flesh on her, liked full, dark-tipped breasts and long black hair, liked thighs with a powerful grip.

In short, he liked the Widow Latrobe.

Rowena flinched at the nickname her lover insisted on using. But she didn't flinch at the touch of his hand. Since the death of her husband two years before, the colonel hadn't been the only man she'd let into her bed, but he was the only one she'd allowed lately, after deciding he was the best.

The two of them were lying face-to-face in the upstairs master bedroom of the Latrobe residence, the high feather mattress on the mahogany four-poster lifting them halfway to the ceiling. They'd finished with the morning lovemaking, but neither liked to get up right away.

She stroked her lover's full head of gray hair. "You're a good-looking man, Billy."

Burr chuckled. "Only woman I ever let call me Billy. The wife calls me Colonel. Ever tell you that?"

At least once a week.

Rowena merely smiled.

"She's proud of your rank."

"Damned if she's not. Proud of being a colonel's wife."

He didn't try to keep the disgust from his voice. What great hopes he'd had for their marriage when they were young, even though she was a pampered debutante from Philadelphia and he a raw lieutenant just out of West Point. She'd not been able to handle the trouble that had befallen them. He was honest enough to admit that neither had he, allowing her the way he had to turn as cold as a mackerel and just as colorless.

He and Eleanor hadn't shared connubial bliss since the day . . . Burr pushed the memory aside. He didn't like to think about what had ended their marriage.

Eleanor had to know he'd taken up with other women, but she was the kind to create a make-believe existence that more suited her fancy. The perfect wife with a perfect husband and child, that was more to her liking. By perfect, she meant no one got in anyone else's way.

Burr preferred a grittier life filled with complexities and hard work and passion. He slipped his hand between his lover's legs. Especially the passion. At fifty, he wasn't the man he used to be, but he liked touching Rowena, even if sometimes he couldn't follow through with anything other than a few active fingers.

Rowena sighed with pleasure. She surely did like a man with callouses. Too, she liked companionable talk after the sex.

"How are things at the store?" she asked, nesting his hand more firmly in place.

Burr returned her smile. He liked the way she referred to Fort Hard. Took the vanity out of what he did. He'd been in the Army too long, had seen too many ugly sights, to glorify his job.

But the smile didn't last long.

"Latest dispatch says there's signs of Indian trouble all along the border clean to Arizona. More renegade Apaches keep cropping up. Victorio still causes trouble, raiding over the border like Black Eagle, although we've not heard much from old Blackie lately."

"Any idea why not?"

"He knows we got us a scout who'll cut off his privates and fry 'em for breakfast, if he gets the chance. The men are well trained, too. Matt Jackson sees to it. Few months back, Blackie could have wiped out an entire patrol and a stagecoach full of passengers, but we had some of Fort Hard's finest there for protection. Sent him running back to Mexico."

The colonel experienced a rare moment's regret. "Gave Jackson a hard time about the scrape, since we lost a few good men in it, but things could've been a hell of a lot worse."

"It feels downright comforting," Rowena said, "to

know a helpless woman can rest peaceful in her bed."

Burr grunted. "There's another one of the savages, too, a medicine man goes by the name of Geronimo. Supposed to have the power to know what's going on anywhere in the territory. The Nednhis have taken him in, made him a war leader. They cross the Arizona border on a regular basis. Sure as hell hope they stay away from here."

He glanced over the woman's white rounded shoulder to the clock on the mantel. The time was shortly past noon.

"Weenie, I got to be going." He eased his hand from between her legs and rested it on her hip. "But I was thinking maybe you could give me some woman-type advice."

"I'll give it a try." She eased from beneath the covers and reached for the clothes scattered on the floor beside the bed.

Burr got up on the far side. Uniform and longjohns were folded neatly across the back of a bedside rocker. Too long in the military, he kept to the trained ways of neatness, even while his Weenie was tossing garments willy-nilly across the room.

"It's Melody," he said as the two of them got dressed.

"She in some kind of trouble?" Rowena fastened the waist closing of her underdrawers and eased her full breasts into an ecru chemise.

"Liable to be, the way she hangs around men." Burr tugged on the blue Army breeches. "Got herself engaged to a fine young lieutenant, but he was killed in that stagecoach raid I mentioned. Gave his life in an act of bravery. Damn shame. He would have been a fine son-in-law."

While Burr watched, Rowena eased on her stockings, then with one foot and then the other propped on the bed, she anchored them in place with a pair of thigh-high, lace garters. Slowly lowering a petticoat over her head, she smiled at her lover across the rumpled bed.

"So now she's looking around, and on an Army fort there's lots to look at."

Burr cleared his throat and straightened his breeches, as he turned his thoughts to his daughter.

"I hope looking is all she's doing. But maybe not."

Rowena saw the worry in his pale blue eyes. She'd never had children of her own, but she could understand a father's worry. She knew, too, that Burr loved his daughter in a gruff, don't-show-affection kind of way, and from the way he talked, she suspected the daughter loved her father right back.

What she didn't get was the mother's role in all this. Eleanor Burr must be as cold a fish as Billy claimed.

"Get her engaged again," she advised as she donned her dress. Plain black it was, like the others in her wardrobe. Since the death of her husband, she'd always worn black, not because she was in mourning, but because she wasn't a woman given to vanity.

"Melody's not one to accept managing," said Burr with a shake of his head.

"She might if you arranged it for her. Pick someone she can respect. Someone strong who will talk her language. She's an Army brat, so she'll need a military man like her daddy."

"You sound like you know what you're talking about."

"I was a ranch girl," Rowena said as she brushed her waist-length hair. "So I married a rancher. Howard Latrobe ran a fine herd of cattle, until he tried shortchanging one of the hands. Gunned down in his prime. Pity, but then that's the way life goes sometimes. Howard's fatal flaw was he squeezed a dollar too hard. Except for this house, of course. He didn't stint on anything here."

Howard Latrobe had built the sprawling edifice at the southern edge of his property on a hilltop overlooking Little Sandy. Columned like a Mississippi plantation, it had been his pride and joy. Next to Rowena, he'd always said, but sometimes she'd wondered whether house or wife came first.

She'd held her husband in affection, but not enough to worry about changing his priorities.

Burr didn't mind her talking about her late husband. From time to time he talked about Eleanor in the same blunt way, except he had trouble coming up with good talk to balance the bad.

"The lieutenant's been gone only a few weeks," said Burr. He sat in the rocker to tug on a pair of polished Army boots. "You don't think it's too soon to look for a replacement?"

"The sooner the better. Trust me on this one, Billy. No matter what age, a woman doesn't like to be alone."

Rowena knew whereof she spoke. She'd celebrated her fortieth birthday the previous summer, and not once in all those four decades had she craved more than a day or two of solitude. What companionship she didn't get from the ofttimes-busy Billy, she got on a less personal level with the foreman and hands on the ranch.

For her, it was a satisfactory arrangement. Sometimes the nights got a little long and a little cold, but she'd learned to cope.

Burr considered her suggestion. "There's someone who might be interested. I work closely with him. Have to approach him just right, you understand, but Melody's a pretty girl and she'll come with a handsome dowry. A betrothal is not out of the question. Not at all."

Rowena felt a moment's sympathy for the colonel's daughter, then brushed it aside. On a couple of occasions she'd seen Melody Burr riding around town in a smart two-seater carriage, eyeing the men on the street. A flirt with a wild cast to her eye. She needed settling down. A husband picked by her daddy might be just what was required.

When her hair was bound into a twist at the back of her head, and both she and Burr were neatly clad, they descended the winding staircase of the large, well-furnished home, then strolled along the carpeted corridor to the back door and on out to the barn, where his gray gelding awaited.

They moved slowly, neither being in much of a hurry to end the visit. He saddled the horse while she watched. A fine figure of a man, she thought. Eleanor Burr was a fool.

Burr led his horse into the open air and mounted. Rowena looked across the landscape, taking note of

273

a ribbon of dust on the trail that looped over an eastern hill.

"Someone's coming," she warned. "Maybe you should wait a while before riding out."

Burr remained in the saddle and watched the lone rider grow nearer. "He's gone on by the cutoff to the house. Must be headed into town."

"Not many use this back way, except the ranch hands. I don't think he's one of mine."

Burr continued to watch. "Looks like Matt Jackson. That's his blood bay, all right."

"Jackson's your Army scout?"

"That's the one. I don't imagine what's going on between us is any secret to him. Been meaning to talk with him. Now's as good a time as any."

He glanced down at her, admiring the fine figure she presented, the proud stance, the returning look of admiration in her eye. Weenie covered herself from neck to toes in somber black, but the easy, flowing way she moved gave plenty of signs that there was a woman's lush body underneath.

"Take care, Weenie. I'll be back before the week is up."

Rowena felt a warm glow inside, knowing her Billy meant what he said.

With a flick of the reins, he was gone down the hill. "Ho!" he called out with a wave when it looked as though Jackson would ride on by.

Matt turned toward the call. He'd known the colonel was at the Latrobe house—he'd seen the easily recognized gray some distance past—but he'd decided on a hasty ride-by. He didn't ordinarily take this route into town, but he'd wanted to show up

274

without giving notice to the gambler Nigel Wolfe that he'd arrived.

He gave the colonel credit for facing the situation directly, once he'd realized he must have been seen. Halting in the shade of a pecan tree at the edge of the trail, Matt waited for the commanding officer to reach his side.

Burr sat tall in the saddle, his plumed hat resting square on his head as he approached. Only a flushed face detracted from his military bearing. The Widow Latrobe must have kept the colonel busy for a while.

Matt thought of his night with Flame. He was probably a little flushed himself, after a few hours of activity with his wife. Men called women the weaker sex, but Matt wasn't too sure men were right.

"Colonel," he said by way of greeting, when Burr reined the gray close to his gelding Pigeon.

"Been hoping to talk to you," said Burr without a trace of embarrassment. He might have been greeting his scout at fort headquarters, instead of within sight of his illicit hideaway.

The colonel proceeded to tell him of the dispatches he'd been receiving from Washington, of the increased Indian activity along the border, of the latest threat, the medicine man Geronimo.

Matt listened carefully, but his purpose in Texas was focused on only one man.

"Any word about Black Eagle?"

"None. I guess after the raid on the stagecoach, Blackie's decided to lie low for a while."

"Spending his time pillaging Mexican villages is more likely."

Using the Winchester rifles, learning just what they could and couldn't do. When Black Eagle came back into Texas, it would be with a plan for more than a hit-and-run attack on a lone stage.

"I'll set up extra patrols," said Matt.

"That's pretty much what I had in mind. You're a damned fine scout, Jackson. I know you've had some problems getting along with Captain Davis, but hell, no one gets along with everybody. As far as I'm concerned, you're a credit to the Army."

Matt wished he could think the same thing of the colonel. He didn't care that Burr was sleeping with a woman other than his wife. But was he buying her expensive gifts that couldn't be provided from his Army salary? The possibility existed.

"Will you be riding into town?" he asked.

Burr shook his head. "Heading the other way." He glanced at the big house on the hill, started to say something, then changed his mind. "Talk to you later about those patrols. Let's bring Black Eagle to justice. Let's do it fast."

Matt watched as the colonel rode away. Oh yes, he thought, he damned sure planned to bring the Apache to justice. Sometimes he got pulled off his track, like with a wife and the distractions that accompanied her, but that didn't mean a hate for the Apaches didn't burn in his heart. And now he had one of the lying, stealing bastards practically under his own roof. It was a Flame-type complication he wasn't going to accept.

Keet might be no more than a kid, but Matt couldn't forget another boy who had not lived past the same age.

He didn't have to force the memory of that terrible day into his mind. It slipped in with familiar ease. Once again he was a terrified eight-year-old crouching with his brother in the bushes of the backyard, while a band of Apaches swooped down in the front. They'd recognized the *boom* of their Daddy's old muzzle loader, and they'd heard their Mama's cry. The infant Sarah gave out only one mournful wail.

And then had come the terrifying yips of the Apaches.

With Matt close on his heels, Charlie had flown around the house and launched himself at the nearest attacker, taking him by surprise and dragging him from his mount. But that was all the good luck he was to know that day. In the midst of his dead family, he'd been beaten down. Again and again and again, until he was little more than blood and torn flesh and exposed white bone.

The boy Matt had watched, frozen as much in terror as by the restraint of the Indian brave who held him to the ground.

The cabin had been left to burn, the bodies to rot under an October sun. Bound and flung belly-down across a bare-backed Indian pony, Matt had seen the circling vultures high in the sky as he'd been taken away.

He'd had no idea where the Indians were headed. In shock, he hadn't much cared. The village that had been their destination wouldn't appear on any map. To this day Matt had no notion exactly where it had been. They hadn't stayed there long, choosing a journey down into Mexico instead of waiting

277

around for the white man's retribution that might or might not come.

The women took charge of him. From his mother he'd experienced kindness and love. From the squaws he learned hardship and hate.

His first introduction to the hardship came with a beating at the hands of the woman to whom he had been given. Each blow of her prickly stick ripped open the skin on his back and shoulders and arms. To a boy who had known only hugs and kisses, the experience planted seeds of hate that flourished yet.

He was put to herding the stolen horses and cattle on the raids into Texas, running barefoot across the rugged ground and then, only because it made him work more efficiently, learning to adapt to the moccasins he had to make for himself.

He didn't mind the herding duties. What he hated most was something far more ordinary: removing lice from the savages' buckskin clothes. The nits burrowed into the seams. Extracting them was done with the teeth. Some of the Indians enjoyed biting into the crunchy insects, seemed actually to relish the taste, as much as they did the rats that were roasted whole in an open fire.

Young Matthew retched the first few times he was given the task, but as in so many other areas of his existence, he learned to perform it without visible signs of complaint.

Not once in all the years he spent traveling back and forth across the Rio Grande, did he receive a kind word or gentle touch. He soon forgot to miss such signs of affection. He adjusted to the life.

Until he was twelve. That was the year Black Eagle arrived in camp. The newcomer, only a few years older, had witnessed the slaughter of his family by white soldiers in Arizona. In other times, other places, Matt might have shared a sympathetic loss. But Black Eagle made certain this white boy captive was tormented more than ever, staked to nearly perpendicular limestone cliffs on hot or stormy days, beaten when he dared to cast surly looks at his captors, bound each night by ropes that cut bloody grooves in his wrists.

He bore no visible signs of the ordeals; his scars were on his soul.

Three years the torment lasted. When he was fifteen and Black Eagle not yet twenty, he saw his chance one evening when a knife was left carelessly close to the fire. He concealed it in his buckskin breeches, even as he was led out to a high and distant tree where the approaching storm could vent its wrath on his unprotected head.

Slowly, laboriously, under the protection of a darkness broken only by occasional streaks of lightning, Matt sawed at the ropes. Black Eagle scrambled up the cliff for his inspection and the special goading he'd taken to providing.

Matt had seen a growing wildness in the Apache's eyes. But he was not afraid. Never had he been afraid of his special tormentor. With his heart filled with hate, he had no room for fear.

The fight was short and vicious. Matt lashed out with all the pent-up might of the torturous, thwarted years. Black Eagle fell backwards, his head striking a rock, but not before Matt had opened his cheek with a ferocious slash.

Like Matt, Black Eagle bore the scar of those years, except that his was worn across his face for all the world to see.

Matt disappeared into the night, using the skills he had learned from his captors to hide his tracks. With his knowledge of the Sierra Madre and the northern Mexico desert, he was able to reach the border and at last enter into Texas.

He had no destination except to get away. He'd drifted around the West, picking up odd jobs, educating himself to the ways of the white man and to his language, determined to leave all vestiges of the past seven years behind. He'd even taught himself to read, taking up the acquaintance of a schoolteacher in San Antonio. He knew she'd hoped to gentle him to a domesticated state, but he'd proven hard to tame.

Restless, he'd traveled across the continent. Until he'd read in a San Francisco newspaper about the exploits of a heathen Apache who wrought havoc along the United States and Mexican border. The Apache went by the name of Black Eagle. Word had it that he was the most vicious marauder among his people.

Worse than Victorio, worse even than the legendary Cochise.

There were those who said the redskin wanted only to reclaim the lands that had been taken from them. That they were doing nothing more than avenging decades of wrongs.

Matt could not become an apologist for the Indian. He knew them far too well.

And now someone was selling them arms.

Maybe an Army colonel, or his subordinate captain, or even the sutler at the fort.

Or maybe it was an English dandy who gambled with the soldiers and drifters who came into the Kitty Cat Saloon in Little Sandy, Texas, a man who spent more money than he gave evidence of earning at the tables, a man with slicked-back hair and hard, dark eyes. A man who made Matt uneasy just to look at him.

Nigel Wolfe was appropriately named. Like the lupine predator that bore the same name, he threatened just by being close.

Matt had made several futile trips into town to talk with him, the first time being the day he'd rescued Flame in the alley. The day she had watched a half-breed street boy rescue a tormented dog.

As though that made Keet human.

And she had brought him into their home.

Complications, that's what his wife meant to him. And distractions. It made no sense that he missed her, even now while he was riding down the ruts of Little Sandy's main road, getting hot inside when he thought of her womanly ways.

He reined to a halt in front of the Kitty Cat, advised himself to put her out of his mind, then strolled inside to see if he might catch the suspiciously successful Wolfe in residence at one of the back tables.

Eighteen

Nigel Wolfe stood in the shadows of the Kitty Cat's second-floor balcony and watched as Matt Jackson entered through the saloon's swinging doors.

Jackson spoke to the bartender and received a quick, negative shake of the head for his efforts. He studied the room, thickly yellow from kerosene lamps and tobacco smoke, selected one of the tables at the side, and with his back to the wall, settled into a chair that gave him unobstructed views of the room, the bar, and the swinging doors.

Little good his observations would do him, not if he were looking for Wolfe.

The gambler smiled to himself, smoothed a pencil moustache, and felt a surge of sensual pleasure because his luck was holding strong. He had no desire to talk with the crude and rude man, to answer the questions Matt wanted to put to him.

Wolfe could imagine what those questions would include.

He covered a cough with a monogrammed handkerchief. There was no need to get agitated over Jackson's presence. None whatsoever. Even if the questions were asked, the scout could prove nothing. He wasn't smart enough. No Americans could best an Englishman who was in his prime.

Still, a little caution never hurt, and so he remained in the shadows above the saloon's main floor.

A movement caught his eye, and he shifted his gaze to the vulgarly swollen figure in black satin that was emerging onto the balcony from the far room. It didn't take a second look to recognize the whore Myrtle. She really was a pig, he thought. The idea of plunging his clean staff into all that mass of flesh sent a shiver of disgust through him.

But she had her uses. He would use her now.

He gestured once. She frowned. He gestured again, eased through the open door at his back, and waited for her to appear.

"What do you want?" Myrtle asked sullenly, as she joined him in the dim, damp room, hands smoothing the black satin gown over her hips. Her lips were a pouting slash of red in the midst of a lard-white face, her eyes brown puddles of dislike as she met the gambler's glare.

Wolfe waved the handkerchief under his nose, wishing he'd taken the time to perfume it before leaving his room at the Little Sandy Hotel this afternoon. He'd been too eager to arrange an assignation for the day, and he certainly hadn't planned on getting this close to the malodorous saloon girl. Unfortunately, Matt Jackson's presence required he conduct his business with her in the privacy of an ill-ventilated room.

He viewed her bulbous bosom with revulsion. He had no taste for girls, overblown or otherwise. Or women. Or even men. His proclivities were far more selective. Too much so for this primitive town.

But there would be time enough later for his proclivities. First to the brute down below.

"Mr. Jackson has returned to the Kitty Cat," he said.

Myrtle's scowl lightened. "Matt? Here?" She turned to leave.

"Stay," said Wolfe, as he might to a hound.

She straightened her shoulders, the Army scout's nearby presence seeming to give her strength.

"I ain't doing nothing for you no more, Mr. Wolfe. No matter what you say."

"Ah, the lovely lady has grown a conscience, has she? Is it strong enough to guide your feet up the steps of the hangman's scaffolding? Will you bravely smile while the rope is lowered around your neck?"

Myrtle shuddered, her strength fading fast. "Don't talk that way."

"I want only to prepare you for an inevitable fate, should you defy me. After all, a man did die in your arms. Smothered, I believe, by your . . . er, charms."

"He was a skinny, little thing," she whined. "We was drinking. I didn't mean him any harm."

"That, I believe, has been the defense of countless murderers and murderesses through the centuries. Never has it proven especially efficacious."

She blinked in confusion.

He altered his assessment to a more mundane,

"The sheriff isn't interested in intent. Results are what matter in the West. And the result of your evening with the Bible salesman from Louisiana was most decidedly his demise."

Myrtle continued to stare at him blankly.

"You killed the poor man, Myrtle, whether or not it was your intention. That's all the sheriff will want to know."

Thank goodness the sheriff, a rather obtuse man far beyond his peak years, remained most of the time in the county seat some twenty miles farther west. Otherwise the threat of Wolfe's lust for justice might prove as insubstantial as his lust for girls.

At any rate, the gambler suspected the unfortunate salesman had died of heart failure, as the whore's breasts descended upon his face. Too much excitement, rather than suffocation, should have been written on the death certificate, if such a civilized document existed in this barbarous country.

"You helped me get rid of the body," said Myrtle.

"A friend in need, as the saying goes. Oh, never mind. Just get down there and entertain Jackson. Find out why he's here. I've never seen him do much gambling, and he hasn't availed himself of any of the girls."

"If that means what I think it does, Matt ain't one much for availing. Not lately, at least. Not since he got hisself a wife."

"Ah, yes, I've heard of the woman. A rather flamboyant redhead, is she not?"

"Comes from a bottle probably." Myrtle sighed. "Oh, peanuts, I'm just jealous. Matt's the kind of man a girl likes to wrap herself around on a cold winter's night. Maybe even the whole winter." She sighed again, more deeply. "Then there's spring and—"

"There is no need to catalogue the seasons of the year. Just go below and entertain the man awhile. I suspect he will inquire as to my whereabouts, but I want to know for certain. Under no circumstances are you to reveal I am upstairs."

His eyes narrowed, and he forced himself to grip her chin in one long-fingered and very strong hand. He squeezed tightly, until her painted lips puckered and her white flesh bulged into a grotesque caricature.

"I repeat, under no circumstances are you to tell him where I am."

He let her go, dismayed to see the reddened skin where he had held her. "Powder your face first, however. Don't stay any longer than you have to. I'll be waiting to ask you for another favor. And I'll be growing quite impatient. You know what a dangerous thing my impatience can be."

Myrtle stirred nervously. "That other favor. I don't want to do it again."

"Oh, but you must."

"It's a sin against God, that's what it is."

"And you, dear Myrtle, are naturally an expert in sin. Neither of us, I suspect, will find ourselves gifted in the afterlife with a heavenly reward."

Giving her little time to continue her protest, he shoved her out the door, then watched as she disappeared into her room for a moment, returned once again white-faced, and hurried down the stairs, where she joined Jackson at his table.

Even from a distance, she appeared agitated, but Jackson would probably believe she needed a drink. The scout signaled the bartender. Good. Wolfe watched the pair for a few more minutes, saw Myrtle toss back the drink that had been promptly served, then growled in anger as she cast a none-too-hurried glance toward the balcony.

For that, she would pay.

She stood, as did Jackson. Wolfe retreated into the room, threw the bolt, and edged toward the window. A drop to the ground was a relatively simple task for a man who kept himself in a fit condition.

He hesitated. A timid knock brought him back to the door.

"It's me, Myrtle."

Wolfe let her in, closed and locked the door, then backhanded her across the face.

She cried out, stumbling backwards, catching herself by the door handle.

"Why'd you do that?"

"You looked up here, you fool."

"Course I did. 'Cause I told him I had a customer waiting." She rubbed at her cheek. "He don't know it was someone couldn't poke it to a woman if a pistol was punched into his balls."

Wolfe decided striking the fool again would only be a waste of time. Besides, she was correct in her assessment. As though he cared.

"What did you find out?"

"Oh, he's looking for you all right. I told him you ain't been seen around lately. Which is the God's truth. You hide better'n a tick on a hound, but I didn't put it to him that way."

Myrtle had actually told him that the gambler was running scared, afraid that Jackson would catch up with him one day. She kept that part of the conversation to herself.

"You're holding something back, Myrtle. It would not be wise to do so."

Myrtle swallowed. If only she wasn't such a sniveling chicken, she'd give the snotty little Brit some advice on what he could do to himself, kick him between the legs where he needed kicking more than anybody she knew, and leave town on the first stage.

Instead, she stood there shuffling her tired feet and trying to figure out how to get out of the room.

"He talked about his wife some."

Wolfe eyed her ever more carefully. "What did he say?"

"Nothing much, nothing he volunteered exactly. I brung up the subject, and it made him real concerned. She's got him worried, is my guess, for some reason or other." She shook her head. "It's hard to picture Matt Jackson being overly concerned about any woman in particular."

But he was concerned now, she thought. And he hadn't tried much to hide it.

For just a moment she forgot that she was in the room with her hated enemy. She remembered only the way Matt had looked when she'd said *Mrs. Jackson*. She didn't know what was going on between the two of 'em, but she figured Matt cared for his wife more than he was willing to admit. It was only a guess, but she was confident she was right, not being quite as stupid as Nigel Wolfe thought.

Someday she'd show him just how smart she was.

Well, well, thought Wolfe, as he watched the softening of the whore's expression. She was at heart a sentimental fool. More than once he'd known her to give away her services to a lonely drifter down on his luck. What a simple mind she had, one ridiculously easy to read. Right now she was thinking of Matt Jackson and wife. She was considering the possibility that the two were involved in some kind of foolish romantic love. Which weakened Jackson, and which in turn gave strength to his enemies.

If the scout really had formed an emotional attachment to his redheaded wife, there were others who would find the news most interesting. One in particular. He must pass the knowledge on.

But later. Now was the time for pleasure.

"You know what you must do as soon as Jackson leaves."

"He's already gone."

"How fortunate. Then you must do what I want immediately."

"It ain't right."

"Perhaps not. But the only justice I am interested in concerns the death of that poor Bible salesman."

"What if I can't find him?"

"Oh, you will. You always do, after making a rather pitiful protest to ease your inconstant conscience. Now leave. Use the fire escape, and make sure no one sees you. I'll be waiting right here."

He watched her departure, looking out the window as she hurried down the narrow, outside stairs that led from the end of the second-floor hallway to a dark and little traveled alley behind the saloon.

She returned shortly with a companion. The two of them hurried up the stairs. Wolfe opened the door to them before either could knock.

"Go along," he said to Myrtle, blocking her entrance to the room.

"But—"

Giving her no chance to finish, he closed and locked the door, then turned to smile, his mouth pulled thin beneath an even thinner moustache.

"Herman, how nice to see you again."

The boy facing him started nervously, his full lips twitching, his young eyes darting around the room. At last they settled on the bed.

Wolfe removed his coat.

"You gonna pay me?" the boy asked, his voice breaking.

"Why, of course. Don't I always?"

Wolfe worked at the buttons of his vest as he looked the boy over. Red-faced and pudgy, but he preferred them a little fat. Most definitely only a little. Not grotesque like the whore.

"Come, Herman, you know what to do by now. Uncle Nigel needs some help with his clothes. If you do everything just right, then uncle will see that you get an entire apple pie just for you to eat. And Uncle Nigel always keeps his promises, especially to well-behaved boys like you."

Matt took the main road back to the fort, the more circuitous route of the morning having gained little except to send Nigel Wolfe cowering on the Kitty Cat's second floor. If Wolfe wanted any subtlety in his subterfuge, he would have to send down a more skilled interrogator than Myrtle.

The poor woman must have a crick in her neck from trying so hard not to glance upstairs.

But she'd been quick enough to reveal what he wanted to know. Nigel Wolfe was hiding something, and he didn't want Matt to discover what it was.

And the gambler thought all he had to do was avoid a direct confrontation. Which made him easy to investigate.

On the half-hour ride home, Matt settled on a plan of action, but he'd need a dispatch delivered to the sheriff at the county seat. The Fort Hardaway telegraph was risky; he wanted soldiers willing to undertake the delivery and to wait around for the answer.

Trustworthy soldiers who would never be suspected of involvement in a secret mission. Dependable soldiers who were hardworking and overdue for time off.

He knew just who to ask, three Irishmen who complained to everyone but Flame that if they'd wanted to spend their lives digging in the ground, they could have remained in County Cork. He could get them a few days' leave without arousing suspicion. Anyone interested would think he was keeping them away from the hospital, his home, and his wife.

The plan satisfied at all levels. Now, if he could think of a way to involve the half-breed. Some task that would ship him to Arizona or beyond.

Matt cursed under his breath. He shouldn't need an excuse to ban the brat from his home. He didn't want him there, and that should be the end of it.

The boy had left fast enough early in the day. Matt had done no more than level an eye at him, and he'd taken his foul mouth back out the door and disappeared.

The little bastard. If he was smart, he wouldn't return. But smart might be asking too much of him.

Arriving at the fort, Matt arranged through the Micks' captain—a young Californian who sometimes joined him at the poker table—for the leave.

"This is serious business," he said solemnly to the three soldiers as they gathered outside the stables. "Can you ride?"

"Can we ride?" Brendan Faulkner threw back his head and laughed. "Can the wind blow? Can the stars shine? Can the flowers bloom in the spring?"

"I get your point," said Matt.

He entrusted the sealed dispatch to Michael Mallon, who usually seemed the most responsible of the three.

Michael accepted the packet solemnly. "We'll not breathe a word o' this, Mr. Jackson. You have our word as sons of the Emerald Isle."

Matt took responsibility for checking out three horses to them, then watched with satisfaction as they saddled the mounts, their normal jocularity veiled by the seriousness with which they took the assignment.

And they knew their way around horses, too, just as they'd claimed.

When they were gone, he brushed, fed, and watered Pigeon. At long last, with the sun edging low over the western horizon, he turned toward home and the night after the night he'd finally slept with his wife.

Distinct choices awaited him. The hearth or the bed. Cold hours spent alone or hot sessions with Flame.

Matt had never considered himself a genius, but he could figure out which choice he would make.

As his long stride took him across the fort, he studied the cloud formations topping the distant hills. Clouds that caught the dying sun. Clouds the color of his wife's hair. He wanted very much to bury his hands and his face in all of her crimson glory, and to bury his sex in her sweet, wet warmth.

He couldn't deny she was a constant temptation to him. Maybe it made him weak, maybe not. But he wanted her. He wanted her badly, even at those times he considered wringing her lovely neck.

Even before he stepped onto the front porch, he could smell supper cooking. The mingled odors of bread and meat and burning wood stopped him. They were scents reminiscent of another place and another time . . . of a woman known as Betsy—or Mama—who had just called for two boys named Charlie and Matthew.

It was peculiar how the memories of such simple, everyday events kept coming back to him lately. Until the time he'd gotten himself married, the only part of his previous life he'd remembered with any clarity was the horror of how it came to an end.

The good times had seemed lost to the past. He didn't see the point in bringing them back.

And yet—

He shook off the burdens of sentiment and

stepped inside. Flame stood at the stove, her back to him, her hair pinned carelessly atop her head. She was wearing a dress he hadn't seen before, a shade of green that was like the wild grasses down by the creek. He didn't know much about fashion, but he did know it fit her well, following the lines of her back, narrowing at the waist, rounding out the way it should at the hips.

She'd probably made it herself. Bought the cloth at the sutler's with her own money, spent the evenings sewing in front of the fire, while he'd been away.

Something caught inside Matt, something twisted hard. Not unpleasant, just firm and sure and different from anything he remembered feeling before. Something warm, too. And then he felt the urges he was used to feeling around his wife. No sense in denying them. If she turned and got a good look at his trousers, she would know what was on his mind.

But she wouldn't know everything. Hell, he didn't know all his thoughts himself.

She was concentrating on stirring a large pot on the stove. Forgetting the stiffness that had been between them this morning, Matt concentrated on a different stiffness that was urging him on tonight.

Hooking his hat by the door, he crept slowly across the room, his target the tender skin just behind her ear. If there was one thing Matt knew how to do, it was creep. She didn't hear him, didn't suspect his presence, until he gripped her around the waist and kissed her neck.

Flame yelped, dropped the spoon, and shot an

elbow straight back, catching her unexpected—and very much surprised—attacker in the solar plexus.

"Oof," he said and let her ago.

Wielding the spoon once again, she turned. "Matt!" Gravy dripped unnoticed onto the floor.

He rubbed his chest. "Who the hell did you think it was?"

"Did I hurt you?" she asked, her eyes round with concern.

Matt fought back a grin. "Yeah, a little."

"I'm sorry!"

He began to unbutton his shirt. "You need to kiss it. Maybe give it a little tongue."

She sighed in exasperation. "How about a chunk of ice? I got some at the sutler's today. You could rub it on your chest. And," she said after a moment's thought, "any other parts that might need special attention."

"Oh, I've got parts that need attention, all right. But I was thinking of rubbing them with something hotter than ice."

Flame could come up with no immediate response. She'd already said too much, flirting with him as though they had some kind of serious relationship . . . as though everything in their world was all right.

A deafening silence descended over the room, broken only by the bubbling of stew on the stove and the pop of green wood in the fire. She tried not to stare at him, at the rugged features, the bristled cheeks, the watchful eyes. She tried not to acknowledge the sense of well-being that warmed her at no more than the sight of him.

She tried, but she failed.

So she did the only thing she could think of, she turned back to the stove and stirred with great vigor the beef and vegetables she'd prepared for the evening meal. And she thought of all the reasons she shouldn't be glad to see him, beginning with his treatment of Keet and ending with the impossibility of their marriage.

The latter was too painful to consider, and she returned to the half-breed, even though in her solitude of the late afternoon—after they'd fed their newborn pet and Keet had taken off for wherever he slept in town—she'd sworn not to mention his existence.

"What did you do with the boy's breakfast this morning?" she asked. "Eat it yourself?"

She couldn't have chosen a more deflating subject for Matt, or one that would raise his ire faster.

"I threw it to the strays."

The stirring slowed, then ceased altogether.

"I was afraid of something like that. Why, Matt? Why did you do it?"

"I don't want him hanging around."

"But he's my friend," she said in protest, wishing her feelings would make a difference to him.

"Get you a dog. They're more dependable than an Apache. And more grateful."

"You can't compare an animal to a human being."

"I'm not."

Forgetting the stew, she turned to face him once again. "And what's that supposed to mean? That he isn't human? No, don't tell me how you feel. I can read it in your eyes."

"Smart woman."

Matt's censure of Keet struck Flame as a censure of herself. She'd already begun to think of herself as damaged goods—like the crushed tins that were sometimes delivered to the Chadwick store—and now her pleas in behalf of a sweet, vulnerable boy were being met with acrimonious scorn.

Caring little about whatever it was in Matt's past that caused him to react this way, her own anger—and her frustration and her hurt—rose to match his. How quickly and completely the mood between them could change. She threw all caution aside.

"You can just forget ordering me not to see him. I'll see him when and where I choose."

"Like hell. He's not only half-savage, he's a street kid. He'd strip this house of everything he could sell, if he got the chance. Hell, he's so foul-mouthed he'd fit right in over at the barracks. The little bastard can't put two sentences together without including an obscenity."

"Ha! Have you listened to yourself lately?"

"I'm a man, not a child."

"Are you?" she said, ignoring the fire in his eyes. She liked this confrontation, or at least she found it easier to handle than the sexual tauntings in which he liked to indulge. It might be tearing her apart inside, but she could handle it.

"Then let's get the man some dinner." She reached for a plate, and with little ceremony or neatness slapped a spoonful of stew in the center. Stepping around him, she dropped his supper on the table. Juices stained the tablecloth, but Flame didn't care.

"The bread's on the shelf. I bought some ginger beer. That's what the ice is for. Help yourself. I suddenly find I'm not in the least hungry."

Without another look at him, she flounced into the bedroom and slammed the door closed.

Before she could draw a deep breath, he'd thrown the door open and was standing in front of her, his tall, strong body outlined by the light, soft as fog, that filtered through the portal at his back. Purple shadows, all that the waning day would allow through the windowpane, flickered across his face, marking the hard planes, the taut lips, the eyes filled with a fury she had never seen.

"Don't defy me in this, Flame. I won't have it."

Flame swallowed, fighting a burgeoning feeling of intimidation.

"And maybe I don't care what you won't have. You think you have some kind of power over me? Well, you don't."

Rage trembled through Matt, and his hands fisted at his side. If he were confronting another man, he'd have smashed in his face by now.

Instead, he stared down at a defiant woman who claimed he had no power over her.

Her fine chin tilted upward, her gold-flecked, green eyes burned bright. And her full red lips . . . he ought to curse those lips and everything else about her.

His rage turned to something else, something equally compelling, something equally hot.

"You're wrong, Flame. I have power over you."

She read the change in him.

"Don't touch me."

"You're lying to yourself, if you think you don't want me."

"I don't," she threw at him, but her voice was not so strong as she wished.

He pulled her hard against him. Somehow she managed to get her hands between them, and pounded with little effect against his chest.

"Let me go. For God's sake, Matt, we're having a fight."

"Yeah, baby, that's what we're having all right. And I know just the way to bring it to an end."

Before she could answer, his mouth took possession of hers.

Nineteen

With all her heart Flame wanted to resist Matt. Even before this moment, she'd felt ugly and broken and damaged, and now it seemed her wishes were no more consequential than a shifting breeze. Why would any man want her, except to satisfy his animal hunger?

Her heart, her soul, her wounded spirit were nothing to Matt, anymore than her will. His thoughts were turned to breasts and thighs and lips. He was most certainly thinking of her anatomy now, with his arms holding her tight against his chest, his legs melded to hers, his mouth soft yet firm and insistent as it urged her without words to acquiescence.

Everything about him was filled with promise and temptation, and worse, an aura of certainty that he knew what was best for them both. She was trapped by all that tantalizing warmth, and as she tried to struggle in his embrace, the fight melted out of her and, heaven help her, she changed her wants.

A woman could be strong for just so long. Eventually she had to submit to her own needs.

Flame needed Matt. Needed his touch, needed his attention, needed to know he was close by.

And she needed him in ways far more basic, more primitive, more primal. Ways Matt understood better than she.

Her fists eased open, and she pressed splayed hands against his buckskin shirt. With his arms enveloping her, she was wrapped in warm leather, breathing in the scent of the wilderness that Matt carried with him, listening to the rasping of his breath, responding with a rush of heat and pulsating urges she could not . . . did not dare to deny.

If she were damaged, truly ugly and broken, Matt didn't seem to notice. For the moment he made her feel beautiful and whole again, a woman passionately desirable to a man.

A thousand yearnings surged like wine in her blood; she grew dizzy from their rapid flow. Wanton that she was, she teased her tongue against his mouth. He groaned, held her tightly, and sucked the probing tongue inside his close, damp chamber.

Exhilaration sang within Matt as he tasted her sweet goodness. He grew impatient for an immediate sampling of all her honeyed offerings. The rancor of a scant minute ago became lost in a heady jumble of triumphant joy and allayed fears, both building from the knowledge that his wife was where she belonged, and she knew it.

Until this instant, he had not realized the existence of those fears. But he had no time to consider them, not with Flame's eager body pulsing in his arms. The scents of the kitchen clung to her skin, mingling with a hint of roses. She was everything she ought to be—wife, temptress, partner in this erotic dance of love—and for her as well as for himself, he wanted everything to be right.

She'd made it clear she hadn't wanted this lovemaking, not until he'd forced it on her. And he would have stopped, if she had kept up her resistance. But she had complied . . . no, more than complied, she had wrested from him the initiative. A rare woman was Flame.

Matt changed the tenor of the kiss, easing his tongue inside her waiting mouth, his hands roaming across her shoulders, her back, down to her waist and beyond, cupping her buttocks and pulling her hard against his arousal.

A kittenish cry came from her throat. He ended the kiss, but he continued to hold her against him.

"I missed you today," he said against the curve of her shoulder. It was a rare confession for a loner.

Through a fog of thickening desire, Flame understood the import of his words. She kissed the spot at his temple where the lush, black hairline met weathered skin. "I missed you, too."

"Let's make this good," he said.

She held still, for a moment caught by the recently born but ever present feeling of self-doubt. "Wasn't it good last night?"

He lifted his head and grinned down at her. Flame's heart did somersaults within her breast. How much different was his grin from his scowl. The grin sent pleasure leaping and dancing to her very soul.

It was a miracle to a woman who lately had known despair.

Everything about Matt seemed a miracle . . . the roughness that could turn gentle in an instant, the eyes that could speak of hungers more readily than words, and the hands. Oh, the hands, she thought as he squeezed them tight against her rear. His shaft pressed hard against her lower abdomen, so close to her wet throbbings, so close and yet so far.

"Last night was good," he said, and kissed the freckles on her nose.

She grew giddy with a feeling of weightlessness, as though the shackles of unhappiness had for a while been loosened, allowing her to float into the balmy sweet air of sensual release.

"Nothing more? Just good?"

He caught the glint in the depths of her jade eyes. "The best."

Flame lowered her gaze so that he could not read the dismay that seized her. *The best* sounded as though he were comparing her to other women. She wanted to be held in his mind alone. And in his heart. Tears sprang to her eyes, but she willed them away. She'd be stupid to cry. Theirs was a temporary arrangement . . . one that did not involve such things as the heart.

Just bodies and hungers and a fervent attempt to keep out the loneliness that must inevitably envelop them both in such a place as Fort Hard. Matt would deny that loneliness, but she knew he must experience it, too. Otherwise, why would he miss a woman for whom he felt no special affection? He could find others in town . . . or at the fort . . . to take to bed.

But he had returned home to her. She was not without value. She had not totally lost her womanhood.

The thought was one that had occurred to her before, but it was one that needed reenforcement. Every day.

She forced her eyes to his. "Let's make it great, then."

His voice turned husky. "For both of us."

"For both." She worked at the fastenings of his shirt, tugging it free of his trousers, spreading it wide so that she could see the hard, slick contour of his chest, could touch it with her hands, could tickle it with her tongue.

She gave her attention to a nipple. Oh, how she loved its salty taste.

Matt trembled. Under Flame's delicate assault, he turned to jelly. Or at least part of him did; part of him remained hard and demanding. Pulling the pins from her hair, he thrust his hands into its fiery thickness. Light from the doorway turned the fire to molten gold. He wanted to wrap himself in those long locks and never emerge.

When he could stand the assault on his chest no longer, he eased her face upward and slanted kisses across her lips. Light, quick touches that struck sparks between them. She moaned, and Matt heard an involuntary answering hum issue from his own throat.

He lost control. With one hand he pulled her skirt up to her waist, and thrust eager fingers inside the waistband of her several undergarments. She wore too many clothes, he thought. As if he'd spoken aloud, she eased all the necessary fastenings, allowing him access to her hungry heat.

He stroked her stomach. She shifted an inch away. His hand moved lower, across her flat abdomen, into the triangle of wiry hair he pictured in his mind as the color of her name. The curls were flames from the heat of her womanhood. Fingers found her secret folds, used the moisture of her own body to wet the protected, pulsating bud, stroked in tiny little circles until she cried against his chest, her hands clutching his open shirt.

He brought her to climax. She convulsed against him, whispering his name again and again, her fingers curled into the leather fringe of his shirt, as she rested her whole body against his strength. The suddenness of her satisfaction left her stunned, weak-kneed, unsure as to what was expected of her next.

Matt ended the wonder as he lifted her into his arms and laid her on the bed, then proceeded to undress and lie down beside her, his long, naked legs lying atop the green skirt that spread over the covers.

Expert fingers worked at the fastenings of her bodice, pulled the fabric aside, eased the camisole down to expose the taut-tipped breasts that grew heavy with impatience for his touch.

"Exquisite," he whispered as he took one nipple between his lips. *Exquisite* seemed a curious word to issue from a man who seemed only a few steps from savagery. How little Flame understood him, and how much she wanted to.

She ruffled the thick hair away from his face, midnight locks dampened by his sweat, then roamed down to the expanse of ropy shoulder, the upper arm, the muscled chest with its dark, damp chest hairs curling provocatively beneath her fingertips.

She wanted to explore every part of his body with the same thoroughness. Eagerness drove her to push him away. Tugging her skirt from beneath him, she stood at the side of the bed and, without shame, undressed, knowing he watched every movement, every patch of skin that was bared to his velvet eyes.

When she joined him once again on the bed, it was to shove him firmly onto his back, to run her tongue across his lips and down his throat, to rub her palm in concentric circles across his chest and rock-hard abdomen, his erect sex beckoning her with such intensity that at last she could control herself no longer, and she enfolded him in her hand.

He moaned. She laughed softly, rejoicing in the power she had over him. All she could think of was bringing him pleasure, a kind he had never known. She was all he needed, all he would ever need, just the two of them locked in carnal explorations, their only quarrels arising from who would bring the other to ecstasy first.

"Flame," he said, his voice urging and caressing at the same time. She thrilled to the sound on his lips.

Flame she was, hot as her name, sharing her heat with him. She was not respectable, not restrained. True to her nature, that's what she was. And her nature told her to explore her lover with more than just her hands.

Did women do such things to men? She had no

idea, but it seemed right to touch the tip of his shaft with her tongue, to surround it with her lips, to take him in deeper while his calloused hands massaged her shoulders, his trembling fingers caught in the tangles of her hair.

And then he was lifting her upward, bringing her face to his, tasting his own musk on her lips as he kissed her. She spread her legs and positioned herself over him, easing downward until they were fully joined, then the rhythmic thrusts began.

She felt the thrills right away, more intense than ever. She wanted to prolong them into forever, holding all other considerations at bay, thinking not at all, only feeling, soaring, peaking, consumed by a pleasure of the most unbridled kind.

Too soon the sweet spasms came for them both, and too soon they ended. She curled against him, felt his arms encircle her ever more tightly, gripped her thighs to hold him in place, wishing their bodies could remain just as they were, Matt filling her emptiness through endless time, providing a place where she truly belonged.

He couldn't let her go. She'd brought him a kind of satisfaction he'd never known, willingly, wildly, performing an act of such intimacy that he felt transformed into a man he did not know. A man who wanted to hold onto one woman, a man complete only when that woman was in his arms.

On this cool autumn night, with his life as unsettled as it had ever been, powerful forces had taken hold of him, and he wasn't sure those forces would ever let go.

He eased her to her side, but he did not ease his

embrace, wrapping one leg over hers, resting her head against his chest, stroking her long, damp hair as he welcomed the whisper of her breath against his still-tingling skin. His heart approached a steady beat once again, but his thoughts seemed as tangled as the cover on which they lay.

Flame rested an arm across his waist, but otherwise she did not move. The moment was too perfect for change. She had not expected such perfection on any day of her life, ever again. But as he had done so often before, Matt proved she was wrong, only this time she was joyous that he had.

He continued to stroke her hair until he felt her settle into a peaceful rest. But somehow he knew she did not sleep. He tried to settle his thoughts into some kind of order, going back over what had led to this moment, the angry hot words in front of the stove, the sweet hot actions in the bed.

It took a moment to recall what had brought on the argument, and when he remembered, he knew there was something he had to do . . . something he had never done before.

For the first time in his life, he felt an undeniable compulsion to reveal to another human being his memories of a long-ago Apache attack and the subsequent years of hellish captivity.

Not just the fact that the tragedy had happened, but all the particulars that had combined to make him the person that he was.

When he first began to speak, Flame wanted to hush him . . . to plead that any talk at all would bring a too-soon return to the world. But when she realized what he was saying, she held still and mourned for the little boy Matthew, who'd suffered a harshness and loss more severe than she.

Tears dampened her cheeks, but she made no move to brush them away. She barely drew breath, unwilling to interrupt her husband's narrative in any way.

He spoke flatly, with no shift in inflection or pitch, no hint of the turmoil his story aroused in his breast. Flame pictured the frontier home, the brother Charlie, the mother and father and the baby girl that had fallen victim to the attack.

She found the infant sister's death the hardest to accept, although she suspected it was the brother that Matt mourned the most.

He spoke quickly of the captive years, mentioning Black Eagle in the briefest of ways, but she understood how difficult that time of Matt's life had been, and her heart broke for him.

She understood, too, why he did not want an Indian boy, even a half-breed, to take one step inside his home. She understood, but she did not believe he was right. Keet had done nothing to harm Matt. The boy was a victim as much as anyone, denied all touch with his Apache ancestry, scorned by the white man despite the white blood that flowed in his veins.

She pictured the lanky, copper-skinned youth with his laughing dark eyes. That he could find humor in anything was an amazing feat, that he could face each day with zest, a miracle.

Matt ended his tale with a brief, "When I was fifteen, I found a knife and got away."

He spoke with finality. She did not ask him to tell

her more. On an earlier day he'd talked about traveling across the country, about returning to Texas to settle old scores. It was the time he'd found her rummaging through his clothes. He'd been angry she'd turned up something that might reveal details of his past. And now he was telling her things she had long wanted to know.

At last she understood some things about him that had always been a puzzle—the savagery battered into him in his youthful years, the poise self-taught as he traveled his way into manhood.

And the frustration he must have felt when he was forced to take a wife. His memories of hearth and home were distant, broken by disaster, while Flame knew what succor and serenity they could provide.

She felt as close to him as she had ever done. And as far.

"Thank you, Matt," she said, and he did not ask her what she was thanking him for. Let him assume it was for the telling of his past. She was thanking him for that, and much, much more.

"The stew must be cold by now," she added. "I could heat it, if you'd like."

He held her close. "Later. We can eat it for breakfast. I've got other things I want to do during the night."

"Oh," she said in a small voice, welcoming his embrace with mixed happiness and sadness.

Earlier in the day she'd compared Melody Burr to a chameleon—changing colors of attitude as her thoughts flitted from Doc to Abraham Lilly to Matt. Flame was a chameleon, too, one moment despairing, the next raised to heights of joy, only to be thrust into a contemplative mood in the least expected times.

Maybe all women were like that clever little lizard, never the same person for very long. If they were, she knew the reason why. It was because most every day of their lives they had to deal with men.

Just as Matt had suggested, they ate cold stew for breakfast. It tasted better than Flame could have imagined, better than it would have the night before, because now it was seasoned with the memory of a peppery kind of night.

Matt spoke little, complimenting her on her skills as a cook and a seamstress, asking if she had made the yellow gown she wore this morning and the green dress she had worn last night. Inordinately pleased, she admitted that she had, then talked of her work at the hospital, and of how it filled her days.

"I guess you need that," said Matt.

"I do."

"Then I was wrong to object. Besides, I have no business telling you what to do or not do with your time."

You could make it your business.

Flame wanted to say the words, although she didn't know why they had jumped so quickly to her mind. Could he really make her concerns important to him? Did she want him to?

And it wasn't entirely true that he wasn't telling

her how to spend her days. He'd ordered her not to spend them with Keet.

She supposed the boy was waiting somewhere at the edge of the fort, until he was certain the man of the adobe house was gone. The two of them had taken to visiting briefly before she reported to the hospital. From one of the soldiers who gambled at the Little Sandy saloons, Keet had learned he could earn money by collecting the flattened bullets from the Fort Hard firing range and selling them as scrap metal.

He was starting what he called his new job today. Except that he put in a colorful adjective or two to let her know he wasn't entirely pleased about having to go to work, but she saw that he wanted the independence his own income could bring him. Right now he depended upon handouts from the saloon women and drunken gamblers in town.

She felt in her heart that were circumstances different, Matt would like the kind of boy Keet really was.

But as much as the half-breed, Matt was trapped by the color of the boy's skin, by the straight black hair and the high cheeks that told of an unwelcome part of his heritage. He might be as rangy as any boy in Savannah, all arms and legs like any adolescent across the country, not in the least squat and solid the way the Indian was most commonly formed. But his color and his hair and his sharp-hewn face were features that could not be changed.

No more than could her husband's long-festering hate.

When the meal was done, she felt a change come

over Matt . . . a tension she could read in the brown depths of his eyes.

She read the meaning of the tension clearly.

"He won't come into the house again," she offered without prompting.

No need to say the *he* she meant.

"But you won't quit seeing him."

She swallowed hard, but she did not look away from his steady, piercing stare.

"He needs me."

"Like hell."

"Please, let's not argue," she said, brushing a strand of her unbound hair away from her cheek. "Not this morning."

She tried not to sound pitiful, she tried very hard, but she could see from the slight softening of his expression that she had failed. She didn't want him to acquiesce because he sensed how much she wanted someone to nurture.

The way Papa and Mama had nurtured her. The way any parent worthy of the name nurtured a child.

She wanted Matt to ease his objections because of a change that came from within him.

She wanted another miracle.

She wasn't going to get it.

He pushed away from the table and stood. "Don't let me see him or hear him. And don't turn your back on him, Flame. Not for a second. Let him know he has nothing to gain by hanging around—" He paused. "You're not giving him money, are you?"

Flame's cheeks burned. A time or two, against Keet's objections, she had forced a coin on him, but it was always taken from her private store of funds.

313

Oh, to be a good liar, but her quivery voice and blush were two handicaps she'd never been able to overcome.

So she resorted to the usual incomplete truths.

"I've given him food, as you very well know."

"And?"

She felt like a child at school, sitting there with the master looming over her, all dark and powerful and probing. Last night they'd been equals. She would have liked to be equals with him during the day.

She stood. "Beginning right now he's on his own."

But only because he had found a way to earn his own cash that didn't involve charity. Matt would not have understood.

How quickly the atmosphere between them was darkening. Flame had a sudden idea about how to bring the lightness back.

"I'd like to show you something, if you've got the time," she said. "I'll need to pin up my hair and get my shawl."

Matt would have liked her to leave it loose against her shoulders. A few minutes ago he could have told her so, as though he were a full-fledged husband asking a favor of his wife.

But talk of the bastard half-breed had changed things between them. He had no real hold on her. She had no real hold on him.

She gathered up the few dishes on the table, setting them at the back of the stove before putting a dollop of stew into an empty tin she'd saved from last night, making sure there was plenty of liquid along with a small portion of meat.

"I'll be just a minute," she said, setting the tin on the table and heading for the bedroom.

When she returned, her thick hair forced into a knot at her nape, the black, knitted fascinator wrapped about her shoulders, she found Matt standing by the door, his gun strapped to his thigh, the dust-colored hat pulled low over his eyes, the fitted buckskin trousers tucked into a pair of tooled leather boots.

He wore the red bandanna, too. At that moment it was impossible to picture him in a three-piece suit. Especially if the waistcoat were made of red velvet.

Flame liked the way he looked, a frontiersman, half-tamed. She liked the fact that she'd managed to tame him last night.

Picking up the tin, she headed straight for him. She'd like to kiss him flat on the lips as she eased past him through the door, but that would be a wifely thing to do. And she didn't want to remind him of what he already very well knew—that she was not truly a wife, even though she'd given a pretty good imitation of one last night.

Matt saw the gleam in her eye, and then the dying of that gleam. He didn't understand Flame, didn't know why she could be a passionate mate part of the time, and an almost spinsterish opponent the next.

But he had no right to ask for an explanation. As long as he could arouse her passions, he'd keep all unrelated questions to himself. Including one about why she was taking a spoonful of stew out of doors.

315

She led him on the path Keet had taken the day before, toward the brush-dotted field that lay to the east of the house, not stopping until they came to the particular shrub that she sought. She dropped to her knees, unmindful of the stain that might mar her yellow gown.

She set the tin beside her and lifted the branches that obscured the object of her quest, whispering tiny little encouragements of *It's all right* and *Nobody's going to hurt you* as she reached into the darkness.

Kneeling beside her, Matt had a hard time not thinking she'd lost her mind. He had an even harder time of it when she sat back on her heels and he saw nestled in her palm the unmistakable fur of a small skunk.

It was one of the most obnoxious pests in this part of the country. And here Flame was, stroking the black and white stripes and offering endearments to a creature that ought to be shot.

From a distance, of course. As great a distance as possible. He doubted this one was old enough to emit much of an odor. But the repulsive ability would be increasing every day.

"It's November, for God's sake," he said, choosing the least combative of several observances that occurred to him. "What's a baby animal doing being born now?" He glanced around at the nearby brush. "And where's the mother? They don't care for anyone interfering with their young."

"You don't like skunks, do you?" Flame asked, her eyes wide and green as summer grass as she looked at him.

"Not particularly."

The truth was he'd been sprayed by one shortly after making his escape back into Texas, and he'd been damned afraid the scent would lead his trackers right to him. He'd carried the repulsive odor on his skin for more than a week.

"This one's helpless, Matt," she said, once again devoting her attention to her ill-chosen pet. "Keet—" She stopped herself, and then saw no reason she shouldn't go on, the damage already having been done. "Keet says freaks are born out here occasionally."

Like half-breed brats.

Matt didn't think the observation would move the conversation along with any peace.

"The mother has obviously abandoned him," Flame went on. "Maybe he was the weakest of the litter, and she didn't think he could survive."

The tiny animal blinked amber eyes up at her, as if to say he most certainly could become a full-grown skunk. She set him on the ground beside the tin. She had to brush the gravy across his mouth before he got the idea that here was sustenance. She watched as he ate.

"I've named him Range."

"You named him?"

Flame caught the displeasure in her husband's voice, but it didn't stop her. "He's black and white. I have a sister who's dark and one who's fair. Raven and Angel. Range. I started to call him Rangel, but that seemed kind of silly, since it isn't even a word."

Matt could have told her something else that was far sillier . . . naming a cursed skunk in the first place.

317

When the animal backed away from the tin, Flame eased him into his hiding place and tried to see that the protecting branches appeared undisturbed.

Matt could have told her that any carnivorous animal worthy of the name could find him if he so chose. Something held him back from uttering his real observances. Flame had already suffered enough encounters with loss. If she returned to find him missing, she could assume he'd either wandered away or his mother had come to reclaim her lost offspring.

They were walking back toward the house, when he spied Sergeant Gibson riding fast across the field toward them. He reined to a halt, his brown mare snorting in displeasure at the sudden stop.

"We're saddling up," the sergeant said. "Injuns been spotted down near that new settlement. Rider just got here with the report."

Matt stared up at the sergeant with a look of cold harshness in his eyes. "Black Eagle?"

"Looks like maybe it is. Colonel says this time he's ridin', too. By the time you get over to the stables, we'll be ready to head out."

Without waiting for a reply, Gibson whipped the mare back in the direction from which he came.

Frozen with fear, Flame grabbed for Matt's sleeve.

He pulled her hand away.

"No telling how long this will take," he said, as he turned his attention to her.

She nodded once, unsure of her ability to speak. Something had closed her throat, had stopped her heart, had left her unable to breathe. A gust of wind stirred the dust and stubble of brown grass around them, bringing in a coolness that hinted of the winter to come.

They stared at one another for a minute.

"I'll need to get my rifle from the house," he said.

It wasn't what she wanted to hear.

"Of course," she said without inflection.

Without another word, he was gone, his long stride taking him across the field toward his home, toward his gun, away from her.

Flame stood still as marble and watched him depart. He'd be gone before she could reach the front porch. The possibility existed that he wouldn't return.

And, in that moment, she saw the way things were with her.

"I love him, Annie," she whispered into the morning breeze, hugging the fascinator tight. "If he doesn't come back to me, what am I going to do?"

Twenty

Green Harbor had been the settlement's name, so called because of the spring-fed grasses carpeting the valley for a brief period each year. Matt had never been impressed with the place. The few times he'd seen the cluster of crudely built structures, everything had had an unfinished look to it, as though something essential was missing, the way sugar would be missed from a cake.

In retrospect it had been a place of beauty.

No grass remained now, not even the brown clumps of November stubble that last week had dotted the countryside. Gone, too, was everything that could have burned—the roofs, the framework of the adobe homes, the rough, wooden structure that had served as meeting place, school, and church for the hundred people who tried to make Green Harbor a civilized place in which to live.

Everything was gutted or reduced to charcoal and ash. At least, thought Matt, whatever had been missing was of little importance now.

A strong, cold wind swept out of the surrounding

hills, over the top of a limestone escarpment a quarter mile to the west, and across the ruins, whipping cinders and dust into the gray afternoon air. Matt sat astride Pigeon in the center of the lone, rutted street, surveying the disaster. Like the buildings, he burned inside.

"Damned miracle so few people were killed," said Colonel Burr, mounted beside him, the wind snapping against his blue wool coat, whipping the feather in his officer's cap, watering his pale blue eyes.

Matt knew the safety of the settlers had nothing to do with miracles. On his last foray to Green Harbor, when he'd seen that both men and women were determined to stay despite the dangers he described, he set up a system of defense that had worked as well as he'd hoped. The system included sentries to watch the outlying areas—especially the waterholes—for the trouble signs he described, rotating on a regular basis to give every man and youth over sixteen a turn to participate, and a predetermined line of retreat if the need arose.

He'd chosen a series of caves halfway up the limestone bluff, with a connecting ledge where they could draw a bead on anyone who tried to attack. He'd taught them how to block the trail to horses, and advised they stock the caves with supplies, especially ammunition for their guns, containers of water, and tins of food, in case they had to hole up for a while.

And he'd told them to practice their retreat, to make sure everyone knew his part if the message to leave were ever delivered. Some had scoffed openly, but others had listened. The listeners won out, and in the early morning attack they'd lost only two men, who stayed behind to hurry up the stragglers and a cocksure youth who rode into the first wave of Apaches, little realizing the finality of death.

"Damned miracle," the colonel repeated. "Expected to find the lot of 'em slaughtered."

Matt nodded in response, then turned his attention to the survivors, who walked in a daze amongst the ruins. Their lives had been spared, but they'd lost their stock and just about everything personal that they'd owned.

He saw no tears, only stunned disbelief and a clinging together to share their strength, friend to friend, parent to child, husband to wife.

For a moment he considered that had it been the Jackson home that was destroyed, Flame might be clinging in such a way to him. He didn't let the thought linger, except to wonder if he would be holding onto his wife with the same purpose, drawing grit from her to do what must be done.

But she wasn't here. And Matt was used to dredging up his own mettle without any help.

"They've headed back toward Mexico," he said, still smarting because the troops had arrived too late for an immediate confrontation.

"We'll never catch them," said Burr with a shake of his head. "Blackie will be safe across the Rio Grande before we're within twenty miles of them."

"Maybe," said Matt. "But we know they've got a few braves injured from the gun battle. And they don't know we're ready to follow in pursuit. Black Eagle will figure he's got at least twenty-four hours head start on us."

Burr scrutinized the rugged terrain that led southward out of the valley, then glanced toward the sky, searching for a sun that was hidden behind a ceiling of thick gray clouds.

"They rode out by mid-morning. It's well past the noon hour, Matt. They could have had as much as six hours traveling time already."

Matt studied the colonel, the full head of gray hair beneath the feathered hat, the pale eyes, the furrows on his face. Burr was showing all of his fifty years, especially in the weariness that he wore on his shoulders along with the epaulets. He had no stomach for a fight.

Matt had enough for the two of them.

"I'm going after them, colonel. I'd like back-up, but if I don't get it, it won't stop me."

"And if I order you to remain with the troops?"

"Then I'll submit my resignation."

The flat tone of his voice, the burning look in his eyes, told Burr he spoke the truth.

"I guess maybe this is as good a chance as any to bring Blackie to justice," the colonel said with a shrug. "Can't have the best damned scout in the Army riding solo on this one."

"I'd like only the fastest riders and the best shots," said Matt. "We're not tracking more than a couple of dozen men. We go after them with the full company, and they'll know we're on the way before we get more than a few miles out of the valley."

"Agreed," said Burr, reining away to bark orders to the officers who were keeping their distance down the road.

A contingent of twenty-four officers and men was

assembled in short order. Matt added three more who came riding up at the moment of departure.

The three Micks were eager to join. They'd heard about the raid as they were headed back to Fort Hard from the brief leave Matt had arranged. News traveled fast in the desolate land, with or without a telegraph.

"That matter we discussed," said Michael Mallon when he'd got Matt aside. "It's taken care of just as you wanted, Mr. Jackson."

Which meant the sheriff was assigning one of his men to watch Nigel Wolfe, a tracker who was—if the sheriff had followed Matt's request—also a stranger to Little Sandy, someone the gambler wouldn't recognize.

"Good," said Matt. "And thanks."

"Glad to be of service," said Brendan Faulkner with a broad smile.

"Thank you for the leave, Mr. Jackson," said Ian Craig. "And for including us on the scouting party today. 'Tis an honor we'll not be letting you regret."

Without glory or ceremony, the tracking party departed before dusk from Green Harbor; its sad residents were augmented by the remaining company of Fort Hard men, who would be helping the most dispirited of them to prepare for the hundred-mile journey to the fort.

Most indicated they planned to stay on.

"Ain't gonna be run off land what's rightfully mine," said one of the settlers, echoing the sentiments of most.

Matt rode ahead of the main body of troops, picking out signs of the Apache departure, noting how

324

the trail wound far to the right, then cut to the left. Too many clues, he thought. Were the Apaches growing careless? Or, more likely, were they trying to throw off anyone who might try to track them down?

Black Eagle should have known Matt would be one of the followers. He should have known Matt could determine where he would cross the Rio Grande. For all his unexpected slash and run ways, the Apache was a predictable sort. Like a faithful dog, he always headed back to the same camp a hundred and fifty miles into the Chihuahuan desert, high in the Sierra Madre, the place that came as close as possible to being his home.

From the few Apaches Matt had managed to capture, he knew of Black Eagle's predilection. And so he wasn't confused by the circuitous path. Instead of following its twists and turns, he directed the troops straight for the river, a route that would carve hours from the search.

Without benefit of a moon, night found them far from their destination. Matt did not want to make a long stop. There would be time enough for sleep after Black Eagle was in shackles . . . or better yet, after he was dead.

They paused only to rest, feed the horses, and grab a quick meal of jerky and hardtack for themselves. The first full stop didn't come until close to noon the next day, when they were in the sanctuary of oak and mesquite a mile from the bend in the river that provided access into Mexico.

All down the line of cavalry, the men sensed Matt's urgency as he moved on ahead. None spoke except to soothe their mounts to silence. The cloud-covered sky cast an appropriate gloom over the scene, marked only by the rustle of leaves and the song of an occasional bird.

In a world of shadow even the Micks kept quiet, their young faces solemn as they waited for Matt to come hurrying back. Maybe he would fire a warning shot, and the colonel would follow with the order to ride. Or maybe the Apaches had crossed into Mexico and were lost to them once again. It was an unpopular idea that communicated itself from man to man.

Unaware of the communal fear shared by those he left behind, Matt rode forward slowly through the brush, right hand resting on his thigh close to the handle of his rifle, close, too, to his holstered gun. Nerves prickled at the back of his neck. Black Eagle was nearby. He didn't bother looking for telltale signs of the Indian's passage. Instinct, honed by hate, was enough.

Besides, far back on their route the Apaches must have ceased leaving markings. This close to Mexico, they'd be thinking they were home free.

Planting one sure hoof after another, the gelding Pigeon worked through the low shrubs and trees, scarcely disturbing a single leaf. Something—someone—stirred behind thick brush a dozen yards to the right. Matt sensed the quick blur. In one fluid motion the rifle slipped from the scabbard into his hands, the trigger cold and hard and taunting beneath his forefinger. He bent low over the gelding's neck. The woods were quiet, still, like a leaden-aired stretch of day before the eruption of a violent storm.

Another movement. Matt and the Indian spied each other across a clearing of wilderness. Rifles belched fire. The Indian fell. In the echoing of the twin explosions came the war cries of the Apaches, and behind them the thunder of the Fort Hard troops riding to respond.

In an instant, the once-still air reverberated with the cacophony of battle as the soldiers spread through the trees, the bellow of their commander scarcely heard. Scattered before them, the Indians turned from their flight with a barrage of rifle fire. Winchester guns meant for other than Apache hands took down too many of the brave troops. In cold fury, Matt rode amongst them, firing, dodging, searching for the savage leader who seemed more than ever an invincible ghost from hell.

The world teemed in confusion before his watchful eyes, until, through the smoke and dust and gloom, he spied his enemy and forgot all else. Black Eagle lurked just beyond the scene of battle, seated on the spotted horse he'd ridden in the assault on the stagecoach, bare-chested, ebony hair bound by a slash of braided, red cloth around his forehead, the scar across his cheek a streak of puckered gray against the hairless slick of copper skin. He returned Matt's stare in solemn silence, as if to say *This is the time.*

Two rifles raised. Two rifles fired in unison, and the roar echoed through the trees, seemingly back to distant Fort Hardaway, bounced against the low-hanging clouds, and hurtled forward all the way across the brown, snakelike sliver of water misnamed the Rio Grande.

* * *

Flame ripped into the sheet, then folded one fragment before placing it on the bed beside a growing stack of bandages. The Army had a supply of regulation dressings, but she feared—when she allowed herself to think—that the number was insufficient.

Her fingers trembled as she worked and she felt hot and hollow inside, but nothing induced her to rest. She had tasks to perform. She must consider nothing else.

Standing in the doorway to the hospital ward, watching his grim-faced worker who seemed far too thin, too determined, too quiet, Doc shook his head. "You keep that up, Flame, and there won't be a sheet left to cover the mattresses."

"We may need more than this," she said, gesturing toward the bandages.

God help us if we do, thought Doc.

"You get anything to eat?" he asked, thinking she looked as pale as the white smock covering her green gown.

"Later," she said, then added, "I promise," lest Doc bring her an immediate bowl of soup.

Hunger was far from her mind. She thought of the settlement survivors who'd come straggling in two days before, herded like lost cattle into the protection of the fort. Only sixteen men, women, and children had asked to leave Green Harbor. They'd been distraught and tired, and a few of them angry, but otherwise they'd been unhurt. Most had ridden double with the soldiers. Despite their weariness, the children stared about them as they came in off the western trail, a glint of adventure in their wide eyes.

As they mingled with the men who greeted them, the soldiers had expressed disgruntlement at not being included on the search to track down the marauders. Flame wished with all her heart and soul that Matt could be here to make the same complaint.

Late in the day she was consulting with the cook in the kitchen, when she heard the arrival of a horse outside the hospital's main entrance. Feet became wings as she hurried to the sound. Standing in the double doorway of the building, gripping the skirt of the white hospital smock, she stared up at the dirt-streaked, exhausted face of Michael Mallon.

"Mrs. Jackson," the Mick said with a ghost of a smile, his horse shifting nervously beneath him, " 'tis a sight for weary eyes I see afore me."

Flame looked past him toward the trail he'd ridden. The empty trail.

"Did no one—"

Her voice failed. Brushing nervously at the unkempt knot of hair at her nape, she swallowed once and tried again. "Did no one else return?"

"They'll be following close behind. I'm to report there will be need for beds and medicine and, aye, need for the chaplain, too."

"Oh," she said in a small voice, understanding what he meant. Men had perished, and more might die from their wounds. She sought the framework of the door for support, but Doc was there to take her hand and offer a helping arm.

Fear wrapped an icy fist around her heart. "And Matt?" she managed.

Mallon shook his head. "Mr. Jackson—"

He had no chance to finish, for a column of battle-weary soldiers appeared in the distant gloom of early evening, drawing all attention. Colonel Burr, his uniform covered in dust, his head held high despite the broken feather in his hat, rode at the head of the line.

The returning company moved toward them with maddening slowness. Burr reined to a halt in front of Doc. "See to the men, Major Kirby. I'll want a report on their condition as soon as possible."

"You'll get it," said Doc, then dispatched one of the hospital orderlies to summon help from the barracks.

Burr rode on past the hospital, past the Jackson home, reining to the right on a path that would take him to the parade ground and on to headquarters. The sun was low on the hills behind him, and it was close to time for taps.

With a mixture of panic and relief, Flame stared at the row of solemn soldiers who followed, some riding double, most slumped in the saddle, a few patched together with crude bandages. Some continued on behind their colonel, others reined aside seeking succor for their own wounds or the wounds of the comrades with whom they rode.

She would help them all—shortly—after she'd done what she had to do.

Walking down the line as if in a dream, she saw the bodies of fallen men lying across saddles, their mounts pulled aside so that they might, when the living were seen to, find a last measure of dignity in their final care. She counted six such men. Her

330

anxieties turned to despair, until she realized that all wore the uniform of the United States Cavalry.

No buckskin shirt or trousers, no tooled leather boots were in sight.

A rush of relief left her weak, and she whispered to God to forgive her, but the relief that Matt had been spared did not go away until she found herself wondering where her husband might be. She thought the worst—of a brave man so damaged he was not returned for burial. Or maybe he'd been taken prisoner by Black Eagle, thrown once again into the captivity that almost destroyed him as a boy, forced into Mexico where the colonel refused to go.

And then she spied the Apache warriors who sat astride their saddleless ponies, wrists bound behind them, their mounts tied in a row. A surrounding contingent of soldiers barred attempts at escape. Robert Anderson's assailant, the scar-faced Black Eagle, was not among the cluster of savages.

It was here at last that she saw Matt. He rode at the rear of the sad parade. A jagged slit rent one sleeve just shy of his shoulder, but otherwise he showed no visible scars of battle.

Flame cried out, but the plaintive wail was lost in the stamp and snort of horses, in the conversation of the men, in the barked orders of Doc Kirby, as he gave full attention to the injured.

For the first time since Michael Mallon had arrived, she drew a deep, although shaky, breath, and once again her heart began to beat. Tears dampened her cheeks. She did not brush them away. She wanted to hurtle herself toward her husband, to drag him from the gelding, to hold him close and tell him what was in her heart.

She wanted to cover his weary face with kisses, and search his body to make certain he truly was without injury. She thought of other things she wanted to do, erotic acts she had never known were possible before the past few weeks.

She wanted him to teach her more.

Instead, she waited until he caught her eye. He stared for a moment, then looked away, bleak resignation carved on his hard-hewn features. She hardly knew if he recognized her as his wife.

Yet she was certain that he had. And he'd been unwilling to leave the guarding of the Indians to the soldiers. Not even to hold her briefly in his arms.

A lump formed in her throat, and more tears threatened to fall, but this time she held them back. When he left a week ago, he hadn't given her a satisfactory goodbye, so why should she expect a different kind of greeting now that he'd returned?

She had work to do, and so, apparently, did he. Stiffly she turned toward the hospital. One of the injured turned out to be Brendan Faulkner, the Mick who'd often sworn his love for her. An Apache bullet had dug a groove along the inside of his thigh.

"Don't worry, lass," he assured her, as she saw him carried to one of the ward beds. "It missed the vital part."

She knew to which organ of his body he referred.

"I want your soothing hands upon me," he said, as she cut aside the trousers to expose the wound.

"Doc will do the actual tending," she informed him, "but I'll do the dressing, if you'd like."

He grimaced in pain, then managed a brave smile. "Aye, I'd like. 'Twill make me rejoice I took the shot."

"You're full of blarney," she said, then added with complete sincerity, "I'm glad you are."

How much she wanted her husband to come to her and say something of the same kind. Even if he lied. She would not care. Anything was better than rejection. Anything.

She glanced around the ward at the fast-filling beds, and she listened to the groans of men who were at last giving in to pain. Rolling back the sleeves of her smock and her gown, she brushed an errant wisp of hair from her face.

"I've got work to do, Annie," she said. "Too much to stand here feeling sorry for myself."

Twenty-one

Matt had wanted to forget the prisoners and ride right up to Flame, to pull her up with him onto the gelding, to hold her close and smell the scent of roses on her soft skin. Maybe roses would erase the stench of blood and failure that filled his nostrils. Maybe the feel of a woman's arms around his neck and a woman's body pressed to his would mute the memories of defeat.

Especially Flame's arms and Flame's body. His wife was well named. Infuriating or arousing, either way she could heat him when he thought he'd never be warm again.

They'd captured most of the Apaches, all but two of the braves and their leader. Once again, Black Eagle had gotten away. Matt's bullet had caught him in the shoulder, a better hit than the returning fire that inflicted only a tear in his buckskin sleeve.

He drew little pleasure from the memory of his enemy's spurting blood. Through the years he'd injured Black Eagle three times—in the face, the arm, and now the shoulder. It seemed as though he were carving away at the devil, working toward his evil heart.

For Matt, the legions of marauding savages from Texas to Arizona could be captured, yet if one in particular got away, he would view his battles as ending in failure. But it didn't have to be this way.

When the Apaches were safely locked in the stockade and Pigeon turned over to a soldier at the stable, Matt headed for the headquarters building. Lieutenant Abraham Lilly, clean-shaven and alert, stopped him at the colonel's door.

"Sorry I couldn't have joined you, Mr. Jackson," the officer said, then added almost shamefacedly, "A bad leg held me back."

"If I recall right," said Matt, pulling off his hat and wiping a sleeve across his forehead, "one of your superior officers used much the same excuse the last time the Apaches were on the prowl."

Stung, Lilly snapped to attention. "That would be Captain Davis. Not at all the same thing," he said angrily. "I'd have been right behind the colonel, except that Doctor Kirby gave me something to make me sleep. I didn't know about the trouble until the patrol was a day on the trail."

Matt studied the upright young officer and liked what he saw. "Next time I'll make certain you get the message sooner," he said.

"I'll make certain I'm awake to receive it," Lilly returned. He glanced toward the commanding officer's closed door.

"Colonel Burr left word he was not to be disturbed, unless it's news from the hospital." He picked up a stack of papers on his desk. "I need to summon an orderly to get this information to the barracks. I'll have to depend on your promise that you'll wait until I return."

Matt had always figured the lieutenant as a stickler for going by the rules. More and more, he liked the man.

"You can depend upon me to do what's necessary," he said.

Lilly was barely out the headquarters door before Matt had entered the colonel's forbidden sanctum and planted himself in front of the colonel's desk.

"We've got to ride into Mexico and bring him back," he said. "Treaties be damned."

Burr glanced up wearily and rubbed at his pale eyes. The lower part of his face was covered by gray stubble that looked like hairs shed from his moustache. He looked a hundred years old. "How did you get in here? Oh, never mind. There's nothing you can count on anymore. Not even the adjutant. I swear, Matt, it's time I was getting out."

"Don't change the subject. We're talking about Mexico."

Burr set down his quill pen and shifted back in his chair. "No, *you're* talking about Mexico. Blackie's a broken man. You'd know it, if you were thinking clearly. We got most of his braves today and sent him flapping across the river like an injured bird. He can't fly anymore. You know it as well as I. Not that there won't be others to take his place. Victorio is still raising hell, and there's this Geronimo to contend with. A report out of Washington claims he may be leaving Arizona and heading this way."

"Victorio and Geronimo be damned! Black

Eagle's the bastard who's causing us the most misery."

"Put that in the past tense. I've been serving out here since the Texas forts reopened after the war. I know what I'm talking about."

Matt saw his protest was hopeless, just as it had been at the scene of battle, when he'd wanted to track down Black Eagle no matter where his trail led. But there had been so many injured soldiers, and so many captured Apaches that Matt hadn't wanted to risk losing. Once again the thing he most wanted in the world had eluded him.

Studying the colonel's bristled, lined face, he came to a decision.

"Did you notice the guns they were using?"

Burr nodded once, and the weariness on his pale face hardened to anger. "Winchesters. Army issue. Someone's dealing with the Apaches. May they burn in hell."

"Remember the attack on the stagecoach? They were using them there, too."

Burr's eyes narrowed. "Why didn't you say something? Afraid maybe I already knew it?"

"It could have been that way. I didn't want to take the chance and let you know I was investigating."

Another time, Burr might have flown into a rage. Not now, not after a week on the trail, not after all that he and Matt had gone through.

"What made you change your mind tonight?" he asked.

"I saw you in battle. You are a brave man, colonel. And not stupid. You wouldn't put yourself or the

337

troops in needless danger, not even to turn a neat profit on an illegal sale."

The colonel grimaced. "Now there's a line that ought to go on my tombstone. What about this investigation of yours? Turn up anything?"

"Suspicions mostly. I did hear rumors about one of the wagon drivers who brings supplies up from the coast. He's been heard bragging in some of the taverns down toward the coast, about how he takes in more than just Army pay. Made me think of the sutler."

"Asa Underwood? You think the guns are being passed through him?"

"The driver takes supplies from the ships and travels overland directly to the store, without anyone between there and here checking what he's carrying. Wouldn't be hard to unload more than just flour and tinned beef."

"Wouldn't be hard except for one thing. I've been conducting a little investigation of my own. With the help of my adjutant. Lieutenant Lilly's a good man, even if he's not worth a plug of tobacco as a guard. He's been checking the invoices against the goods Underwood puts up for sale. Not nearly enough go on the shelves. Lilly figures he's skimming staples, and selling them for inflated prices to some of the townsfolk. Wouldn't be the first time a sutler got caught padding his pockets like that."

"And you don't think he'd be running guns as well?"

"Wouldn't put it past him. But we've been watching for some time. It's not a detail Lilly would miss."

Matt tended to agree, and with reluctance he

338

crossed Asa Underwood off his shrinking list of suspects.

The colonel glanced at the report he'd begun to write, then back up at Matt. "You look dead on your feet. Dead as I feel. Get on out of here and back to that fine wife of yours." He fell silent for a moment, his thoughts turned inward. "Man ought to appreciate a good woman. They're damned few and far between."

Sometime past midnight, after being ordered home by Doc, Flame found Matt lying facedown across the bed, still in his clothes, his booted feet dangling off one side of the mattress, his arms hanging limply off the other.

For one terrorized moment she didn't think he was breathing. And then she heard a soft, sonorous snore, muffled in part by the quilt on which he lay. She had never heard a more beautiful sound.

He looked so tired, so innocent, so dear lying there, that she forgot the distance he'd kept between them only a few hours ago. How could she feel resentment, when love for him filled all the corners of her heart?

She'd heard from several of the soldiers how he'd narrowly missed his chance to bring down his old nemesis . . . how he'd ranted in frustration as the fury of a continuing battle kept him from abandoning the men and following the wounded Black Eagle across the Rio Grande.

She knew how close to mad desperation he must have come.

Dear, tenacious Matt. Courageous Matt. Infuriating Matt. He was all those things and more.

Setting the lamp from the main room just outside the doorway, she stood in the muted light and drank in the sight of him. All the weariness she'd carried from the hospital seemed to lift from her shoulders, and she was struck with a spurt of energy she hadn't suspected possible at this late hour and after such a day and night. Stripping down to her chemise and petticoat, she turned her hand to undressing him.

The boots proved difficult, especially since she didn't want to awaken him, but as exhausted as he was, he did little more than change the pattern of his breathing as she toiled. Somehow she managed shirt and trousers and undergarments. She worked slowly, steadily, until he was naked, not allowing herself the luxury of really looking at him, intent only upon making him comfortable.

As she worked, she smiled to herself, thinking how Matt would be surprised that he had managed to sleep through everything. He might even ask for a repeat of the undressing, so that he could observe her methods while in a conscious state. And Flame just might comply.

Sitting beside him, her hip close to his, she felt an urge to do more. She heated water from the pitcher on the bureau, gathered towels and rags, and returned to the bed, where she proceeded to bathe him in long, languorous strokes. She was his wife, she told herself, and she had the right.

She also had the right—more, the obligation—to observe him closely, to make sure he had not been injured in any way that he might be inclined to keep secret. She didn't find a single flaw, a single impediment. Even in a relaxed state, Matthew Jackson was all long, lean muscle and artful sprinklings of body hair, some of which was concentrated in a few very special areas. He was, in truth, a perfect specimen of manhood. She'd been looking at injured and ailing soldiers all evening, and this time she could say from experienced observation that she was right.

She felt a tingle of delicious evil as she turned him to his back and wiped the rag softly over his neck and chest, his stomach, and down to his private parts. He stirred and grew erect. With great forbearance she abandoned her play. He was fatigued, and she was beastly to take advantage of him this way.

A cold wind rattled the windowpanes, and she saw a shiver ripple through him. Chastising herself, she worked the quilt free and eased it over the length of his body right up to his chin. Not good enough, she thought. She couldn't let him catch a chill. Stripping away her underclothes, she crawled beneath the cover and snuggled her naked body close against his side, wrapping her arms around him and holding him close.

She jumped when he shifted and wrapped his arms around her.

"You're awake," she said in surprise.

"Yeah," he said, running his fingers down her arm.

"For how long?"

"Long enough."

Guiltily she said, "You should have stopped me."

"I'm a little tired, Flame. Not crazy."

"But you need your rest."

"I need a lot of things."

She liked the huskiness in his voice.

His hand drifted to her face, and he lifted her chin so that he could look into her eyes.

"That was a nice thing for you to do. The cot's still folded up by the fire. You could have left me alone and slept out there."

She lowered her lids lest he see, even in the dim light, what her expression must surely reveal about her heart.

"And give up rights to the bed? You don't know me very well."

Matt had to agree. He felt a moment's displeasure, then told himself he was being a fool. Since the unfortunate circumstances under which they had met, she had done more for him than any woman before her, and he was irritated because he couldn't figure out why. The truth was she was making the best of a difficult situation. He ought to leave it at that.

He leaned close and brushed his lips against hers. She moaned softly. All the frustrations, the bitterness, the weariness of the past days dissolved in the warmth of that moan.

"I need you, Flame," he whispered into her parted lips.

"Oh, Matt—" She broke off, alarmed by what she almost said. "I need you, too," she finished.

Matt lost control, plundering her mouth with his tongue, running rough hands over her torso, massaging her breasts with his palms, then teasing the tips with his thumbs. He kissed her face, her throat, her valleys and curves, suckling at the nipples, then lowering his lips to her concave abdomen, licking the navel, tickling the pubic hair with soft blows of air.

She protested weakly when he thrust her thighs apart and continued his downward pursuit, letting his tongue part the precious folds of skin until the small, pulsating nub of her sex was exposed.

"Matt," she cried out, but as his tongue continued its relentless teasing, the cry turned to soft mewings that urged him on. She came against his lips, her body writhing in frenzied ecstasy. He shifted upward to lie beside her and hold her in his arms as the pulsings slowly subsided. And then he touched her again, this time with his fingers.

"You can do it," he said when she reached for his wrist to pull his hand away. "It'll feel even better, too."

Flame didn't see how that was possible.

"I'm tender," she whispered, embarrassed to admit such an intimate detail of her condition, yet realizing how absurd it was to be embarrassed now by anything that she and Matt did to one another.

He lightened his touch, but he didn't stop. And soon she didn't want him to. She reached for his erection and gave him an equally thorough massage. He didn't take it for long. Parting her legs once again, he settled himself on top of her and thrust deep inside her chamber of wet, tight heat. He shared her frenzy, and just when he thought he would go mad, he shared her ecstasy as well, spilling his seed inside her as spasms of unparalleled intensity racked them both.

Flame felt the hot liquid fill her, and she clung to Matt with all her strength, as if holding him this way would make her body heal, would make it provide a place for the seed to settle and grow.

As the tentacles of passion slowly released them, he held her just as tightly, and she knew that he, too, wanted more than just the sex. He wanted release from the tormenting memories of his failed hunt. She longed to tell him he was wrong in his pursuits. She longed to tell him that he wanted death, while she wanted the creation of a new life.

But, of course, she couldn't say a word. Her sorrow was her secret. To put it into spoken words would only draw his pity, and maybe his suspicion that she was looking for a way to trap him into a permanent alliance, the way he'd once accused her of trapping Robert.

I love you, Matt. It was something else she had to keep to herself.

Nestled beside him, listening as his breathing grew regular and the low snore returned, she welcomed the weariness that would bring her, too, to sleep. In sleep she might dream, but she could not think.

When she awoke, she lay in bed alone. The brightness of the day outside the window told her it was late. Doc needed her this morning, and so did the wounded soldiers. Her conscience struck her that she could be so indolent.

She dressed hurriedly in the lavender skirt and blouse, gulped down a quick cup of the coffee that Matt had left on the stove, and hurried out the front door. Sounds of angry voices brought her to a halt. They came from just around the corner of the house on the side away from the hospital. She recognized the shrill tones of Melody Burr and, after a moment, the military-brisk inflection of Lt. Abraham Lilly.

"You're the stupidest man I've ever met," Melody was saying.

Flame had never heard the young woman speak so stridently.

"You go too far, Miss Burr," Lilly protested.

"I can go a lot farther, Lieutenant Lilly. You don't know me very well."

"Indeed," he threw back right away, "I'm beginning to think I don't know you at all."

"At least we agree on one thing."

"What I don't understand," Lilly continued as if she hadn't spoken, "is how the daughter of a fine military man like the colonel can find it wrong for a soldier to want to go into battle."

"Maybe the daughter of a fine military man realizes how dangerous such a mission can be. To accept an order into conflict is one thing. To mourn because it was missed is something else entirely."

"I am not mourning, as you so inaccurately put it."

"Of course, you are. When I saw you just now leaving the ward, I thought maybe your closest friend had passed on. And then I find it's because you're jealous of the wounded. As though it would be more noble to have lost an arm or a leg or even been winged ever so slightly, instead of remaining behind like any sensible man would prefer."

Melody paused, and Flame could imagine her drawing breath after the long harangue. Conscience said she ought to get away from the porch and leave the couple to their argument. But she couldn't forget the way Melody had looked at the lieutenant when he'd been sleeping in a hospital bed. And she couldn't forget that here was a woman who had openly—and lewdly—set her sights on Matt. Both re-membrances created a curiosity she couldn't ignore.

"I am beginning to think," said Lilly, with more than a hint of acerbity in his voice, "that you would not recognize a sensible man if he were quartered in your own home."

"Hell's fire, you're not telling me you're moving in, are you? And don't look at me like that. I'll use whatever language I want."

"I wouldn't consider telling you anything, Miss Burr, since you seem to have developed a hearing problem this morning. You have misinterpreted everything I said."

"Misinterpreted, have I? When a man makes a claim like that, it usually means a woman's got him figured out."

"And how much do you know of what men say?"

The sharp clap of flesh striking flesh drifted around the corner, and Flame realized that Melody had slapped the honorable young lieutenant.

"Please," Lilly said stiffly after a moment of silence, "do not bother to answer. It was an ungentlemanly question, and I apologize for the asking. I think it best if I bid you good day."

Flame could picture him bowing sharply and taking his leave, something she should have done the moment she heard the voices. She felt suddenly ashamed that she had intruded herself into what was a very private conversation, even if she got away undetected.

Melody came around the side of the house and spied her on the porch.

The two women looked at one another, Melody in her blue velvet gown and matching feathered hat, Flame in a simple lavender gown.

"I'm sorry—" Flame began, not quite sure what she was sorry for, but the girl looked so miserable with her full lips trembling and her blue eyes filled with tears, that an apology was the first thing that came to mind.

Melody covered her face with her hands and gave in to a bout of sobbing that rent Flame's already sore heart. Forgetting all the suggestive comments the young woman had made toward Matt, forgetting that she had shifted Robert Anderson's affections from his hometown-intended to her very available self, forgetting everything that had been unlikable about Melody, Flame hurried down the steps and took her in her arms.

Melody did not try to pull away. Instead, she rested her head on Flame's shoulder and cried until she had no more tears to shed. Flame discovered that the giving of comfort brought a responding kind of comfort in return.

At last the girl backed away and dabbed at her face with a handkerchief that soon became soaked. Flame found a replacement in a pocket of her skirt. The girl wiped beneath her eyes, blew her nose, and looked up to acknowledge her consoler, her once-neat, yellow sausage curls in disarray, her face splotched with red.

"He thinks I'm a tramp," she said without prelude, her voice shaky. She blinked away another rush

347

of tears. "And he's right. Lieutenant Abraham Lilly would be a good judge of such matters. Even his damned name is pure."

"You're too harsh on yourself," said Flame, unsure if she really believed what she said.

"No, I'm not. I'm my father's daughter, that's what I am." She threw her head back proudly and cast defiant eyes from under the brim of her tilted bonnet. "Have you heard he keeps a mistress? I'm not supposed to know anything about it, but I do. Mother knows it, too, but she pretends otherwise. Oh, we're a fine family, we are."

Flame touched the girl's arm. "Maybe they've made their peace with one another. Maybe"—she floundered for a moment, not knowing just what she meant to say, only that somehow she must say something—"maybe they've given each other all that they can give."

Melody seemed not to hear. "Did you know I once had a little brother? Oh, he was a charmer. Died in a riding accident when he was ten." She spoke rapidly, as though once she'd begun a confession of her troubles, she had to hurry through their catalogue before she changed her mind.

"It broke my mother's heart," she said. "She's not been the same since. Daddy threw himself into the Army, worked his way to command. He didn't have much time for us. But he found time for the Widow Rowena Latrobe."

She made the name sound like an obscenity.

"I'm like my Daddy, you know," she went on. "We both need something, we go out and get it. I guess maybe I should have been born the boy." Her voice almost broke.

"Oh, curses," she muttered, "listen to me carry on. You've got other things to worry about besides my stupid story. It's just that I hadn't ever told anyone, and here you were."

Flame listened in silence, realizing she could not judge the girl. How would she have felt if Thomas Chadwick ever once betrayed his loving wife Anne? She could not imagine the pain it would have brought.

"Anytime you want to talk, I'll be close by."

Melody shrugged, and her red-rimmed eyes cast nervously about. "I've said it all, I guess. Too much."

Flame looked toward the corner of the house. "You don't care for the Army life, do you?"

"What makes you say that?"

"You didn't want the lieutenant to fight."

"No," Melody answered, "I didn't want him to fight. Don't tell me you felt differently about Matt when he rode out of here."

"No," Flame said slowly, "I didn't feel differently about Matt."

Melody looked suddenly wiser and older, too, as she glanced up at Flame. "We women don't look at things the same way as men, do we?"

Flame thought of a hundred arguments she'd had with her husband, beginning the day of their strange marriage and coming right down to the arrival of Keet. "No," she said softly, speaking more to herself than Melody, "we don't look at things the same way at all."

"You love him, don't you? Mother and some of

the other women say there's something suspicious about the quick way you two got married, and I thought so, too. At least at first. But I can see now the way you feel about him. Does he know?"

As much as Flame felt sympathy and understanding for the girl, she couldn't bring herself to confess the secrets of her heart.

"What about Lieutenant Lilly?" she asked. "I suspect you have some strong feelings for him."

"Little he cares."

"He might, if you let him know. He didn't seem uninterested in your opinions a few minutes ago."

"He may not have been uninterested, but he certainly didn't like the way I expressed them. And there are other things about me that he didn't care for, either. Things that are perfectly acceptable in a man."

Melody's sigh seemed to come from her toes. "I guess the problem is men and women don't understand one another. And they won't, not ever, not in a million years."

Flame might have smiled at the exaggeration, but along with the arguments, she remembered too well all the ways Matt had misunderstood her.

"You're right," she said. "I don't believe they will, not in a million years."

Twenty-two

"Hello, Keet. I haven't seen you around the last few days."

Without waiting for a response, Flame knelt in the dirt and grass beside the boy, and set a small tin of meat and another of water on the ground in front of them. Both stared into the thick brush sheltering the den of the baby skunk called Range. It was late afternoon, time for the animal to venture out in his nightly forage for food.

Flame was still proud of the name she'd selected for him. She'd written Raven and Angel about having a skunk as a namesake, but had yet to receive a reply.

She stole a glance at her companion. Despite the harsh bite of cold in the December air, he was, as usual, barefoot. At least, she thought, he was wearing a shirt, even if it was a faded, threadbare cotton whose sleeves came two inches short of his wrists.

"Where have you been?" she asked, pulling the fascinator tightly around her shoulders.

"Away. Didn't want my arse whipped," Keet said matter-of-factly.

"Why would it be whipped?" said Flame just as calmly, determined not to be shocked by anything he said.

He glanced sideways with a condescending shake of his head. "The soldiers just got back from killing Apaches. Figured they'd want to go right on killing."

He didn't sound in the least afraid.

"But you're only half-Indian, and besides, you're just a child. Oh, sorry. But you certainly aren't an adult."

Keet picked up a rock and sent it skittering over the surface of the stubble-covered ground. "Shit, they don't care about nothing like that. I'm Injun, don't matter who my ma was, or how long I've been hanging around."

Flame fought an urge to give him an affectionate pat. Coming from a family of girls and an Irish father—huggers every one except maybe for Raven—she didn't know much about young boys, but she knew this one didn't care for being touched.

"You haven't had any trouble gathering metal out on the firing range, have you?"

"Not as long as I work at night. When there's a shortage of bullets, no one bothers about where they come from. What with all the shooting, there'll be a shortage now."

Flame looked away to gather her composure. The soldiers had been shooting at a band of warriors who might very well be Keet's kin, and he talked calmly about giving them ammunition to shoot at more.

"You're a practical boy, Keet." And brave and tough and, to Flame's way of thinking, totally lovable.

He cocked a dark brown eye at her. "What's that mean?"

"It means you look at things the way they are, and manage them the best that you can."

Keet's face twisted in thought. "Don't everybody do that?"

"No, not everybody."

Not me, for instance.

If Flame were looking at things the way they were, she wouldn't be staying on at Fort Hardaway, working long hours at the hospital, coming home to two cold and empty rooms, stoking the fire and preparing supper, most evenings for just herself, then after working on a few gifts to send home, falling into bed, and turning to her husband when he finally tromped in, throwing herself into his arms for frenzied lovemaking that sometimes went on half the night.

And she wouldn't let him turn silently from her each night, wouldn't listen to the sounds he made in his sleep, wouldn't suffer the leaden heart that came with unrequited love.

If she were practical, she wouldn't do any of these things. But no one had ever called Flame practical. Impetuous, fun-loving, caring, even clever at times, and certainly foolish at others. There were those who thought she looked presentable. She would have to add passionate to the list, and shameless, too.

But practical? Never.

She looked about her . . . at the hills turned purple by the setting sun, at the dark windows of the adobe house far to her left, at the stretch of rocky, open field, and the distant squat stone buildings to her right and behind her. Very little green except for some live oaks that never seemed to shed their leaves. Everything looked dry and dying, without a sign of life, but she knew that was deceiving. There were rattlesnakes and copperheads, horned toads and wild boar, and hawks that circled overhead in a never-ending search for carrion.

It was a harsh land that required a harsh people to settle it. People like Matt and, yes, even Keet.

Not someone like Flame, who'd been raised in the lush, green, humid land of coastal Georgia. She liked her air thick and sweet and damp, not dry and searing and dust-laden. She longed to run through a field of waist-high summer grasses, to breathe in the heavy scent of magnolias, to see a riverbank covered in ferns, instead of a creek bank jagged with stones.

She longed for her mother's flower garden. That's why she wore attar of roses as her scent. It reminded her of home.

So why was she staying here, when there was really nothing to keep her?

The answer came in one word. Matt.

He was expecting her to leave. She could see it in the way he stared at her on the few occasions he returned home before she'd gone to bed. When he entered through the front door, he always looked a little surprised to find her there, as though she might have slipped away during the day.

She'd like to believe he looked relieved to see her, maybe even a little glad, but that was her imagination telling her what she wanted to view as fact. He'd been back a week from the trek to protect Green Harbor. Not once had a word been said about how it was time to end their marriage, but she knew it had to be on his mind.

She would have told him that she couldn't leave the hospital, as long as there were wounded who needed her care. And that would have been the truth, although not the full disclosure of her motivations. The major reason she didn't even mention the subject was that she couldn't bring herself to tell him goodbye. Maybe another few days or weeks in his arms would be enough to send her on her way. Maybe she could love him so much that she would get her fill of sex and never, ever want to lie with him again.

She knew beyond doubt that she would never want to lie with any other man.

She stirred from her reverie and found Keet watching her with wide, unhappy eyes.

"What's wrong?" she asked.

He looked away, as if embarrassed he'd been caught at something bad.

"Nothing."

"I don't think it's nothing. Friends confide in friends. You are my friend, aren't you?"

He rubbed at his nose, then pitched another stone. "It's just that sometimes you go far away, like

355

maybe you was thinking of other places you'd like to be."

"Sometimes I'm remembering my family," she said, and he nodded. She'd already told him about the Chadwick clan. "I do miss them, but there's a stagecoach that leaves here every two weeks. You haven't seen me get on it, have you?"

"Nope," he said, shrugging as though to say he didn't care what she did.

"I'm not claiming that I won't. Just not anytime soon."

It was then that she made up her mind. She'd stay until after Christmas, which was two weeks away, and then into the first days of the new year, catching the first stagecoach that came along. There was one going through on Christmas Eve, but that seemed too soon to leave . . . too soon to even contemplate.

She'd stay into 1877. That is, if matters didn't bubble up before then and force an earlier departure. Matters like Matt's telling her to pack and get the hell out of his life.

Oh, dear, she thought, she was beginning to think in the terms of her husband and Keet.

And why should Matt be so eager to see her go? She cleaned for him and cooked for him, and gave him a good time in bed. He was always accepting where dinner and sex were concerned. And what did she get in return? An uncommunicative husband who kept himself apart, until it was time to satisfy a few of his hungers.

She knew he was questioning the prisoners, visiting the wounded, seeing to the burial of the dead. She knew, too, he was going into town from time to time to take care of business. Army business, he said, that he couldn't talk about. She was trying very hard to believe he told the truth.

"You're doing it again."

Flame looked at Keet. "Doing what?"

"Going away."

She smiled and ruffled his hair. "Sorry," she said, glad that he didn't jerk away.

Something moved beneath the shrub.

"Oh, shit, here he comes," said Keet.

"You don't want to see Range? I thought that's why you were here."

"I ain't talking about the skunk. Least not the four-legged kind."

Flame glanced over her left shoulder and saw Matt's long legs covering the ground fast, his boots kicking up dust as he walked. His hat was pulled too low on his forehead for her to see his eyes, but he communicated determination by the pace of his stride.

"Oh," she said, her heart taking a little leap.

She looked back to Keet, but he was gone, his thin-limbed, dark figure scurrying toward the stand of trees that stood at the edge of the fort.

Before she could rise, Matt stood beside her, and she settled weakly back on her knees.

He thumbed the hat to the back of his head and stared down at his wife. "What's the half-breed doing here?"

She looked up the long length of Matt, trying not to show how much she liked the view—all except the light of displeasure in his eyes. "Keet's helping me with Range."

357

"Range?"

"You know, the skunk."

Just then, as if recognizing his name, the small, black animal with the curious white striping on his back emerged from his sanctuary, amber eyes blinking, a small, active nose sniffing the air as he waddled into view. He headed straight for the tins.

Flame stroked his back.

"Goddamn it, get away," said Matt, taking a half-dozen steps backwards, and then a second half-dozen for good measure, remembering too well his youthful encounter with another one of the beasts.

Enjoying her husband's retreat, Flame smiled sweetly at him. "Who are you talking to, me or Range?"

"Don't fool around with me, Flame. Get on back to the house before something happens."

No mistake about his tone, she thought. He was laying down orders.

"So that you can fool around with me?" she asked.

Flame had no idea why she said what she did. She didn't even know she was thinking it.

Flame and Matt stared at one another. For a moment the anger was gone from his eyes. "If that's what you want," he said.

It was exactly what she wanted, but something of her father's Irish temper and a great deal of his stubbornness kept her from letting him know. A man who didn't bother to come home in the daylight forfeited his right to rule. Any of the Chadwick women—with the possible exception of Angel— would have agreed.

She returned her attention to Range, stroking

him once again. "When I'm through here. Before long, he'll be old enough to wander off and find another den that's bigger. That's what Keet says."

Little did Flame know she chose the wrong time to be difficult. Matt had just returned from Little Sandy, where he'd been talking to the deputy assigned to follow Nigel Wolfe. Except for some nasty suspicions about a boy from town who paid visits to the gambler's room, he hadn't turned up anything to report.

And now here was his wife, in the green gown that matched her eyes, her gold red hair in its usual half-done knot, giving her affections to a damned skunk. It was bad enough that every man on the fort had been telling him what a wonderful woman he was married to. So sweet, so hardworking, so kind.

Saint Flame, the Micks had taken to calling her. Especially since they'd brought the barracks cook over to talk with her about seasoning up his meals.

Saint Flame wasn't acting so saintly now.

"You come with me, or you won't find me waiting for you later," he said.

She sat back, hands on hips. "And what's that supposed to mean?"

"Simple enough. It means I won't be home."

"And I imagine that's supposed to break my heart. Like I'd miss the conversations we have in front of the fire. Like taking care of supper and eating alone and cleaning up by myself would be different from most other nights of the week. Is *that* what it means?"

"You make your life sound pretty miserable. I hadn't heard you complain."

"And when should I do this complaining? When you're climbing naked into bed? I don't imagine you'd listen to much I had to say."

"You got anything you want to criticize, you go right ahead and do it whether or not I'm naked."

"I'll do just that. When you're naked, I'll probably think of several additional complaints."

Flame knew their voices were rising in anger, but they were out in the field and she didn't think anyone could hear.

She forgot about Range.

And so did Matt, who didn't see the animal abandon his food and start waddling his way . . . didn't see him until he was a couple of inches from Matt's foot, turning his backside toward him, emitting a thin stream of liquid that scored a direct hit on his trouser leg. It wasn't much of a shot, Range still being in his infancy, but it had an immediate and violent effect.

Matt let out a yell and ran toward the house, his hat falling into the dust. He didn't bother to retrieve it. Flame bounded to her feet and scurried backward in the opposite direction, keeping herself out of range of the odor that fouled the air. From a distance she watched a very unconcerned skunk waddle back to his dinner and continue eating.

Her defender, she thought, unable to hide a smile. He'd made Matt cease badgering her. Maybe he wasn't a knight in shiny armor, but neither was he without a weapon. A very effective one, it turned out. She didn't know he was old enough.

She fanned the air with her hand. She'd been

wanting a change in the odors on the air, but roses and magnolias had been uppermost in her mind.

Poor Matt. It was only mildly unpleasant for her. What must it be for him?

She looked at him from a distance of several dozen yards, grateful the wind was at her back instead of his. He glared back with such anger in his eyes that she could see it even from afar. As much as she loved him, she wanted to laugh at him, too. If he hadn't been so sharp with her, if he hadn't taken to ordering her about, Range would have kept on eating.

Matt's trouble was he didn't know what was good for him. And the best thing for her husband was his wife.

"Don't go in the house," she called out. "Go down to the creek where the laundresses work. Take your clothes off, and I'll be there in a minute."

"Like hell," he shouted back.

"There's no one there now. I'll get some soap and a scrub brush, and some clean clothes for you. Be sensible, Matt. You don't have any choice."

He thought over her words, then called back, not quite so fiercely, "You want me naked, do you?"

"I want you clean. And don't get any ideas. This is hardly the time to be thinking of—"

She fell silent. What it was, was hardly the time to be shouting about such personal matters across the field. No one could have heard the conversation when they were closer together, but by now half the patients in the hospital—at least those who could walk—must be crowded outside to hear the Jacksons argue.

And if Doc didn't watch them, they'd be hobbling toward the creek to get a good seat for the second act.

Hurrying toward the distant creek, as if he could outrun the smell he carried on him, Matt thought of a hundred ways to get back at Flame, most of which involved violence to her person. He'd never been an even-tempered man, but he'd always kept his anger under control. Not any longer. Sometime in early October, 1876—he hadn't known the exact date—all that had changed.

Saint Flame, was she? Not to the man who knew her best.

She was actually enjoying the situation. He thought of only one thing: killing that enjoyment. He'd feel better when she was as miserable as he.

Little Sandy Creek ran on a jagged north and south path at the western edge of Fort Hard, a quarter mile from the site of Matt's disaster. The area Matt was heading for was bordered by thick shrubs on the fort side, and on the other by a series of large, flat rocks, resembling dinner plates for a race of giants. Here the creek itself formed a pool four feet deep in the center, and a dozen feet wide. During the day laundresses waded across upstream shallows, trudged around a dogleg bend, and came down on the far bank to stand in the water that lapped the rocks, using them as washboards for their work.

Unless someone descended from the limestone cliff that rose a short distance away, the pool was isolated from view. Which suited Matt just fine. He didn't want any witnesses for the mayhem he was contemplating. He didn't think his wife's shrieks would carry back to the fort.

And if they did, he doubted that even to save her, some foolhardy hero would follow the malodorous trail he laid. Bravery could take a man only so far.

Following the route of the laundresses, he made his way to the rocks, stripped, and tossed his clothes into a basin of creek water caught in an indentation in the rocks. Next he pulled his boots back on, as protection from rough ground and from snakes that might crawl out to investigate the proceedings. He contemplated strapping the holster and gun around his middle, then decided he looked foolish enough in the tooled leather boots.

Any villains that managed to creep up on him would have to take their chances with his bare-fisted fury.

And that included his wife.

He wanted to distance himself from the befouled garments, but he'd forgotten something in the trousers pocket. Gingerly he moved in on them again, found that what he was after was still dry in its pouch, and made a very careful journey up the sloping ground to a shallow cave a dozen yards up the side of the limestone cliff, gathering twigs and small logs as he went.

The cold air didn't bother him, nor, at this point, did the indignity. What did rankle was the smell that had burrowed its way into his pores. And the memory of Flame stifling a laugh.

If all went as planned, he'd be doing a little stifling of his own.

Unsure as to the ventilation of the cave, he laid the wood at the entrance and used the matches he'd rescued from his trousers—matches that bore a faint, foul memento of the evening's assault—to light a fire. Selecting a spot out of its light but not out of its heat, he sat, then rose again, cursed the rocky ground, and squatted back down on his haunches to wait for Flame.

Night was coming on fast, its long shadows devouring the last pale streaks of day. She didn't take long to get under way. He saw her lantern swinging as she walked across the flat, hard ground toward the creek. He imagined she could see the fire. She would wonder what was going on. He'd let her know soon enough.

When she disappeared into the trees on the far bank, he descended from his perch to greet her. He stood in the dark on one of the massive rocks close to the cold, still pool, feet apart, and listened to her splash across the shallow creek bed around the bend, spied the lantern light as she strode down the bank toward him, and, best of all, he saw the look of astonishment on her face when she picked out his unorthodox figure in the dark.

"Welcome, wife," he said evenly.

"Oh," she said, almost dropping her bulky bundle of supplies onto the damp bank. She'd been picturing Matt cowering behind a shrub, waiting impatiently for her arrival, and, of course, cursing the day she had ever crossed his path.

That wasn't the picture he presented at all. She should have realized how he would be.

From the moment he stalked away from her, she'd had misgivings about her offer of help. Not because he didn't need or deserve whatever she could do for him, but because of what he was planning for revenge. In his place, she'd be thinking the same way. It wasn't unreasonable for a man of the wilderness to doubt the affections offered by an animal with Range's particular traits. And it wasn't unreasonable for a man to take offense when his wife laughed at him, especially when he'd been made to look like a fool.

Men had their pride. Mama had told her that even Papa did not like to be the butt of jokes. It was one of several of Mama's teachings that she had, to her regret, let slip from her mind.

Looking at the formidable figure of her husband as he stood on the rock, legs apart, practically every inch of him—certainly the inches that mattered—exposed to view, she caught her breath. It took a minute for her to catch his scent.

Just as she'd feared, he was definitely not a happy man. She wasn't fooled a second by his even-toned greeting.

She forced her feet to move forward. "Aren't you cold?"

"Not in the least," he said, not entirely truthfully. "I've had a few thoughts to keep me warm."

She didn't care to ask what those thoughts might be.

"I brought some soap and a scrub brush and some

clothes. Oh, and a couple of blankets and some towels."

"How thoughtful of you."

The surrounding night seemed inordinately quiet, and his voice carried with insistent menace, even though his words were kind. When she was almost upon him, she set the lantern down on the ground and beside it placed the heavy bundle. Standing, she stretched to ease her muscles and saw that Matt had not moved a step.

She got the distinct idea he was posing. Irritated, she did some fast rationalizing. He'd brought this on himself, she told herself, refusing to accept a simple request that she be allowed to feed her pet. She was sorry for the results of that stubbornness, but she really didn't see how it had been her fault.

He was trying to intimidate her, that's what he was doing. And, a small voice said, doing a rather good job of it. He really made a formidable picture standing there in the altogether, the soft lantern light fashioning rather interesting shadows on his torso.

She felt tight and tingly inside and decidedly warm, even though she wore only the fascinator over her green cotton gown. She forgot that he didn't smell very good.

This was absurd, she told herself, and to him she said, "I'm surprised you didn't strap on your gun."

"I considered it. But then I remembered my quarry, and decided another weapon might be more effective."

"Your quarry?"

Her eye fell to the only weapon he could possibly

mean. From her angle he appeared loaded and ready to fire.

"Don't even think it, Matt," she warned.

"Think what?"

"You know what."

"My, you're an interesting conversationalist this evening."

"You'll pardon me if I'm not very entertaining. Conversation with my husband is not something I've had much practice at."

"Then we must definitely talk. Come here, Flame. I've got something I want to say."

"Matt—"

"Come here."

As usual, he seemed to have her on a string, and he was tugging at her now.

Against her will, she took a step forward, and then another and another, until the damp hem of her gown was brushing against the tip of his boots. She took a deep breath to steady herself, and was reminded of why they were here.

She looked up into his eyes. Lascivious purpose glinted in their depths.

Oh, no, she thought, as she placed her hands on his chest and pushed him into the creek.

Twenty-three

Icy water gripped Matt and pulled him under. He came up spluttering, and he came up enraged.

Shocked by what she had done, Flame was rooted in place. Matt took advantage. Grabbing the hem of her gown, he pulled hard. The fascinator fell backwards onto the rock, and Flame fell forward into the creek beside him.

She came up cursing.

He stood, the water lapping low on his abdomen, but when the cold air hit him, he went back to the relative warmth of the creek. "You've been around the half-breed too long," he observed when the curses subsided.

"Every one of those words I learned from you," she managed when she could draw a breath.

Even in the dim light he could see her lips were already turning blue. His conscience struck him. Inflicting permanent damage was not really what he'd had in mind.

He put his arms around her.

"Don't you ever th-think of anything else?" she stuttered.

"Shut up," he said, rubbing her arms and shoulders, briskly, to get the circulation going again, then working at the buttons of her gown, adding a few curses of his own at the difficulty they presented.

"Don't say it," he warned. "I want you out of these clothes and into one of the blankets, before pneumonia sets in. You did say you brought blankets, didn't you?"

A nod was all she could manage.

Flame recognized the urgency in his voice, and she helped him remove her sodden garments. He tossed them up on the rocks, and when he was done, he lifted her into his arms and carried her out of the water. The December night air was a knife that cut more keenly than even the creek, but the heat of his skin next to hers kept him warm.

Leaving her to stand for a moment, making sure she could lean on him if the need arose, he pulled a blanket from the bundle and wrapped it around her trembling body. One of the towels went around her wet, streaming hair. Without ceremony, he sat her down and pulled off boots and stockings, the only articles of clothing he hadn't been able to deal with in the creek.

"Are you all right?" he asked.

"Y-yes." She saw he didn't believe her. "I really am," she said, managing to make it sound like the truth.

"Then I'll take care of why we're here."

He grabbed for the soap and scrub brush and, with what she considered monumental courage, stepped back into the pool. He made short work of scrubbing himself down. He rose up and out of the water, applied a towel briskly to his tall frame, then wrapped himself in the second blanket and lifted her into his arms.

By this time Flame trusted him to do what was right and necessary. His boots squeaking damply with every step, he made his way in the dark up the slanted, rocky ground to the cave and its waiting fire, placing her where she could huddle on the ground close to its warmth.

She looked up at him with a tremulous smile. He brushed wet tendrils of hair from her face. Neither said a word.

He turned and disappeared into the dark. The time he was gone seemed interminable. What had once been a quiet night turned noisy with rustlings in the brush that clung to the limestone around the mouth of the cave. With forced nonchalance, Flame edged closer to the fire and studied the star-studded sky and the sliver of a moon resting on its surface. Wrapping the towel around her head turban-style, she tried to recall the constellations Papa had taught her, and the legends that went with them, but she couldn't get Matt out of her mind.

At last he returned with the bundle and the lantern, placing them on the ground behind the fire.

"What took you so long?"

"Just doing what any well-behaved husband would do."

"Not having a well-behaved husband," she teased, "I can't imagine what that would be."

"The laundry, of course. I laid our clothes out on the rocks to dry."

"Oh," she said, inordinately grateful. She looked

at the blanket in which he was wrapped. It came three inches shy of the tops of his wet boots.

"I brought you some dry buckskins," she said.

"So you did. It didn't seem fair to get dressed, when you didn't have anything to put on. Except that black thing you wear sometimes, but it's full of holes. I brought it up anyway. It's in the bundle."

Flame laughed. "You mean the knitted shawl. It's called a fascinator, but don't ask me why." She hesitated a moment. "Speaking of fairness, Matt, it wasn't fair of me to push you into the water."

"I'd have ended up there anyway, unless you figured out a way to scrub me down while I was dry."

His reasonableness took her by surprise, and she looked into the fire. Still slightly chilled, caught at a nighttime hour in a cave far from home, naked as the day she was born, she felt a rare contentment. She was afraid to speak lest the mood shatter.

Matt felt no such compunction. He sat on the ground beside her, unwound the towel, and began to dry her hair. The action took even him by surprise. Somehow it seemed like the right thing to do.

"Did I ever tell you that you have beautiful hair?"

"Not that I recall," she said. Her voice was barely above a whisper.

Setting the towel aside, he combed his fingers through the damp curls. She looked up at him, and their eyes locked.

"I'm not one for poetic words, Flame. But I like the way you look. I like it very much."

"Oh," she said tremulously, "that's poetic enough." Her lips twitched into a grin. "I have some even plainer words for you. You don't smell nearly as bad as you did when I first got here."

"Woman, you'll turn my head with compliments."

"Then that's the only one you're getting tonight."

Moving very close, he kissed a corner of her mouth. "Sounds like a challenge."

He kissed the other corner. She parted her lips and kissed him right back, getting a little tongue into the action.

He moaned. "We've got to do something about these blankets."

"I trust you to figure out the necessary maneuvers. You're clever about such things."

"Careful," he warned. "That sounded almost like another compliment."

"Sorry. I take it back."

He stood and moved into the shadowed recess of the cave. "The heat's collected back here. Almost like a summer's day."

She joined him, walking gingerly over the rough ground in her bare feet. "You're right." She dropped the blanket. "I won't be needing this."

Matt let out a long, slow breath between his teeth. Firelight played over the tantalizing surfaces of his wife's body, the long, slender neck and sloping shoulders, the high firm breasts with the darkened nipples puckered from the cold, the narrow waist, the flaring hips, the orange red curls of hair guarding her sex.

He liked everything he saw, including the long sweep of legs that wrapped like fiery tentacles around him whenever they made love.

He wanted them wrapped around him right now.

Whatever damage the cold creek had inflicted on his readiness was cured by one look at Flame. As always, she heated him with amazing efficiency.

His blanket joined hers on the ground. "Come here, baby, we've got things to do."

She melted into his arms.

"I'm going to pick you up," he said. "I want you to put your legs around me."

"But we're standing," she protested, feeling foolish for offering the obvious.

"I don't want you to get bruised on the ground."

"But—"

He bent his head and licked one of the puckered nipples. She had to grab onto his shoulders for support. He gave equal attention to the nipple's mate, then ran his tongue from the valley between her breasts all the way to the pulse point at her throat.

He stroked the length of her spine, cupped her buttocks, and kneaded her into compliance. When he lifted her, she wrapped both arms and legs around him, and he lowered her onto his shaft. Wet and waiting, she allowed easy entrance. He rotated his hips. His sex touched her in a very appropriate spot.

She balanced her forehead against his.

"This is the most erotic thing I've ever felt," she said. She slanted a kiss across his mouth, then outlined his lips with her tongue. "And you can take that as a compliment."

He managed a grin. "I've never done it freestanding like this."

She rotated her hips in imitation of him, and the thrills of promised ecstasy shot through her. "I don't want to hear what you have or have not done, Matthew Jackson. Just do it to me."

He did as she ordered. Their joined climax was quick and violent, but the passionate spasms that followed seemed to extend forever. She wanted him inside her into endless time. She loved him with her heart and with her soul, as much as she loved him with her body. Out here in a wilderness cave she felt as one with her savage lover, the civilized man who had left the big cities and returned to a rugged land he swore he'd be leaving one day.

But this was home to Matt, even if he didn't realize it. And it could never be home for her.

What foolish, maudlin musings, she thought. And coming at such a time.

She lowered her feet to the ground, but she continued to cling to him.

"I don't know how you managed that," she said against his hairy chest.

He kissed the top of her head. "If you want to know the truth, neither do I."

He removed her arms, but only long enough to spread the double blankets close to the fire. After tugging off his wet boots, he pulled her down beside him. They wrapped themselves in the covers and in each other. It was as though they were encased in a cocoon.

"We can go back to the house, if you'd like," he said.

"If that's what you want."

"Is the ground too hard?"

"Not for me," she said.

"I can't promise to leave you alone."

She snuggled closer against him. "I'd be insulted if you did."

They fell silent. She was the first to speak.

"I really meant it when I said you didn't smell so bad."

"That's a matter of opinion. I think I smell like a rose garden.

"It was the soap. I thought it might work against the other . . . you know, the other smell."

"I know all about that other smell."

An edge to his tone made her change the subject.

"Tell me something." She traced a figure eight on his chest. "Do you ever find the scent of roses arousing?"

"Now that's a damned peculiar question to ask."

"It's just that I'm getting aroused, and I was thinking it could be because—"

He covered her mouth with his. He didn't allow her to speak again for a long, long time.

They fell into a pattern of sleeping and awakening to make love. Once, after Matt had added logs to the fire, she sat on the blanket and pulled the fascinator around her, letting various parts of her anatomy show through the lacy openings. Matt told her he'd figured out where the shawl got its name.

In retaliation, she wrapped it around his waist. Nothing seemed to show. She played around with him a little, and as she pointed out, he managed to rise to the occasion.

She agreed the garment was well named.

An hour before dawn, Matt dressed and went down to retrieve her clothes, claiming his buckskins still needed a decade or two of fresh air before being wearable again. He'd leave them right where they were. Her clothes were still damp, especially the shoes, but she pulled them on anyway and wrapped herself in both the fascinator and blanket for added warmth. Leaving the cave, they made their way down the slope. Matt carried her across the shallow water around the bend, and decided he might as well carry her on home.

They passed a couple of soldiers out on patrol. Matt grinned at them and they grinned at Matt, while Flame pretended to be fast asleep. No one spoke.

He made a wide berth around the shrubbery housing Range, scooped up his hat where he'd lost it yesterday during his hasty retreat, and continued on carrying her all the way up the porch, through the front door, and into the bedroom. "Get some dry clothes on," he said as he set her down. "I've got something I want to ask you."

He saw the surprise on her face. She wasn't any more surprised than he. Maybe what he was going to say was a mistake. If he thought about it, he'd likely change his mind.

So he didn't think about it. He put on a pot of coffee and when she came out in her yellow gown, her hair brushed so that it hung loose and shiny down to her shoulders, he handed her a cup of the warm brew and gestured for her to sit.

She sat.

"About your leaving—" he began.

She choked on a swallow of coffee.

"Please," she said, patting her chin dry, "you

ought to warn me, if you're going to bring up something like that."

"And what else is 'like that'?"

She couldn't think of a thing.

Suddenly she felt frightened. She wished he'd do as he usually did and disappear for the day. When she'd complained about their never having a conversation, divorce wasn't the topic she had in mind.

"I'm all right, Matt," she said, wondering if he realized the courage it took for her to speak. "Go on."

He stood by the fireplace and watched her a moment, then he looked away. "I just wondered if you'd given any thought to the arrangement we originally set up."

"Annulment is out of the question," she said. "Neither of us is a big enough liar to claim we've never made love."

Their eyes were drawn to one another. Flame got all fluttery inside.

"Is life here so bad?" he asked.

"I never said it was bad. Well, maybe I did, but not in a long time."

"You like working at the hospital, don't you?"

She started to tell him that it was the only thing keeping her here, but she knew he'd detect the sarcasm in her voice. She limited her response to a nod.

Matt turned and poked at the fire. "This is a bad time of the year to travel, what with winter storms."

Flame set down her cup, walked over to the hearth, and took the poker from him, resting it against the wall. Hands on hips, she looked up at him. "Say what you have to say."

"I think you ought to stay at least until spring."

"Why?"

Matt didn't know quite how to answer her. Wanting her around didn't make good sense. She'd turned his life inside out, and even managed to stink him up with flowers and skunks. But he also knew he wasn't ready to start coming home to an empty house again.

These were not sentiments he could or even should put into words.

"Because you don't want to travel during Christmas, and then there's the two worst storm months of the year, and by then it's only a short time until the bluebonnets come out. You really ought to see of field of bluebonnets, before you consider going back to Georgia."

"Missing them would be a real shame, wouldn't it?" Oh, she was proud of the strength of her voice.

She shifted away and pulled out a skillet to cook breakfast. When she felt in control, she turned to face him. "Tell you what, Matt. I'll stay until after the new year begins, and if we haven't killed each other by then, I'll see about staying on a little longer."

Her crispness got to him. Hell, here he was asking her to stay, hinting—if she was sharp enough to catch it—that maybe she shouldn't go at all, and she was taking his offer under advisement.

"You do that," he said. He reached for his hat. "I'm taking some of the troops out on patrol. I'll be gone a couple of days. You'll be all right?"

"I'll be fine."

"Good." There seemed nothing more to say. He pulled her into his arms and kissed her long and hard. Settling his hat on on his forehead, he left her in stunned silence by the hearth.

Flame watched the door close behind him and fought to sort out her jumbled thoughts. Two firsts had just taken place, she decided with a shake of her head. An unemotional, no-feelings-declared request for her not to leave, and a kiss goodbye. Forgetting breakfast, she returned to the bedroom and sat on the edge of the bed.

"Annie," she whispered, "what's going on?"

But Annie could only listen to her mother's questions; answers were beyond her spiritual realm.

Flame sighed. She hadn't had a good cry in a long while. Maybe it was time she had one now.

An hour later, after she'd washed her reddened eyes and bound her hair tightly at the nape and worked off some remaining frustrations by sweeping both rooms of the house, she prepared to leave for her work at the hospital.

Melody met her on the front porch. She hadn't seen the young woman since the day of her confessions, and she'd decided the colonel's daughter had regretted saying all that she had about her family and the redoubtable Lieutenant Lilly.

"I've got the carriage tied up over at the hospital," said Melody, as though nothing untoward had passed between them. "Please ride into Little Sandy with me."

Wearing a smart gray bonnet trimmed in red lace and feathers and a matching gray cloak, her golden hair in a swirl of wisps and curls, she looked as fetching as ever.

"I can't," said Flame.

"Doc says there's not a thing for you to do today. He says it'll do you good to have a change of scenery."

Doc had a habit of talking too much about her to others, thought Flame.

Still, he had a point. And contrary to Melody's once-brusque manner, she *had* managed a rather sweet *please*.

In the mood Flame was in, the request couldn't have come at a better time.

"Just a minute," she said, going back into the house to don her green bonnet and cloak. She joined Melody shortly, and with a cold clear December day opening before them, they were soon under way.

Melody cracked the whip sharply over the rump of the black mare pulling the smart, two-seater carriage, and the wheels fairly flew over the uneven roadbed. Flame found herself liking the sting of wind against her cheek, the bounce that had her grabbing for support, the edge of danger offered by the fast ride. Concentrating on what was happening at the moment, she couldn't think of anything else.

"Mother wants some supplies from the store in Little Sandy for the Christmas ball," Melody said loudly over the wind, the creak of leather and springs, the pounding of hooves on the hard ground. "You'll be there, of course. It's Christmas Eve."

"No, I won't."

Melody spared her a quick, surprised glance. "Whyever not?"

"Because I've not been invited."

"I'm inviting you now. Both you and Matt."

How long it had been since Flame had been to a party . . . had whirled around a dance floor . . . had laughed over trivial matters that eased the serious moments of life. She tried to picture Matt sipping punch with a gathering of officers and their wives and making small talk, but the image wouldn't form in her mind.

"Thanks, Melody, but I'll have to decline."

The girl jerked back on the reins, and the mare snorted to a halt at the side of the road.

"I've done some confessing to you, Flame, and now it's time you did the same. Am I the reason you won't come? It never was serious between Matt and me. I did the chasing, and he let me catch him a time or two, but all that stopped a couple of months ago. Oh, I get upset sometimes and talk bad when I'm around him, but he knows it doesn't mean anything."

Flame wasn't so sure she was right about Matt.

"Besides," Melody went on, "I'd never call a man I really cared about *sugar. Precious,* maybe, or *darling* . . ." Her voice trailed off and for a moment she was lost in thought.

"It's not you," Flame said truthfully. "It's the officers' wives. They've not exactly asked me to visit for tea."

"Hell's fire, they don't much care for me, either, but they can't do anything about it, not with Daddy being in command."

"We're a little bit alike," said Flame with a smile. "I wasn't all that acceptable back in Savannah. Papa and Mama owned a mercantile store, and my sisters and I worked there as soon as we were old enough."

Under Melody's questioning, she passed on a few details about the Chadwick clan and their life in Savannah, leaving out the fact that like Melody, she had once been engaged to Robert Anderson.

As she talked, Melody took up the reins once again and proceeded toward Little Sandy at a slower pace. "Why'd you come to Texas?"

"It was supposed to be an adventure," she said, hoping the lie wasn't evident in her voice. "And I was supposed to join a friend, but . . . things didn't work out."

"You didn't know Matt, did you? You just saw him and fell in love."

"Not right away."

"I don't believe it. All that shooting and killing and you were frightened, and he saved your life. I can see why anyone would go crazy over him."

Her blue eyes darkened with private thoughts. "It's easy to fall in love with a man at first sight."

Flame chose not to question her about the lieutenant, but she knew the man was very much on her mind.

"What I don't get is how you got him to say 'I do,'" said Melody with a sideways glance of puzzlement.

"It was a sudden decision," said Flame, her

cheeks burning. "I've always been a little impulsive, and I guess that evening so was Matt." Desperately she searched for a change of subject. "I was traveling under a different name. Frances Chadwick had a more dignified sound to it than Flame."

Melody giggled. "Flame's no worse than Melody. What do you suppose gets into parents when they have a baby?"

Flame thought of Annie. "I guess they just go a little crazy inside."

They spent the rest of the ride recalling all the strange names they'd ever heard. As they rode into town, Melody spied a black-clad woman on the wooden walkway close to the general store. Full-figured, with hair as black as Raven's bound at the back of her head, she moved with a long, determined stride.

"Now that one's got the ugliest name I've ever heard."

"What?" said Flame, for a moment lost.

"Rowena Latrobe."

Oh, my, thought Flame, recognizing the name of the colonel's mistress, the source of her information being, as usual, the three Micks.

A wild light came into Melody's eyes. "I've never met her. Maybe it's time I did."

She reined the carriage smartly to the side of the street in front of the store, dropped to the ground, and tethered the mare to a post so quickly, Flame had no time to issue a word of caution.

And who was she, she asked herself, to lecture anyone against impulsive acts?

Melody swished her way directly into the path of the Widow Latrobe.

"How do you do? I'm Colonel William Burr's daughter. And you are, I believe, the woman he sleeps with."

Her voice drifted loud and clear around the small town, and the few pedestrians on the street turned to listen.

The woman's dark eyes narrowed, but to Flame she didn't look in the least embarrassed. "Does he know you're here?"

"Mother sent me. That would be Mrs. William Burr, the colonel's wife. I don't believe you've met her, either."

"Melody," said the widow, touching the girl's arm. "If you want to talk, let's not do it here on the street."

Melody wrenched free. "I don't want to talk, and if I did, I'd do it anywhere I pleased."

"I'm sure that you would. I was thinking of your father."

"That's natural enough. Aren't you his whore?"

Rowena jerked backwards as though she'd been slapped, but she did not turn away. "I'm certain you look at it that way. I doubt if he's called me any such thing."

Flame looked back and forth between the two . . . the young, fair Melody and the dark, buxom widow, staring at one another with wounded eyes. Her heart pounded as she stepped between them and faced the younger woman, slipping into the place of an older sister with some wise advice to impart.

"Melody, we need to get the supplies you wanted

for your mother, and then hurry back to the fort. Doc will be expecting me at the hospital, even if he said I wasn't needed."

"But—"

"Please," insisted Flame. "You've done all you can do out here. Anything else you'll regret. Believe me, I know what I'm talking about."

Melody hesitated, her eyes bright with unshed tears. "The supplies," she said at last. "We must get them right away."

Without another glance at Rowena, she made a wide circle on the walkway and strode, head high, into the store. Flame started to follow. A hand at her elbow held her in place.

"She's hurt by what we're doing, isn't she?" said the widow. "I hadn't realized. When Billy finds out, he'll share her pain."

Flame saw something in the woman's dark eyes she hadn't expected to see . . . concern for the girl, as well as affection for the father.

"She's got a great deal on her mind just now."

"Yes, I'm sure she does." Rowena stared through the closed door of the store. "She needs a friend. I doubt her mother can fill that role." She glanced back at Flame. "Can you? I don't know who you are, but you seem like a sensible young woman."

Flame wanted to tell the widow how wrong she was. She didn't feel sensible in the least. But she could be one thing, and that was a friend to Melody.

"I'll do what I can," she said and followed Melody into the store, where she told her she would be delighted to attend her mother's Christmas ball.

The girl was silent on the return ride, allowing

Flame to consider all the relationships she had discovered could exist between men and women. She'd once thought matters of that sort so simple. A girl fell in love—truly, deeply, eternally because that was the nature of love—and she married and lived happily ever after.

Except that life rarely worked out in such a way. Raised in a loving home, she'd always considered the relationship between her parents natural and even traditional. Now she saw that such wasn't the case at all.

The scandalous, unhappy Melody in love with the upright Abraham Lilly, the Burrs at war with one another, the colonel finding affection with a willing widow, and Robert falling in love with whatever woman was closest at hand.

And Matt. Could he ever find love with her? He wanted to bed her, he even wanted to keep her around, but could he ever take her into his heart?

It was a question she could barely allow herself to ask.

Twenty-four

"Saint Flame," Mrs. Ruby Broome said with a twitter. The small, birdlike woman assessed the newcomer from head to foot. "The captain says that's what the men call you. Whatever for?"

Flame smiled sweetly, but the effort made her cheeks ache. "Well, Flame is my name." She spoke to Mrs. Broome as well as the three other women who had cornered her the moment she arrived at the Fort Hardaway Christmas ball, not, she could tell, as a potential friend, but as an object of curiosity.

"A rather unusual choice for your mother to make."

"My father did the naming. He saw my red hair and declared he would call me nothing else."

At that moment, Flame felt pride in the designation her father had bestowed upon her. Papa had chosen it out of love. It would have been cruel of her to change Flame to Frances, because of something so inconsequential as dignity.

"But *Saint* Flame?" Mrs. Broome said. "I do believe that's what the captain claimed."

"I can't imagine that your husband would be concerned about such a small thing. I've helped with the patients at the hospital. Perhaps that's where it comes from."

"Ah, yes, so I've heard," piped up Mrs. Thelma Fike, a buxom matron who made two of Mrs. Broome. "How noble of you."

"Not at all. I'm paid for my work."

Mrs. Fike frowned. "When we lived in Albany, I volunteered my services at the charity hospital. I don't believe I could have accepted wages."

"You could if you needed the money," said Flame, then bit the inside of her cheek. She was being disloyal to Matt, who had repeatedly offered her an allowance. Her resistance to using any of his funds was too complicated to explain, however, and she searched about for a change of subject.

"You ladies have done wonders with the decorations," she said, waving a hand around the soldiers' dining hall. Most of the tables and chairs had been removed for the evening, only a few remaining under the overhang of the railed balcony that outlined the perimeter. Supportive posts every ten feet had been used for stringing red and green bunting, and candlelight sparkled everywhere a sconce could be hung.

The room really did look nice, thought Flame. Melody had said her mother was in charge. The colonel had declared the decorations would remain for the enlisted men's Christmas dinner the following day.

Upwards of fifty uniformed officers and wives milled about the room, sampling the food and drink from the tables. The dance floor was empty, the fiddler and the accordionist, both from the enlisted ranks, having paused between lively tunes.

"What an unusual shade for a woman of your coloring," said Ruby Broome, once again eyeing the picture Flame presented.

Flame had been waiting for someone to mention her scarlet silk gown. She'd bought the material at the sutler's the day after promising Melody she would attend the ball. With Matt gone so much, she'd had plenty of time to turn the bolt of fabric into fashionable attire.

Or what had been fashionable back in Savannah—small capped sleeves and scooped neckline with small, lace-edged roses created from the same silk decorating one shoulder and falling like a cluster of flowers on a bough to the center of the bodice. The fitted waist billowed to an overskirt draped over a series of red ruffles that rippled in vertical lines to the floor. The skirt was trailed in the back, but she'd decided against a bustle.

Flame wore her hair away from her face, curls piled high and falling to her nape. She had chosen to entwine her parents' just-arrived Christmas gift— a pearl necklace—in the curls. The teardrop earrings from Raven and Angel hung from her ears. Otherwise she was without jewelry.

Except for the brass wedding ring she'd bought herself months before.

The women around her were in black or deep purple, each gown throat-high and without a ruffle in sight. Flame felt somewhat like a ripe red cherry, dropped by mistake into a bowl of prunes.

"Flame, you're here," a young voice trilled, and she watched with genuine pleasure as Melody approached through the crowd.

The girl wore a gown of white faille, fashioned not too differently from Flame's. A cameo was at her throat, and white silk flowers nestled in her golden sausage curls. She looked lovely and young and innocent—until Flame looked into her far-too-worldly eyes. She'd been crying, and she had a brittle smile pasted on her face.

"Can we talk?" Melody asked, draping her arm through Flame's. "You ladies won't mind if I take her away for a while." As she spoke, Melody dragged her into a quiet corner underneath the balcony.

"Are you here alone?" she asked.

"Matt's on patrol."

As he had been most of December, scouting the area river crossings and waterholes for signs of Apache activity. She'd had plenty of time between her regular chores to sew, hence all the flowers and ruffles.

She'd even had time to finish her Christmas presents, fascinators for the Chadwick women, a wool scarf for Papa, and blue linen shirts for Matt and Keet. Regretting her tardiness, she'd mailed the Savannah gifts on the morning stage.

Matt had made it clear that he didn't want to go to the ball, although he'd promised to get back if he could. She hadn't felt well earlier in the day, but she didn't want him to arrive home and think she was there because of him. She'd laid out the black suit, white shirt, and red vest he kept stored under the bed, and she'd waited until the last minute to leave.

The Micks had walked her across the fields, otherwise she would have had to get to the dance alone. She didn't mind, she told herself. She really didn't mind.

"Daddy wants to make an announcement tonight," Melody laughed sharply. "He wants to introduce my fiancé."

Flame studied the girl's face. "Is that what you want?"

"I've forbidden him to do so."

"Do you mind if I ask who's the gentleman he has in mind?"

"Captain Arnold Davis." A shudder accompanied the name.

"Oh," said Flame, picturing the narrow-faced captain with the calculating eyes. She floundered for something nice to say about the man. Which wouldn't include the false-kind concern he showed for her every time Matt was away from the fort, and it wouldn't include the fact that he never seemed available when Matt needed a troop of men to go on patrol.

"He's way up in his thirties," said Melody. "Hell's fire, he's practically ready for the grave. I doubt he could even—"

She stopped herself. "There I go again. I'm trying to quit talking dirty, but I swear, Flame, sometimes it's hard to be good."

"Did your father say what made him choose Captain Davis?"

"Daddy had a lot of say on the subject. He thinks I need an older man to settle me down."

Privately, Flame could see the colonel's point. But not Arnold Davis, if for no other reason than he and Melody would be at each other's throats before the marriage was a week old.

"And does anyone else know about the possible engagement?" she asked.

"Mother, of course, but she's been too busy hanging decorations to pay attention to anyone so unimportant as a daughter."

"I was wondering about someone else."

"Lilly the pure? Is that who you mean? I might have mentioned the possibility to him in passing."

"And?"

"He offered congratulations. The dunce! He was supposed to congratulate the groom and offer best wishes to the bride." Her eyes filled with tears. "Oh, Flame, what am I going to do?"

Trapped herself in a love that was not returned, Flame understood the young woman's misery. Except that she wasn't so sure Abraham Lilly's affections were not involved. Too well she remembered the argument overheard outside her home. He'd been as distraught as Melody.

The lieutenant was not a man to be so shaken, unless by matters that struck his heart or soul. She thought the heart might be wounded right now, but like most of the men she knew well, he was proud. And stubborn. Flame was certain he would speak up, if he had any idea how Melody felt about him.

Which meant Melody must be goaded into action. Perhaps by making her believe that the lieutenant was interested in someone else. Raven's favorite poet had written plays on such a theme.

> *Trifles light as air*
> *Are to the jealous confirmations strong*
> *As proofs of holy writ.*

Flame rather thought the quotation came from *Othello*. Her problem now was to use the observation to her purpose, and come up with a trifle that would send the young girl into a jealous rage.

A trifle such as . . .

She seized upon an idea.

"If you'll excuse me, Melody," she said, "I'm rather thirsty. Can I get you a cup of punch?"

As expected, the offer was declined, and in rather surly tones, too. Departing, Flame mingled with the crowd, spied Doc, and hurried to his side.

"Have you see Lieutenant Lilly?" she asked.

"And a happy Christmas to you, too," he said, taking a moment to admire her gown. "Much better than that smock you wear in the ward."

"But rather impractical for tending the patients, don't you think?"

Doc studied the rise of her bosom above the neckline. "Dunno. Might strengthen a heartbeat or two. That's hardly a clinical observation, you understand. We could give it a try."

"Have you seen Lilly?" she repeated with insistence. "It really is important I talk with him."

Doc looked around the room. "Ah, there he is now. Just coming in the door."

Flame spied him at the same time. He stood with

military bearing, hat under his arm, the blue dress uniform sharply pressed, his fair head held high. He did not, in her opinion, appear to be in a festive frame of mind.

She hurried over to him before anyone else could get the chance and took him by the arm.

"Good evening, Lieutenant Lilly. I haven't had an opportunity to talk to you since you were a patient at the hospital."

He looked down at her in surprise. "Why, Mrs. Jackson. I was asleep so much of the time, I was hardly aware you knew me."

"A handsome young man like you?" She touched his hand. "I'm not blind."

He looked past her. "Your husband—"

"—is out on patrol," she finished for him. "He won't mind if we talk." The first strains of an air drifted over the crowd. "Or even dance. You do dance, don't you?"

Lilly barely heard her, so intent was he on searching the crowd of celebrants. Flame let him look until he spied Melody standing by the punch bowl talking with Captain Elroy Broome. She seemed particularly animated, throwing back her head and laughing with such enthusiasm that the sound came to them over the dance music.

He looked back at Flame, blue eyes cold as ice. "You were saying?"

"That I would love to dance."

"Good. So would I."

He tossed his hat aside. It landed on a cloak-laden table by the door. Taking Flame by the hand, he tugged her onto the dance floor; she had to scurry after him to maintain her footing.

Pulling her into his arms with rather more force than the action required, he proceeded to demonstrate that his dancing dexterity was not nearly so carefully developed as his military skills. Flame stepped lively to keep her slippers from falling beneath his boots. She also managed to keep a smile on her face, laughing as animatedly as Melody when the lieutenant said nothing more witty than, "Sorry for stepping on your foot."

He didn't seem to notice the inappropriateness of the laugh.

At last the music ended. The lieutenant kept stomping until he was directly in front of Melody and the captain.

"Thank you, Mrs. Jackson," he said with a bow. "I can't remember when I've enjoyed anything more."

The music started again. He looked at Melody, then at Flame, and it was to the latter he said, "Shall we?"

Once again Flame was whirled into dizziness. She was beginning to feel decidedly sick to her stomach, when both fiddle and accordion ground to an unscheduled silence. She looked toward the raised platform at the end of the room. Colonel Burr was standing in front of the musicians, Melody on one side, Captain Davis on the other.

"Oh, no," whispered Flame.

The lieutenant muttered something decidedly stronger.

"Ladies and gentlemen," said the colonel, a cup

395

of punch raised high, "Mrs. Burr and I wish you the merriest of Christmases."

"Hear, hear," echoed around the room.

"And," the colonel went on, "we wish to make an announcement that fills us both with great joy."

Mrs. Burr, who was standing beside the platform, gave little evidence of that joy, but she looked decidedly giddy compared to her grim-faced daughter.

"Our daughter Melody has accepted the offer of marriage from one of the men I depend upon most to keep Fort Hardaway running smoothly. Captain Arnold Davis."

The news was greeted with somewhat less enthusiasm than the wish for a merry Christmas, but there were still cries of "Good show" and "Well done" from the crowd. Lieutenant Lilly stood close to Flame and watched the proceedings with all the enthusiasm of a stone.

"Captain Davis," said Burr, "would you care to say a few words?" He stepped aside so that the captain could take his place closer to his bride-to-be.

The captain cleared his throat and ran a hand through his thinning brown hair. "I'll keep it short and simple, so that you can get back to your celebrating. On this night I am the happiest man on earth."

He certainly didn't sound it, thought Flame. Even halfway across the room from Melody, she could have sworn the girl flinched while he talked. But she was staring at another man in the audience, and so Flame couldn't be sure exactly what brought on the reaction.

Lilly reached for a cup of punch on the table and

raised it high. "A toast to the happy couple," he said loudly.

The sentiment was echoed, and other cups were raised.

Melody smiled brightly. "I think this calls for another kind of celebration, don't you, darling?"

She turned to Davis, threw her arms around his neck, and kissed him. The kiss lasted longer than the previous dance. At last she stepped away and stared in triumph into the audience.

"Two can play that game," muttered Lilly, who grabbed Flame into his arms and covered her mouth with his. Midway in the kiss, Flame decided she preferred her husband's lips.

Lilly stepped backwards. She looked past him to see Matt standing in the door, watching her with all the concentration a hawk gave to a mouse.

She muttered one of Keet's favorite vulgarities.

Matt strode across the room toward her, the crowd parting to get out of his way. He was wearing the black suit and red vest and ruffled white linen shirt, and looked as handsome as she had ever seen him. Her heart twisted. She wanted to run to him and throw herself in his arms.

He didn't look as though he would be interested.

He came to a halt in front of her. "I can explain," she said.

"No need. I've been gone a great deal lately. I understand."

"Mr. Jackson—" Lilly began.

Matt was in no mood to hear excuses from the man who'd just kissed his wife. Silencing him with a glance, he took Flame by the wrist. "It's time to go home."

Flame considered causing a scene, but the evening had already contained enough disaster. In as dignified a manner as possible—as though leaving were her idea, too—she hurried beside him, grabbing for her cloak as they passed the table by the door and dragging it behind her as they emerged into the dark.

She barely noticed the cold. Flinging the cloak over her shoulder, she held her skirt high, her dress rustling like windblown leaves as she ran to maintain Matt's pace. By the time they crossed the parade grounds and then hurried down the long path to the hospital and on past to the adobe house, she was out of breath and rubbing at the stitch in her side.

Matt gestured for her to precede him into the house. A fire was burning in the hearth, and she saw he had opened his gift. The shirt lay on the table in the midst of the wrapping paper, still neatly folded as though he hadn't cared enough about it to see if it fit.

She rubbed at her wrist and stared at him. "What do you mean, you've been gone a great deal lately?" she asked, as though he'd just made the comment here in the house instead of back at the scene of the ball.

"Just what I said."

"And what has that got to do with Lieutenant Lilly kissing me?"

"Was that the way it was? I couldn't tell who was kissing whom."

He studied her disheveled hair and scarlet gown more thoroughly than anyone at the ball had done, and with a decidedly more unsettling effect.

"Do you like what you see?" she asked.

"I'm a man, Flame. Of course, I do."

She swiped at an errant curl. Tears burned at the back of her eyes. What was wrong with her lately, crying so easily the way she did?

"Do you know what a bastard you can be?" she asked.

"You haven't reminded me in a while, but I know."

"Do you really think I seek out other men while you're not here?" She gave him no chance to respond. "Of course, you do. I could see it in your eyes as you stood in the doorway. Men like Flame, and Flame likes men. You had that figured out the first time you ever saw me. I guess you're just too smart to fool."

He stepped toward her. Firelight glimmered in her hair and in the depths of her green eyes. Chin tilted, she stared at him in defiance. She had never looked more magnificent. Fool that he was, he had never wanted her more.

Desire conquered the fury of seeing her in another man's arms, but it did little to gentle him.

"Did you like his kiss?" He tossed his coat aside. Next came the vest.

"Not especially," Flame said, watching his every move.

Matt unfastened the top buttons of his shirt. She stared at the triangle of sun-browned skin and black hairs that were revealed.

She backed against the table. Her body began to throb for him, to grow hot and wet. He moved close and pulled up the yards of crimson silk, bunching the ruffles around her waist, pulling up the petticoats, tearing at the underdrawers until he found what he was after. His fingers probed deep inside her, then stroked her small, hard nub. She had no will to pull his hand away.

He paused long enough to unfasten his trousers and free his swollen penis. He licked her lips, then kissed her.

"Do you like this better?" he whispered huskily.

Flame's heart pounded in her throat. "I like it better," she managed.

He took her in his arms and eased her backwards until she was lying on the table, her buttocks at the edge. She wrapped her legs around him while he thrust deep inside her, pulled back, then thrust again and again, the poundings of their bodies becoming one long desperate striving for completion.

They stared at one another throughout the frenzied coupling, daring the other to submit to their separate demands, not looking away even when their shared climax took possession of them. Matt's hands dug into her buttocks, while hers gripped his shirtsleeves. Neither let go until the last spasms had subsided.

They breathed raggedly, almost in unison. He backed away and fastened his trousers. She stood and smoothed her skirt. They moved slowly, deliberately, as though they did such things to each other every day. Flame would have felt cheap and used, except that she had used her husband as well. Her body still thrummed with the excitement of their joining.

There was an emptiness, too, that the thrumming could not fill. Flame needed more than just the thrills that came with Matt's lovemaking. She needed his love, as well. And she remembered how he had hurt her with his false assumption. The pain would last long after passion had died.

The fire crackled and popped and sent out uneven waves of heat into the tense air. Removing the pearl earrings that had been a gift from her sisters, she stared at the opalescent teardrops in her hand.

"Lieutenant Lilly wanted to make Melody jealous," she said, forcing her eyes to Matt's. "He has no interest in me, nor I in him. I've been with no other man except Robert Anderson, and that was a long time ago."

Matt listened to the emotionless declaration, and he knew she spoke the truth. What had come over him tonight? He'd seen her in another man's arms and something inside him had torn apart. He knew that if he were to hold on to any kind of life with his wife, he must put that something back together again.

A long time ago he had lost what had meant the world to him. He could not suffer such a loss again.

He stepped closer. "Flame—"

She raised her hand as though she would push him away, and he could do nothing less than give her the room for which she asked.

He stared at the pearls woven in the once-neat curls, at the high, slender neck, and the crimson silk gown that shimmered in the firelight.

"You looked beautiful tonight."

"And so did you," she said, "but neither of us behaved beautifully, did we? Please, Matt, stay away from me. We've taken all the pleasure we can from each other tonight. I'd like to sleep by myself."

He felt powerless to do more than nod.

She turned, glancing at the Christmas shirt, which still lay miraculously folded on the table. She saw no sign that he had brought a gift to her. Perhaps he thought his body was enough . . . if, indeed, he thought of things like gifts.

It seemed a selfish, hurtful thought, but tonight seemed made for suffering hurt.

In the privacy of the bedroom, she quickly changed into her nightgown, tossing aside the dress on which she had so carefully labored, unpinning her hair, but leaving the brushing until morning.

Exhausted, she crawled beneath the covers. Sleep came blessedly fast. A pounding on the front door brought her to wakefulness Christmas morning. She struggled out of bed. A wave of nausea hit her, and she sat back until the feeing passed. By the time she got into the other room, Matt was standing in the doorway, wearing only the white shirt as he talked to someone on the porch. The cot was set up by the fire.

Closing the door, he turned to her and caught his breath. Hair a fiery tangle, her graceful figure gently clothed in white, she'd stood just that way the first morning of their marriage, when Melody had pushed her way into his home. Since that morning, a great deal had happened to them all.

"That was Sergeant Gibson," he said.

She rubbed the sleep from her eyes. "What did he want?"

"Melody Burr is missing, along with her carriage. She could have ridden out as long as eight hours ago."

"Oh, no," said Flame.

"There's more," said Matt. "She's not the only one gone. Abraham Lilly hasn't been seen since he left the party late last night."

Matt dressed quickly in his buckskins and, with a promise that matters between them would be resolved, he left to confer with the colonel. Flame remained behind with her thoughts.

The nausea of minutes earlier returned. This wasn't the first time she'd been in such distress early in the day. It had been happening with regularity the past two weeks, along with a proclivity to seek solace in tears. For the first time she allowed herself to speculate as to the cause.

It couldn't be.

The words circled in her head while she dressed.

Doc said it wouldn't happen again.

She remembered he'd said he couldn't be positive. She had taken the comment as an attempt to ease her pain.

She folded the ball gown and petticoats and packed them away, made the bed, put coffee on the stove, thinking all the while, *What will Matt say?* The question hung over her like a cloud, dimming what should have been the bright sunshine of joy.

He returned to announce that he'd be riding out with the colonel in search of the missing couple.

"I don't want to leave you alone like this," he said, "but I gave my word."

"And you're an honorable man," she said, looking at the shadowed face she loved above all others, looking at it with great intensity, as though she might be seeing it for the last time.

"I don't feel honorable right now," he said. "Last night—"

"No, please wait. Anything we have to say to one another should not be said as you're walking out the door."

"Yeah," he said with a rueful smile, "I've got a lot to say."

Flame's heart twisted. "Oh, Matt, why can't the colonel just let them ride on? Then you could stay here and—" She broke off, not knowing what they would do if he remained.

"Good question. He wants to be sure they're all right. In case they've gotten into trouble, he's making Davis ride along. The sergeant's going, too."

"Why not an entire patrol?" she asked, suddenly angry. And then she sighed. "Oh, never mind. It's long past time he acted like a father."

In her heart, Flame hoped that Melody and her lieutenant got away. Couples had a right for happiness . . . couples in love.

Couples who wanted the same things out of life.

"Tell me something," she said as she poured his coffee. Her hand shook when she handed him the cup, and she prayed he didn't notice. "Did you ever in your life think about settling down and having a family? I mean a real one, with children?"

He studied her over the steam rising from the cup. "That's a strange thing to be asking now."

"I just wondered," she said, knowing she sounded too bright, too nonchalant, and knowing, too, he must not realize this was the most important moment of her life. "The colonel hasn't handled parenthood very well. Some men don't."

Matt stared at her for a long time, and she began to stir uneasily.

"You're not pregnant, are you?" he asked at last.

Her heart pounded so hard she thought it might break. "Oh, Matt," she said, making no attempt to hide the pain in her eyes, "you know what Doc said. I was only wondering."

He drank the coffee, then set the cup aside to rest his hands on her shoulders. "I'll tell you the truth, Flame, I never thought much about it. Now that you put it to me, I'd say a wife is about all I can manage. And I'm not doing a good job of that."

"Maybe you don't have confidence enough in yourself," she said, her lashes spiked with tears. "Maybe you need to have a son dangling on your knee, or maybe a daughter cuddling in your arms."

"I wouldn't know what to do with a child," he said, wanting to kiss the tears away.

They stared at each other for a long while, until the sound of horses outside the house shattered the moment of fragile peace.

Matt shook his head in disgust. "I've got to leave. We'll talk when I get back."

"Of course," she said, forcing a smile. "We'll

talk." But there was nothing more he could say that would undo what he'd already revealed.

He kissed her, then paused in the doorway. "I wish I had been gentler last night. I wish I had loved you until dawn."

"I wish you had, too," she whispered after he was gone. She stood unmoving in the middle of the room, hurting too much to cry.

At last she stirred herself to action. Perhaps she was wrong about her condition. And if she were, could she truly be glad? How simple life had once seemed to her, and now, how complex.

She grabbed up her cloak to keep out the wintry cold and hurried next door to the hospital. Half an hour later, her suspicions confirmed, she walked slowly home, sad resignation mingling with the joy she could not ignore.

Doc had said she seemed healthier this time. He gave her a good chance to carry her baby the full nine months.

"You've told Matt of your suspicions?" he'd asked.

"Not yet," she'd said, avoiding his eye. "It's going to be quite a surprise."

Arriving home, she found Keet waiting on the front porch.

"He gone?" the boy asked.

Flame nodded.

"I've got bad news," he said. "The skunk's disappeared. Been watching for him the last couple of nights, but shit, he musta found himself another place to live. Chances are we ain't never gonna find him again."

"Range has moved on?" she said. She looked past the boy to the brown-stubbled field beyond the house. She looked, too, into the future and all that it might hold.

I wouldn't know what to do with a child. He'd stated it clearly enough. Opposite longings tore at her, but she knew in her shattered heart that there was only one she could choose. Matt knew the kind of life best suited to him. After all he had done for her, she would see that he got it.

Christmas, it seemed, had turned out to be a good day for running away.

Gesturing for Keet to come inside, she presented him with the shirt she'd made. It was a little long in the sleeves, but he'd grow into it before it wore out.

"I ain't got a gift for you," he muttered, stroking the front lapels.

"There's something you can help me do that will be worth more than a hundred shirts." She went on to explain what she wanted of him. None too happy with her proposal, he nevertheless agreed.

As she went about her meager packing, she considered the irony of returning home in the same condition that drove her to leave. Except that this journey was different. This time she bore the name of her baby's father.

It offered little consolation.

Twenty-five

"The bitch." Arnold Davis cracked a whip against the rump of his Army mare. "I'll beat her for embarrassing me this way."

He rode beside Matt on the road to Little Sandy, his thin face twisted into a snarl. A quarter of a mile to the rear, the colonel followed on his gray gelding, and behind him, Sergeant Gibson.

Matt kept his mouth shut, otherwise he'd be telling Davis that running away was the smartest thing Melody ever did. He'd already mentioned something of that nature to her father, who hadn't been in a mood to agree.

Besides, Matt had another matter on his mind. One that always filled his thoughts—a sexy, red-headed wife with a hot temper and a stubborn streak, and more goodness in one corner of her heart than he'd known since his family died.

And how did he treat such a treasure? He insulted her on a regular basis.

He couldn't clear his mind of the questions she'd asked before he left . . . and the dark, lost look in her eyes. He hadn't been very convincing in his answers.

He should have said that above all else he wanted her. He should have said that he might have been a fool last night, but he'd kill the next man who touched her. He should have said a lot of things.

She wanted conversation? When he returned, she would get all she could handle and more.

When they reached Little Sandy, Davis was still muttering imprecations against his betrothed. The sun was halfway to noon on a bright and cold Christmas morning, and the street was deserted. Except, Matt noted, for an oversized drunk in baggy trousers who staggered down the uneven walkway near the Kitty Cat Saloon.

"Buck Grady," he called, reining Pigeon toward him. The rest of the search party came to a halt in the street.

Grady paused, swayed, and blinked into the light. "That you, Matt?" He scratched at his crotch. "Damned sun. Can't see a thang."

"It's me, all right. I'm looking for someone."

Grady grinned. "Don't tell me that purty wife of yours got away."

"It's another woman I'm after."

"Now, Matt, that seems kinda selfish."

"This is absurd," Davis growled behind him. "The man's a fool, and we're losing valuable time. They're probably out of the county by now."

Matt ignored the captain. "This one's almost as pretty, only she's got blond hair instead of red. She'd be driving a black carriage. Could be a man in uniform with her."

"Don't recall—"

"I'm riding on," said Davis.

"Matt, he's right," said Burr. "We're wasting time."

The sergeant was the only one who kept his opinion to himself.

"Unless you mean that couple hidey-holed up over to the hotel," said Grady. "Myrtle at the Cat was just saying how she seen 'em ride in awhile ago. Fine carriage, she said. It's over to the stable."

"Did she describe the man and woman?"

"Said they was all kissy-face."

"Goddamn," Davis muttered.

"I'll kill him," said Burr.

"Did they ride in from the direction of the fort?" asked Matt.

"Don't recall—" Grady paused, again scratching his crotch. "Naw, she said they come the opposite way. He was wearing a uniform, just like you said, and she figured he was reporting for duty. Only she said he had some other duties to tend to first, seeing as how they went right to the hotel in broad daylight. That Myrtle. She sure knows how to put thangs into words."

Matt flipped a coin in Grady's direction. Grady caught it in midair.

"Merry Christmas, Buck."

"Merry Christmas to you."

Grady staggered on down the walkway, and Matt turned in his saddle to face Burr. "I'll check it out."

"We all will," said the colonel, his face flushed beneath gray stubble, his usually pale eyes darkened with resolution.

For once, Davis had nothing to say.

"Matt," called Grady, who'd stopped in the doorway of the Kitty Cat. "You take it easy over there. Something funny going on in one of the rooms, according to Myrtle. As a rule she don't get upset, but I swear she was scairt when she was talking this morning. Face cut up a mite, too, like someone hit her."

He disappeared inside the saloon. Matt shifted his attention to the unpainted clapboard building across the street. A tilted sign nailed over the door identified it as the Little Sandy Hotel. He tethered Pigeon to a post and made his way toward the door.

"Come on, Davis. What's holding you back?" said Burr.

"Waste of time," snapped Davis, who was still astride his horse. "You heard yourself the couple was riding from the west. Besides, we've got only Jackson's word that they came this way to begin with. I'm not sure what his word is worth."

"I'm not going on 'til I know for sure," said Burr. "Now get down off that horse. That's an order."

Reluctantly, the captain complied.

"The sergeant and I will check things out first," said Matt. Walking ahead of the others, he entered the dim lobby. His eyes adjusted to the light. Lobby was too fancy a name for the small entrance with its bare walls, single desk, and ladderback chair. The air was damp and stale, and smelled of smoke and kerosene.

The clerk sat slumped over the desk, fast asleep. Matt shook him awake.

He jerked upright, sputtering. Matt put a few

questions to him, and learned that there were a half-dozen rooms opening three to a side off the corridor directly ahead. Only two of the rooms were currently occupied, one by a local gambler and the other by a young couple who rode in only an hour ago.

The description he gave matched that of Melody and Abraham Lilly.

Matt reported outside to the colonel. When he mentioned the nearby presence of Nigel Wolfe, he watched the captain. Davis blinked twice and looked down the road, as though he were considering the wisdom of riding on out of town. Matt was convinced he was acquainted with the Englishman.

Reluctantly, he put all thought of Wolfe aside. "Colonel, you're calling the shots now."

"Forget the colonel business, Matt. I'm a father. That's the only role I can deal with right now. Truth is, I'm out of practice. Haven't told Melody what to do since she was a little girl and couldn't talk back. Except to get her engaged. And look how she handled that."

He glanced sideways at Davis, a look of disgust on his face. "You're the enraged fiancé. Leastways you're supposed to be. Back me up. Can't picture Abraham taking a gun to me, but I'm beginning to think I don't know that boy. I sure as hell don't know the girl."

More than anything, Matt decided, Burr sounded sad, as though he'd lost something and didn't know if he could ever get it back. Burr straightened, and for a moment he was the colonel who had led his troops into battle against tribes of marauding Indians . . . the man who as a captain had fought under General Grant at Appomattox.

With Davis following slowly behind him, Burr followed the directions of the hotel clerk and stopped at the last door on the left. He knocked once, hard. "Lieutenant Lilly, open this door immediately," he barked.

He heard a woman's low cry, hurried voices, and a scrambling before the door creaked open a fraction. Burr shoved it the rest of the way.

Abraham Lilly, clad only in the blue wool shirt that went under his uniform, jumped backwards out of the way. The shirt was wrongly buttoned, his fair hair tousled, his blue eyes dark from lack of sleep. Through his anger, Burr thought the lieutenant looked a little silly when he attempted to snap his long, bare legs to attention.

He glanced past Lilly to the woman sitting up in bed, a yellowed sheet pulled to her chin, her eyes both defiant and afraid. With her hair a mass of golden curls and shadows under her eyes, she looked innocent and wanton at the same time.

"Sir," said Lilly, "I can explain."

"Hell's fire," said Melody, but there wasn't much vigor in the curse, "we don't owe him an explanation. It's Christmas. You've got the day off."

Her voice tapered off, and father and daughter stared at one another as though from a great distance.

Burr looked back at Lilly. "I ought to put a bullet through your balls."

"Not if you want a grandson," said Melody.

"What are you talking about?" asked Burr.

413

"Sir, we're married," said Lilly.

"You're *what?*" asked the colonel, feeling a little stupid.

"I'm Mrs. Abraham Lilly, that's what he's saying, Daddy." Melody's voice took on strength. "And there's not a thing you can do about it. We just got through with the consummation."

Lilly glanced back at the bed. "Be quiet, Melody. I'll handle this."

"Yes, dear," said Melody, her look of defiance softened. Burr stared at his daughter in amazement. He hadn't heard her so meek since . . . Hell, he'd *never* heard her so meek.

Burr stared at the man who was apparently his son-in-law. "Married, you say."

"Yes, sir. We rousted a preacher out of bed early this morning. His church is near the county seat."

"Can I say just one thing, Abe?" Melody smiled at her husband, and he smiled back at her.

"Just one."

She looked at her father. "Abraham Lilly is the noblest, best, smartest, most honorable man I've ever met. He wouldn't consider taking me to bed, until we had the papers making everything legal."

The lieutenant cleared his throat. "Melody, I don't imagine your father's interested in such matters."

"Oh, yes, I am," said Burr. He stared at his daughter for a minute. "I'd like to talk to her alone, if you don't mind. You're her husband. It's up to you."

"Yes, sir," said Lilly, reaching for his trousers. Pulling them on, he headed for the hall.

"Arnold Davis is out there," the colonel warned.

"I can handle him," said Lilly, and he closed the door behind him.

In the aftermath of his departure, an uneasy silence descended on the room.

"Do you mind?" asked Burr, sitting on the side of the bed by his daughter. "Why didn't you tell me you wanted to marry the lieutenant? I could have gotten you engaged to him instead of Arnold."

"Oh, Daddy, a girl doesn't want her marriage arranged. Besides, I didn't know if he wanted me, being spoiled goods the way I am."

"What are you talking about?"

"Don't lie to me. You know I've been with men. Mother probably hasn't let herself admit the truth, but the same can't be said of you."

Burr started to protest, then saw the futility of it. "I didn't let myself consider the possibility, although somewhere inside I figured the way things were. Why'd you do it, girl? Why'd you have to give yourself away?"

Tears brightened Melody's eyes. "You haven't called me girl since my brother died. Truth is you haven't called me much of anything. Lately your time's been taken up elsewhere. And I decided, what was good enough for you, was good enough for me."

He knew without asking that she referred to Rowena Latrobe. "A man has his needs, Melody."

"And so does a daughter. I know you and Mother don't get along, but you didn't have to shut us both out."

"That's what you think I did? Shut you out?"

Melody nodded.

"And I suppose your mother thought the same

415

thing. Strange, I always thought it was the other way around."

He stood, every joint in his body aching, his heart heavy in his old soldier's breast. "I'll get your husband back in here, then I'll leave. Natural enough for you two to want to be alone for a while."

Melody came out from under the covers and, kneeling on the mattress, threw her arms around her father. They hugged one another, then he pulled the sheet up over her once again. "You're naked, girl. Show some modesty."

"I'll have to," she said, grinning through her tears. "Abe is going to make me respectable yet."

Burr started to leave.

"Daddy, he really is a good man. He knows I'm not pure, but he doesn't care. I told him he wasn't the first man, even before we went to the preacher, and he said that the important thing was he planned to be the only one from now on."

Choked up, Burr didn't trust himself to speak. In the hallway he shook Lilly's hand and gestured for him to return to the room. He found Arnold Davis waiting in the hotel entrance, along with Matt and Sergeant Gibson. The clerk was nowhere to be seen.

"Looks like you'll have to find yourself another bride," he snapped. "I pity the woman. You made yourself scarce back there. Good thing there wasn't trouble."

Davis popped his knuckles. "I was afraid of what I would do."

Burr didn't dignify the comment with a reply. He looked at Matt. "I'm going outside. The air's a mite close in here." He hesitated. "No, I won't be outside. I've got some business to take care of. Something I should have done a long time ago. I'll see you back at the fort."

Davis stepped forward as if to follow.

"Just a minute," said Matt. "There's another matter we need to clear up. I'm talking about Nigel Wolfe."

Davis's eyes shifted slightly, and a band of sweat broke out above his thin lips. "Wolfe? I don't know the name."

Davis was a terrible liar, thought Matt. Maybe it was time to call on all his old poker skills and pull a bluff or two.

"He says he knows you."

"And you believe that tinhorn gambler?"

"I thought you said you didn't know him?"

Davis cleared his throat. "I might have heard the name."

Matt glanced at Gibson, who eased sideways to block the door to the street.

"He's back there in his room," said Matt. "Number three, the clerk said. Why don't we go ask him whether he lied?"

"I'm getting out of here." Davis turned toward the exit, saw the solid figure of the sergeant, and turned back to Matt. "See here, I'll have you both charged with insubordination."

"You've got me quaking in my boots." Matt nodded toward the hallway. "Let's go."

Gibson edged up behind the captain, who moved with reluctance in front of Matt, not stopping until he came to the gambler's room.

Matt motioned for Davis to knock, but when the captain shook his head, he did the honors for him.

"Herman," came the gambler's voice from inside the hotel room, "just a moment."

A shuffling sounded behind the door. Matt tried the knob. Locked. Remembering who was waiting for him at home, he grew impatient, raised a boot, and kicked hard. The door slammed open. Wolfe stood in the middle of the small, dim room, his back to the door, polished shoes resting neatly by the bed, his shirttail dangling outside his trousers.

The gambler whirled, eyes blazing with fury, lips pulled back from pearl white, snarling teeth. "Davis!" he growled. "What the—"

The roar of an Army pistol filled the room, reverberating from wall to wall. Wolfe stared in disbelief at the blood spilling from his gut. He looked up at Davis, who stood in the doorway, a smoking gun in his hand.

"I thought he was armed," the captain stammered. "I thought he was going to shoot."

Wolfe opened his mouth, arms wrapped around his middle as if he would hold in the life's force that seeped from the open wound. He staggered once, then silently slumped to the floor.

Back at the fort, Matt wrote a brief report detailing Nigel Wolfe's death at the hands of his accomplice, Army Captain Arnold Davis, now residing in the Hardaway stockade. Copies of Army invoices for Winchester rifles were found in the gambler's room—invoices that had once crossed the captain's desk—

and beneath a broken floor slat, a cache of bills and gold coins.

More incriminating were the gambler's dying words. He'd lived long enough to curse his partner and outline their scheme of trading guns to the Apaches for stolen cattle and horses and goods. An order for the arrest of the wagon driver who delivered the weapons would be forthcoming.

Matt was about to leave the headquarters building, when the colonel walked in.

"I left something on the desk for you to read," he said. "A Christmas gift."

The colonel barely seemed to hear. "You ever get into something, Matt, that tears you apart? Something that's all right and all wrong at the same time?"

An image of Flame flashed across Matt's mind. "I thought I had. I've decided the situation has nothing wrong to it."

"And I've decided there was nothing right with mine. Nothing that would justify continuing." He glanced toward the western hills. "Weenie's a good woman. I hurt her today, but hell, I guess I'll go on hurting a little bit for the rest of my life."

He moved past Matt, disappearing inside his office.

Matt turned his thoughts to his wife. He remembered the shirt she'd made him. He hadn't even thanked her. He hadn't told her how he felt about her. He hadn't done a damned thing right concerning her, since the day they met.

Except to make love to her and to fall in love with her. It was time she knew.

He had a gift for her, too. He'd left it back at the house. There hadn't been time to give it to her. If she would take it. He wouldn't give her a choice.

His long stride took him across the fields to the house. Both rooms were empty. He searched them twice. The shirt was lying on the table where he'd left it. The bed was made, her trunk in its usual place against the wall. Something told him to open the lid. Half the contents were gone.

He stared in disbelief, unwilling to believe the evidence of her desertion. A horse's hooves pounded near the house. He hurried to the sound. The half-breed boy jumped from the back of an Army mare, and landed at the step to the porch just as Matt came outside.

Boy and man stared at one another. Matt saw he wore a shirt like the one Flame had made for him, and he cursed her for what seemed a cruel betrayal.

"They got her," Keet gasped.

Matt felt the forces of life drain from him, and he forgot all else except his wife. "What are you talking about?"

The boy swiped back tears. "We was riding to catch up with the stage."

"The stage?" Matt felt stupid, confused.

"I was supposed to bring the horses back after she got on board—" He strained for breath.

"Go on," Matt said, fear and rage a burning furnace inside him. Flame had left him. Why hadn't she spoken up? Why—

He stopped himself. He had far worse matters to handle than the breakup of his marriage, no matter how shattering it was.

"You said somebody got her."

"Three of 'em rode out of the trees, before we knew what was happening. Black Eagle said to tell you he was making her his woman. Said you'd know where to find her, if you wanted back what was left of her."

The boy's words came at Matt like arrows, and he stared wildly about him, unsure for a moment what to do. Flame was all he could think of, wanting her back in the protection of his arms, sinking in a quagmire of helplessness because she was not there. Flame—precious, darling, vulnerable Flame—in the hands of the Apache bastard who'd already made his life hell. Nothing the savage had ever done compared to now.

He couldn't think for a second. Where had she been taken? Black Eagle said he would know. Only one place was possible—the Indian camp that lay deep in the Chihuahuan desert of Mexico.

Determination cold as a grave settled on him. He went inside for his rifle and a supply of ammunition. When he came out, the boy was sitting astride the mare, his long, thin legs in their torn trousers bent to accommodate the short stirrups, the reins held firmly in his hands.

"I'm going with you," he announced.

Matt started to argue, but it wasn't worth his time. He set out on a run toward the stable, the half-breed riding close on his heels.

"Wait, Matt," he heard someone call. He looked back to see Doc running toward him. Impatient, he forced himself to hold still.

Out of breath, Doc stopped beside him. "I heard

the boy," he managed. "Before you ride out, there's something you need to know. Flame came to see me shortly before she rode out. I didn't know what she was planning, or I sure as hell would have tied her down, until you got back."

He looked at Matt with pained and sorrowful eyes. "She's carrying your baby, Matt. And she didn't know how to feel about it. All she could do was sit there and hold her middle and blink back the tears."

Matt listened in stunned silence. Looking toward the house, remembering the scene before he'd ridden away, he knew what had made Flame leave. She had asked if he wanted children, and he had told her no. Half-fearing her answer, he'd asked if she were pregnant, and had accepted her ready lie.

Self-revulsion engulfed him. How devastating his words must have been to a woman bearing a beloved child she'd thought she could never have . . . devastating enough to send her into a peril she could not comprehend. And he had taken her departure as a personal affront.

He wanted to be out of his skin, out of his mind, someone else who had the strength and the goodness to make things right, not a half-savage monster who saw everything through self-serving eyes. Not want a child that was born of Flame and him? He wanted nothing else.

In that moment of revelation, he promised the God he hadn't believed in for years, and the family he'd lost so long ago, that he would save his wife and unborn baby, and he would bring them home. If she would let him, for the rest of his life he would love them and cherish them and see that they never again were faced with harm.

Without a word to Doc, he set out on a run toward the stable, Keet's Army mare close beside him. Above the man and the boy—enemies to one another without apology—a thin blue Christmas sky stretched from horizon to horizon, and a cold breeze drifted across the fields, as they hurried to rescue the woman they both loved.

Twenty-six

Craggy peaks and jagged ravines shielded Black Eagle's encampment deep in the Sierra Madre. To get there, Matt and Keet had to cross a hundred and fifty miles of Mexican desert, and this after they traversed the ungracious terrain between Fort Hard and the Rio Grande.

"You fall behind," Matt warned the half-breed when they were under way, "and I'm not coming back for you. You won't be slowing me down."

"I ain't falling behind."

Keet sat stiff-backed in the Army saddle on the Army mare, his straight, black hair plaited away from his sharp-hewn young face. He wore his blue linen shirt, and over it, the darker blue woolen coat of the United States Army. On his feet were regulation Army boots. Except for Flame's gift and the worn trousers that the saloon women had bought him last summer, his outfit was courtesy of the Micks, who had bade them an agitated farewell at the stables. All of the government issue was oversized, but Keet wore it with pride.

"I ain't slowing you down," he added, as he whipped the mare alongside Matt's gelding. It was the last communication either attempted until they were across the Rio Grande late the next day.

Matt chose the crossing where Black Eagle had escaped him less than a month ago. He read the signs of recent passage. How recent he didn't know. Under ordinary circumstances, by stealing replacements for the horses they rode to exhaustion, the Indians could travel up to a hundred miles a day. But they were traveling with a white woman. Matt prayed she didn't try to delay their journey by being difficult.

She might try it once. He knew she wouldn't try it again.

In late December the heat of the day was bearable—more so than the cold of the night, when ice formed on the surface of streams and a bitter wind stung exposed flesh. Matt knew what to expect. The years slipped away from him, and he became the boy who had learned the Indian ways of survival. Traveling in the valley of the Rio Conchos, he ate the seeds and winter fruit of wild grasses and cacti, and from the occasional ravines he made a quick harvest of walnuts and the soft inner bark of pine trees.

In other circumstances, he could have taken the time to catch and cook the turkeys, quail, rabbits, even the field mice or prairie dogs that abounded throughout the land. But the only time Matt allowed himself pause was to care for Pigeon.

He'd named the gelding for his ability to handle steep slopes and narrow trails, as if he knew he could sprout wings if the need arose. Pigeon's skill would be important on the route they had to ride.

Keet copied Matt's diet and his care of the horse, but the two did not talk. Matt rarely looked at him directly, the half-breed's Apache features too reminiscent of the young Black Eagle who had ridden into camp and destroyed what little peace a white boy had found in captivity.

Matt had ample time to remember those years of torment, the beatings, the hours exposed to scorching suns and fearsome thunderstorms, to the sleet and rare snow that fell in the Sierra Madre—all because Matt was white, and Black Eagle had watched the white soldiers slay his family. With the love for his own lost family having returned to him a hundredfold through Flame, he understood now the torment that had driven the savage to such cruelty. And maybe in other circumstances, he might have learned to forgive.

But not now. Not with Flame at the mercy of that same cruelty. Now, he wanted to tear out the Apache's heart.

He did not try to follow the path of the Indians. Instead, he moved directly toward the Sierra Madre encampment. They passed the ruins of a half-dozen hamlets that had been destroyed through the years by the Apaches. In a few, the hollow-eyed natives came out to watch the passing of the American man and an Indian boy, but they did not call out and they did not wave.

The undulating land gave way to steep hills of lava and limestone, and they tore their way through jungles of thorny vegetation as they moved toward

426

the higher peaks. The air grew thin, the under-growth sparse as they journeyed higher, their passage made more difficult by the countless ravines that must be crossed.

Climbing steadily, they reached the crest of one ridge only to find that a higher ridge awaited. Majestic pines towered over them, perfuming the air with their scent; below were thick clusters of scrub oak. Along the sides of the trail, either discarded or stored in the hollows of trees, were the goods left behind by bands of Apaches—bolts of calico, clothing, horse-hides, dried meat.

They moved on in silence, traveling by daylight now because of the treacherous footing, huddling close to a fire at night, staring at the stars, trying not to think.

At noontime two days into the year 1877, Matt announced their destination lay over the next and final ridge. With Keet crouched close beside him, he sketched the encampment in the dirt.

"It's at the base of a narrow gorge. Rock walls make it hard to get to. A stream flows through the middle. There's walnut and ash and some cotton-wood growing on the banks, and up there's pine and cedar and some oak. All of it can be used for cover. The problem lies along the ridges that surround it."

Keet looked up from the drawing. "Is that where they put the sentries?"

Matt nodded, giving the boy grudging respect.

"Can we kill them?" Keet asked.

"Take too long to work our way around the perimeter. There's a hidden trail that twists down through the trees. I doubt it's changed much."

Matt thought about the last time he had walked that trail. It was the day he'd found the knife and slashed his way to freedom, scarring Black Eagle's face and wishing he had done more. He'd been fifteen, but by then, the seventh year of his captivity, he'd become a man.

"We'll travel as far as we dare during the afternoon," he said. "Tonight I'm going in alone."

"The shit you are."

"Don't mess with me, Keet. I'll bind and gag you and leave you for the Apaches to find. They'll see the white blood in you, even if I don't."

The boy fell silent, his black eyes watchful as Matt stood and prepared to mount. They moved out, their progress slow and cautious as they kept to the covering trees. Toward dusk, they made a crude camp well off the narrow path, and Matt announced he was going in on foot.

He checked the pistol and pulled the rifle from its scabbard, holding it loosely at his side. "You be here when I come out. We'll need to ride fast."

Keet nodded once, then looked away, his dark eyes unreadable as Matt disappeared into the brush. He counted the seconds, and then the minutes of solitude, before making preparations to follow. When he was certain Matt was far down the trail, he took off his boots, then removed the knife hidden inside his coat, before tossing the garment aside. He hesitated, then removed the shirt, baring his thin, hairless chest to the night's cold.

Clad only in threadbare trousers, his straight black hair falling free, he moved swiftly, surely, through the unfamiliar land, departing from the trail and scrambling on a diagonal route through the trees and shrubs toward the flickering campfires far below, intent only on his purpose and his destination, ignoring the thorns that tore at him and the rough, rocky ground over which he trod.

He was at one with the night that shielded his movements, and his young heart pounded with the knowledge that for the first time in his life, he felt the heritage of his unknown father. For once in his fourteen years, he accepted the Apache blood that flowed in his veins.

Under cover of darkness, Matt descended unseen to the narrow valley separating the monoliths of limestone and lava that served as the encampment's protective walls, moving with stealth through the trees and shrubs toward the babble of moving water and the crackle of burning logs. He came so close to the camp, he could hear the talk of the women as they squatted outside their tents, ignorant of the danger that lurked a dozen yards away.

The language came back to him as though the past decade and a half had never been. He remembered the quiet laughter and ribald jokes of both men and women, and as a boy he'd wondered that they could be so harsh by day and so human by night. Listening to them now, he heard only desultory talk of work and children, nothing that might provoke even a smile.

As the night lengthened, they talked in more somber tones of the dwindling number of Apache braves. One squaw timorously suggested a move to the reservation across the border, but she was quickly shamed to silence, and at last the women retired into the tents.

Matt listened in vain for news of his wife. Swallowing the bile of impatience, he circled the tents, but outside the aureole of the few campfires, he could make out nothing in detail except a few old men moving slowly through the trees, along the banks of the stream, disappearing one by one inside their tents. Where were the young men, he asked himself, the braves who fought at Black Eagle's side? Were the women right? Were they really gone?

He asked himself, too, if he had arrived before his enemy. Certainly he was here long before Black Eagle would be expecting him. But he felt his wife's presence somewhere close, not with the prickling at the back of the neck that warned him of the Apache, but with a pounding of his heart and a quickness of his breath.

She was within his reach and his help, frightened, no doubt, and cold on this January night in the mountains, tormented . . . tortured. He could not allow himself to go on. Instead, he concentrated on sending her his thoughts, willing her to a sense of peace and hope, instructing her to cooperate with her captors, until he could set her free.

For a watching post, he chose a dense outcropping of shrubbery on a slope at the edge of the valley. Here he could make out the stream moving darkly beneath a cloudy sky, the campfires, the tents, the few squaws milling about. He crouched amidst the thorn-laden bushes, the rifle trained onto the center of the camp, and he waited for the first rays of dawn to arrive.

The sky was a rosy glow over the eastern escarpment, the morning star twinkling into view, when Matt decided to move out. Anything was better than the waiting that had lasted a dozen lifetimes during the long hours of the night.

He heard rustling behind him and whirled, the rifle snapped into firing position, his finger pressured against the trigger.

"Don't shoot," a young voice whispered, "it's me."

Incredulous, Matt lowered the gun. "What the hell—"

The shrubs parted, and in the dimness he could make out the face of the half-breed Keet peering through the leaves.

"She's up there," the boy said, gesturing toward the western wall, his voice barely audible in the quiet morning air.

Matt's eyes darted to where Keet was pointing, but he could see nothing except shadows and the dim outline of trees.

"You ain't an Apache like me," the boy said. "She's up there, all right. Tied to a post like an animal." His voice broke. "I've been looking all night for her. I don't know if she's all right. There's someone watching over her, and I couldn't get close."

Matt closed his eyes, remembering his own grim past, and he knew exactly where his wife awaited rescue. The bastard Black Eagle had tied her to the same stake he had used to fetter a captive boy so many years ago.

He wanted to grab Keet and hug him close for what he had learned, but he contented himself with a touch on the boy's bare shoulder, feeling the bones beneath the cold skin and, too, the hint of muscles soon to be formed.

"Scrambled all night to find her, but she was easier to spot than you," Keet said with a slight smile.

"You've done good work."

"Only if you get her free. Here," he said, holding out a knife. "Use this to cut the rope."

Matt exchanged the knife for the Colt pistol. "You know how to use a gun?" The boy nodded. "Stay here. Fire a warning shot if they come after me."

"I'll do better than that," he said. "I'll shoot 'em."

Matt didn't argue. The valley was growing alarmingly light, and he left the boy in the protection of the shrubs and moved out toward his wife. Behind him he heard the first stirrings of morning in the camp, but he did not look back. He was halfway toward his destination when he spied the sentry, a young buck clad in leather shirt and leggings, a Winchester rifle in his hand.

With a wishful prayer for the moccasins he'd once scorned, he placed one booted foot carefully after the other against the jagged path, closing the distance between them, keeping to the shadows and the protection of the scrub oaks clinging tenaciously to the rock wall. One shot would have taken the sentry down, but it would also have alerted the camp and Black Eagle, who must be lurking close by.

He crept higher than the Indian and came at him

from above, easing behind him and cracking the rifle butt against his ear. The Indian fell to the ground in silence. Matt dragged him into a stand of shrubbery and hit him again for good measure, ensuring that he wouldn't wake up anytime soon and sound an alarm.

Onward he climbed, noting the signs of the path over which he'd so often been dragged, at last coming to the clearing where he expected to find his wife. Blood pounded in his ears. The stake was there, protruding like a stiff snake from a crevice in the limestone. Flame was nowhere in sight.

There was, however, a small scrap of green wool he recognized as coming from her cloak. He held it in his hands and prayed it could tell him where she'd gone. A rustle in the bushes jerked him from prayer, and he whirled to stare into the barrel of a Winchester. He fired without thinking. A second Apache stumbled into the clearing and fell at his feet, this one almost torn in half by the rifle shot at close range.

Matt cursed the explosion that reverberated from wall to wall of the gorge. In the valley below, he could hear the excited voices of the women, but he did not look down. Nerves prickled at the base of his neck, and his eyes were drawn upward, past the sloping rock and dawn-dusted trees, all the way to the top of the ridge. Silhouetted against the yellowing sky, on a triangle of limestone jutting away from the towering pines, were the unmistakable figures of Black Eagle and Flame. Her cloak whipped lustily in the winter gusts that raked the high, exposed land.

The Apache had her by the wrist, and Matt knew without seeing it that the savage wore a smile of triumph on his face.

"Come, *sikisn*," the Indian called out, his voice echoing through the gorge. "We await you."

Matt watched in horror as Flame jerked her arm against his hold, yet the horror was tempered with elation that she still had the spirit to fight.

He raised the rifle, but Black Eagle shifted around until Flame stood as his shield. He continued to circle, never presenting a possible target for more than an instant. Lowering the gun, Matt began to climb. He found Flame standing on a flat plateau of rock and dirt that extended out from the main crest of the ridge. Directly behind her, holding a knife to her throat, was Black Eagle.

Matt stopped within twenty feet of them, and he looked at his wife. She stood with back straight, the red hair whipping wildly in the frigid wind, face streaked with dirt, cloak ripped and stained. The look in her eyes was a mixture of fear and relief.

He stared at the knife blade against her white throat, and he trembled with a greater fear than he had ever known.

Her lips parted. "Don't speak," he said.

"He's sick," she said anyway, as always defying him. He loved her for it, even as the danger of her situation tore at him and blurred his will.

He looked at Black Eagle and saw the feverish madness in his eyes.

"Your fight is with me," he said. "Let her go."

"Even as the soldiers let my family go?" Black Eagle said, his voice thick and dark and clipped.

The puckered scar that ran diagonally across his cheek looked luminescent in the early morning light.

"Your people killed my family an equally long time ago," said Matt.

"They should have taken your life as well."

Black Eagle's free hand wrapped around Flame and stroked across her breasts. "The gambler who sells the guns has said you care for your woman. I have vowed to take her as my own. You will watch."

Matt stared at the brown hand against the green cloak and imagined cutting off the fingers one by one. His eyes moved upward, to the shoulder where his bullet had penetrated the last time the two met. He saw the inflammation, and he knew the reason for the Apache's fevered look.

"You can barely stand upright," he said. "Unless you get treatment, you will not live through the day."

"You sound like the women," Black Eagle scoffed. "And the braves who have lost their manhood. Did you look for them amongst my people? You will not find them except in the stockade of the white soldiers, or in the prison you call a reservation. Only Black Eagle remains to wage the battle of his ancestors."

"Today you fight a woman," Matt said. "This does not make you a man."

"I *take* a woman. This makes me very much a man."

Matt felt the power of Flame's eyes on him, and the pleading to set her free. He set the rifle on the ground and pulled out the knife Keet had given him. "We will duel for her."

"I am not a fool—"

A gunshot echoed from the incline below, and another and another, each explosion following quickly on the other and seeming to come from closer to the crest.

"But you were alone," Black Eagle said in disbelief, as he wheeled toward the sound. With his hold on Flame slackening, she bent her head and sank her teeth into the restraining hand.

"Aiii," the Indian cried as the knife fell to the ground, and Matt snatched up the gun. Flame flung herself away from the Apache and out of the line of fire.

All happened in an instant. Matt leveled the rifle at Black Eagle's gut. The Apache stared at the barrel, looked toward a hawk circling over the pines, and at last settled his dark eyes on Matt. The fevered madness was gone, replaced by a sadness Matt had never before seen.

Overhead the sky brightened, as if to announce the start of a new day.

"The white man wins," Black Eagle said.

Matt nodded slowly. "Once the battles began, your people did not stand a chance of victory."

"But still, we had to fight." He stared once again at the gun. "I think you will not shoot me, *sikisn.* I think on this day I choose my own death. You will see I am well named. I fly with the hawk."

Turning, he moved to the edge of the ridge, where the land dropped away into blue emptiness. Matt stroked the trigger of the rifle, but he could not bring himself to fire. Not even when he remembered Charlie, and his mother and father, and the infant sister taken from him so brutally a long time ago.

Without a word, the Apache leaped into the void and disappeared, swallowed by both earth and sky, for all time robbing Matt of the revenge he had sought for so long. But he felt no regrets, no loss. He thought only of his wife.

Dropping the gun, he turned to Flame. "Are you really all right?"

Smiling through a blur of tears, she said, "I feel as though I could run all the way back to Texas. In truth, I never want to get on another horse as long as I live."

With a sob, she threw herself into his arms, and the wind tore at her cloak until it was wrapped about them both. Neither saw the boy Keet creep quietly onto the ridge, observe the scene, and quietly ease away, the Colt pistol hanging limply in his hand.

"And the baby?" Matt asked, stroking her back, her shoulders, her hair.

"I've had no problems the way I did before." Flame's voice was muffled against his chest. "Oh, Matt, I'm so sorry—"

"No," he said, "now is not the time for apologies, when I've got so much to say."

Matt held his wife tightly, as though he would bring her inside his skin. "I love you," he whispered into her hair. "I want you to bear my children, and I want to keep all of you with me forever. Remember that, Flame. I love you. It took me a long time to say it, and now I don't know how to stop."

He eased away and lifted her tear-streaked face. "If you still wish to leave, I will see that you return to Savannah safely. But you will go knowing you take everything that has meaning to me."

He kissed her, savoring her sweet goodness and the warmth of her breath against his cheek. She was alive, and he knew it was all he could ever ask of life.

"My home is wherever you are," she said, and then, needing reassurance, she couldn't keep from asking, "You really don't mind the baby?"

"I want our baby as much as I want you." He eased his embrace to pull a cord from around his neck, and reveal the object he'd worn hidden beneath the buckskin shirt.

"A ring," said Flame, and looked into his eyes. "Oh, Matt, you bought me a ring."

"Merry Christmas," he said as he removed the brass ring she'd bought for herself and substituted its gold replacement. "I planned to give it to you the night of the ball, but other matters got in the way."

Suspending the brass jewelry from the cord, he dropped it beneath his shirt. He felt its warmth close to his heart.

"I could renew my vows right now, if you'd like. I'll even call you Frances. Frances Jackson isn't so bad a name."

"Oh, Matt, my darling, darling, darling. How much I love you." Her words caught in the breeze and seemed to circle around them. She ran her hands over his bristled cheeks and stroked his parted lips.

"A lifetime ago I thought I wanted to be something I wasn't. Now I know that whatever else life holds for me, I want to face it as your wife and the mother of your children. And I can do that only as myself. Papa named me right, and you knew it the day we met. I'm Flame Jackson, and Flame Jackson I'll always be."

Epilogue

"Keet fired the warning shot that distracted Black Eagle, and when he realized everything was lost, he jumped. That's all there was to it."

Flame smiled reassuringly at her family—at her disbelieving Papa and worried Mama, at a skeptical Raven and an awestruck Angel. They were sitting in the parlor of the frame home behind the Chadwick store, and for what seemed the tenth time that spring afternoon, Flame was relating the story of her rescue.

She wouldn't have told them anything about the incident except that Colonel Burr, in a final act of duty before resigning his commission, wrote the family that she was well, despite her harrowing experience, and that she had proven herself a fine and strong resident of Fort Hard.

She wished the colonel well in his new life as a civilian back in his former home in Pennsylvania. More, she wished him well in mending his marriage. But she also wished he'd minded his own business and not stirred the Chadwicks to worrying about her more than they already had.

"I should never have insisted on the riding lessons," Thomas Chadwick said with a shake of his head. His once-black locks were streaked with gray, and there were lines on his round, ruddy face that Flame did not remember. During the last year and a half, he'd lost most of his stockiness, and her heart twisted when she considered the possibility that she was the cause of the changes in him.

"Papa," she said with a smile, "after the Indians took me, I was wishing the same thing, otherwise I never would have dared leave the fort. I went over two hundred miles astride that poor mare, with my skirts twisted between my legs. And then I had to turn around and ride right back."

She glanced at Mama, who sat close beside her husband on the settee, holding tightly to his hand. Anne Chadwick was short like her husband, and her fair hair was faded, but her blue eyes were as lively as ever.

"Would it be impolite, Mama, to mention I suffered chaffing in some rather intimate areas?" Flame asked.

Anne Chadwick answered with a smile. "I can imagine you didn't want to sit for a week."

"What about the Micks?" Papa asked.

"They'll be mustering out of the Army soon. It's not a life they've taken to. There's nobody back in Ireland to return to, and I suggested they consider settling here in Savannah. You'd like them, Papa. They're fine young men."

"They befriended me daughter, and I'd like a

chance to return the favor," Thomas Chadwick said, beaming.

"I swear," said Raven, who stood by the hearth close to an open window, "Papa enjoyed your letters the most when they mentioned those three. He said the Irish can always be depended upon, when troubled times arrive."

"The young girl Melody," said Mama. "She married a lieutenant, isn't that right?"

"She hated the Army, and now she's an officer's wife at the Presidio of San Francisco, while her father has retired." Flame glanced at Raven. "You ought to appreciate the irony in that."

Raven smiled. "Oh, I do."

Flame studied her sister with the same concentration she'd been giving to her parents, wanting to impress on her mind sharp images of them all, images that would not fade after she had gone. Raven was the most striking member of the family, she decided. The tallest, the most imposing despite her slender frame, primarily because of the way she held herself, rather like an English queen. Black hair and eyes, tawny skin, a strong mouth and deepset, expressive eyes—oh, yes, a beauty, and a woman of mystery because she always held something of herself back.

Except her opinions of her middle sister.

"I still don't know why you did it," she said.

"Did what?" asked Flame.

"Left in the first place. I'll never believe it was because you wanted some of the Anderson money. You're too good a person for that, and I thought you were smarter, too."

Flame hid a smile, thinking how Raven managed to compliment and insult her at the same time. She glanced at Mama. Anne Chadwick was the lone member of the family who knew the reason for the hasty departure. Mother and daughter looked at one another for a long moment, then Flame turned back to Raven.

"You know how impetuous I've always been," she said. "I was engaged to be married, and Robert was a world away."

"I know why she left."

Everyone looked to Angel, who sat with her back straight in a rocker across from her parents. Short like her parents, with a more voluptuous figure than either of her sisters, she had an innocent air about her that went with the golden hair and wide blue eyes. Trusting, gentle, sweet-natured, but Flame, like the rest of the Chadwicks, knew she was nobody's fool.

"Why did she leave?" asked Raven. Flame stirred restlessly in her chair.

"Because she was looking for true, deep, and eternal love. We used to talk about it sometimes late at night." She smiled at Flame. "And you found it, didn't you?"

"Oh, I most certainly did."

"Glad to hear it," a deep voice said from the doorway.

Flame's heart thudded as she looked at her husband and at the baby in his arms. Matt was in shirtsleeves and a pair of fitted, worsted trousers, the only thing remaining from his days of Indian scouting was the pair of tooled leather boots. Black hair

443

trimmed to his collar, he was as tall and lean and handsome as she'd ever seen him, the blanket-covered infant only making him appear more of a man.

"Charlie woke up and wanted to attend the party," he said with a grin.

"I didn't hear him cry," said Flame.

"He didn't have to. He opened those green eyes of his, and I could see what he was thinking."

Flame stood and went to her husband's side. She touched his arm, wanting to reassure herself that this happiness was real, and then she stroked the fine red hairs that covered the head of Charles Thomas Jackson, the first grandchild of the Chadwick clan.

And the first offspring, Matt was quick to point out, in the Jackson dynasty.

Charlie had made it with a gusty good nature all the way to his eighth month, despite a pair of parents who hovered over him and let him want for naught.

Flame took the infant from Matt and walked over to her mother. "Would you like to hold him?"

"I'm next," said Papa.

"You'll get your turn," his wife said, and she held the baby close, a rare light of defiance in her eye, as though she would dare anyone to take him from her.

Thomas looked at his wife and then, one by one, at the girls they'd brought into the world. How different each was from the other . . . unique in her own right. There were those who thought him foolish for the names he'd chosen, but both he and his beloved Anne knew the names were apt.

What would the future hold for his unwed daughters? Raven, so outspoken yet secretive at the same time, determined to live a single, independent life. And Angel, thought to be gentle and of a passive nature. He suspected that in actuality, she was the stronger of the two.

He looked at his middle born, the one who lived closest to danger. He shuddered as he thought of all she'd been through. "Why do you have to live in Texas?" he asked.

Flame looked at Matt, and they shared a smile. "Because that's where we belong now. The ranch is still small, but we'll be expanding it soon. The widow that owns the neighboring property is planning to sell off some of her land, and she's promised Matt first bid."

Flame gave a thought to Rowena Latrobe, and how she had changed her life since the colonel left. Learning about the abuse of the street children of Little Sandy, she'd taken them in as her wards. Even Herman had lost his baby fat, and had seemed to put the harsh memories behind him.

One of the saloon women—Myrtle at the Kitty Cat—had quit her job to help.

Flame was thinking of maybe setting up a decent mercantile store in town. She knew the business well enough—Papa had seen to that—and Little Sandy showed signs it was ready to grow beyond a stable, a run-down hotel, and a few saloons.

"I don't know," said Anne with a sigh. "Texas is so far away."

"It's closer than Savannah is to London," said Flame.

"What's that got to do with anything?"

"Papa and you ran off to a new world to make a new life. That's all Matt and I are doing."

"But—"

Thomas patted his wife's hand. "The lass has a point, my dear." He looked once again at Flame. "You've got that boy in charge of the ranch while you're gone, don't you?" asked Thomas. "Do you think that's wise?"

"Keet's practically sixteen, Papa, and in Texas that makes him a man." Flame looked to her husband. "We trust him, don't we?"

"Yeah," said Matt, "we trust him." He walked over and put an arm around his wife. "He proved himself down in Mexico, when the proving was needed most. As far as I'm concerned, Keet can do no wrong."

Flame was the only one who knew how far Matt had come to make such a declaration, and she loved him all the more.

"Keet's learned to read and write, so that he can help the Indians on the reservations," she said. "Maybe study the law, although we'd like him to stay with us."

Matt stroked his wife's cheek. "A man has to find his own destiny. Although I have to admit, sometimes it shows up at the most unexpected times."

"It most certainly does," said Flame.

Charles Thomas Jackson chose that moment to gurgle out a laugh, and everyone joined in.

Including Raven, who decided that for some members of the family, marriage was a very good thing.

Author's Note

While the physical descriptions of Texas and Mexico are as accurate as research and travel can make them, Fort Hardaway is fictitious—an amalgam of the nineteenth-century frontier posts that protected settlers from the marauding Indians they were trying to displace.

Flame is the first book in a trilogy recounting the adventures and misadventures of the Chadwick sisters. Raven, the oldest and most private of the three, is the subject of Book Two, which will appear at the end of 1994.

Determined to root out the source of threatening letters to her beloved mother, Raven travels to London and finds herself at odds with a very handsome English lord, who believes she is up to no good.

Angel's story will appear in the fall of 1995. The sweetest of the Chadwick offspring, she comes to Papa's rescue by giving herself to the most devilish hero of them all.

Evelyn Rogers
San Antonio, Texas
June, 1993